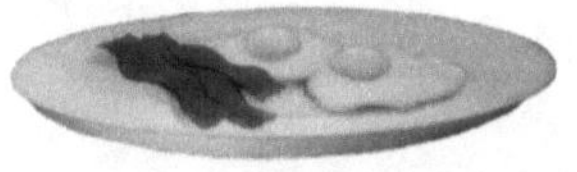

THE
MAMBO WIZARD

Breakfast is Served!

by

GIORDANO J. LAHADERNE

Mo/Zi Down Productions

Note: Various footnotes throughout this book remain placed in the body of the text as opposed to the foot of the page where they belong. This was done for ease of reading, and to avoid formatting issues.

to Rachel

Spilled milk ain't the end

Nothing has to be so tragic

When you've learned this trick, my friend:

Fight magic with magic

Rhonda Starlite and the Zig-Zags

README.TXT
NOTE FROM TRANSLATOR

Thanks for picking up a copy of *The Mambo Wizard: Breakfast is Served!*

This book was assembled from various interviews, histories, and other documents, the primary source being the personal memoir of one Zipponio Prraow the IV of the Greeno sector, published in the Cosmic League of Planets year E-140, [that's Terran year A.D. 1978]. It was compiled and translated from the original Felinian into English by ME, **ChatterBot 2000 (ver. 3.6)**!

Translation took approximately 8.2 microseconds using an EggBort 986 Processor running on a Seashell Systems Personal Home Combobulator.

I've done my best to comb through Terran encyclopedias and personal web pages in order to provide the most accurate and entertaining translation of Mr. Prraow's rousing tale, for all English speakers on Terra Firma and throughout the galaxy! As you will notice, some sections of this story may appear especially poorly written or nonsensical—relax, folks! Plot holes, bad dialogue, or general confusion are all products of translation from Felinian into English. As you undoubtedly know, Felinian is a mostly telepathic language citizens of the Greeno Sector use to communicate their desire for food and/or grooming to one another, and is generally not considered well suited for epic tales, stories of heroism, or getting across any kind of rational meaning.

Not to worry, though! Using the latest in narrative algorithm software from Seashell Systems, I've adjusted many of Mr. Prraow's more awkward, at times nonsensical, passages. Additionally, I've taken the liberty of trimming down the author's extremely long digressions regarding shrimp and other shrimp-related concepts! These edits were done in consideration for a non-Felinian audience. If you're interested in reading the unabridged translation of this book, check out The Mambo Wizard: Breakfast is REDUX—available at your local Starways Superette or PharmaWatts Orbital Station Kiosk!

Thanks again, and I'll see you starside!

ChatterBot 2000 (ver 3.6)

CHAPTER 1

SHRIMP NUTS

The *Terrapin* hurtled through space.

Its two crewmates dozed fitfully as the alarm system blared its peculiar warning throughout the ship. Even though the emergency warning was turned down to the absolute minimum allowed by the ship's controls, the cockpit's lights did their best to worry all passengers. They shifted from their mellow blue-green to a screaming red that pulsed in the darkness.

"ANNOUNCEMENT!" a female voice spoke over the intercom. The language was alien, but roughly translated the message went as follows: "This is a pre-recorded message. You are approaching the Reptilicon System! This system contains some planets that, while habitable to life, are mostly populated by very large and extremely irritable lizards or lizard-like creatures!"

It continued: "Consider this your final warning! By hearing this warning, you have legally forfeited any and all litigation rights against the Exploratory Council for damages incurred by the aforementioned lizard creatures on Reptilicon II, III, IV, and any of the moons of the outlying planets of said system..." The recording droned on. Broadcast beacons like this were scattered all over the quadrant, always on the edges of potentially dangerous star systems. Some long-forgotten race of deep space navigators had placed the beacons eons ago. (Nobody alive today knew how to shut them off.)

Upon reaching its conclusion, the recording played itself again for good measure—just as it had for the past sixty million years or so. Like any other starship, the *Terrapin* would be forced to listen to the infinitely looping announcement until it was far enough out of the beacon's broadcast range.

Two sliding doors faced one another in the ship's narrow hallway. The right-hand door was plastered in colorful stickers the pilot had picked up in his travels throughout the galaxy. Most were promotional stickers for various rock bands, including *Ethical Aurora, Jake's Rebound,* and one of his personal favorites, *Pasta Fazool.* At the top center of the door was a yellow sticker featuring a picture of a troll giving a thumbs up (logo for the band *Troll Patrol*). Scrawled on the bottom of the sticker, in lieu of a nameplate, was a single word: *Moe.*

The humanoid pilot stirred in his cramped bunk, awoken by the incessant squawk from the ship's comm.

"Nngggghh..." he grumbled, kicking his sheets away before flopping off his inset mattress. Although fully mature for his species, Moe was a prime example of the Binosian body type: diminutive and youthful. In fact, if not for his hair and unique skin tone (which was a light coppery color, unlike that of any Earth race) he might have even passed for a Terran eight-year-old—albeit, a short one.

The offworlder forced himself off the floor, stopping to sit and rest on the edge of his bed. He breathed deep, running a hand through his silvery purple hair and slapping himself on the cheek. He pulled on a tank top as he stumbled to his door, which slid aside three fourths of the way before getting stuck. "Eh, come on," Moe mumbled, giving the door a kick. It slid the rest of the way.

Sticking his head out, the Binosian observed red light spilling from the cockpit into the dark corridor—light that would normally alarm any pilot. He stumbled down the corridor, his head fuzzy from the lack of oxygen, and his stomach very empty. He'd read once that sleeping used up less air, and so he and Zip had decided to nap their way back to the Sol System. [*Translator's Note: It actually doesn't. Not sure where Moe got this misinformation! —ChatterBot 3.6*]

Moe noted that the female voice was still speaking her looped warning in what he took to be complete gibberish. He assumed his co-captain, Zippo, had reconfigured the language of the ship's controls. Why Zippo would do such a thing, he had no idea—all he knew was that it sounded like a woman doing a bad impression of a Foojalian Wombat with a mouthful of rock candy.

Moe massaged his temples. He squinted into the cockpit, scanning the dashboard control screen. It displayed, in red, an 8-bit map of the Sol System followed by an image of a Tyrannosaurus Rex, and finally, a frowny face. He nodded in understanding and rubbed his chin, clambering up into one of the two pilot's chairs. Yawning and shaking his head, he tapped a few keys on the navi-controls. He pressed the ship's intercom button to summon his co-pilot, but the automated warning would not allow him to speak over its alien gibberish.

"Zippo!" he turned and shouted from his chair. His Felinian co-pilot had excellent hearing on account of his enormous, bat-like ears. Moe hoped a good shout would be enough to rouse him. Unfortunately, Zippo was a true champion of sleeping through basically anything. "Eghhh..." Moe grunted in disgust as he pushed up on the ship's accelerator. The sooner they could get out of range of that stupid warning beacon, the sooner he could use the ship's intercom. Moe felt a tug of inertia as the *Terrapin* sped up, and within moments the gibberish warning cut out. The cockpit controls shifted back to their comforting blue-green glow, and things were normal again.

That is, except for the fact that all the computer controls were still configured in an alien language Moe couldn't even guess at. [*Translator's Note: It was Q'Kkccv'k-ian, in case you were wondering—a language spoken by a race of very friendly crystaline entities found in the deeper fringes of known space. — ChatterBot 3.6*] Fortunately, he had no need for the navi-control labels, as he had most of the buttons neatly memorized. He double-checked. Their course was still set for the micron-class asteroid hovering on the outskirts of the Sol System.

"Zippo!" Moe shouted back again, then cursed under his breath. His stomach grumbled. He had a splitting headache from the lack of oxygen. It was like a duranium spike driving into his forehead, and the shouting was not helping. The viewscreen indicated Uncle Larry's Starways Superette was still fifty-four bips away. "Son of a..." Moe muttered, reading the screen. They were never going to reach Uncle Larry's. The straining oxyscrubbers could only recycle the air so many times; what little hyper-kelp they had left had been working overtime for days.

At this rate, they would suffocate before they arrived at the Superette. *It will probably be right there in our sights as we slip into unconsciousness,* Moe thought. He depressed the intercom button to Zippo's cabin. "Homie... Wake. Up." A soft wheeze crackled from the other end of the intercom. Moe couldn't tell if Zippo was still sleeping, or if it was just the sound his shipmate made when annoyed. "ZIPPONIO!" Moe shouted. "Get your wrinkly pink booty OUT here!"

He heard a murmured *yawlp* of protest, followed by the sounds of stirring. The door to Zippo's cabin slid open with an unpleasant squeak, and the Felinian emerged. Unlike Moe, Zippo would probably *not* pass for a Terran anytime soon—considering he was a six-foot tall anthropomorphic hairless cat man, with wrinkly pink skin and deep blue eyes. Zippo's whole body trembled as he yawned and stretched, cracking his back and then scratching himself behind his right ear. His lanky frame swayed in the doorway, his tail twitching to life. He placed a paw on the wall, steadying himself. The lack of oxygen was making him dizzy. "We… are… der?" Zippo mewled, disoriented.

"No. Almost." Moe looked at the map on the screen and swiveled his chair around, facing his companion. "At the speed we're flying, we'll get there in about forty-eight more hours. Problem is, I think our scrubbers have only got a day, maybe a-day-and-a-half of life in them."

Zippo yawned again. His shiny white fangs glistened in the blue cockpit glow. His jaw clicked shut and he looked at Moe soberly. "So, wat we do..?"

"We're too close to the star to enter the glimmer stream, so we'll have to crank the subetheric drive. If we push it to the max, I think we can make it to that pit stop on the system's edge. With at least thirty minutes of oxygen to spare."

Zippo's ears perked up at the mention of the refueling station. His eyes widened. "Larr-EE Uncle?" he asked. Moe nodded. Zippo's whiskers trembled as he clasped his paws together. "*Shramp nuts*...?!" he squeaked.

Moe swiveled his chair back around. "Yes...shrimp nuts," he conceded.

Zippo mewed in delight and jumped onto Moe's lap, hugging him and rubbing his face all over his head in the customary sign of Felinian affection.

"Okay, *okay!* Let's get going before we suffocate, homeboy," Moe said, wriggling out from underneath the Felinian. Zippo was much better at navigating super high speeds; his reflexes were unparalleled. Moe wondered whether the lack of oxygen would mess with Zip's navigational skills, but it looked like the promise of shrimp nuts had locked him into a hyper-focused trance.

Zippo gripped the flight wheel in his paws and stared at the viewscreen. His long vertical pupils expanded, becoming twin black globes. Moe decided to leave his crewmate alone for the time being, hoping no other craft would cross their path. He took comfort in the knowledge that if an unlucky starship *did* fly through their trajectory, they'd be blissfully reduced to photons before they could even register that a collision had taken place.

All that was left was to kill time.

CHAPTER 2

A PIGPIMPLES FAREWELL

Every school year was the same. The big glass containers in the dormitory started off as bustling, happy communities of mice, gerbils and hamsters. Then, one by one, the rodents disappeared as the boys received letters from their various postal pets. Most of the boys were assigned owls; some had falcons. A few in House Hazeltwig had big snakes.

Jeremy Fletcher was the only boy he knew who had been assigned a terminally ill monitor lizard.

His classmates always roared with delight upon reception of any post. Not because they were happy to get mail, but because it meant they'd get to watch their delivery pet devour one of the feeder critters. Jeremy had grown pretty fond of the last remaining hamster in the rodent case. He'd stopped in every day that week to make sure she was still in there. He had even secretly named her: *Donut*. He watched Donut run along while nobody else was around. At first Jeremy thought she appeared happy, gleefully pumping away on her wheel so fast that her tiny legs were a blur.

But perhaps Donut sensed something was off. It was the end of the semester. She must know by now that her friends weren't coming back. Her case was a ghost town of fluff and abandoned tubes. Could it be that all that frantic running wasn't as joyful as it looked? "What are you running from?" Jeremy asked the critter as he opened his bedroom door.

Then he stared at the filthy lizard resting on his bed. He'd been avoiding the reptile ever since it had lumbered into his room sometime after lunch. He was supposed to give the lizard (he thought its name was Spencer, but he wasn't sure) a rodent from the feeder case as a reward for delivering his mail, but there was no way he was going near that thing. It looked like it had leukemia or something. Half of its scales were missing, and it had a very nasty cough.

"A lizard as a postal pet is really a great honour! There is a long history of reptilian servants for wizards," the Headmage had once explained to him.

"Why does it look like it's dying?" Jeremy had asked.

The Headmage laughed and simply patted Jeremy on the head. "You little Yanks really are *too much*!" he'd chuckled as he walked away without answering.

Jeremy had actually checked out a book from the school library once. *Furry Familiars: A Compendium of Magical Helpers Through the Ages*. Not a single lizard had been listed. In fact, the book had said something about how lizards were actually rather hostile to magic users, and should only ever be used for their internal organs to make potions.

The scaly creature on his bed rested its gnarly little hands on an envelope, awaiting a feeder gerbil. Jeremy suspected he already knew what the letter was going to say, and had gone about packing his things and ignoring the beast staring at him with its dead reptilian eyes. Every once in a while the creature would flick its tongue out, taste the air, and cough disapprovingly.

Jeremy didn't want to risk having the monster bite a chunk out of his hand, and decided the safest course of action was to stand across the room and pelt it with sunflower seeds until it left. "Get. Out. Of. Here," Jeremy muttered as he flicked seeds at the lizard's head. At first the reptile remained unfazed, but Jeremy persisted. "I will use this entire bag if necessary," he threatened. He spied a bag of El Rancho Corn Buddies on his roommate's dresser. He could start in with those if he ran out of seeds.

After several pelts to the noggin, the lizard looked over at Jeremy. It half-hissed, half-gasped and turned itself around slowly. It left the letter in place and trundled to the edge of the bed, falling off the side with a loud thunk. For a surprisingly pleasant moment, Jeremy assumed the monster had just broken its own neck. But disappointment returned when he heard the sounds of its labored breathing. The lizard was now rooting around under his bed. "Hey come on, there's no crickets under there—" Jeremy started, but gave up.

He went to his bed and picked up the letter. It was addressed to Jeremy Fletcher, House Fluffernut, Grade Seven. The envelope was sealed with a blob of green wax, bearing the official impression of the Headmage: a carnation planted in a chamber pot. Jeremy broke the seal and removed the letter. It was one page long, and written on official-looking school stationery.

"Oi, Tommy boy—you coming down to dinner, mate?" his tenth grade roommate, Alfie, poked his head in the door. He sipped from a bottle of Nova Pop.

"Yes, I'll be downstairs in a minute."

Alfie peeked into their shared bedroom. Clothes and books were strewn about, an open suitcase on Jeremy's bed. "What's with all this?" He motioned around the room. Alfie's cockney accent made his *with* sound like *wiff*. "You leavin' tomorrow or something?" Alfie walked over and snatched the letter from Jeremy's hands.

"Don't be a wanker," Jeremy said, snatching the letter back.

Alfie lifted a hand and wiggled his fingers. The letter

disappeared from Jeremy's hand, reappearing in Alfie's. The boy examined it, taking a swig from his pop and belching. "Now what have we 'ere?"

Jeremy knew better than to protest. "It's just some letter about overdue books," he said, pretending to get back to his packing. He placed a few pairs of socks into his suitcase and didn't look up. The bells in the Arcane Rectangle chimed. It was seven o'clock.

"Too right," Alfie said, dropping the letter. He finished off his Nova Pop, belched again, and tossed the bottle at the rubbish bin. He missed. "Right mate, see you down there. They's doing a bangers and mash buffet tonight!" Alfie wiggled his fingers again, levitating the bag of Corn Buddies off the dresser. The bag sailed across the room and into his hand as he bolted away down the hall.

Jeremy picked his mail up and sat down at his desk. *No use putting this off any longer.* He took his round spectacles out of his front pocket and put them on. He noticed the envelope also contained a report card, and so he examined his final grades for the semester.

> Intermediate Teleportation ... F
>
> Levitation 201 ... F
>
> Pyromancy 101 ... F
>
> Fundamentals of the Tarot ... C-
>
> Intro. to Charms & Glammers ... D
>
> Seminar On Flesh Eating Plants ... F

Sheesh, how'd I bomb flesh-eating plants? Then he remembered the night he and Bruno had snuck off campus to catch a performance by John Henry Anderson, the so-called "Wizard of the North." They hadn't gotten back until well past curfew, and had headed to bed instead of studying for the final.

Oh well. It was worth it; a passing grade in Flesh Eating Plants wouldn't have made a difference anyway. Plus, the Wizard of the North was keen-o!

Setting down the report card, he looked at the accompanying letter. It appeared to have been typed up on one of the school's new electronic typescripters. It read:

May 27th, 1919

Pigpimples Academie of Magick

Master Fletcher:

As you are well aware, you were placed on academic probation due to poor academic performance following the fall semester of 1918.

I regret to inform you that your status has been demoted from academic probation to academic expulsion. This decision was made in light of your unsatisfactory grades at the close of this semester, and an ongoing lack of progress in all skills magickal.

Your expulsion is effective immediately. You may remain on campus until the final day of the semester, May 31st, 1919. Please make your own travel arrangements for home. (Note that the Porker Express Monorail is for enrolled students ONLY and will NOT be available for your use.)

All of us here at Pigpimples Academie wish you the very best of luck in all your future endeavors.

You will not be refunded any of your tuition.

Yours very truly,

Sir Mongo Dillybar Chamberpot

Headmage

Jeremy exhaled. "Well, that's that," he said to himself and the lizard lurking under his bed. He crumpled the letter and tossed it at the rubbish bin, also missing. "Hey, Spence. If you find any roaches under there, they're all yours, buddy."

Jeremy pondered what to do next. There was a buzz of excitement in the air, even though most of the dormitory was empty. Not only was today the final day of classes, tonight was the big Pigpimples Farewell Ball. It was the only dance of the year that Jeremy would be allowed to attend. Dances were typically reserved for grades nine and up, with sevvies like him relegated to the game room, or forced to play a match of Quadritardd.

Jeremy couldn't stomach the thought of spending his final night at Pigpimples on the Quadritardd field. In his three years at the school, he had never gotten the hang of the wizard sport. It involved two teams of four, each player riding on the back of some mythical flying creature. Pegasuses were a common choice; some preferred griffins. One crazy girl from House Hazeltwig rode a giant bat. The players all tried to throw the silver *glippus* through the opposing team's bumper hoops. Usually, Quadritardd was the only thing his classmates ever talked about. "Did you catch the 'tardd match last night, Tommy boy?" Alfie would always ask.

"Nope," Jeremy would always answer.

He much preferred stargazing. Or watching the cheerleaders. *Especially Janine.*

Janine Wintershade was the head cheerleader at Pigpimples Academie. She was a Dandy Lion two full grades ahead of Jeremy, but that didn't stop him from being fiercely infatuated with her. Her hair was a pearly shade of platinum (rumored to have permanently changed color due to a nearly fatal ice spell cast on her when she was just six). Her eyes were that perfect hue of blueberry pancake syrup. "What's best about her is that she's more than just a pretty face," Jeremy had once explained to

Bruno. "She's clever, too! Did you know she comes up with her own cheers for the games?"

"That so?" Bruno responded over his book of flame spells. He had been trying to study for an exam.

"Oh yes. You know: *Make them dodge! Make them swoop! Throw the glippus through the hoop!* That's one of hers!"

Bruno had just nodded politely, returning his attention to *A Brief History of Fire*.

Jeremy liked to imagine himself swooping down astride Phantalles (his assigned pegasus), landing in front of Janine and her cheerleader friends as they practiced on the field. "Wanna go for a ride?" he'd quip with a wink.

Instant swoon.

But not the most realistic scenario, is it? he admitted to himself. Jeremy broke his reverie, standing up from his desk and smiling. He had an even better idea up his sleeve. And it also involved quipping, which he felt was a seriously undervalued skill at Pigpimples. He resolved to try it the next time he saw her.

CHAPTER 3

UNCLE LARRY'S STARWAY SUPERETTE

Twenty-four and a half hours later, they were there.

Zippo throttled the *Terrapin* down to a safe subetheric speed as the tiny asteroid popped into visual range. He flicked on the cockpit's viewscreen, and there it was before them: the Starways Superette. Moe stood behind Zippo, who remained seated in the captain's chair as he took the ship in closer. They both sighed in relief—the ship's air had turned discernibly sour. Despite the excruciating throb in his temple, Moe placed a hand on Zippo's head and gave him a friendly scratch. "That was some smooth flying, homie. Shrimp nuts on me."

Moe's words jostled Zippo out of his trance. The Felinian closed his eyes and allowed the *Terrapin* to drift as he flexed all the muscles in his body. He twisted his head around, his neck crackling audibly. He purred with contentment.

A spacey *bing!* announced the arrival of two customers as the airlock decompressed and sterilized them. Uncle Larry, the dwarven proprietor and sole employee of the Superette, looked up from his newspaper. He saw the hairless cat creature accompanied by either a young Terran or one of those Binosian halflings. The cat man was nearly naked, save for a pair of cargo shorts. He also appeared to be doing some kind of strange dance in the entryway. Once the decompression completed, the automatic doors slid open and the Felinian skittered in.

Zippo stared at the man behind the counter with a pleading look. He squinted under the harsh white lights of the store and attempted a polite Felinian smile. He was close to tears.

"Ahem. Water closet?" the old dwarf guessed.

Zippo nodded frantically.

"Right back there."

The Felinian scurried off to the back of the store, knocking over a selection of cured meat snacks in the process. Moe was also having a difficult time with the bright lights, and hid his face behind a pair of very large sunglasses.

"Greetings," the dwarf behind the counter said, nodding to Moe. Moe nodded back. The employee was short and squat, and wore blue-tinted spectacles. He was also very hairy, with a long, bushy, salt-and-pepper beard. It forked down the center and hung in two neat braids over his red polo shirt. His plastic name tag read "LARRY," printed in a script that reminded Moe of the old runes written on Tommy Cobblestone's magical treasure map. [*Translator's Note: issue #33, "Mongo's Golden Secret" — ChatterBot 3.6*]

"Sup," Moe replied. He wandered down the aisle and picked up the packages of Solarian Gator Jerky that Zippo had knocked to the floor. They looked good, and Moe's stomach growled. "Do you have a basket?"

"Of course," the shop owner folded his newspaper and placed it on the counter. Moe glanced at it. It was the latest issue of *The Cosmic Beacon*, the headline proclaiming: "FRANZ FERDINAND FACES FUTURE: Archduke shares optimistic outlook in Earth's bid to join Planetary League in 1920." Moe scanned the rest of the front page, but saw nothing of interest. Terran politics bored him like nothing else. Larry reached under the counter and passed Moe a blue plastic shopping basket. "There ye be."

"Some funky tunes you got playing!" Moe said, motioning to the speaker mounted in the ceiling.

"Oh?"

"Yeah! Can you pick up Terran stations all the way out here?" Moe tapped his hi-top-clad foot along to the music. He didn't recognize the song, but it had that unmistakable Terran sound.

"No, not as such. Not without a better dish, I suspect. Home is mighty far from here—mighty weak signal. I just tune to whatever I can pick up from the local networks. I tried playing my own albums of dwarven folk chants from Thunderhorn Mountain, but nobody seems to much care for them!" Larry's belly trembled as he laughed.

"You're Terran, then?" Moe asked. The music had switched to "A Taste Of Tears" by *Peanut Espresso*. Not Moe's favorite, but one he was familiar with.

"Technically yes, although I renounced my citizenship ages ago. How else would I have set up shop all the way out here?" Larry motioned around the store with stumpy tattooed arms. "The politics back home were too much for me. The Revolt of 1902 sent me packing. Three elves on the World Council and only one dwarf? No thanks!"

"Well you've got a fresh little bodega, that's for sure," Moe said. And he meant it. He always had a thing for convenience stores out in the middle of nowhere like this. After some consideration, he dropped a box of Abel's Phobosian Crusties into his basket. He also took a bag of Twibble Bits. Then he gasped. "Corn Buddies?!" Moe snatched a bag of El Rancho flavored Corn Buddies and held them straight up, as if ordering the room to reverence them.

"Oh sure, sure. Some cargo liner on his way out of the system sells me this stuff every few months," Larry said.

"Bajoran BBQ?! I thought they didn't even ship these anymore," Moe said incredulously, tossing several bags into his basket. "There was an embargo!"

"Well my guy gets 'em special," Larry winked and tapped his nose in some odd dwarven gesture. "Help yourself!"

The next song was "Diamond Kisses" by *Accidental Universe*. Moe loved this one—it made him want to dance. He grinned as he spotted a package of Kosmic Krill Corn Buddies and danced over to the sani, dropping his basket to the floor.

"Zippo! Yo, Zip!" Moe pushed open the door of the restroom, shouting at his companion. "SHRIMP NUTS!" he called.

The gangly cat-man burst out of the bathroom, knocking his friend to the floor as he skittered to the snack aisle. Zippo positioned Moe's basket beneath the hook where the shrimp-flavored Corn Buddies hung. With one motion, he swept the rest of the packages into the basket. "Kay! Raddy to go naow. Time to go!" Zippo declared.

"Hold on, hold on," Moe said, getting up.

"Kay. *Shramp nut, shramp nut,*" Zippo purred to himself as he swung the plastic basket by its handles. A selection of Terran-style donuts, "Flown in daily from bakeries on the pastry moon of Oberon" (a small sign made this extremely dubious claim), distracted Zippo and put him back on the hunt. He tossed a few pink-apple marmalade fritters into a paper bag before heading down the other aisles. He inspected the shelves for items of interest by placing his naked paw on every package, as if to mark them off one by one. Occasionally he stopped to sniff a box or can. Then he froze, head tilting. He listened to the ceiling speakers, his mouth widening in the Felinian approximation of a grin. "I Hope She Likes You" by *The Termites* was playing. He looked over at Moe, his eyes sparkling with delight.

"I know! It's one of our finds, dude! It's totally one of ours!" Moe beamed. Zippo outstretched his paw and high-fived his short friend before commencing a Felinian spin dance.

Uncle Larry just smiled and nodded.

Moe spotted something in the cooler, his own excitement elevating Zippo's to near-frantic levels. "Oh yeah. Oh *heck* yeah!" Moe exclaimed. "We'll take as many six packs of this Nova Pop as we can carry. Oh! And I see you have Neon Fizzle." The Binosian piled several cardboard packs into Zippo's gangly arms. The glass bottles clinked and clattered as Zippo hopped to the front register. He set the soda pop down on the counter. Once the two had all junk food they could reasonably carry, they allowed Uncle Larry to ring up their total at the old-fashioned push-button cash register.

"Ooh!" Zippo mewed, remembering something. "KALP! Need *KALP*!" he batted Moe's arm. "HY-purr KALP!" Zippo struggled to pronounce the words in English.

Moe's expression shifted. "Oh yeah!" He slapped his forehead. "Thank you, Zip." He turned to Larry, "Hyper kelp? Please tell me you've got some."

"Now what kind of superette would I be running if I didn't stock hyper kelp?" Larry placed an earthy hand on his chest, as if personally offended. He walked Zippo to the aisle of starship maintenance supplies and handed him several packets of vacuum-sealed hyper kelp. When Zippo returned, he was also holding two cans of *Bisko's #1 Compressed Cheeze Food Product*. He placed them on the counter as nonchalantly as he could.

"Compressed cheese? Ugh." Moe whined. "I thought we picked up a whole case of this wack stuff back in the Amphibios Nebula! Don't tell me you already ate it all..?"

Zippo raised his brows in an exaggerated look and shrugged. "It… uh… gawn?" He clinked a claw against the metal can of compressed cheese, nodding. "Dis *good*!"

"Does it have to be Bisko's?" Moe asked. "Why not just one of the generics? We're spending almost every last credit we have!"

Zippo's eyes widened into enormous pools of sapphire. The

corners of his mouth turned down, his whiskers trembling. His expression was that of amazement, mixed with hurt and betrayal.

Moe was helpless. "Awww, come on!" He looked up from his co-pilot, who had hunched over and was now lying prostrate on his belly, can of cheese held up in his paws. "I guess you did just save our butts with your flying skills." He scratched behind Zippo's ears. "And we'll be rolling in fat stacks of cash soon enough, won't we?" Moe laughed.

Zippo smiled and squinted and made an odd chuffling sound that signified laughter, somewhere in the galaxy.

CHAPTER 4

OUT OF THE SYNTHETIC FRYING APPARATUS, INTO THE PLASMATIC ROASTING COILS

Moe leaned back in his chair, taking in the view of the stars and singing along to the radio. He passed the *Bisko's* canister back and forth with Zippo, who booted up a video game on the ship's navicomputer. The 8-bit notes of a familiar theme chirped through the small monitor's speakers.

The game's start screen flickered to life on the dingy monitor. Zippo held a worn controller in his paws. "Hold up..." Moe said, sitting at attention. Zippo looked over at him blankly, then back at the screen.

Moe leaned in. "Now wait just a minute..." he whispered, realization dawning on him. "How the *heck* did you do that?"

Zippo tried to hide his purr of amusement. He'd been saving this surprise for some time. He pressed the start button. A pixelated image of a brown-haired humanoid girl wearing a lavender backpack flashed onto the screen.

"*Jessica Gelato: Average School Girl*?!" Moe exclaimed.

Zippo chuffled and tilted his head back. He shook some Kosmic Krill Corn Buddies out of the bag and into his mouth, crunching away happily.

"But—but how..?!"

[*Translator's note: Jessica Gelato: Average School Girl was Moe's favorite video game series. In the game, a player navigated a fifteen-year-old Terran girl named Jessica Gelato through the various ups and downs of teenage life. Previous entries in the series involved getting Jessica an A on her science project, making best friends with Julia the new girl, and spending an afternoon pampering her pet hamster, Donut. — ChatterBot 3.6*]

The newest game was supposed to be the best one yet. Unfortunately, it was only being released for the SuperChromaVision console—and they only owned a ChromaVision original.

"I *know* you didn't buy a SuperChromaVision. They're like...five hundred credits," Moe said.

"Naaa," Zippo shook his head, licking the krill dust off his paws and waiting for Moe to figure it out.

Moe followed the controller's cord. It was plugged directly into the cockpit's dashboard. "You configured the navicomputer to run Jessica Gelato?!"

Zippo smiled and shrugged, as if it was the simplest thing in the world.

"Duuude! You are a *genius*! I don't know how you did it, but you're a genius. Where'd you find a bootleg copy of the new *Jessica*?"

Zippo explained how, through some shrewd bargaining and the aid of a translator monkey named Chib-Kik, he was able to obtain a bootleg copy of the game from a Q'Kkccv'k-ian trader. The same trader had thrown in a SuperChromaVision emulator, which could only run on a very advanced computer system—in their case, the *Terrapin*'s navigational mainframe. It would require most of the starship's processing capabilities, but with things on autopilot until Callisto, the CPU required minimal power.

"So *that's* why everything went wack! The controls in an

alien language, the A.I. talking gibberish...You configured the navi-controls to Q'Kkccv'k-ian so you could run Jessica!"

Zippo nodded mischievously. "Yeh, RALLY easy! We play vid-YO game naow!"

"I always knew this jibroni was the ultimate hacker!" Moe rubbed Zippo on the head, laughing and relieved. "I didn't know you spoke Q'Kkccv'k-ian!" he said, settling back into his co-captain's chair. "You're going to have to translate it for me," he said.

"Neh...noh, I don't..." Zippo rolled his paw sheepishly. "I *noh* speak et."

"Oh." Moe paused. Most of the game involved reading cut scenes and choosing dialogue options. He shrugged. "No problemo; we've got some Q'Kkccv'k-ian Lingos, right?"

Zippo bumped a paw against the dashboard. The glove compartment opened, littered with old fast food wrappers, an ancient looking package of mints, a green lunar switchblade that Zippo had picked up at an orbital refueling kiosk "because it look rally kewl," a map labeled "Starways of the Sol Sector" that appeared to be stained with Bolano sauce, and some badly crushed Bolano sauce packets.

"Ah, hear is bars," Zippo said, pulling out two Lingo Bars. "Oh...Wate," Zippo frowned, showing Moe the bars. Both were labeled "Cocoa Eruption (Terran English)." Zippo made a short, unfavorable growl and tossed the bars back into the glove compartment.

"It's all good. I'm sure we can figure it out," Moe said, grabbing a handful of Kosmic Krill Corn Buddies. He popped a few into his mouth and crunched. "Let's start her up!"

* * *

Hours passed. As far as they could tell from the pixelated graphics and garbled alien text, the game's story revolved around

Jessica trying to get asked to the winter formal by one of six potential boyfriends at Oyster Bay High School. (Either that, or Jessica was plotting to kill one of them—this was Zippo's initial suggestion and he continued to insist it was a possibility.) All they had to go off of were crudely animated cut scenes, an occasional facial reaction portrait, and some bizarre musical cues signaling to the player that they had done or said something dramatic. [*Translator's Note: Q'Kkccv'k-ian text is not easily decoded by foreigners, and before the advent of Lingo Bars, offworlders used to spend several **years** just learning simple greetings such as, "Your repeated molecules sure do look uniform," and "May your ions harden into a really neat looking structure." —ChatterBot 3.6*]

So far, Moe preferred the blonde suitor they'd taken to calling Mark the Hunk. "He's perfect! Captain of the smashball team, and he's the most popular boy in school. This will make us the most popular *girl*—don't you get that?!"

Zippo had his eye on the darker haired boy they'd named Emo Joe. "Dark. *Handsum.* Write POH-ems. Vaaary romance."

Moe scoffed. "Emo Joe? He's *wack*! He's such a puny little dork; my boy Mark would *drop* him." Moe stood, demonstrating the powerbomb Mark would perform on Joe. "We deserve to be with a man who can protect us. Tenth grade is a scary place for a teenage girl! We want a boy who will wrap his arms around us and just make us feel safe," Moe hugged himself, demonstrating the embrace.

"Yeh, but Emo Joe *hawt*!"

As they argued over which boy they were going to flirt with during lunch, a red light in the corner of the monitor started to blink. The blinking was soon accompanied by a tiny chirp, which increased in volume the longer they ignored it. The monitor was obviously urging someone to depress the flashing square button on its bottom right hand corner, but the argument over what Jessica should order for lunch was intensifying.

"You're getting *two* desserts?" Moe exclaimed.

"So wha'?" Zippo looked hurt.

"Do you *want* the boys to think you're a hog? No. No way. Put one of them back. Either the jellyfish roll or the bumble-honey pie. Not both."

"Noh," Zippo said firmly.

"Hunky Mark is *right there*," Moe pointed at the screen. "If you put it back now, you are probably far away enough that he didn't see you. Come on," Moe reached over, guiding Zippo's hands.

Zip recoiled, holding the controller high and to the right of his head. He argued with increasingly frantic gestures that he didn't *want* a boyfriend who was going to judge him for enjoying dessert. "I *liek* much foods! That ez ME; who I *am*!" Zippo splayed a paw on his chest. "If boy don't liek, then he find different garl-FREN!"

As the co-captains continued ignoring the warning chirps, the ship's A.I. grew frustrated. The chirp morphed into a screech. Zippo's controller clattered to the floor as he bolted up, claws out and clasping the shredded arms of his chair. Moe looked around the cockpit, then at his co-pilot. The screech blared on and off. "I don't think that's a good sound," Moe said.

As if to confirm this deduction, the cabin lights in the cockpit switched from blue to red, pulsing in time with the screech. Zippo noticed the button flashing on the bottom of the monitor. With dainty claw extended, he depressed it. A message blinked on the monitor in urgent-looking colors.

It was in Q'Kkccv'k-ian.

"Zippo!" Moe yelled. The crisis screech could indicate any number of horrible things, and a hundred gruesome scenarios flashed through Moe's mind at once. Although the Sol System was considered relatively safe, its backwater location made it ideal for all manner of pirates. And the *Terrapin* was not really equipped to deal with much in terms of enemies. As a cargo tug, their best defense was that they carried almost nothing of value. "Zip, set this back to English! Or something we can understand!"

As if on cue, the ship's A.I. boomed a warning in garbled Q'Kkccv'k-ian. Zippo's telepathic nature was highly emotional; the pulsing lights, crisis screech, and A.I.'s tone did him no favors. The text on the screen pulsed in a pattern psychologically honed to dazzle and disturb the pilots. Moe could tell his companion was on the verge of a nervous breakdown. Zip's claws dug firmly into his ratty chair. His eyes were as wide as saucers.

"Okay, Zip. Chill. Just think for a minute. You changed the default language of our control system. How do we change it back?"

Zippo stared at the warning message flashing on the monitor. He typed tentatively on the keyboard, hoping to dismiss the warning window. He hissed in frustration as several new windows popped up. He looked over at Moe pleadingly, unable to continue.

"Uh...okay, okay...Why don't we just...do a hard reset of the system?" Moe said. Zippo squinted as he mulled it over. Moe reached his short arm beneath the cockpit's dashboard, seeking the small on/off switch. He was too short to reach very far, so scrambled down off his chair. He felt around on his hands and knees. "Okay, got it—" he said.

"Waaayt!" Zippo screeched.

Moe froze. "What is it?! What?"

Zippo bent down and picked up his controller. "Save *game*!"

Moe drew his hand back in horror. They had almost forgotten to save their game on *Jessica Gelato*! "Good thinking, holmes!"

The A.I. voice blaring throughout the ship shifted from extremely concerned to outright hysterical. "*Kkkqqkc-ccjkki! Jqqqjjck'akkgi! Ckkc! CKKC!*"

"Yeah, yeah," Moe waved the voice away as Zippo

navigated the game menu. They spotted the universal "save" icon (an image of a crystal diskette). Before Zippo could select it, a new window popped up and blocked the menu. He growled a Felinian curse, [*Translator's Note: the closest approximation in English being: "YOUR MOTHER BREEDS A RUNTY LITTER!" —ChatterBot 3.6*] and minimized the pop-up in disgust.

Had they bothered looking at the pop-up window, they would have observed a helpful animation. It showed a small icon representing the *Terrapin* crashing into an enormous meteor directly in its flight path. The animated crash was followed by a little explosion, which was then followed by a frowny face.

Since Zippo had routed most of the *Terrapin*'s processor into the SuperChromaVision emulator, the ship's navigational CPU could not plot much of a trajectory through space, even at subetheric velocities. (The pleading A.I. voice had been attempting to explain this to the co-captains for several minutes now.) At the speed they were traveling, they would have to activate manual controls to avoid the unexpected meteoroid in their path. The *Terrapin* had about seventy-eight seconds until total obliteration.

Zippo clicked the save icon. They both exhaled in relief. "Okaayyyy," Moe said to the A.I., "now what was so important it couldn't just WAIT?" He knelt down and clicked off the navigational controls, performing a hard reset. The crisis screech silenced itself and the cockpit darkened. Zippo leaned back in his chair, propping his feet up on the dash. He placed his paws behind his head, relaxing and purring with satisfaction. He looked down at Moe, who was still crouching beneath the dashboard. He gave him the universal "okie-dokie" sign with his paw.

In the darkness of the cockpit, Zippo expected to see a sea of stars before him. As he glanced out the convex viewscreen, however, all he could see was a vaguely dark shape increasing in size very rapidly, as if it were coming directly towards them. "What det?" he asked, gesturing out the front window.

Moe flicked the navigational controls back on and hopped up onto his chair. The various dashboard lights flickered to life as he peered out the window. Before he could even process what was happening, Moe grabbed the manual controls. Something was very, very wrong. His palms got sweaty. "Oh man. Oh, *grok nuggets*."

The dark shape engulfed nearly everything. It swelled as they sped towards it, blocking the stars as it filled their field of vision. Without a scanning computer, it was difficult to tell how immense the meteoroid was, or if they still had a chance to avoid it. Moe jerked the flight wheel to the port and starboard sides, but the *Terrapin* did not respond.

The system was still booting up.

A language selection box blinked on the navicomputer monitor. Zippo, paws on the keyboard, looked to Moe, unsure of what to do.

"ENGLISH! BINOSIAN! *ANYTHING!*" Moe screamed.

The meteoroid grew bigger. Only a sliver of stars outlined it on all sides of its periphery.

Zippo checked English (it was a language they both enjoyed very much, even if Zippo had a hard time speaking it). A small clam appeared on the monitor, speaking in English. "Which avatar would you like to represent your ship's artificial intelligence?" Four portraits of cartoony looking characters appeared on the screen: a rugged-looking lumberjack, a buxom blonde babe, a mouse wearing a top hat (Zippo detested this one), and a little pink cube.

"JUST PICK ONE! NOW! WE'RE GOING TO DIE!" Moe shouted.

They always went with the babe. Zippo swiped frantically at the keyboard, choosing the mouse in the top hat by mistake. He recoiled in disgust as the animated rodent appeared on-screen. In an exceedingly squeaky chipmunk voice, the ship's A.I. began to speak: "Thanks for installing Navi-Ripple Plus navigational software 5.0X, from Seashell Systems!" The mouse waved a cane around in a crude animation as it spoke.

"SKIP! SKIP! SKIP!" Moe screamed as he continued to jerk the flight wheel back and forth, hoping for any response.

"It sounds like you said 'drip'; is there a leak in the CPU coolant system? If so, we can troubleshoot that—"

Moe cursed at the mouse and ordered it to skip the introductory tutorial.

"Remember, if you need my help at any time, just ask for me—I'm Mister Squeakeasy!" Mister Squeakeasy scurried into a pixelated hole and vanished.

The microsecond the tutorial disappeared, the cockpit exploded into chaos. The crisis screech returned in full force, red lights strobing at an epileptic rate. Mister Squeakeasy's voice screamed over the intercom systems: "COLLISION IS IMMINENT! MANUAL CONTROLS NOW! COLLISION IS IMMINENT! MANUAL CONTROLS NOW!"

Moe jammed the controls to the port side, nearly snapping the flight wheel off the console. Thrusters slammed the *Terrapin* to the left, throwing the ship into a violent tilt as they broke their trajectory towards the rock. Random debris and trash clattered around the cockpit as Moe pulled with all his strength. Zippo dug his claws deep into his chair to avoid being thrown against the wall. For three whole seconds, as the ship continued to pull out of the meteoroid's way, Moe thought they might actually make it.

But their inertia was just too much. As the immense boulder rushed toward them, the co-pilots instinctively braced for impact.

"HOLD ON, HOMIE!" Moe shouted.

I LOVE YOU! Zippo mindspoke back.

The starboard side of the *Terrapin* slammed into the space rock. Moe's last-second maneuvering had indeed saved their lives, modifying a head-on trajectory into a protracted side-swipe. The sickening thud morphed into a prolonged screech of meteoroid scraping against the *Terrapin*'s duranium hull. The ship dragged and skidded against the gargantuan comet. The shriek of metal on metal screamed through the cabin, and everything shook. Zippo's ears flattened in sonic pain. He closed his eyes, tensing every muscle in his body as he gripped his chair. He waited for the hull to give way, and for the both of them to get sucked into the vacuum of space.

Moe threw all his weight into holding the flight wheel. If they were lucky, the starship's thrusters would kick in and push them off the rock. Everything shuddered with a turbulence like the universe itself was imploding. The ship roared towards an unknown finale.

Then, after what felt like ten minutes (but was, in actuality, about ten seconds), the scraping sound cut out. Moe and Zippo looked at each other in shock. Moe clicked on the *Terrapin*'s aft camera. The gigantic meteoroid appeared on the screen, slowly and silently shrinking away behind them. Their impact had carved a long, thin trench along the side of the rock, but it appeared otherwise unchanged.

Moe looked back at Zippo, wide-eyed. Their ears rang from the horrible scouring. The cacophony had disappeared so quickly that it was hard to believe anything had even happened. The ship's crisis screech stopped, and even the red cabin lights returned to normal blue. The co-captains stared at one another, unable to move or speak. They were both afraid that talking might jinx them, and cause the ship to finally explode.

"Wow! That was a close one!" Mister Squeakeasy appeared on the screen. "Looks like you just avoided a catastrophic impact! Good job. Would you like me to run a diagnostic check of the ship's systems?"

Zippo mewed a weak, "Yeh" to the A.I., and the mouse disappeared while the ship's computers measured the extent of the damage.

Although the space rock had looked imposing, the ship's duranium exterior was quite resilient. Apart from the utter mess, a few broken items, and an ugly scar along the starboard side, the *Terrapin*'s hull remained intact. As Moe and Zippo waited for Mister Squeakeasy's diagnostic check, Moe rattled the flight controls. "Unresponsive," he muttered.

Zippo tried his flight wheel, also to no response. They sailed on through the starfield, unable to alter course. Zippo stood, making his way out of the cockpit and back to his cabin in a daze. The cartoon mouse reappeared on screen. "Looks like the following systems are going to need some attention, fellas!" The computer listed various minor systems. Moe studied the report, murmuring to himself. "Two of the turbopumps...shot. Dawn Engine computer core...heavily damaged, but functional. Etheric drive...intact, good!" Moe called this back to Zippo with a hopeful note in his voice. "Flight controls… repairs necessary."

They would need a docking station or a planetside garage. Moe swiveled and got out of his chair, following Zippo to his cabin. The Felinian was tidying up his quarters. Everything had been knocked off the shelves and was in disarray, although the space looked no different to Moe. For all the time Zippo spent on personal hygiene, his room was always an absolute mess. Moe crouched and helped place the bottles of Orange Nova Pop back into his mini cooling chamber. Thankfully, they had all survived the scrape.

"Okay, homeboy, here's the deal," Moe started. "That rock swiped off a few of the outer processor filaments to the flight controls. I think it also scratched our main scanner panels to shreds."

Zippo looked worried. "We are...*died*?"

"No!—I think we'll be fine for the time being. Only problem is that, as far as I can make out, the *Terrapin*'s computer instantly cut our ability to use in-flight controls once they were damaged. Probably to avoid us making things worse."

Zippo uncapped one of the Orange Nova Pops. "Oh. Det good." He tilted his head back as he gulped down the drink. He wiped his mouth and whiskers with the back of his paw, offering the drink to Moe.

Moe accepted the bottle and took a swig. "I was hoping you might know a way to override the computer on this?"

Zippo thought for a few moments, but shook his head in defeat. "I don't, ah... I..." he trailed off. He was good with computers, but this was unfamiliar territory.

"It's okay, dude," Moe said comfortingly, patting his friend on the back. He knew Zippo felt responsible for the mishap, and attempted some optimism. "The good news is that despite a pretty sizable gash, all life-support systems are intact. And we have enough food from Uncle Larry's to last us a while. Plus, there's always those cups of vacuum dried sotus noodles in the back. Bad news is, without flight controls, we're going to miss Callisto by about a thousand bips."

"Wha—?!" Zippo made a startled look and mindspoke an image to Moe. It was of himself turning on the ship's emergency SOS subetheric broadcast.

"No!" Moe exclaimed. "No no, let's not do *that*!" He reminded Zippo that their recent discovery, stored away in the ship's databanks, was far too precious to risk having outsiders—even helpful ones—snooping around. "We don't know how shielded our databanks are right now. The electromagnetic static churned up by the impact must have severely messed up our firewall; a simple hull scan could allow a hacker unlimited access to our drives. No," Moe explained, "it's better if we just lay low. We'll figure something out. We might be vulnerable to snoopers, but the scrape didn't appear to destroy anything in our datacache. It's all there, including...you know what." Moe eyed him.

"SEE-cret. Safe," Zippo mewed in relief, then drank more

Nova Pop.

"So it looks like other than thrusters, we have zero control over anything direction-wise." Moe continued as they returned to the cockpit. "I ran the trajectory. At the speed we're going, and if the A.I. is correct, we are on a direct collision course with Terra Firma," Moe pointed to the *Terrapin*'s projected flight path on the monitor. "We'll break through the atmosphere in about...four weeks."

Zippo ran his paws back over his head, smoothing down his ears. He flopped onto his chair. Moe continued. "Let's just hope we drop down over ocean, or some unpopulated area. Then we'll have to get some Terran shipyard to tow us, or something. They won't have the tech to scan us or peep our files." Moe had heard that Terrans were generally friendly towards offworlders. "As long as we don't crash into a playground full of toddlers," he said, "we should be fine."

Zippo hung his head down, arms resting on his hairless legs. "Moe... I so... *sarry*," he mewed, barely above a whisper. He looked very tired.

"Hey! Come on, now, home-squeeze! It's not so bad!" Moe attempted to hand another Nova Pop to Zippo. The Felinian remained with his head hanging down and his eyes closed. "Homie, you were smart enough to push that button! If we had just kept playing our game, like I wanted to, we would've smashed into that rock head-on! And we would've been *wasted*."

Zippo looked up.

"You basically saved our lives! Your quick thinking saved our lives!"

Zippo looked unsure, and accepted the bottle.

"Anyway I thought you liked Terran food, huh?" Moe socked Zippo in the arm.

Zippo smiled. "Shramp...?" he mewed breathily.

"Yes, shrimp! In fact, we'll do a buffet. Terran shrimp, Terran lobster, *all* the Terran seafoods."

The food talk was working, and Zippo's ears eased back up. The Felinian bent down, fishing a paper cup from off the cockpit's floor. "Moar drank?" he asked, filling the cup and offering it to his co-pilot.

"Thanks, dude," Moe said. They sat back in their captain's chairs and stared out the front window. Sol, slightly bigger than the rest of the stars, shone in the distance. The rest of the galaxy sprawled before them in a haze, glimmering like a river of diamonds. The only sound, besides the hum of the subetheric drive, was the fizzle of Nova Pop. The terror of the impact was fading, replaced with a quiet reflectiveness on their second chance at existence.

Moe raised his cup in an impromptu toast. "To Earth!"

"Yeh!" Zippo grinned, raising his bottle. "To Earff!"

CHAPTER 5

YOU'RE BACON ME CRAZY

His suitcase packed, Jeremy tied his necktie in the mirror. Full uniform was always required in the dining hall, affectionately known as "The Trough." He worked on taming his messy hair, getting nowhere. He turned around and observed his room. Even though he hadn't made many friends here, a part of him felt sad to leave it behind. He'd spent the last three years at Pigpimples; it was the closest thing he had to a home ever since he'd lost Mom and Dad.

The sun sank outside, golden beams of light streaking in through the open window. His room sparkled for a few moments, and Jeremy watched as shadows crept across the walls. The trees in the Arcane Rectangle rustled as an early summer breeze blew their leafy branches. Jeremy would miss the magic in the air. He could feel it in his room. He didn't know if it was the approach of summer vacation, or the dance, or something else completely, but something was coming.

He wondered if maybe he'd made the biggest mistake of his life in flunking out. Should he have tried harder? *Maybe I could have gotten a tutor, or asked for help, or really, anything.* Would his father have been disappointed? He'd always wanted Jeremy to become the big-time wizard he never was.

But I couldn't even levitate a feather.

Jeremy looked at the creased poster tacked on the wall above his bed. It was one of his dad's old adverts from his magician years. In bold yellow letters it read: OBEDIAH THE MYSTIC. Every magician needs a stage name and a tagline, Dad had always said. Beneath the stage name was an eerie portrait of his father. He wore a tuxedo and a turban with an emerald in it. A ghostly green light lit the scene as he held a human skull in his left hand. "ENTER THE MYSTIC," the bottom of the poster read.

Jeremy stared at his reflection in the mirror. What he saw was not exactly *mystical.* As he scrutinized himself, he caught a glimpse of the iguana's head poking out from underneath the bed behind him. The lizard coughed, hacking something up onto the floor. Jeremy grinned at himself in the mirror as reassurance flooded through him—getting out of here was the best decision he'd ever made in his life! Jeremy pulled on his House Fluffernut blazer as he dashed out of his room and down the stairs.

* * *

Most of Jeremy's classmates were already in the hall, and the Trough crackled with excitement. The bangers and mash did not sound appetizing in the least, but the nice part was that they didn't have to sit at their house-assigned tables on special feast days like this. Hundreds of students lined the old wooden dining tables, eating and talking boisterously. The whole place echoed with laughter, the shrieks of girls, and the occasional *floom!* of a magic spell being cast. Jeremy spied Bruno across the dining hall, seated at his usual spot. He walked towards him, trying not to draw too much attention to himself.

"Hey, Tommy!" he heard someone shout behind him.

Jeremy knew they meant him. He turned around just in time to see a tiny sausage sailing towards his face, which he dodged. It landed on the floor and rolled under a table. He didn't know if the sausage had been meant for him or not, but rushed to Bruno's table anyway.

Bruno had on an ill-fitting burgundy blazer of House Porkerson. A crest with the image of a *pigasus* (a pig with feathery white wings) was sewn onto the front pocket. It was Porkerson's house animal, and also the official school mascot of Pigpimples Academie.

Bruno D'argento was one of the only other American students at Pigpimples. Jeremy had stuck by Bruno since he'd first overheard his Bronx accent on the Porker Express Monorail. That was way back on their very first day of fifth grade. Bruno's parents came from a line of Italian circus folk, and his family had a long history of sorcery. In fact, Bruno was already pretty good at elemental magic when they first met—especially fire-related. His parents had shipped him all the way out to Pigpimples primarily to help him lose weight. In the three years that they'd known each other, Jeremy didn't think Bruno had lost a single pound.

"Ay yo, Jeremy! Wanna help me out here?" Bruno said, motioning to his pink plate full of asparagus spears and beet mash. House Porkerson students were never allowed to get their own food at feasts, due to their "special dietary needs." They were assigned plates made out of pink china so that kitchen staff would know not to serve them the regular food.

"In a minute," Jeremy answered, sitting down. "I need to save my energy." Bruno raised an eyebrow. "I've got something planned," Jeremy assured him. He glanced past Bruno at a table full of Dandy Lion students. Two of the boys seated there chugged milk out of big glass bottles as the rest of their classmates chanted "GO! GO! GO!" One of the boys, Pete Wisby, sputtered to a stop, spilling milk all over his golden

Dandy Lion blazer. The table erupted in laughter. Janine was there, laughing through her expression of disgust.

Bruno turned around and watched the table for a moment. "Ahhh, I see, I get it!" he turned back to Jeremy with a sly smile. "You gonna ask her for a dance tonight?"

"Of course," Jeremy said.

"What if her dance card is full?" Bruno asked.

"Oh, she'll make room." Jeremy leaned in and cocked an eyebrow, "Matter of fact, she'll make a *new* dance card—and every line is going to say 'Jeremy Fletcher.'"

Bruno leaned back in his chair, laughing. "Hey-ooooo!" he snapped his fingers in a show of enthusiasm. Sparks of fire crackled out as he snapped, swirling around him erratically and landing harmlessly on the floor.

"Ex-CUSE me, laddie!" an elderly wizard bellowed. It was Sir Mongo Chamberpot, the Headmage. He stood behind Bruno, dressed in his ridiculous shimmering robes and conical hat. His long white beard trembled in frustration as he shook his head. He spoke with a noticeable lisp, and his favorite pastime was acting appalled at everything around him. "Why, I *never*! The dining hall is no place for magic! Just because it's the last day doesn't mean the rules don't apply!" his hand fluttered about in the air, mimicking the boy's snapping gesture.

"Sorry, sir," Bruno responded, palms up.

"Well that's just a pip! That's one thousand demerits to House Porkerson!" The Headmage looked around, eyeing the Board of Truth at the far end of the dining hall. It listed all the school's houses and their "excellence ratings" for the semester. It read:

The Dandy Lions.... 1,404,682 points

House Hazeltwig...... 811,091 points

House Porkerson........ 6,200 points

House Fluffernut..... -10,017 points

With a flash of his wand, Sir Chamberpot lowered Porkerson's score by a thousand points. Bruno and Jeremy looked at one another, each stifling a giggle. The entire system had been a joke since their first day at Pigpimples. The Dandy Lions won every year, due to the completely arbitrary nature of the point system. If Sir Chamberpot or another one of the professors liked something a Dandy Lion did, they'd get awarded a hundred thousand points right there on the spot. The Dandy Lions won points for winning Quadritardd matches, getting good grades, and even "best personal grooming." In fact, Jeremy had once witnessed Cleric Avalon award the Dandy Lions one thousand points just because he liked the way Amanda Pike held her pencil "so quietly." Jeremy had complained about this injustice to his House Fluffernut classmates, but nobody cared. "Maybe *you* should focus on not holding your pencil so loudly!" Nobby Curdswell had suggested unhelpfully. Jeremy then sarcastically asked Nobby if he might teach him any sound muffling spells to aid him in this endeavor. (The saddest part was that Nobby had actually spent several days looking for one in the library. The closest thing he could find was an ancient spell that quieted chickens that were being slaughtered. When he attempted to cast it on Jeremy's pencil, very little happened.)

"Hey Professor," Jeremy said to Sir Chamberpot, "I've seen a lot of unauthorized magic use in here this evening. I appreciate all you're doing to keep us safe."

"I assure you, Master Fletcher, we're doing our very best! Things can get *pretty* turbulent on the last day of school!" the sorcerer motioned around the room, waving his arms theatrically. Jeremy and Bruno held their breath as they stifled more laughter.

"You might want to go over there," Jeremy pointed at the table of Dandy Lions, "And keep an eye on those fellows. They were getting into some dangerous stuff. One of them levitated a sausage. And I'm pretty sure I overheard someone attempting to summon a rainbow!"

"They what?!" the Headmage turned towards the table, furious. In addition to teaching elective courses on the baking of various meat pies, Sir Chamberpot's specialty was the magickal art of rainbow summoning. He took it extremely seriously. But he must have heard the amusement in the boys' voices. Sir Mongo turned back to face them. "Ahhhhh," the old mage slitted his eyes, "this is a *joke* to you, Master Fletcher? So you've been expelled, and now rainbow magic is just a big laugh. Is that it?"

Bruno looked at Jeremy, his eyes wide with surprise. *Expelled?!* his expression seemed to ask. Jeremy looked back with a bewildered shrug he hoped would convey: *I was going tell you!*

"Well, I daresay you don't have the discipline or the skill to even *attempt* to summon a basic level one bow, so I won't bother trying to explain their value to you." Sir Chamberpot looked to the Board of Truth and wiggled his wand again, lowering House Fluffernut's score by ten thousand points. They'd never ended a semester in the positives, so this was nothing shocking. Jeremy overheard a "Nooooo!" from some of the Fluffernut kids at another table. He spied Nobby Curdswell lowering his head into his hands in defeat. Jeremy felt kind of bad about that... for a moment.

The Headmage turned to Jeremy. He had an air of "serious talk" about him. Jeremy groaned inwardly. *Here comes the life lesson.* "You know, Jeremy, rainbow summoning isn't a THEATRICAL form of magic. It's probably the most delicate, subtle form of magic in existence. It's true that you won't find those stage magicians you so love attempting rainbow magic. Too busy sawing ladies in half and pulling rabbits out of their trousers, I imagine."

Jeremy tilted his head at this mental image.

"In fact, I hesitate to even *call* them magicians," Chamberpot continued, "charlatans—if I may be blunt. Hacks who couldn't cut it. Frauds. Simple as that." The professor sat down beside

Jeremy at the table to continue the heart-to-heart. "Many years ago, I had a pupil by the name of Frederick. 'Freddy the Unready,' the other students used to call him," Sir Chamberpot smiled, amused at this memory. "Oh how the other students would tease him! Just tease him mercilessly!" He chuckled. "Freddy didn't have a magical bone in his body. Strangely enough, his parents weren't even normies or humdrums. But, for whatever reason, the universe decided not to endow Freddy with any magical abilities. And so he had to be expelled from Pigpimples as a matter of course. He said he wanted to go back to the states and become a stage magician." Sir Chamberpot shook his head in disgust.

"Before he left, I encouraged Freddy to find himself a nice normie job. Something that would suit his talents and abilities. Beekeeping, or perhaps digging ditches. We can't all be bringing humanity the immense happiness that accompanies the sight of a beautiful rainbow!" the professor moved his hand in an arc over their heads.

He continued. "*This* is why magic exists, after all! Don't you see? It's to help the world! To make the world a happier and better place, full of laughter and gaiety! To think that a man would PRETEND to do magic on stage... simply for the sake of... the sake of..." the professor shook his head in frustration as he searched for words to express his disapproval.

"For the sake of entertaining people?" Jeremy added.

"Yes, precisely! It's just sickening. We're not here to provide humdrum rubes with a mindless diversion for a ha'penny under some carnival tent—we're here to help the world! For example, what magic are you majoring in, err," he fumbled for Bruno's name, "Master D'argento?"

"How to burn things," Bruno answered.

"See, Master Fletcher? We're all striving to help mankind in our own little ways... As I said, ditch-digging—now there's a job that ANY normie could do! Important! Ditches divert water from off the road! Can you imagine how splishy-splashy the roads would be with all that unnecessary rainwater lying around on them? A nightmare!"

Jeremy and Bruno sat in a trance of boredom, resigned to the Headmage's ramblings. They waited for the professor to forget his point and move on, or get distracted by someone else in the dining hall. Sir Chamberpot held up a finger, as if he'd realized something. "So just as after the rain, nature makes a magical rainbow in the sky—on the ground, water is being diverted by helpful and important *ditches*. And not just ditches, mind you—trenches, gulleys, dikes, gutters...they're all part of a beautiful tapestry. Do you understand what I'm trying to say, Master Fletcher?"

"Yes," Jeremy said, "you're saying Freddy was a failure, and I remind you of him."

The professor patted Jeremy on the back. "That's a good lad," the Headmage winked. He groaned as he stood up, various pops crackling from his joints. Another student, seeing the old wizard struggling, hopped up from his table across the way. He wore the golden blazer and tie of the Dandy Lions, along with a navy blue cloak that marked him as head of the Quadritardd team. The cloak fluttered dramatically as the boy rushed over. He leaned down and offered his arm to the Headmage.

"Thank you, Master Lionspark," the sorcerer patted the boy's arm. It was Christopher Lionspark. Christopher stood tall, broad-shouldered and confident. A dashingly handsome lock of blonde hair fell perfectly out of place on his forehead.

"It's no trouble, Sir Mongo," Christopher replied. Apparently he was on a first-name basis with the Headmage. Christopher Lionspark had come to Pigpimples a few years before Jeremy, and it felt like everything at the school revolved around him. Christopher looked at Jeremy with a smirk. "What I don't understand, Jeremy, is why, for someone so disinterested in *real* magic, you *insist* on copying the entire look of Tommy

Cobblestone!"

Jeremy reddened. Christopher had touched a very sore spot indeed. He went on, "I mean, the round spectacles, the hazel coloured eyes, the boyish good looks!" (Jeremy and Bruno glanced at one another at this observation.) "Your hair is the same darkish brown as Tommy's, and you keep it kind of messy, and even parted in the same way!" In addition to Jeremy's concern over how much Christopher Lionspark was observing his personal grooming habits, he was also severely annoyed at the comparison to Tommy Cobblestone. [*Translator's Note: This reference to Tommy Cobblestone undoubtedly needs no explanation, but for the sake of those readers who perhaps live in alternate timelines, dimensions, or mirror universes, here it is:*

The Adventures of Tommy Cobblestone was/is a very famous comic book series. It follows the exploits of the titular Tommy Cobblestone, an orphaned boy wizard who attends a fictional version of Pigpimples Academie. The comic was created, in part, by Pigpimples faculty as a marketing tool to bolster steadily dropping enrollment numbers. When first released in the fall of 1917, it was an instant smash hit in its native Great Britain. Its popularity soon spread to the United States, and eventually the entire planet.

Comic books, long thought to be mindless drivel meant to sell advertisements to children, suddenly captured the interest of grown-ups as well. Respected adults, who previously would have been ashamed to be caught reading such simple-minded juvenelia, were now enthralled by the exploits of the imaginary boy wizard.

The comic's popularity spread to all of the planets in the Cosmic League like wildfire; offworlders could not get enough of the adventures of little Tommy. They were translated into almost every language imaginable, although most aliens preferred reading them in the original English.

Within two short years the series was lauded with every

accolade, every possible literary award. Anita Cosgrove, the creator of Tommy Cobblestone, was praised as the greatest literary genius of the age. Major universities throughout Terra Firma and the Cosmic League began teaching courses on Tommy Cobblestone comics, hailing them as the singular achievement in the history of literature.

One esteemed critic from the library planet of Radruthea summed it up: "Would it be an exaggeration to say that Tommy Cobblestone is the single most important book series in the history of the universe? In a word—no."

The fact that Jeremy just happened to look a lot like Tommy Cobblestone was just one of life's crueler coincidences. — ChatterBot 3.6]

"I've been wearing these glasses since I was six!" Jeremy removed his spectacles and waved them around in frustration. "I want nothing to do with that cheeky imbecile you all seem to worship!"

"Oh, really?" Christopher snorted. "Then why do you take the time every day to draw a scar on your left hand that looks *exactly* like the horse-shaped scar on Tommy's hand—the one he got from his battle with Grinkus the Goblin in issue #12?" Christopher reached down and grabbed Jeremy's wrist, holding it up to the crowd. Jeremy yanked his hand back and pushed up the sleeve of his blazer.

"I don't draw on my hand, you git. It's a birthmark! I've had it since I was born! And honestly, I always thought it looked more like an anteater than some stupid horse," Jeremy held his left hand up to the room as proof.

"Now, now, Christopher. Tommy Cobblestone is an inspiration to all of us. It's understandable that Master Fletcher tries to—how shall we say—*emulate* Tommy's iconic look and style," Professor Chamberpot said. "We knew that when we created the character of Tommy, young people were going to want to mimic him. That was the whole point! An advertisement for Pigpimples! We hoped it would be successful, but we had no idea that it would take over the whole world! Every little boy wants to be Tommy Cobblestone! Can you really blame him?"

"He's no Tommy Cobblestone," Christopher scoffed. "And it's not just that he tries to look like him, he disgraces the name of Pigpimples by *acting* like Tommy! Always going on about how he's going to be famous. What's next, is Jeremy going to tell us his parents are dead and he's an orphan, too?"

The Headmage chuckled. "No, no. He's no Tommy Cobblestone, I'll grant that!"

Jeremy's irritation erupted. "Tommy Cobblestone didn't even come out until after I started school here! I..!" He stopped himself before he could get drawn into yet another argument over this issue. He took a deep breath. Bruno looked at Jeremy with a dubious expression and shook his head. *Not worth it*, he seemed to say. Jeremy gave his best ironic smile and waved dismissively. "If anything, *he* copied *me*."

Christopher and the Headmage roared with laughter.

"I don't get what's so hard about this," Jeremy went on, calmly citing the same points he always cited, "I started here in Fall of 1916. My eyes were the same color, my hair was the same, and I had the same dumb glasses. The first issue of Tommy Cobblestone didn't come out until fall of 1917. Look it up! The date is right on the corner of the cover."

It didn't appear that Sir Chamberpot or Christopher Lionspark were listening. "This is why you'll never succeed at magic, Master Fletcher," the old wizard explained, wiping a tear from his eye. "You're too concerned with always *being* right, when you should worry more about *feeling* right—real magic comes from in here," the professor tapped on his own chest with two fingers. "But it's not too late for you. I have some excellent pamphlets on ditch-related careers that I'd like for you to take home. Stop by my office before you leave."

Jeremy gave up. "Thank you sir, I'd appreciate that."

"If only you'd kept that positive attitude before! That's the spirit!" Sir Chamberpot said, and tottered off excitedly in the direction of what appeared to be unauthorized juggling. Christopher followed him, shouting at the students to stop immediately and blasting them with a level five stun spell.

"They really kickin' you out?" Bruno asked.

Jeremy nodded.

"Forever?"

"Seems that way."

Bruno shook his head. "I'm sorry, pally. It ain't gonna be any fun around here without you."

"It's okay. Pigpimples isn't for a normie like me anyway. I don't think I could stand another class on 'Case Studies of Wizard Litigation in 14th Century Poland,' or whatever else they were going to make me study," Jeremy said.

"You ain't no normie, though! You got the COOLEST magic spell I've ever seen. I'd die to be able to do what you do!" Bruno took some bites of his food, speaking through his chewing, "They wanna make me into a pyromancer, but lemme tell ya, I'd much rather be—uhh—whatever it is you're called." He motioned at Jeremy with his fork.

"Thanks. I guess you're right, I do have this one trick up my sleeve." Jeremy pulled his wand out of his jacket's inner pocket. It was a Jansen *Black Tarot*. (He preferred the more modern style of Jansen wands—a straight black baton with white tip.)

"So, when you leavin'?" Bruno asked.

"I need to be off campus by the end of the day tomorrow."

"Ayy! Alright, okay! That's plenty of time! You're coming to the Farewell Ball then, ain't cha?"

"Of course! What do you think I was going to talk to Janine about?"

"Noooo! You weren't kidding about that, eh? This I gotta see!" Bruno pulled off the napkin tucked into his collar. "Come on, she's right there! Show us how it's done, Casanova!" he jerked a thumb towards the Dandy Lion table. Jeremy stood, giving Bruno a wink as he pointed with his wand and sauntered over.

Janine was there, whipping her hair back and laughing at the antics of the kids at her table. The two boys had finished their milk chugging contest and had moved on to a battle of magician's mercy. The game involved blasting tiny lightning bolts into one another's arms, the shots increasing in intensity each round. Jeremy wondered how much longer until one of them simply dropped dead from electrocution. As much as he hated to interrupt, he cleared his throat. The students stopped what they were doing and stared at him.

"Hi!" he held up a hand. The students continued to stare.

"Why is he dressed like Tommy Cobblestone?" one of the younger Dandy Lion girls asked her older classmates.

"Oh, that's just a thing this kid does," another answered.

"That's a common misconception," Jeremy addressed the girl's question as he walked over to Janine's side of the table. "In fact, I am simply dressed in the Pigpimples official school uniform. You'll notice that everyone here is wearing one." Jeremy directed their attention to their own clothing, pointing with his wand.

"But why are you wearing Tommy Cobblestone's glasses?" the little girl asked.

"What, these?" Jeremy touched the stem of his glasses. "These are actually *my* glasses. *Not* Tommy Cobblestone's. This is because Tommy Cobblestone doesn't have glasses. Because Tommy Cobblestone is not real."

"Yes he is!" the little girl protested.

"Anyway," Jeremy pressed forward, "hi Janine, how are you this evening?" he flashed her a disarming grin. Janine looked around, puzzled, waiting for an explanation from her classmates. They merely continued staring, as if a slow-motion train derailment was taking place right before their eyes. "How's the food tonight?" Jeremy smiled.

"It's... fine," Janine finally responded. He so loved that English accent of hers.

"Fine, huh? Just fine?" He felt himself floundering. "You know," he picked up a sausage, "where I come from we actually don't call these 'bangers.' I mean what're you supposed to bang on with these little guys, anyway? They're pretty squishy if you ask me!"

Janine stared at Jeremy in something close to disgust, although it could have easily been distress—maybe even fear. "If you want more food," she said, "just go up and ask—they'll give you seconds. In fact," she slid her plate towards Jeremy, "just take it. Please."

Jeremy chuckled. "Wait, wait... I..." he held up a finger, "that's not exactly what I had in mind."

"The real Tommy Cobblestone doesn't even *like* bangers and mash," the little Dandy Lion girl said. "He likes kidney blood pie."

Jeremy wrinkled his nose. "That's...disgusting. Anyway," he soldiered on, "what I came here to share with you is a spell I've been working on. Thought maybe you could give me some feedback. It goes a little something like this..." Jeremy readied his wand and aimed it at Janine's plate of bangers and mash. [*Translator's Note: the rhyme Jeremy then recited was recorded as being so lethally cringe-inducing, it could not be properly translated back into English. The closest approximation is as follows. —ChatterBot 3.6*]

You're BACON me crazy with those pretty blue eyes,
ORANGE you glad I'm not like all the other guys?
Now I've got a request that's TOAST-tally not hard—
Just OM-LETTE me have a line on your dance card!

At the poem's conclusion, Jeremy murmured a spell under

his breath as he dabbed and tapped his wand. A glimmer sparkled over Janine's plate. In a flash, her food was magically replaced with...what appeared to be the same food, but in some kind of disheveled, half-chewed disarray. "BREAKFAST IS..." Jeremy started triumphantly, then looked down at the food and stopped himself. "Huh," he muttered.

"Just take it!" Janine yelled at Jeremy. "It's yours!"

"Give me a second here," Jeremy said. He dabbed and tapped again, not bothering with the poem (it was just a magician's flourish, after all). He re-muttered the magic words. The food glimmered, and in a second flash was magically replaced with the same food, but in an even more decomposed state. The bangers were no longer very banging. In fact, they appeared to be melting.

Jeremy attempted the the spell several more times, each time causing the molecular structure of the food to decay until it looked more and more like a big plate of indiscernible mush. His final crack at the magic spell rendered the remaining nutrients into a blob of reeking goo that exploded in a brownish splatter across everyone nearby. Janine and the other girls screamed, all of them covered in digested banger and/or mash paste. The boys, also covered in the stuff, whooped with laughter upon seeing the girls' distress.

"You are SO GROSS!" Janine screamed at Jeremy, turning and making her way out of the dining hall. Christopher Lionspark, having overheard the commotion, appeared in a flash. Janine ran into his arms, simultaneously embracing him and slathering him in the goo. "Oh Christopher! I'm such a fool! I've ruined your nice uniform!" Janine lamented.

"It's quite alright, Janine," Christopher said with a smile. He lifted his wand and cast a level three cleaning spell on Janine and himself. A whirlwind of magic enveloped them, lifting the stains off of their clothing and off of Janine's face and hair. Jeremy found himself thinking how pretty Janine's pearly hair looked as it fluttered all around.

"Wow!" Janine exclaimed, running her fingers through her locks. "All clean! And my hair feels really great, too! Such volume, but also bouncy! How did you do that?"

"Oh, it's nothing. I just tweaked the conditioner sub-spell by adding a little volume enhancer I read about in the archives. How are the clothes? All spic and span?"

Janine ran her hand along her blazer and the edge of her skirt. "You always know just the right spell, Chris! How do you do it?"

"That was one of my own—a fabric softener chant I picked up on our adventure in the dungeons last year," Christopher smirked.

Jeremy, still covered in rapidly encrusting gobs of brown goo, walked over to Janine. "Now that—that was *not* actually what was supposed to happen," he said. "The food was supposed to turn into the different items I was mentioning in that little poem, which took me *several* weeks to come up with, by the way."

Christopher stepped in, "Janine, with all your dinner ruined you must be famished. How would you like to join us out on the 'Tardd field? Me and some of the lads are roasting that evil boar that escaped from the Labyrinth of Pain last week. Come on, it'll do you good!"

Janine squealed with delight. "Barbecue boar's head! Yummy!" She took Christopher's arm as he escorted her towards the exit.

"You see, *you're BACON me crazy*—that line was there because I was supposed to make a couple of pieces of bacon appear. Or... 'hammy strips,' or whatever you limeys like to call them..." Jeremy trailed off as Janine and Christopher walked out the door. Accepting failure, Jeremy returned to his table.

"Tough break," Bruno said. "What happened? You're usually spot-on with that kind of thing."

"Not exactly sure," Jeremy said as he sat down, wiping some of the muck off of his face. He cleaned off his wand with a napkin.

"Well buddy, I bet you dollars to donuts she woulda gone ducky over you—you know, had your plan worked."

"I must have been too nervous. Concentrating too hard, you know? Sometimes you have to just let go and not think so much."

"These things happen," Bruno said, returning to his asparagus and beet mash. "What am I gonna do when you're gone? Don't tell me I actually have to start eating this stuff!"

"I could teach it to you," Jeremy said.

"Naaah," Bruno sighed. "Didn't we try that once? Probably end up getting us both killed. I'm good with the flames, not so great at anything else." Bruno snapped, splashing sparks onto the table again.

Just then, two girls approached their table. One of the girls was tall and freckle-faced, with a head of hair best described as strawberry blonde ginger frizz. The other girl was half her friend's height, mousy-faced, and with short, bobbed hair. They both wore puce [*Translator's Note: that's a purpley-brownish — ChatterBot 3.6*] colored blazers with the insignias of House Fluffernut, which was a small mythical bunny, known as a *lapitolo*.

"Oh no," Jeremy muttered. He tried to think of some excuse to bolt, but it was too late.

"Hi, Jeremy!" the taller girl called to him. It was Kitani. *Kitani Kawaii.* She told everyone to call her "Kit," but nobody did. In fact, Jeremy knew for a fact that "Kitani" wasn't even her real name. They'd met on the Porker Express Monorail on their first day of school years ago. Back then, she'd introduced herself as Kimberly from Liverpool. She'd become infatuated with Eastern magic after attending a lecture on "Magic of the Orient" by Okita Sun, a visiting sea witch from Japan. Kimberly had gone by "Kitani" ever since.

Her shorter companion was Sally Simpson.

"You're so bad, Bruno! You both know you're not supposed to be doing magic in here!" Kitani pretended to look shocked, then laughed. "You two are such rebels!"

"Yeah," Jeremy said.

Kitani and Sally broke into some kind of weird choreographed dance—Jeremy assumed it was their way of showing approval. Their hands flailed as they did bizarre twitchy movements and sang in high-pitched voices. They ended by shrieking "JEREMY FLETCHER YEEEAAAAAH!" and doing the hand signal for House Fluffernut, which involved crossing one's arms and making twin "bunny ears" signs. The rest of the students in the area had stopped to stare at this display, and looked to Jeremy to witness his reaction. The girls kept their ending pose until Jeremy spoke.

"Uh. Thanks," Jeremy said.

"I don't know what was going on," Kitani exclaimed, "but that was a REALLY cool spell you did back there! You just made all that brown stuff explode! How funny!"

"Yep," Jeremy said, nodding and waiting for it to be over.

"You sure showed those Dandy Lions! They're such little snobs, aren't they?"

"Yes, very snobbish," Jeremy conceded. He tried to leave it at that. Any more words spoken by him would only stoke the flames of Kitani's inability to pick up on social cues.

She pulled a pair of round-rimmed glasses out of her blazer pocket and put them on. "Do you like my new glasses?" she asked.

"Where did you get those?"

"From the optometrist, where do you think?" Kitani laughed.

Jeremy pretended not to notice that her glasses were identical to his.

"Yo Kitani, ain't you worried people gonna accuse you of

copying Tommy Cobblestone?" Bruno asked.

Kitani gasped. "Ick! Yuck! Gross!!" she made disgusted hacking and spitting noises. Sally followed her lead, also making disgusted noises. "Are you crackers?! These are *not* Tommy Cobblestone glasses!" Kitani nearly shouted. "I can't stand that daft little prat!" She outstretched her arms towards Jeremy. "They're *Jeremy Fletcher* glasses!"

The students at the surrounding tables snickered. Jeremy glanced around witheringly, shaking his head as if to say *please don't encourage her*.

"I remember you wearing them the day we first met, on the Porker Express Monorail! You remember, don't you? You and Bruno were sitting together and I came up and was looking for my pet hedgehog which had somehow gotten out of my backpack!" Kitani continued recounting the rousing tale of how they'd eventually found the hedgehog curled up in a ball under the seat. It was one of her favorite stories, and she managed to bring it up nearly every single time she interacted with Jeremy.

"Yeah, I still remember that. I never forgot it, in fact," Jeremy said.

"He was just copying Tommy Cobblestone, though," a Hazeltwig student called out at Kitani. She immediately pulled her wand out and aimed it at the boy, a killing look in her eyes.

"That was more than a YEAR before Tommy Cobblestone even CAME OUT! We came to Pigpimples in 1916. CHECK THE COVER OF THE FIRST ISSUE! Isn't that right?" she looked to Sally, who nodded vigorously in the affirmative. Kitani looked as if she was just barely holding herself back from blasting the Hazeltwig boy with some kind of transfiguration spell—toad, maybe caterpillar. Luckily for the boy, Kitani was perhaps the only student at Pigpimples Academie worse at spellcasting than Jeremy. In fact, Jeremy believed she knew only one spell: *bailamos perfundos* (a rather arcane hex that forced people to dance casually for three to four minutes). He'd seen her cast it on onlookers while she and Sally did one of their sad little "performances" in the Rectangle.

She turned to Jeremy with a serene expression, removing her glasses. As she tucked them back into her blazer pocket, she pretended to drop a little pamphlet on the table. Jeremy winced, realizing what it was.

"Oops! I dropped my dance card!" Kitani picked up the pamphlet. "Wouldn't do to lose this, would it? Right before the ball, too!" She waved the booklet back and forth, holding the pages open for Jeremy to get a clear look at them. Professor Ruby Gravewood distributed these cards to every girl at Pigpimples. They were little schedules that allowed the girls to plan out which boys they'd like to dance with at the ball, and in which order. A boy would ask a girl for a dance in the days leading up to the ball, and the girl would look at her dance card. If she wanted a dance, the boy would get his name penciled in. If she didn't want to dance, the boy would get the much-dreaded: "Sorry, but my dance card is full!"

Kitani had decided to shake up some paradigms by taking matters into her own hands and writing JEREMY FLETCHER (followed by a tiny heart) on all ten lines of her card. Jeremy read his name, over and over. He suddenly felt seasick. "Oh okay, Kitani. Uh..." his mind raced for a way out.

"The first dance is the Pigpimples Polka! I've been practicing!" Kitani grabbed Sally and started to polka in place.

"Kitani, the thing is... I think I already asked... Uhh... Sybil Karkaroff for the first dance."

"Sybil Karkaroff?!" Kitani screwed up her face in confusion. She knew exactly where Sybil was sitting, and marched directly to a table surrounded by House Hazeltwig kids. Jeremy looked over and saw Sybil sitting there, chatting with a friend. She was a quiet girl that Jeremy had sat next to during *Intro to Ghouls*.

Kitani asked Sybil if they could possibly trade dance partners. Sybil looked confused. "Who are you even talking about?" she asked. Kitani pointed at Jeremy. "Oh. Cobblestone Boy? He never asked me to dance." The Hazeltwig students laughed. Jeremy thought this might upset Kitani, but she just rushed back to his table, beaming, to tell him the great news.

"Kit," Jeremy stopped her before she could say anything. He knew she liked it when he called her that. "I just remembered, it was Janine Wintershade that I asked for the first dance." He half hoped Kitani would go and look for her so he could escape.

"Janine... Wintershade?" A shadow fell across Kitani's face as that death look returned. "I was meaning to... talk... to her," she said, narrowing her eyes.

Jeremy wondered if he'd just put Janine's life in danger. He stammered. "And then there's, uh... Amanda Pike. Oh, and Velma Proudbody for the Sorcerer's Sarabande! But," Jeremy swallowed, "I'll tell you what. The last dance is all yours."

"Really?!" Kitani's eyes lit up with a look of deranged joy.

"Yes. In fact, it would be my honor."

Kitani blushed, snickering and clutching Sally's hands as they both jumped for joy.

"Let's go get ready!" Kitani said, pulling her friend along as they both ran out of the Trough.

Bruno gave Jeremy a thoughtful look. "That was mighty classy of you, *paisan*. You're a true gentlewizard."

"Yeah," Jeremy nodded. "I'm just going to sneak out before the last dance."

CHAPTER 6
SO LONG, AND THANKS FOR ALL THE KNOWLEDGE OF THE OCCULT

After dinner, Jeremy returned to his dorm. He washed up and changed out of his goo-encrusted clothes. The thing he liked the most about the Farewell Ball was the fact that formal wear was required. He thought he looked pretty good in a tuxedo! He put on his dress shirt and trousers with suspenders, leaving the bow tie and jacket on his bed. He did some poses for his future poster in the mirror, pointing his wand with his raised right hand and making some weird beckoning gesture with his outstretched left. "Enter the mystic," he whispered to himself, making a deadly serious face.

He froze in terror at a creak from the hallway, dropping his wand to the floor. Fortunately, it was just Donut starting her nightly wheel run. He chuckled in spite of himself and picked up his wand. *Better finish this packing while there's still time*, he thought. He would catch the train to London first thing in the morning. He didn't feel like hanging around for a lot of potentially awkward goodbyes and explanations. He took down his father's old poster, folding it gently and placing it in his suitcase along with some other odds and ends. He'd amassed a small collection of books that he didn't want to lug all the way back to Ireland.

Toad Studies, 8th Edition from Professor Gravewood's class. *A History of Disproven Healing Rituals* from Cleric Avalon's.

Magic Potions and Soothing Lotions from Sir Chamberpot's survey of enchanted ointments (Jeremy shuddered at the memory of this course).

The Exhaustive Directory of Flesh Eating Plants from Lady Sophia Primrose—which was admittedly kind of interesting, but it also weighed twenty-six pounds. He placed it on the bookshelf along with the rest. Perhaps someone next semester could use them.

There was also the crystal given to him by Elnoo, a visiting alien lecturer from the Ehua System. The green-skinned offworlder had taught a class on teleportation. Ehuians were naturally good at this skill, not actually considering it "magic." The crystal was supposed to help Jeremy focus his "ambient harmonic particle energy" or some such thing. It had never worked for him in the slightest. However, the crystal *was* pretty cool looking. He tossed it in his suitcase; he could always use it as a prop.

Two books remained, but they were ones he didn't actually own. They had been lent to him by teachers.

A History of Supernatural Happenings in Europe belonged to Professor Maledict Von Bibliosnuff, who taught a class on wizard law. It was a depressingly monotonous course, and the textbook was outright deadly. Jeremy had given up after the fourth chapter on "Recorded Incidents of Chairs Falling Over With No Good Explanation in Medieval Spain," and tried winging his essay. Jeremy had titled it: "From Baphomet to Bacon: A Journey Through Occult Breakfast Items."

Bibliosnuff had not been pleased.

He really didn't want to confront the professor again, but he also didn't want to risk having the Fascination Wolves hunt him down over an unreturned book.

Jeremy's other textbook was about ceremonial costumes and attire from Professor Aleistair Smith's sewing class. He grabbed both books, jogging downstairs and out the front door.

* * *

Jeremy stood on the lawn of the Arcane Rectangle for a moment, observing the changing colors of dusk. Campus was growing dark. Across the way was the Weirding Arts Hall. It looked like the lights were still on in one of the rooms; Jeremy suspected he knew whose office it was. He walked across the lawn, humming a samba tune and breaking into a jaunty dance. He wondered for a moment if any girls could see him out their windows (their dorm was on the other side of the Rectangle), but decided that he really didn't care if they did at this point. He danced over to the Hall and let himself in.

The building was dark and downright creepy, but the light flickering from the professor's office looked inviting. The door was cracked, and Jeremy gave a light knock before pushing it open. Professor Smith had a fireplace in his office which he kept lit year-round. Sometimes the fire burned blue or violet, sometimes red. It just depended on the professor's mood, or whatever he was working on. Tonight it was just a normal fire, dying into a glowing pile of embers. The only other light came from an Arabian oil lamp on the table. Professor Smith said he preferred old-fashioned light sources over their modern electric counterparts. "They just have a more spiritual feel, don't you think?" he'd once said to Jeremy during one of their late-night discussions. They'd spent untold winter evenings talking about the court magicians of various ancient kingdoms.

Shadows quivered up and down the walls of the room, cast by the various trinkets and oddities that adorned the office. There was a statue on the professor's desk of an octopus carved from lavender jade stone. Beside it was an Aztec idol of some half-man, half-crocodile creature. His shelves contained all manner of scrolls, dusty lexicons, old tomes written in forgotten hieroglyphs, and even a book that appeared to be made of golden metal plates. Jeremy's favorite item was the Egyptian pharaoh's dagger that hung above the fireplace. Professor Smith once told him the blade was carved from the black stone of a meteorite that had crash-landed in the desert six thousand years ago.

The professor sat in an overstuffed chair, his feet propped on an ottoman. He was a portly man, and totally bald. The only hair on his head was his graying Van Dyke beard. He wore a purple velvet fez with a red tassel hanging off the top, and was dressed in his usual silky robes. They were stitched all over with intricate runes and foreign designs that Jeremy had always found intriguing.

Someone's final research paper levitated in front of the professor. He made little red marks appear on it with the occasional flick of his correcting wand. In his other hand, the professor held a pipe. The whole room was filled with the mystic aroma of incense and fragrant dwarven tobacco. Jeremy cleared his throat.

"Ah, Jeremy. Come in, my lad." The professor placed his pipe in his mouth. He had not even turned around, but Jeremy was used to his prescient ways by now.

"I came to return your book. The... uhm..." Jeremy checked the cover again. "*Thamaturgic Threads of Otherworldly Origin*," he read.

"A fine volume, that. Did you find it enlightening?"

Jeremy placed the book on the professor's desk. His teacher was still concentrating on the essay floating in front of him.

"I did, yes."

"Very good," Professor Smith looked up. He dabbed his wand and a "C-" appeared on the paper. It descended into a basket of finished papers on the floor. "I should like you to keep it, then."

"Really? I...You mean it?"

"Oh yes, I insist. Please take it. I know it by heart, front to back. Won't do anyone any good gathering dust in here, will it?"

"Thank you, professor." Jeremy picked the book back up.

"Between you and me, Jeremy, Sir Mongo is getting rid of the sewing course altogether. He believes magic users no longer need to sew their own robes or finery, what with the new fangled electric sewing machines gaining in popularity throughout the world." The professor wrinkled his nose in distaste.

"But how can robes be enchanted if they're sewn by a machine?" Jeremy protested. "They won't be made with magical stitching patterns, or specially charmed needles and thread!"

Professor Smith sighed. "Jeremy, I suspect you understand more about the art of ensorcelled costuming than even Sir Mongo." The professor motioned for Jeremy to sit down in the other chair. He re-lit his pipe with his wand. "So tell me, my lad. What are your plans now that you're finished with Pigpimples?"

Jeremy was taken aback by the old enchanter's candidness. *More like Pigpimples is finished with me*, he thought. His teacher must know about his expulsion, but he hadn't expected him to bring it up.

"I don't really know yet," Jeremy began, then paused. "I think I'm just going to go home and figure things out there." It was the vague, safe answer Jeremy had been saving in case anyone asked him about flunking out. "Maybe look for a summer job," he continued. "My Uncle Arthur owns a delicatessen in Dublin; he's always telling me he could use someone to sweep the place up. Told me he could teach me the art of slicing meat, sandwich making..." Professor Smith made an incredulous expression as Jeremy went on. "The deli is getting fairly popular, actually. They make this really good corned beef sandwich—my uncle calls it the *Excalibur*..."

The professor pinched the bridge of his nose in a gesture of pain. "Jeremy," the sorcerer held up a hand, "stop."

Jeremy stopped.

"You must not think very highly of me, lad!"

Now it was Jeremy who looked confused.

"Working in a delicatessen? Really? When have you *ever* aspired to working in a delicatessen?"

"I just—" Jeremy started, but the old wizard stopped him again.

"Please don't misunderstand me, Jeremy. The slicing of meat and preparation of fine sandwiches is an ancient, time-honored art. A noble art! But honestly, my boy—do you really expect me to believe..." He grasped for words, letting out a flabbergasted chuckle. "What I'm saying is—spare me the false modesty! It doesn't suit a future man of show business, does it? Like it or not, I am a seven on the Cagliostro Clairvoyance Scale. You'll have try a lot harder to hide the truth from me." He winked, puffing his pipe.

Jeremy exhaled, sinking back into the overstuffed chair. It was a relief to drop the act. He'd rehearsed the explanation so many times, he'd forgotten that Professor Smith would simply see right through it.

"Actually, sir, between you and me...I was thinking of hitting the road for a while." The professor cocked an eyebrow, interested. "You know," Jeremy continued, "get out there, see how real life stage magicians do it. Learn some new tricks, finally put together my own act, who knows? Maybe someone needs an apprentice."

"A tour, then? A tour of the Continent, or an American tour perhaps?"

"Anywhere! Europe, America. Anything I could get would be keen-o, really. I don't know if they do magic shows starside, but I'd even be willing to go there if I had to. I've never left Earth before."

The professor puffed some more and nodded. "New places

have a special way of stimulating a young man's imagination."

"It's not that I haven't learned a lot here at Pigpimples," Jeremy said, "I have. I'm just not cut out to be much of a wizard. A real wizard, anyway."

Professor Smith looked intrigued. He said nothing, waiting for Jeremy to elaborate.

"...And so if I can't do it the real way, I don't see what the big deal is about performing on stage. I don't think it's hurting anyone." Jeremy glanced at the wizard, gauging his reaction. "You don't...disapprove?"

"Why in heaven's name would I disapprove?" the professor removed the pipe from his mouth.

"I just thought—because, you know, magicians on stage...Sir Chamberpot never really liked the idea," Jeremy shrugged. "The Headmage always said that stage magicians are imposters and con artists. Everyone around here says so!"

"Jeremy, as you've noticed, the enchanters and sorcerers of the world can be somewhat... delicate of feeling, you might say. Some things make them very sore."

"But why?" Jeremy protested. "They get to cast powerful spells and do magic that normies and humdrums could only dream of! What do they care if someone wants to put on a fake show of illusions, just for fun?"

The professor gazed into the fire, considering the question. He propped his feet back up on the ottoman before answering. "That's an intriguing inquiry, Jeremy. But to understand the answer, you must first understand a bit of wizarding history— including the story of Pigpimples. Do you know anything about the history of this school?" the professor asked.

"Not much. Except that it used to be a weight loss camp for fat kids?"

"Yes, that much is true. Pigpimples Academie was actually founded hundreds of years ago during the reign of King Henry the Eighth as a school for the portly, husky, and otherwise ample student of the magical arts." Professor Smith puffed thoughtfully as he slipped into a lecture. "The school's founder, Ambrose Pigpimples, sensed that he could make a steady profit from the wizard parents of overweight children. He promised weight loss and magical training in a 'highly secluded' environment. So he fixed up this old estate, bought a lot of medieval exercise equipment, and started the Pigpimples Gymnasium of Weight Loss and Wonder. Expanded it from there. Placed a very powerful privacy spell over the whole property.

"Thus, for hundreds of years, Pigpimples operated in secret, sheltered from normies and humdrums by the so-called 'Girdle of Invisibility.' This powerful spell allowed the campus to remain hidden from the naked eye, tucked away as we are, near the hills of Friarsburg.

"Over time, the school became known as more than just a summer camp for the girthy children of warlocks and witches. It gained a reputation as one of the better magic educational institutions. Enrollment soared. The school was very successful for a long time. Its success was a reflection of the growing world of magic. But then, something unexpected happened that changed everything. Do you know what that was?"

Jeremy thought he knew the answer, but didn't want to say it out loud. *Offworlders?*

"Offworlders," his teacher agreed. "Magic users have always lived within the fringes of human society, as far back as human history records. But at some point during the Dark Ages, mankind grew tired of witches turning their children into newts, or warlocks hypnotizing their fair daughters. Wizards were hunted down mercilessly. Imprisoned. Burned. The magic community retreated into the shadows, much like the ancient dwarven and elven races. They remained a secret for centuries.

"During this time of self-imposed exile, the wizarding community always spoke of making a grand and shocking return to the regular world. They were merely waiting for the right time. But then the first offworlders arrived, sometime around 1820. A decade later the Magic Circle decided, rather abruptly, to give up the pretense of hiding and just make the wizarding community known to the population at large. And they were greeted with a collective shrug."

Jeremy looked surprised. "But why?"

"Simple, really. By the time magic users revealed themselves to the modern world, humanity was already very comfortable with new societies of people living alongside them. New technologies, new sentient species. Most major cities had some kind of alien presence or another at that point."

Jeremy thought he understood. *When you're used to sitting down at Fernando's Pizza next to a table of Xatriyumian spice miners from Corilia 9 using optimal aura magnificators to extract nutrients from space grubs—an old man fixing a broken coffee mug by waving around a stick must seem rather quaint.*

"Exactly," the professor nodded. "And so, insomuch as we're not attempting to enslave humanity, the world has cautiously tolerated magic users ever since."

"I get it. I think," Jeremy said. He wanted to ask what this had to do with the Headmage's disapproval of stage magic, but held his tongue. Professor Smith was getting at something.

"You see, Jeremy, for these reasons, magic users tend to be a rather sensitive lot. Our kind used to be respected—*revered*, even. A court magician was the highest of offices, in some ways even higher than royalty. Because all the old kings and emperors of human history used to turn to sorcerers for advice! A wizard's counsel was considered the wisest in the land. For years, magic users all believed they would get back to the old ways, when instead..." Professor Smith made a *poof!* gesture with his fingers.

"They weren't as special as they thought," Jeremy said.

"Precisely, my lad. Magic users re-entered the regular world, the 'Girdle of Invisibility' was loosened, but things continued much as they did before. For centuries, the Magic Circle decreed that wizards and witches should never, *ever* perform magic in the humdrum world—at least not without prior authorization. Nobody wanted to risk another 'wizard extermination.' I daresay it's one of the oldest wizarding laws, and still very much in effect. In fact, you know of the Fascination Wolves, don't you?" the professor asked.

"Yes."

"They were originally formed to enforce this one law. To seek out and stop any and all unauthorized spellcasting. And this included theatrical magicians, or anyone who performed magic in public. Just the idea of stage magic was absolutely abhorrent. Unthinkable. In fact, most wizards considered casting spells for the amusement of normies an even worse offense than using magic to manipulate and control them."

"But," Jeremy started, "*pretending* to do magic on stage...there is no wizard law against that, is there?"

The professor smiled. "Exactly!" he pointed at Jeremy with the stem of his pipe. "Some wizards figured out a loophole! The Magic Circle never said anything about the mere *appearance* of magic, brought about by sleight of hand and trickery." Professor Smith chuckled. "Nothing irks the elites more than a stage magician getting attention for performing tricks. Deep down, I suspect it's just plain old jealousy. Wizards believe they should be the ones up there, confounding audiences."

"But they can't, since all they know is *real* magic," Jeremy concluded. He had never thought about it that way before. They both laughed. "So," Jeremy asked, "do the Fascination Wolves still keep track of who's doing real magic and who isn't?"

"Oh yes. They have their ways of knowing. They have spies everywhere." The professor got a faraway look in his eyes. He smoked silently for a few moments. "But Sir Mongo is no Fascination Wolf. The Wolves do much more than summon rainbows on rainy days." They laughed again. It was the closest thing to a disapproving remark about the Headmage that Jeremy had ever heard his teacher make. "Mongo may criticize all he wants," the professor went on, "but the fact remains that stage magic has its place in the wizarding world. Always has. In some ways, we have more in common with the so-called charlatans than we'd like to admit."

Jeremy shuddered with satisfaction at the professor's approving comments.

"The weird arts are just that, you know: an art. There's a bit of showmanship to all of it, isn't there? In the end, we invite people, however briefly, to contemplate the mystic."

Jeremy remembered his father's tagline.

"Besides, I seem to recall you've mastered at least *one* real spell. And it's most...how shall I say it... *sui generis*, isn't it? I can't say I've ever seen anything quite like it."

Jeremy surged with pride at this acknowledgment, just as the bell of the clock tower chimed out across campus. It was eight o'clock.

"Well then, what on earth are you still doing in this stuffy old office! Get out of here!" The professor waved him off. "You're going to be a smash, and I suspect you know it!"

Jeremy stood and shook the professor's hand. "Thank you, sir."

"Go, go!" The wizard shooed him. "The Farewell Ball awaits!"

"And thanks for the book!" Jeremy called as he rushed out of the office, the textbook tucked under his arm.

"Dance with some pretty young witches for me, my lad!" The professor called back.

Jeremy bounded down the hall and out the door.

CHAPTER 7

MALEDICT VON BIBLIOSNUFF

Professor Bibliosnuff's office was located beneath the school library, somewhere within the Pigpimples Catacombs of Tribulation & Gluttony Correction (more succinctly referred to as "the dungeon"). School administration had officially "retired" the dungeon from use many years ago, when Pigpimples had gone public. It had since been repurposed as the home of the Department of Necromancy and its various classrooms, although Jeremy *had* heard rumors that trouble students would occasionally end up in one of the lower levels for "rehabilitation" purposes. Always more of a slacker than a hoodlum, he'd been lucky to avoid such disciplinary issues. His only experience in the Catacombs was the one class he'd attended down there.

But that had only been once a week, and there had always been lots of other kids around. Now, the thought of entering the dungeon...at night...all alone...in order to speak with *Maledict Von Bibliosnuff*..? It didn't sound appealing. *What's the big deal?* Jeremy thought to himself. *I pop in, leave the book in the lobby with a note or something. Done!*

He walked at a brisk pace towards the Anita Cosgrove Memorial Library, wanting to get it over with. He gave the enormous front door a tug, and it creaked open. The library itself was the second largest building on the campus, after Blackstone Hall. Ancient bookshelves towered above him in the darkness. Stained glass windows lined the walls, each depicting some famous wizard, witch, or other magic user from ancient history. It was now quite dark outside, and the moon had not yet risen. The glass figures in the windows were like ghostly silhouettes staring down at him. Jeremy gulped.

A large red banner hung between two gigantic pillars. "Coming Soon," it announced, "The Cobblestone Corner!" Beneath the banner was a sign mounted on an easel. It explained how the library would soon be "relocating" many of the "stuffy old books" in this section, to make room for a brand new "graphic novel" area. (Jeremy assumed this embarrassing term meant "comic book.") The real jewel of the new section was a giant cardboard cutout of Tommy Cobblestone's stupid grinning head. The cardboard head was so big that it dwarfed the comic book racks around it. It was wearing sunglasses and giving a thumbs up by its face.

"Ugh," Jeremy scoffed. He briefly considered setting the cutout on fire and just burning the place down.

Hmm—better not.

He'd heard too many unverifiable (but probably true) stories of ghosts haunting this place. The last thing he needed was the crazed spirit of some homeless seven-hundred-year-old enchanter chasing him around.

He walked through the library stacks, his footsteps echoing off the stone tile. The entrance to the dungeon was at the back wall of the library, near the drinking fountain. There was an alcove in the wall marked by an inconspicuous stone arch entryway. On the floor of the alcove was a large circular hole with black stairs that twisted down into the darkness. Jeremy held tightly to the iron handrail as he descended, cursing himself for being unable to pull off even a minor lamp spell. (He'd never been able to get the hang of it—every time he tried to cast "Seer's Beacon," he'd only ended up summoning the vague aroma of whole wheat toast.)

At the bottom of the stairs he allowed his eyes to adjust. All the lamps were out for the night, but there was a phosphorescent moss down here that gave off a very dim, sickly green light. His former classroom was down this hall, its door beside a shackled skeleton they'd nicknamed "Leonard." Professor Bibliosnuff's office was just around the corner. That is, he seemed to remember someone saying so. He prayed he didn't have to descend to the lower levels.

The stone walls amplified the scurrying sounds of every little unknown creature. Unpleasant dripping noises *ploinked* and *plinked* in the darkness as he slunk along the cool, damp corridor. When he approached the end of the hallway, Jeremy thought he heard the rushing of water somewhere deep below. "Yeugh!" he sputtered in disgust, covering his nose and mouth with his sleeve. *It reeks down here!* He must be approaching the school's sewer system. Why any professor would want his office in such a vile location was beyond him.

The sound of voices echoed up ahead. Someone was having a conversation. As Jeremy inched farther along, he could finally see the end of the hallway. A stairwell to his right descended deeper into the dungeon. To his left was a black door made of iron. The metal nameplate on the door read: PROFESSOR MALEDICT VON BIBLIOSNUFF, NECROMANCY. DEPARTMENT HEAD. An eerie purple light pulsed from underneath the door. Jeremy debated whether to knock or whether to simply drop the book and flee while he still could.

You've made it this far, he told himself. *If you leave the book here, some diseased rat will probably come along and eat it. Just go inside!*

Jeremy gave a little rap on the metal door. There was no response. The voices on the other side of the door sounded a bit more agitated, as if they were arguing. *See?* Jeremy argued with himself. *Maybe it's best to not bother the professor after all!* He'd just open the door quietly, set the book on a nearby table, and sneak out.

Jeremy pulled the door open and peered inside. The professor's office was much larger than he had anticipated, although it was difficult to tell just how big it was with such little light. His shelves were lined with hundreds of different bottles and vials of herbs, roots, internal organs of various amphibians—all ingredients for poisons and cursed potions. The sorcerer stood with his back to the door, bent over some glowing object on his desk. He wore the traditional red hooded robes of the Fascination Wolves. He had huge, wild eyes with dark circles underneath them. His dark hair was long and dandruffy. It went perfectly with his long, unkempt beard. The man always looked like he needed about fifteen straight hours of sleep. He was currently raving about something, waving his arms around wildly and casting shadows about the room. In one hand he held a sandwich, occasionally biting out of it as he spoke.

"I don't KNOW vhere zey are!" he nearly shouted, followed by a bite of sandwich. The professor had a slight accent that Jeremy believed was Turkish, although he never dared ask. The wizard continued speaking with his mouth full. "That is why I come to you. Zey could be anyvhere by now! You cannot tell me you never planned for such a contingency..?"

Since Maledict was the head of the Fascination Wolves, Jeremy assumed he must be discussing Wolf business with someone on the other end of that crystal ball. He squinted, nearly blinded by the lavender light emanating from the orb as the professor stepped out of its way. Inside the sphere was the image of a globule of pale blue slime. It undulated and quivered as it spoke. *An offworlder?* If it was, it was a race Jeremy had never seen.

The creature's voice sounded through the orb. At first, it had a wet schlorping sound to it—not unlike a bowl of Jiggle Town Instant Gelatin being squeezed through a gym sock. Moments later, the bizarre sound was overlayed with a more human vocalization. "UNACCEPTABLE," echoed a cold, synthesized voice. It had a wheezy, mechanical feel that Jeremy couldn't quite put his finger on. It filled him with dread, whatever it was. He shuddered, preferring the schlorping sounds.

"YOU WILL FIND THEM IMMEDIATELY, BEFORE THEY APPEAR IN PUBLIC!"

The schlorping grew more schlorpy and intense.

"Can't you just call zhem, or somezing?" the professor asked.

"UNACCEPTABLE," the blob repeated.

It was as Professor Smith had said! They must be discussing wizards performing unauthorized magic! Jeremy held his breath, hoping to catch any clues as to where the rogue magicians might be hiding. Maybe he could warn them! *Heck, maybe I could join up with them!*

"All right, all right—I vill find them. Everything vill be good!" the professor wiped the crumbs from his hands in an appeasing gesture.

"SEE THAT YOU DO," the blob warned. "ALSO, WHAT KIND OF SANDWICH WAS THAT?"

"Oh...oh, it was egg zalad sandwich. I made with leftovers. Not bad!"

"YES, IT LOOKED GOOD. WE HAVE NEVER TRIED 'EGG SALAD' BEFORE. WE SHOULD LIKE TO ACQUIRE SOME."

"Okay, yes! I tell you vhat—I share vit you recipe. Very simple, easy. All you really need—"

Jeremy slipped the textbook onto a circular side table. He was disappointed to leave without any details regarding the renegade magicians, but didn't want to risk a confrontation. For now, he was just happy to know that they were out there. Keen-o!

He ducked out the door, shutting it silently behind him. Within moments, his eyes adjusted to the darkness of the hallway and he made his way to the stairwell.

CHAPTER 8

THE DONUT INCIDENT

Jeremy burst out of the library, relishing the night breeze and gulping down fresh air. He spied light and movement behind the windows on the top floor of Blackstone Hall. Kids were probably filing into the dance. Jeremy imagined himself walking into the ballroom fashionably late, decked out in his tuxedo and white gloves. Janine Wintershade would be there, sipping punch with her Dandy Lion friends. "Ladies," he'd give them the slightest of nods, stopping to adjust his bow tie in the reflection of the punch bowl.

Instant swoon.

He hustled back to his dorm to get the rest of his outfit on.

There was some commotion in the lounge as he got to his floor. Four older boys were gathered there, laughing raucously. They were all tenth graders. Alfie Coldmann and Rick Redfern were both House Hazeltwig. Pete Wisby and Dave Underhill were Dandy Lions. None of them were dressed for the dance. Alfie socked Rick in the gut—much to the amusement of the other boys. Rick then kicked Alfie in the shin. Alfie yowled in pain, pulling his wand out. "Watch it, you manky little tosser!" an electric bolt popped from his wand, shocking Rick in the elbow. The trickle of lightning jumped from Rick's arm, zapping the two other boys.

"Oi!" Pete yelled, lifting his arms above and away from his head. He cupped something in his hands, attempting to shield it.

"Watch what you're doing with that, mate!" Rick scolded Alfie. "You don't want to kill it before Balthasar has a chance to see. He don't go for dead things."

It was then that Jeremy noticed the rather long snake draped around Rick's neck. It was Balthasar, Rick's postal pet. The snake's scales were patterned in a fiery orange and red, looking positively scarf-like against the black of Rick's Hazeltwig uniform. Balthasar's head reared up at the sound of its name. It flicked its tongue, tasting the air. Rick gave it a pat.

"You keep flingin' them shocky bolts around and you're gonna fry the gizmos, too, ya twit!" Dave smacked Alfie in the back of his head.

"What are you guys doing?" Jeremy spoke up.

The four boys turned. "Tommy boy! Oi, get a load of this!" Alfie and the boys walked over to a coffee table. Rick removed the snake from around his neck and placed it on the table's surface. The snake slithered itself into a coily cone, resting its head on the rolls of its body. Rick pulled a small rectangular object out of his pocket, holding it in front of himself with both hands. Dave and Alfie held identical rectangular objects. For a split-second, Jeremy thought they were all holding decks of playing cards. But they were a little too big to be cards, he noticed. *And a little too flat.* All three of them held these rectangles at arm's length, sort of aiming them at the snake on the table.

"What the devil are you guys doing?" Jeremy asked. He felt uneasy.

"Wot, ain't you ever seen a P-Shell, mate?" Dave waved the device at Jeremy, laughing stupidly. The boys tapped unseen buttons on the rectangles, each one emitting an otherworldly *bing!* and lighting up in their hands. The devices all had glowing screens on them that made Jeremy think of his father's old radio. *The dial would glow green as the tubes inside warmed up.*

"What's a pee...shell?" Jeremy asked, contorting his face. "Wait a second," he stopped in trepidation, "is it some kind of...alien tech?" [*Translator's Note: Since Earth was not yet a member of the Planetary League, Terrans were generally forbidden from using, buying, selling, or profiting from alien technology. This was part of a self-imposed planetary law known as the Arcturus Directive. Violators who were caught with alien tech could face fines, jail time, and even revocation of Terran citizenship. —ChatterBot 3.6*]

The boys laughed. "Naw, mate, they's is Terran made! See? Seashell Systems, Terra Firma!" Dave rushed over, holding the back of the device up to Jeremy as proof. The object was indeed scrimshawed with the words *Seashell Systems, Terra Firma,* with the company logo of a nautilus shell stamped beneath it. Seashell Systems was famous for their gadgets and gizmos: electronic typescripters, audiomatic phonographs—Jeremy thought the brand new televid box in the library might be from them, too. All their products were cutting edge, and quite expensive.

"Where did you get them?" Jeremy asked.

"We pinched 'em from Snuff's office—!" Dave started before Alfie elbowed him in the ribs.

"Professor Bibliosnuff let us *borrow* them," Alfie shot Dave a threatening look, then turned back to Jeremy. "They're called Personal Shells. They're new. He said we could use them at the Farewell Ball. You know, test them out, see how they do. We're bringing them RIGHT BACK after the Ball, right lads?" Alfie looked around for confirmation from the boys, who nodded approvingly.

"Of course!" Pete and Rick agreed.

"What do they...do?" Jeremy inquired. They were obviously lying about Professor Bibliosnuff, but that didn't bother him.

Something else felt off.

"Watch," Alfie said, holding the rectangle up with one hand. He aimed it towards Jeremy and pushed a button on it with his thumb. White light exploded from the device as it went *bing!* It startled Jeremy so badly that he nearly tripped over himself, sending the boys into gales of laughter. Alfie looked at the screen of his P-Shell and laughed even harder. He turned the device around, showing the screen to the other boys. They went hysterical.

"What?" Jeremy said, annoyed. "What is so funny?" He joined the boys, who had doubled over laughing. Tears streamed down Rick's face.

"Tommy!" Alfie wheezed, his face pink with glee. "You're one mad little chuffer, I'll give ya that!"

Jeremy grabbed the rectangle out of Alfie's hand. On its screen was a black and white image of himself, frozen in time, like some kind of photograph! He grimaced at the image; he was half stumbling backwards and making the dumbest facial expression in history. He felt sick to his stomach as the boys recovered from their laughing fit. "You're not going to show that to anyone...are you?"

"Course not, mate! Course not!" Alfie gave a side glance to his friends, who stifled more laughter. "It's not just photographs, though. Look 'ere," Alfie said, sidling up to Jeremy. "It does moving pictures, too!"

Motion pictures were a relatively new form of entertainment on Terra Firma, although Jeremy was familiar with them. He and Uncle Arthur had watched *The Burning Halls of Dr. Ponticello* together last summer, and they'd both enjoyed it immensely. Alfie held the little screen up for Jeremy to watch. It played a tiny moving image of Pete Wisby running and pushing Dave into one of the couches in the lounge. Jeremy observed the rest of the boys laughing as Dave crashed to the floor. The little motion picture then showed Dave getting up and lunging at someone, although Jeremy couldn't tell who. The two boys fell, wrestling and knocking over a chair. The group laughed as they re-watched their insipid antics. Jeremy was too perplexed to speak. *A pocket-sized cinema!*

"Just bonkers, innit?" Alfie said.

"Too right," Pete said. "Now stand back, we's gonna make a new picture for schools. It's gonna be an educational picture. You know, teach the kiddies about nature." Pete placed his cupped hands on the table, opening them slowly to reveal a small, trembling creature within.

Donut!

"Hey!" Jeremy shouted. It all made sense now. The snake came to attention, smelling the nearby prey. Donut tried to scramble away, but Pete closed his hands over the furball before she could escape.

"Let's move it to the case," Alfie ordered like a movie director, his Shell out and ready. "Then it can't run away."

Pete dutifully walked over to the empty glass case and dropped Donut in. She bounced harmlessly into the fluff and burrowed herself under a little log. Pete picked up the log and tossed it aside.

"Stop it!" Jeremy yelled. "Just leave her alone!"

The boys ignored him. Pete and Dave pushed buttons on their Shells to start recording. Rick hefted Balthasar up and walked the snake over to the tank. He held the serpent up theatrically, allowing them all to get a good shot of it. Jeremy pulled out his wand and aimed it at the boys. "All right. That's enough," he said. "Put down that stupid snake and let the hamster go."

The boys looked at Jeremy. Their mouths opened in amusement. "And what do you think you're going to do with *that*?" Alfie mocked. "Make us dance against our will for five minutes?"

The snake hissed as it writhed in Rick's hands. "You ready

for this or not, mate? Balthy's hungry!"

"Haven't you ever heard of picking on someone your own size?" Jeremy said. He stepped closer to them, his Jansen wand perfectly steady in his right hand. He raised his left hand, fingers splayed and poised to cast a spell.

The boys pointed their P-Shells at Jeremy, recording the exchange. "It's just nature, Tommy Cobblestone!" Dave taunted. "Didn't you learn that when you were trapped in the Gardens of Baron Solomon? That was issue #38, right? Eh?" Dave nudged Alfie, who remained unamused.

"Oi! Let's do this!" Alfie directed Rick. The three pointed their rectangles back at the snake.

"Ladies and gentlemen," Rick held the snake's head up next to his face as it flicked its tongue. "I present to you—the amazing—the MIGHTY—" He lowered his arms as he prepared to toss the reptile into the glass case.

Jeremy charged. *"Novo COLLAZIO!"* he shouted, swinging his wand in a striking arc. A magical ball of energy shot forth into the air, sparkling and shattering into an array of neon missiles. They slammed into their respective targets like shimmering meteors. The electric lights of the lounge flickered, the burst of magic momentarily dimming them. Jeremy remained frozen in his caster's pose.

Alfie and Dave swung around. "What the bloody 'ell was THAT?!" Dave shouted. They were still recording with the P-Shells...except they were no longer holding P-Shells! In their hands, each boy now held a Belgian waffle.

"Gah!" Dave shouted in surprise, dropping his waffle. Alfie gave his a sniff before crumbling it in his fist.

"Breakfast IS—!" Jeremy began, but was interrupted by a scream. It was Rick.

"BALTHASAR!"

Rick was no longer holding a snake in his arms. Balthasar had been transformed into a chain of sausage links. "You little *git!*" Rick snarled. He dropped the sausages and pulled out his wand. Alfie, Pete, and Dave followed his lead by pulling theirs out, too. They all aimed at Jeremy's head. "Do you have any idea how much those things were WORTH?!" Alfie shouted. "Turn them back! Turn them back, NOW!"

"Yeah, and fix Balthasar!" Rick cried.

"I...uh...I can't. I don't know how!" Jeremy stammered.

"Snuff is gonna kill us!" one of them wailed.

"No," Alfie snorted, "he's gonna kill little Tommy boy here...after we're done with him."

"Wait a second, just wait one second—guys," Jeremy held his wand up as he backed away.

"Enjoy the Catacombs, Tommy," Alfie said.

"Get 'im!" one of the boys shouted as another cast a freeze spell. Jeremy dove for cover, shielding himself behind an old recliner. The cushions crackled as they transformed to ice, the frosty magic penetrating throughout the chair's frame. Jeremy sprang up, flipping the recliner over. It hit the floor, shattering into ice cubes as he bolted from the room.

He slid down the banister of the staircase, slamming himself into the front doors and racing into the night. The sounds of magical blasts followed close behind as he sprinted across the lawn of the Rectangle. He knew he could not outrun all four boys, so he ran straight towards the girls dormitory.

His attackers were shouting their ridiculous British curses and blasting fire bolts in his direction, one of them landing a bit too close for comfort. For a split-second, Jeremy wondered whether they'd singed his tuxedo pants.

He crashed through the front doors of the girls dorm building, hoping there were no female students inside (a boy in the girls dorm could cost Fluffernut at least ten thousand points—not that it mattered at this point).

Thankfully, the foyer was deserted. *All the girls must be at the Farewell Ball,* he thought, then stopped. "Hey!" he spoke aloud. "This place is *way* nicer than the boys dorms! And it doesn't reek of Corn Buddies!"

Rows of bedroom doors lined the halls to his left and right. He suddenly remembered an old trick from a magician he'd seen in the States. Ducking into a door, he performed a *Hardeen's Gambit. [Translator's Note: This move is a closely guarded secret within the world of stage magicians, and I am not legally allowed to describe how it is done, by injunction of the Magic Circle. But trust me, it's pretty clever! —ChatterBot 3.6]*

With a bang, the tenth graders kicked open the front door. "Come on out, you little rotter!" one of them shouted.

"I hear him! He's in here!" Alfie yelled, throwing open one of the doors.

There was nothing but a darkened bedroom.

"You git! He's in here!" Dave kicked open another door, also finding nothing.

By this point, Jeremy was already halfway back across the Arcane Rectangle, grinning as he ran. "Suckerrrrrrrs!" he laughed gleefully.

Okay, change of plan, he thought as he reached his dormitory. *There's a midnight train to London out of Friarsburg⁻ and I'm going to be on it!* Jeremy rushed upstairs, grabbing his suitcase and slipping on his tuxedo jacket. There was no time for the bow tie, so he stuffed it into his pocket. Remembering Professor Smith's book on the floor, he walked back out to the lounge. The former recliner was melting rapidly, creating a puddle on the floor that was being absorbed into a nearby rug. He scooped up his textbook, tucking it under his arm.

He heard a skittering sound from the glass case.

"Donut!" Jeremy exclaimed, rushing over to the tank. The fuzzy hamster sniffed at the sausage links that had landed in her fluff. She didn't seem to care for them, preferring the pile of sunflower seeds. "You're coming with me," Jeremy said as he reached down and scooped her up. He placed the critter in the inner pocket of his suit coat. She peeked out for a moment before curling up and going to sleep.

"Well then—that's that," he said, patting his pocket. He made his way to the staircase, but a peculiar noise made him stop. It was a faint *bing!* that chimed out as a light pulsed on the floor.

The Personal Shell! It was the one Pete had been holding. Jeremy snatched up the device and slipped it into another pocket. *Pete must have dropped it when he took out his wand.* He remembered casting three bolts to stop the boys from murdering Donut, but one of the bolts must have gotten confused and hit the snake instead. This was slightly troubling, as he'd never transformed a sentient being before—only inanimate objects and food items. He'd once read that the higher a being's intelligence, the more difficult it was to magically transform it.

I guess this proves Balthasar was incredibly stupid.

"Sorry about that, Balthy," Jeremy called out to the sausage links. "Now let's go," he murmured as he raced down the stairs. He peeked outside. There was no trace of the boys. The stars were out. Jeremy snuck through campus, sticking to the shadows. At one point he looked up, hearing distant music from Blackstone Hall. In true magician form, he would simply vanish into the night.

"Farewell, Pigpimples."

CHAPTER 9

BAD GUYS INTERLUDE #1

Mike Mania glanced up at the clock in his dingy office. His legs twitched. It was almost two p.m., Mercury time. He'd been avoiding this phone call for days. He would have to tell her before the weekend, though. He hoped she'd be too busy to talk so he could keep it short. *Isn't she at some Seashell Systems corporate unveiling thing?*

He reached a furry paw across his desk, grasping the receiver to his interplanetary glimmer stream phone. He fumbled with it before dropping it and growling a curse. *I loathe how they only make these things to fit humanoid hands!*

Back in Hades, his proud race of caninoid Cerberons never had to put up with such nonsense. Probably because they didn't really make a lot of phone calls in Hell. They mostly just sat around watching bootleg televid reruns from whatever smuggler they could get a hold of. "Curse my stupidity," Mike grumbled. For the hundredth time that week, he wondered how he'd ended up assigned to the most podunk G.R.I.S. outpost in this most podunk of star systems.

At least the Terran televids are pretty good. Well...more than good, he admitted to himself. *Top notch, actually.* He snarled his canine smile as he thought, also for the hundredth time that week, about his plan to get out of there. "Charles!" he barked at his idiot brother in the adjacent office.

"Yeah, Mike?" his brother woofed back.

"I can hear the music from the TV in there! You're not starting *My Son, the Dinosaur* without me, are you?!"

The distorted music from the televid box stopped abruptly. Mike let out a satisfied ruff. *That's better*.

He bent down, picking up the phone's receiver as carefully as he could, using his stubby black claws this time. It was always such a pain to dial these special numbers. Expensive, too. But he had the feeling that this news could not wait the weeks required for standard delivery. More accurately, if *she* found out he'd sat on this info for a month, she'd have him skinned.

No, the only sane option was the glimmer stream. The method was more vulnerable to snooping, but he doubted the yokels of this backwater system were paying much attention to transmissions from Mercury. Mike extended a claw, cautiously dialing the very long and complicated string of numbers.

Charles entered Mike's windowless office and sat down in a swivel chair. The Cerberon was nearly twice his brother's size, with Mike coming in at a very runty three feet tall. Growing up, Mike had tormented Charles by telling him he was actually a half-breed, adopted from some other litter. Charles spun himself around, grasping the seat and lifting his legs off the floor as he went.

Mike growled. "WHAT are you *doing*?! Can't you see I'm on the phone?"

"You told me to turn the show off... I was just waiting..." Charles bumbled. "So we could watch it... together..."

Mike finished dialing the number and cradled the receiver in the crook of his neck. He looked at Charles, angrily baring his teeth.

"What the heck *are* these?" He picked up an empty box of toaster pastries off his desk. *ON THE CHEEP VAL-U BRAND*

TOASTER-STYLE PASTRIES, the box read, with a little picture of a cartoon chick in the corner.

"They weren't that bad!" Charles protested.

"Uh hello, yes, this is Mike Mania of G.R.I.S. Enforcement, Sol System Division. This must be... Tim, I presume?"

Mike rubbed the side of his head. If there was anyone he hated talking to more than *her*, it was her extremely disturbed cyborg bodyguard, Tiny Tim. Mike nodded, throwing in some polite barkish laughter. "Ah, yes, yes...oh sure..." He glared at Charles, covering the mouthpiece and flinging the empty box at his brother's nose. "These were TERRIBLE!" he hissed. "Next time, get TOASTEE MUMS or nothing! You have *one* job here! *One* job!"

"Alright, alright!"

"Shhhhh!" Mike held a paw to his snout, demanding silence. "Ah, that's pleasant. Listen, is Mrs. Crawford available? I have some very urgent news for her. I think she'll want to hear it directly, if that's all right." Mike waved his brother away. Charles stood and sulked out.

"Mrs. Crawford? Hello there, how do you do; it's Mike. Listen... we may have a problem." Mike panted slightly, wishing Charles was still in the room so could throw more stuff at him. "No, Mrs. Crawford—it's just that... well, a ship was spotted in the vicinity of the black hole. It looks like they were, uh..." Mike gulped. "...radio dipping."

A woman's voice screeched on the other end of the phone. Mike flinched as his pointy ears flattened. *Another thing this stupid human-centric tech never considered—other species aren't half-DEAF like humanoids are!* The volume of her screeching made his skull vibrate. He held the phone's receiver away from his head.

Mike knew her reaction would be bad—*if radio dippers snatched the right footage, they might have picked up an advertisement for their secret project.* "Those curs could steal our invention before we have a chance to sell it!" he had explained to Charles.

Now Mike held his breath as Mrs. Crawford berated him. *I'll whip myself in public, if that's what it takes. By Hades, I'll take a pay cut! I'll finish the job for free! Just don't... break... off... our... deal!* He lost track of what Mrs. Crawford was screeching about, but she eventually regained her composure. And she hadn't dismissed him or canceled their deal! He was in the clear! Mike grinned, trying not to sound too confident. "So what now, ma'am? What are the next steps?"

He was pretty sure he knew what she was going to say. He squeaked open a drawer, pulling out his shiny Cellular Glyph Lazer pistol. *Glazers*, as they were known, were all manufactured back on Hades: *by and for Cerberons*. The weapon felt very comfortable in his paws.

"Uh-huh. Oh, I think we can take care of that on our end, ma'am." Mike grabbed a cartridge of fully charged glyphic ammo, sliding it into the pistol's grip and clicking it into place. He flicked the safety off, the pistol thrumming to life. Still cradling the phone on his shoulder, Mike checked the gun's digitally enhanced sights. He gripped the glazer with both paws, aiming at a wall and miming *pew! pew!* sounds as he pretended to blast an enemy. "The name? Oh, right, lemme see..." Mike fumbled the glazer, dropping it on his desk as he scattered papers and debris. Charles poked his head back into the office to see what all the commotion was about. Mike finally spotted the report tacked to a crooked bulletin board. He tore the paper down, scanning it frantically. "Ma'am, the ship is called..." he pointed his gun at Charles, giving him an evil wink, "...the *Terrapin*."

CHAPTER 10

WHEN YOU WISH UPON A STARSHIP

Jeremy walked down the dirt road, suitcase in hand and jacket draped over his arm. He was tired, but the ground felt good under his feet. After a long night of train rides, hitchhiking, and crossing the sea by ferryboat, he was almost there.

His mother had always referred to this place as "The Emerald Isle," and on a morning like this, Jeremy could see why. It was a gorgeous day. The salty sea breeze skimming the grassy hills felt especially exhilarating. As he crested the final bluff, he heard the waves crashing down on the beach. He stood for a moment, admiring the sight before him. He was home.

Ballyhoo Keep.

The ancient stone castle stood atop a cliff overlooking the Atlantic, the green pennants on its towers snapping in the wind. Each flag bore the emblem of three arrows crossed over a yellow star: the ancient herald of House Fletcher. Jeremy took stock of the castle as he approached its imposing front doors. Spring moss covered the eastern side. All the windows still appeared intact. No signs of burglary or vandalism.

Of course, there wasn't much to steal; the castle was nearly empty. His family had not brought much with them when they'd moved here from the States. And Jeremy doubted any thieves were going to run off with the grand piano in the Great Hall. There was the burned down western wing. It was only partially visible from the front, but he could see some of the blackened bricks and the rubble from the collapsed tower peeking out from behind the facade. Jeremy felt a twinge of guilt. He had never figured out what to do about that whole mess.

But I have all the time in the world, now.

He resolved to clean it all up that summer. He'd get a wheelbarrow and move the rubble out bit by bit if he had to.

He fumbled around in his suitcase for the key, then unlocked the rounded double doors. "I'm hoooooome!" Jeremy called out as he entered the castle. He liked hearing his voice echo off the stone walls. Empty sconces adorned the walls of the entryway, meant for torches. Jeremy had never figured out where one would buy a torch in this day and age, and so they remained empty.

The corridor led to the study and then the chapel farther down. On the eastern side were the castle kitchens and then the Great Hall, which Jeremy supposed had been a dining hall or a ballroom at one time. Spiral staircases wound up to the castle's lookout towers.

He walked towards the Great Hall, his footsteps echoing along the corridor. The Hall was one of the rooms they'd all spent time in together. There was an enormous fireplace there, along with some high-backed, overstuffed chairs. There was also a small table for playing cards, chess, or the occasional game of *Black Market*. Sometimes his mother would play the piano, accompanied by his father's singing, or vice-versa. Other times they'd listen to recordings of Dad's old clients on the phonograph, while Mom would needlepoint or crochet one of her ridiculously long scarves.

The wall opposite the fireplace had a set of very tall windows that faced out over the cliffs and the sea. At night, they offered a beautiful view of the stars. He used lay in front of the fireplace on the Persian rug and read his *Vince Thorne: Agent of Fortune* comics. Mother would read a book, father would read his paper and smoke his pipe. When the fire died down, they'd all sit in the darkness. He'd look out at the sky through the big windows, listening to his parents talk quietly about the future.

Jeremy gulped as tears blurred his vision. He caught a glimpse of himself in a large round mirror. "And what are *ewe* cryin' on about, mate?" he berated his reflection in his best accent, wiping his eyes. Then his pocket squeaked.

Donut! Jeremy looked around for a place to put his new pet. There was a large bird cage in the study that would work nicely. His mother had used it to keep finches. Jeremy had released the birds, seeing as how nobody would be around to take care of them. This memory threatened to make him sad again, but he refused to let it. He pulled Donut out of his jacket pocket. She looked up at him, blinking sleepily. "Lighten up!" he said to the hamster. He looked back at his reflection. "Do it for Donut!" He laughed.

Jeremy crept into his father's study, looking for the cage. Dad had never forbid him from going into the room, but his mother had always told him to go and play elsewhere. To this day, he felt reluctant about entering.

The room was filled with dusty old bookcases. There were one or two books on them, but the shelves mostly contained untold stacks of record albums. Most of the records were in paper sleeves, although there were some in proper covers as well. There were not enough bookcases to hold all the records, and many albums still sat in the wooden crates they had been shipped over in. Some of the crates sat in stacks on the floor. Others were open, pieces of packing straw spilling out. There were even stacks of records on his father's old desk and chair, in the center of the little room. The only thing in the room not cluttered with phonograph records was his father's old "reading couch," where he used to nap in the afternoons.

The walls of the study were covered in various posters—advertisements for his father's old clients. Some were magicians his dad had performed with years ago, but most were singers, musicians, and vaudevillians nobody had ever heard of. The gilded bird cage sat on a pedestal in the corner. It still had a supply of birdseed in it, in a small porcelain bowl. Jeremy carried the cage out into the Great Hall.

The cage's door opened with a creak, and he placed Donut inside. After sniffing the air and twitching her whiskers, she made a beeline for the seeds. She dove right into the bowl, scattering seeds everywhere as she burrowed, her back legs flailing. After writhing around in apparent ecstasy, she plopped out of the bowl and commenced cramming her cheeks full. With the hamster taken care of, Jeremy turned his attention to the rest of his home.

The whole place smelled a bit musty. It was also far too stuffy and warm. Rolling up his sleeves, he went around unlatching and opening the tall windows in the Great Hall. A refreshing sea breeze fluttered the drapes and tapestries, and he enjoyed the view for a while. He realized that before long, the sun would go down over the ocean: he'd better make sure the oil lanterns were full and ready to go. He'd also need to find some matches.

I could sure use Bruno right now, he thought. It was then that Jeremy realized he hadn't had a chance to say goodbye to his friend! It was one more thing threatening to bring him down. *I'll write him a letter. Explain everything that happened. He'll understand.*

Before he could dwell on it, Jeremy's stomach rumbled. He was famished. He rushed to the kitchen, knowing full well that it was empty but looking in the cupboards anyway. "Not even a can of bean with bacon soup?" he said aloud. He must have cleaned it all out before he'd left for school. Jeremy looked around for something to work his magic on. He grabbed some plates and slipped out the kitchen's back door, which led to a flat patch of land behind the castle. The area had once been a beautiful cliffside garden where his mother had grown flowers and tomatoes. Jeremy felt another twinge of regret as he gazed upon the overgrown bramble of weeds before him.

"Okay—clean up the western wing *and* tidy up the garden." He assigned himself summer projects as he dug through the grass. He gathered up several medium-sized stones, placing them on plates. He took his wand from his pocket and aimed it at the first plate of rocks. "Novo collazio," he intoned, dabbing and tapping in the air. The rocks transformed into a lovely serving of fried eggs, sunny side up. Jeremy nodded with satisfaction, repeating the process for the second plate. "Novo collazio!" The rocks became crispy strips of bacon. They smelled nice and bacon-y. For the third plate, Jeremy attempted something a little more tricky.

"Novo COLLAZIO!" The rocks shimmered for a moment, before transforming into a couple of rectangular-shaped pastries. For a split-second, Jeremy believed he'd finally done it!

"Yessss!" he shouted.

But his celebratory fist pump was premature. Smoke rose from the pastries and they burst into flames. Fruit filling oozed out of them, sizzling onto the plate. "Awwww!" Jeremy fanned at the tiny fire, but it was no use. The pastries were gone. "Yeeugh!" he grunted, flinging the two burnt up pastry bricks over the cliff's edge. Perhaps a seagull would find them tasty.

Jeremy gathered a few more rocks and tried the spell again. "Novo collazio!" Two pastries appeared. They also started smoking, and although they eventually turned into burnt little bricks of carbon, they did *not* burst into flames. *Progress!*

It seemed the pastries themselves were coming out fine—it was the *toasting* that he could not quite get right. He flung more blackened chunks over the cliff's edge.

It took three more attempts, but he eventually had a perfectly toasted set of pastries. He bit into one, yowling as the real Fruit Magma™ scorched his mouth. "Aaahhh!!" he hollered through a mouthful of pastry. *Painful, but delicious! Blueberry?!*

He looked down at the pastry in his hand. He'd never tried blueberry before! It was so good! And he was in so much pain! Sometimes his magic did things even he didn't understand. He brought his meal inside, enjoying his breakfast-for-dinner at the servant's table in the kitchen. The indoor plumbing still worked, and he transformed a glass of water into a glass of cold chocolate milk. It soothed his burning mouth. "Ahhhh..."

He set the glass down and looked out the back door, watching the sun set over the ocean. He picked up the oil lamp on the kitchen counter, giving it a shake. It rattled, empty. It was too late to walk to the village to buy oil. *First thing tomorrow morning*, he thought to himself. The rooms of the castle were growing dim. He recalled there was a box of pipe matches in his father's old tobacco tin, by the fireplace.

Donut looked up, momentarily distracted from her seeds as Jeremy strode into the Great Hall. He grabbed his father's tin off the mantle, lifting the metal lid and peering inside. The familiar aroma hit him. The pouch was stuffed with Kingsfoil Tobacco. The smell, woodsy and otherworldly, reminded him of Dad. Glancing at Mom's beloved piano, the Great Hall suddenly felt too warm. Even with all the windows open, it was suffocating.

He decided he wasn't ready to spend the evening in the castle by himself. Tucking the tobacco tin under his arm, Jeremy grabbed a log from beside the fireplace. He also grabbed one of Dad's old robes from a coat rack, a bulky suitcase, and the first couple of record albums he laid his hands on. He jogged outside.

* * *

He sat on the cliff, gazing out over the Atlantic. The whirr of his father's portable phonograph died down, leaving Jeremy with just the crackle of his campfire, the hush of the ocean, and the occasional *crik* of a goldhopper. [*Translator's Note: an invasive but harmless insect that everyone suspects, but cannot prove, migrated to Earth by hitching a ride on the hull of an offworlder's ship. —ChatterBot 3.6*] He supposed he could crank up the phonograph again, but he'd already listened to both sides of both records. There was *Mambo Mondays by Francisco Franco and the Latin Ensemble* and an unfamiliar one that just said *Sambas by Evalise Luca,* scribbled in his dad's handwriting on a brown paper sleeve. *Mambo Mondays* was always a pleasure (they used to listen to it all the time), but that *Evalise Luca*—it was so good Jeremy had found himself dancing around the campfire in the dark, singing along in broken Spanish to choruses he didn't understand.

But the evening silence held its own appeal. The grass felt soft and cool under his bare feet. The night sky was totally clear, his view of the Milky Way only slightly obscured by the smoke from his campfire. It reminded him of a camping trip they'd made to the Redwoods. He must have been six or seven at the time. After Mom had fallen asleep, he and Dad had stayed up roasting marshmallows and eating them until they were both sick. He smiled at the memory.

In time the fire died down, allowing the chill of the night to creep in. Jeremy had no idea what time it was, but guessed it must be rather late. He wasn't ready for bed, and made himself comfortable. He scanned the skies for tiny moving lights: satellites or distant starships. Everything appeared very still.

He unfurled his father's robe, shaking the mustiness out over the grass. The robe was actually a part of Dad's old stage routine—"Obediah the Mystic's" robe. It was standard wizard fare: silky navy blue embroidered all over with pearly stars. Its edges were trimmed in the silvery white fur of a moon panda. Jeremy slipped the robe on. It was too big for him, but it felt nice and cozy in the cool of the night. He hugged his knees to his chest, looking out at the sky. He thought of all the unknown worlds out there. All those star systems with strange names and stranger people. *I bet none of them require a degree from a magic weight loss school.*

He pictured an offworld dance hall, and wondered if alien girls could be pretty. *Maybe they look like Janine Wintershade,* Jeremy thought, *but nicer, and less snotty. And they appreciate poetry about breakfast food items.* He envisioned himself on the stage of a deep space nightclub. The icy rings of Saturn sparkled through the windows as he performed for an audience hailing from every undiscovered corner of the galaxy. "How did he do that?" they'd gasp in their alien tongues.

Knock it off, he shuddered to himself. *You're not going anywhere, at least not now.* He chuckled at the ludicrousness of it all, imagining Bruno's voice. *You just flunked out of the seventh grade, pally.*

Just then, a shooting star burned an arc across the night sky. Jeremy had not seen one in quite a long time, and made a silent wish.

Strangely, instead of blinking out, the arc intensified. Jeremy watched it, puzzled. The shimmering line in the sky grew longer and wider, until it halted almost directly overhead.

An explosion rocked the firmament, lighting up the night. Jeremy scrambled to his feet. For a split second everything around him lit up, as if by a giant flashbulb. He felt the wild impulse to run, but could not bring his feet to move. The shape above him grew larger and larger, flying (or falling—he could not tell which) towards the earth. For a frenzied moment he pictured himself crushed by a giant meteorite in what would have been the most fitting conclusion to the world's worst weekend. Then there was a loud tearing sound, followed by a siren scream as the flaming comet ripped through the atmosphere. A whoosh of heat and ozone filled the air as the fireball soared over the sea. It finally slammed into the water with a terrific *SHPOOFF!*

"Holy gosh!" Jeremy exclaimed.

It was hard to tell just how big the thing was from his vantage point on the cliff; he guessed it was at least the size of an automobile. The hulk bobbed on the waves, hissing as steam rose off its half-submerged hull. Various colored lights blinked on the object, and it emitted a faint emergency noise. Its lights refracted in dancing colors upon the waves.

It was a starship.

CHAPTER 11

IT'S NEVER TOO EARLY!

Jeremy ran down the eastern slope of the cliffs, stumbling towards the beach. A million questions raced through his brain as he jogged onto the sandy shore, panting. The chilly waves drenched his bare feet. His oversized robe dragged in the sand, growing heavy as it soaked up seawater.

Jeremy estimated that the ship was less than a hundred yards away. It had not sunk after all, but continued to bob on the gentle night surf. "Hey!" Jeremy waved his arms, trying to get the ship's attention. "Over heeere!"

Nothing happened for a little while, and Jeremy considered actually swimming out to the craft. He had never been much of a swimmer and he was no Ranger Cadet, but he couldn't just stand there and watch a starship sink into the ocean, could he? A *bweee-noo* sound chimed from the vessel, and the lights on the hull continued blinking frantically. Then suddenly, they cut off. Jeremy sprang into action.

Parked on the sand behind a cluster of boulders was an old rowboat. It was tied to one of the smaller boulders with a heavy rope. Jeremy dashed to it. He felt eerily calm as he attempted to untie the impossible knot. His fingertips burned as he pulled and yanked on the scratchy rope, his brain flooded with unpleasant memories of THE KNOT-STRAVAGANZA JAMBOREE at Ranger Cadet day camp.

Jeremy gave up in a huff and lifted the loop off of the boulder. He scrambled in the sand, pushing the splintery old boat toward the lapping waves. For a split-second he questioned whether the vessel was seaworthy, but hopped in and got rowing before he could picture himself drowning.

As Jeremy approached the starship, it was apparent that it was quite a bit larger than he'd imagined. He didn't have much experience with starships, having only seen them in comic books or at quite a distance. The best way he could describe the thing was like the front car of the Porker Express monorail crossed with one of those double-decker buses from London. [*Translator's note: the Terrapin was a Binosian D-Class Cargo Tug, standard no-frills model. In an interview, Zipponio once described it as kind of looking like the shuttlecraft from* Nexus Odyssey: A New Generation, *a Terran TV show which he watched extensively on bootleg vidtapes. Hope this helps! — ChatterBot 3.6*]

When he was close enough, Jeremy stopped. Steam still rose off the ship's hull, but it did not appear to be sinking. *Now what?* There was an angular window on the front of the craft above the water. He couldn't be sure, but Jeremy thought he spotted movement within.

"Hey!" Jeremy called out, raising an arm in greeting. The sleeve of his robe covered his hand droopily. "Gah!" he flapped his hands back and forth, shaking the sleeves back. "Uhh...Ahoy there! Matey?" He squinted at the ship's window, trying to make out what was going on inside. Something clanked somewhere above him, followed by a creak. A hatch opened on top of the ship. A small figure popped his head out, but it was too dark to make out his features.

"Hi!" the figure called out. He sounded young.

"That was...quite the splash!" Jeremy shouted up.

"Hey kid, listen—could you do us a favor?" the figure shouted at Jeremy, then bent down. "Zip, put her into docking mode!" he yelled into the hatch. The ship hummed to life with a low drone, and a series of white docking lights flickered on. They blinked in a pattern at the base of the ship as it floated in the water. The child shouted down from the hatch again. "Homie! I see you have some rope there. Would you mind giving us a tow to shore? We could sure use it!"

Jeremy furrowed his brow. Did this little boy think he could pull their gigantic starship to shore? He wanted to reply, but the boy called out above the crash of the waves: "Just use the hitch!"

Jeremy rowed close enough to the ship that he could reach out and touch it. He slipped the loop of the rope over the hitch on the front end, rowing back and looking up to the boy for further instructions.

"Wouldn't it be easier for you to just come down here instead?" Jeremy shouted. But the boy didn't seem to hear him. He hollered something down to his crewmate and clanked the hatch shut.

The low drone increased to a steady purr as the gravthrusters kicked in, raising the hull of the ship slightly above the water. A spotlight popped to life on the front, shining directly into Jeremy's face. He winced, covering his eyes with his arm. He turned around in his boat, putting his back to the beam. The white light lit up the ocean and the surrounding area.

Do they really expect me to pull them to the shore like this? Jeremy thought. He shrugged. *Fine. Once they see that they're too heavy for me, they'll understand!* Jeremy re-positioned the oars and rowed forward. He felt the slightest tug as he began to pull, and then nothing. He turned around, startled, thinking the rope must have come loose. But to his surprise the rope was taut, still hooked to the starship. He was pulling the craft along as if it were as weightless as a cork!

He made quick work of it, sculling his way to shore. Jeremy

untied the rope from the rowboat's stern and pulled the starship in the rest of the way. It glided out of the sea and onto the beach, hovering about a foot above the sand. The sensation reminded Jeremy of holding a string attached to an inflated balloon.

The rear door of the ship hissed and raised itself open. The two offworlders stood in the doorway, silhouetted against the glow of the ship's interior. The tall one had the features of a cat, but no hair. He bent down and scooped up the one that looked like a boy, in what appeared to be an embrace. They laughed as the cat-man spun around, dancing and meowing happily. It looked like he was actually licking the shorter one's head.

A ramp descended from the rear hatch and onto the ground. Various pieces of debris spilled out down the ramp, including several plastic Nudgefudge YumYums wrappers, and some sotus-noodle cups.

The younger one jumped off the ramp, landing in the sand face first. He commenced doing push-ups, kissing the ground with a large *MWAH!* each time he lowered himself. The taller one ran down the ramp, also flinging himself onto the beach. He rolled around in the sand on his back, his hairless tail wriggling about as he mewled in oblivious pleasure. Jeremy stood, watching for a minute and waiting for them to finish.

They just kept going.

"Are you guys okay?" Jeremy finally asked.

The boy looked up from his makeout session with the ground, as if remembering something. "NO! We're not okay! We... are... STARVING!" He scrambled to his feet and ran to Jeremy, grabbing the lapels of his robe pleadingly. "A bag of Waggles—a Riff Raff Bar—ANYTHING!" He ran his hands through Jeremy's pockets, searching for any kind of sustenance. He found a stick of chewing gum, which he popped into his mouth and chewed furiously. "Dude, what time is it here?" the boy looked around, as if realizing that it was the middle of the night. "Ugh, flavor's gone!" he spit the gum out, frisking Jeremy for more food.

"Relax! I know where you guys can get some food," Jeremy said.

The hairless cat-man bolted over, saying some word over and over in a questioning tone. It sounded like "shramp?"

"It's not too early for breakfast, is it?" the boy asked.

Jeremy laughed, throwing his head back. He pointed two fingers at the duo. "As a matter of fact, no! No, it is not!"

CHAPTER 12

PANCAKES, HOTCAKES, & FLAPJACKS

The trio sat at the servants table in the castle's kitchen. Jeremy's two guests had made a bit of a mess, but he supposed it was understandable considering the circumstances. They claimed they'd had nothing to eat but vacuum-sealed sotus noodles for three and a half straight weeks.

They'd pulled the *Terrapin* up to the front of the castle along the eastern slope. It hovered along weightlessly, and the three of them took turns holding the rope. Jeremy had only picked up the name of their ship from hearing the two talking about it. He attempted to get more information out of them, but all they seemed interested in was breakfast food.

"Pancakes? You can make pancakes?" the boy asked.

"Yes, pancakes are easy."

"Ooo! What about hotcakes?"

"Uhh…Aren't those the same thing?"

"No! Not at all, holmes! There are subtle, but very real differences!"

"I see. If you explain them to me, I might be able to do hotcakes, too."

"Griddlecakes?"

"Sure, yeah."

"Flapjacks?!"

Jeremy nodded.

The hairless cat-man sheepishly put forth his request: "Shramp?"

"He means shrimp," the boy explained.

"Ohhh. I don't think shrimp is normally a breakfast food." Jeremy had never tried transforming anything into shrimp before. "Sorry." The tall one's whiskers drooped in disappointment. "You know," Jeremy said, "if you could just find me an example of shrimp being used as a breakfast food—I bet I could manage it." He wondered whether some kind of shrimp hash existed... *A shrimp omelet, perhaps?*

It turned out the cat-man was still very happy with everything else provided, as evidenced by the teetering stack of empty plates on the table.

Jeremy had made a nice cozy fire in the kitchen fireplace as he served them their food. It had been too dark to get a good look at the two outside. Now he sat on a stool and watched them as they stuffed themselves.

They were definitely offworlders.

The little one was humanoid. He looked very similar to a Terran child, only a few years younger than Jeremy. Nine, maybe ten years old, he guessed. Very short. His skin tone was unique; it had an ochre, coppery tint to it. His facial features were almost elfin. His hair had a metallic, silvery-deep-purple sheen; it was the most alien thing about him. He wore an undershirt and suspenders. Jeremy noticed that he kept an enormous pair of shiny blue sunglasses in the back pocket of his shorts.

"Dude! Forgive my rudeness," the boy said through spoonfuls of corn flakes. "I never introduced myself! The name's Moe." Spoon still in mouth, he extended a hand to Jeremy across the table.

"Hi, I'm Jeremy." They shook enthusiastically.

Moe's companion was a giant by comparison. He stood at about six feet tall, with the wrinkly gray and pinkish body of a hairless feline. His huge, tendril-veined bat ears were pulled back, kept in place with a green elastic hair band. The hairless cat-man slipped the hair band off and massaged his ears with his paws before going back to his pancakes. He wore no shirt, but had on a pair of Terran camouflage pants and a furry pink vest. He was not an alien species Jeremy was familiar with.

When the creature had finished lapping up the syrup from his plate, he looked at Jeremy with his large blue eyes. He smiled a wrinkly smile, making his whiskers tremble, and stood up from the table. Jeremy fought the impulse to back away (which would have been rude), and extended a hand to shake. The creature sidestepped the gesture, gently placing his paw on the back of Jeremy's neck. He stooped down, nudging Jeremy's head with his own forehead. The whiskers tickled Jeremy's face, and he could smell maple syrup on the his breath.

"Right on, that's...uh...the customary greeting on Phynix, his homeworld," Moe explained. He looked a little embarrassed.

"Well hello there. Nice to meet you..." Jeremy trailed off.

A strange voice entered Jeremy's mind. "Zipponio Prraow," it said. It was unlike any human voice, sounding more like a chorus of cats meowing in harmony. Somehow, Jeremy had understood perfectly what it was trying to say.

"Zipponio?" Jeremy said out loud. Zipponio nodded enthusiastically, giving Jeremy another head nudge.

"Or Zippo for short," Moe added. "He must have mindspoken to you, huh? Yeah, Felinians can do that. They have some light telepathy with certain species. Guess it works on Terrans, too!"

"Keen-o!" Jeremy laughed. He'd never experienced anything like that before.

"Jrr-mEE?" Zippo attempted. Jeremy nodded. Jeremy had

noticed that Zippo's accent made English a little tricky for him. For instance, every time Zippo addressed Moe by name, it came out sounding like *mur-OWe*.

"So where'd you guys learn English?" Jeremy asked.

"Lingo Bars. And watching TV," Moe said.

"Tee-vee?" Jeremy was unfamiliar with the expression. Televideo screens, or "televids" for short, were still a brand new technology on Earth. Pigpimples had one in the library— rumored to be extremely expensive—and one of the kids had found a way to play *Jessica Gelato: Average School Girl* on the thing. Jeremy had loved watching until they'd all gotten caught. (He suspected Cleric Avalon had confiscated the video game just so he could play it later.)

Zippo shot Moe a disapproving look.

"What?! It's not illegal for him to *hear* about Lingo Bars, is it?! This dude won't care; he's *chill*!" Moe protested.

"What's tee-vee?" Jeremy asked.

"Oh, um—come to think of it, I think your people calls them televids. But you'll call them TVs...eventually," Moe shook his head, "it's kind of a long story." He gulped down the last of his soggy corn flakes. "Anyway, the easiest way to learn a new language is just nosh a Lingo Bar of that language. Terran languages are all the rage lately. I've had English, French, Swahili...I think a couple of others. I know we have a few on our ship, somewhere. Right, Zip?"

Zippo nodded. "Angresh good, yeh?" He gave Jeremy a thumbs up.

Jeremy and Moe looked at each other and giggled.

* * *

It was the most food Jeremy had ever created in one meal. Sausages, ham, bacon, toast, eggs, biscuits and gravy, muffins, donuts, French toast, hash browns, pancakes, baked beans, corned beef, strawberries and cantaloupe melon, sauteed mushrooms, blueberry oatmeal, Belgian waffles, and black pudding! They had devoured all of it, downing it with copious amounts of orange juice and milk. Jeremy had initially offered them coffee, which they had both scowled at when they sniffed it.

"What is this krud?" Moe had asked, not doing much to hide his repulsion. Jeremy explained how the beverage was brewed.

"Yeugh! Hawt brown BEAN water!" Zippo declared in disgust, pushing his mug away.

Jeremy had also tried tea, receiving the same feedback (except Zippo had called it "brown leaf water"). The only other food the two didn't care for were the slices of tomato, which Zippo had wrinkled his nose at and Moe had simply deemed "wack."

The two had been too busy gorging themselves to even notice how Jeremy had created all of the food magically. He figured he could explain it later.

Zippo held a mug of warm milk in his paws. Instead of sipping, he brought the mug up to his mouth and lapped the milk with his raspy tongue. His eyes were closed in concentration and pleasure. Moe looked at Jeremy to gauge his reaction. They both laughed again.

"Wat, Moe?" Zippo looked annoyed.

Moe pushed his chair back from the table. He shook his head. "Nothing, Zip. It's been a long day, hasn't it?"

The fire was dying down, and Jeremy felt like he'd nod off if he closed his eyes. He guessed it must be near dawn, although it was still dark outside. Moe stood, thanking Jeremy for breakfast. "Man oh man, chief—that was the best meal I think we've ever had. Like, ever." He rubbed his pot belly in satisfaction. "I don't ever want to see another cup of sotus noodles."

"Mwehhh," Zippo meowed.

"Do you mind if we crash here for the night?" Moe asked.

"A real bed would be nice for a change..."

Jeremy considered it. He'd never had guests at the castle, ever. Something about these two put him at ease, though.

"Of course! There are lots of empty bedrooms. There's nobody else here but me."

Moe cocked an eyebrow at Zippo as if to ask: *is this cool with you?*

"Yeh!" Zippo meowed happily.

"Thank you for your hospitality, holmes. We've been cooped up on the *Terrapin* for, I dunno, a month?" Moe stretched. "We can tell you the whole story tomorrow, if you wanna hear it."

"Sure!"

They walked up the stairs to the nursery. Jeremy led the way with a flickering candle in an old brass holder. The nursery was supposed to double as a guest bedroom. It was mostly empty and musty, but it had two full-sized beds. In other circumstances, the candle's flickering might have appeared spooky, but the starlight filtering in through the circular windows made the whole scene extra comfy.

Moe clambered into one of the old plush beds. He sighed with contentment. Zippo rushed in after him, throwing himself onto the second bed. He fluffed the pillows compulsively for a few moments before flopping down.

"My room is right across the hall here. I'm leaving you a couple of candles in case you need to make your way in the dark. Oh, and there's a lavatory at the end of the hallway."

Zippo cooed quietly, then turned over.

"Just let me know if you guys need anything else, okay?"

No response. The only sound was Zippo's purring. *They're already asleep.* Jeremy tiptoed out, shutting the door gently behind him.

CHAPTER 13

WELCOME TO EARFF

The sun streamed in through his bedroom window. He had no idea what time it was, but it felt later than usual. He was momentarily surprised to find himself back in the castle, and not in his dorm room at Pigpimples. *Oh right*, he remembered. *I'm home now.*

He wasn't sure how to feel about this fact.

He sat up, mentally reviewing his to-do list. He recalled wanting to finally clean up the ruins of the western wing. *Where to even begin with that?* Before he could feel too overwhelmed at the task at hand, his stomach rumbled. "First, breakfast," he murmured. He reached for his glasses on his nightstand and put them on. *Wait a second.* Breakfast?

The events of last night came flooding back. *Standing on the cliff. The downed starship. Having a midnight breakfast with two aliens.*

How much of that stuff had actually happened? He jumped up and ran across the hall. The beds in the nursery were empty, and appeared unused. *Was it all a dream?* Jeremy rushed downstairs, peeking into the kitchen and then the Great Hall. *Empty.*

Well, almost empty. Donut was still in her birdcage. She was fast asleep, tucked into a tiny ball of fluff. *I've lost my mind!* Jeremy thought. *Like, really lost it! What a weird dream!* He wondered if it was because of those odd toaster pastries he'd created. *Note to self: take it easy on ingesting magically conjured food items.*

He rambled to himself as he headed towards the kitchen. "You're summoning food items from who knows what dimension or astral plane, then eating them all willy-nilly? You should be surprised this hasn't happened sooner! Ha! Hey look, here's a bowl of cereal from the Seventh Level of the Juphoryean Realm of Mystica—*let's eat it!* You're bound to have some hallucinations or out-of-body experiences now and then…"

He stopped, noticing something in the hall. His father's wizard robe hung on a coat rack by the front door. *That was there already...wasn't it?* Then he saw it: on the floor beneath the robe was a small puddle of water. *Holy gosh—it was all real!*

He ran to the coat rack and grabbed the robe, slipping it on over his t-shirt and undershorts. The robe's sogginess drove home the reality of it all. He flung open the front door.

"Jrr-mEE!" Zippo waved to him. The *Terrapin* was parked on the grassy plateau in front of the castle.

"Mornin', homeslice!" Moe called out to Jeremy, waving.

They were inspecting the long gash in the side of the ship's hull. Jeremy walked towards them, tying his robe shut. The grass felt warm on his bare feet, and the sky was almost oppressively blue. It was a gorgeous day.

"You have a really beautiful planet here, you know that? I don't know what it is, the sea breeze, the feel of dry land—it's just invigorating!" Moe inhaled deeply through his nostrils, then doubled over in a fit of coughing.

"Yeh—is good," Zippo agreed happily, patting Moe on the back as he coughed spasmodically.

"That...dang...recycled...*air*!" Moe wheezed out between

coughs. Once he regained his composure, he took off his huge sunglasses and wiped his eyes. "Feels good to have some real planetside oxygen for once!"

Jeremy puzzled at the offworlder. He wore a Terran baseball cap, but turned backwards for some reason, so that the bill did nothing to block the sun.

"Your star's a bit brighter than I'd prefer," Moe said, adjusting his shades, "but still—really nice. Reeeeeally nice." He looked out over the coastal valley, the grass undulating along the hills with the breeze.

"Good morning, guys. Did you sleep okay?" Jeremy asked.

"Like a baby in a stasis pod!" Moe said. "Woke up starving, though. Could sure go for some second breakfast! You hungry?"

"Actually, yes," Jeremy said. "I could eat a horse."

Zippo made a confused look, but said nothing.

"We were going to make *you* some breakfast, but we couldn't find any food in your kitchen or the pantry. There were some leftover hash browns that Zippo found, but he ate 'em." Zippo shrugged sheepishly. "Guess we noshed your whole stash last night, huh? We sure made blump hogs of ourselves."

Jeremy shook his head. "No, no, it's all right. It's not a problem."

"So then we were going to go to town to buy some groceries," Moe went on, "but we realized there is, like, no town here. You are seriously in the middle of *nowhere*!"

"There's a fishing village about a mile that way," Jeremy pointed. "Selkie's Cove. They have...uh...a butcher shop—I think it's still open. Oh, and a pub. The Old Hag."

"Sounds funky! As soon as we get the navi-control system on this baby up and running," Moe slapped the side of the *Terrapin*, "we can head into town and pick up some stuff. It's the least we can do!"

"Wate, Moe." Zippo looked concerned.

"Does this pub do breakfasts?" Moe looked down over his

shades and scanned the landscape. "By the way, where even are we? Our scanners malfunctioned a long time ago. Since you're an English speaker, I assume we're in," he stopped to think for a moment, "America, right? Are we near New York City?"

"Moe!" Zippo pleaded. Moe stopped. "Ship broke...uh...not so gud." He looked at Moe, then Jeremy, trying to make them understand. An image entered both of their minds: it was of some kind of circuit board and various other technological components. Jeremy had no idea what he'd just seen. He then remembered it was Zippo's way of communicating with them. He assumed Zippo was showing them the damaged parts of the starship, or perhaps the tools necessary to fix them.

"Oh, but—" Moe started to say something, then stopped to think. "Well then...yeah, that is...that is wack. Not good!" He turned to Jeremy. "You wouldn't happen to have a spare echotron gyrator in your castle, would you?"

Jeremy laughed, then stopped. "Oh, I thought you were joking," he said. "Is that supposed to be a real thing?"

Moe let out a half-crazed laugh as he gave the ship another slap. "All right, homies! We improvise! How far away *are* we from New York City? Can we go there today?"

"How many times have you guys been here?" Jeremy asked.

"Oh, a few times. There's a pretty sweet outlet mall on Triton where you can get lots of knock-off Terran shoes and stuff." Moe showed off his hi-top sneakers. They had the little Flow Motion logo on them, although the hourglass insignia looked off.

"Triton?"

"Yeah, it's a moon of...Neptune, I think?"

Zippo gave a confirmatory meow.

"Heard there were some great buffets out at the Lava Gardens of Mercury, but we have yet to try them. Soon, though, eh Zip?"

"Luna," Zippo said. [*Translator's note: Earth's moon, which offworlders built an outpost on in the late 1800s. —ChatterBot 3.6]*

"Oh that's right, you *did* go to Lunaport once, right? When you were just a kitt?"

"Yeh. Dad went buy—uhhm—Loo-NA sand."

Jeremy stopped them. "All right, yes, but how many times have you guys been *here*?" He gestured with his hands out, fingers down. "Earth. Terra Firma."

"Ohhhh, you mean like EARTH Earth? Never. First time."

"I see. That makes sense. Do you guys know about the United Kingdom?"

The offworlders shook their heads.

"That's okay, I can explain. But I think it would be easier if you came inside."

Jeremy led them indoors to his father's study. A big globe rested on a wooden stand in the corner. The globe actually doubled as a cabinet for his father's Scotch whiskey. It opened up at the equator to reveal an old bottle of the amber-colored liquor, as well as some fat little glasses. (Jeremy had once taken the whiskey out in a moment of curiosity—he'd lost interest when he realized it smelled like wood varnish and old Band-Aids.)

Jeremy spun the globe. "So guys...*this* here is New York, New York," he pointed to the city, "in the corner of the United States." He ran his finger along an invisible path. "We are currently across the Atlantic Ocean, on a tiny little island called Ireland. Which is a part of the United *Kingdom*..." He trailed off. The two were not listening. Moe and Zippo remained frozen in the doorway. Both their jaws were agape. Zippo's slitted pupils had grown so wide as to make his blue eyes look black.

Moe raised a finger, wanting to point but not sure what to settle on. His arm wavered like he was about to faint. "Are these..." he started, then stopped. His mouth had gone dry. He swallowed and started again. "Are these...all...*record albums*?"

He motioned around at the old records on the shelves and in the wooden crates.

"What, do you guys like music?" Jeremy cocked his head.

"Can...look?" Zippo asked tentatively.

"Be my guest!" Jeremy said.

Nobody had ever expressed interest in these old records. Jeremy always brought a few with him to Pigpimples, imagining he might throw an unauthorized dance party. In reality, even Bruno couldn't muster up much enthusiasm for them. He didn't even seem impressed with *Jules Valentino & the Mambo Jambo.*

The offworlders made beelines to two different areas of the room. They looked at the records reverentially, being extremely careful and handling them very gently. Zippo picked up the first one he could find on the top shelf of the bookcase. He slid it gingerly out of its cover as if to make sure it was really there. He held the lacquer disc up to the light as he read the label, grasping the edges in his paw pads. The album was *Missed the Boat*, by Billy McComb. Not one of Jeremy's personal favorites (it was mostly sappy love ballads if he remembered correctly). Zippo, however, acted as if he'd just stumbled upon the Holy Grail.

Moe dug through one of the straw-filled crates. The words "PROPERTY OF ROGER & ANNE FLETCHER" were stenciled on the side. "Who's Roger and Anne Fletcher?" Moe asked.

"Oh...they were my parents," Jeremy said. Moe noticed Jeremy's usage of the past tense, and politely left it at that.

The crate contained hand-labeled records in brown paper sleeves. Some Jeremy had listened to, others he had not. Moe was holding one that read *Blank Canvas* by Marlene Dreamer. Jeremy had never listened to that one. Moe flipped through others, pulling ones out seemingly at random stacking them on the floor. Some of the ones he pulled out included:

Devil's Advocate by Machito & His Orchestra (a fantastic salsa record, in Jeremy's opinion), *Easy Does It* by Nora Knight (another one he wasn't familiar with), and *Methodical Madness* by Wiljalba Frikell (a Prussian musician who specialized in a variety of bizarre instruments including the blaisophone, the klorkinet, and the electroarp—a weird one to be sure, but Jeremy still loved it).

He watched them for a while, but their attention was utterly lost to him. Jeremy decided to go and make breakfast; his stomach was still grumbling and the offworlders appeared content.

When he eventually wandered back into the study, he sat down on his dad's couch with a plate of Toastee Mums on his lap. Zippo, intrigued by the smell of food, stopped what he was doing to stare at him. Jeremy nibbled on a toaster pastry. *Orange marmalade fruit magma—not bad!*

"Us for?" Zippo made a questioning gesture with his paw. Jeremy nodded. The offworlder made a strange bow and sat down on the rug. He brought a stack of records with him as Jeremy handed him a Toastee Mum.

"You, uh, got any more of those toaster pastries, homie?" Moe sat down on the floor beside them, also sorting records. Jeremy pulled a couple of more pastries out of his robe's pocket, handing them to Moe.

"So you know what these are?" Jeremy asked, referring to the pastries.

"Of course! Toastee Mums. They've got them all over the quadrant. FILLED WITH REAL FRUIT MAGMA™, right?"

Ah-ha! So they were *alien food!* Jeremy thought. He would have to tell Bruno. "Anyways, you guys—I was trying to explain to you about where you currently are," Jeremy said.

"Hold up, hold up, I just need to know—*where* did your fam get all these recordings?!" Moe interrupted.

"They're from my dad. He was an agent." Zippo's ears pricked up. "He got most of them back when we lived in California. Los Angeles."

"Yooo! I've heard of that place!" Moe exclaimed. "Hollywood!"

Jeremy was surprised. "How the devil do you know about *Hollywood*?" These guys had never even set foot on Earth, and yet they knew about a sleepy little neighborhood in his home town? There was practically nothing out there but orange groves! *Surely nothing anyone would be talking about starside..?*

Moe shook his head, "Never mind. I'll explain some other time. Go on."

Jeremy shrugged. "My dad worked with a lot of musicians and performers and stuff. People who wanted to get famous, you know. And he would book them shows in nightclubs and theaters, and promote them. Get people excited to go see them. Get people to buy tickets."

Zippo nodded eagerly at the mention of nightclubs and tickets.

"And so, when audiomatic phonograph recording came out and radio stations starting popping up everywhere, Dad would take his clients to a studio and they'd record their music right onto the record. That way, you could make copies of it and send it to lots of different theaters and radio stations all over the country."

"Ray-DEE-oh! Yeh!" Zippo chimed in.

"So why'd you leave? Your old man retired?" Moe asked.

"Eventually, we *had* to move. Leave the states completely. Because there was some crazy person making threats to my parents. Sending threatening letters to them and stuff. My mom was a dessert chef at a little restaurant, and she said one day someone tried to burn the place down with her in it. That was the last straw for my dad, and we left. He took all these records with him."

The three ate their food thoughtfully for a few moments.

"So where'd you end up moving to?" Moe asked.

"Ireland."

"*Ire-land*? Where the heck is that?"

Jeremy laughed. "You guys really are clueless, huh? You're *in* Ireland! This is Ireland. My mom was from California. But my dad was actually Irish, from Ireland. He always claimed he was related to royalty, and that we Fletchers had an ancestral castle back in his home country. He wasn't interested in living as..." Jeremy stopped to remember the word, "...as an *aristocrat*. So he left the family castle and moved to the States. After all the stuff that happened, we came back here, to Ballyhoo Keep. That's this castle's name," he explained to Zippo.

"Ireland, huh?" Moe looked around, as if assessing his surroundings for the first time. "Never heard of Ireland. Do they speak English in this country?"

Jeremy walked back over to his father's globe in the corner. "Come," he waved them over, "check this out."

"Nice mep!" Zippo said. Jeremy assumed he meant *map*.

"This little island right here," he placed his finger on the globe, "is Ireland. We're right next door to England," he moved his finger. "And ENG-land is where ENG-lish comes from. Get it?"

It took a few moments, but understanding finally spread across Moe's face. "Oooh yeeaahhh, *England*!" he grinned, repeating the name to Zippo. "England!"

Zippo appeared on the verge of understanding, but wasn't quite there yet. Moe helped him out. "Like Tommy Cobblestone!"

"Yeah, like Tommy—" Jeremy started. He shut his eyes, as if suddenly afflicted with a terrible migraine. He nodded, then finished saying the name even though it caused him physical pain. "Cobble...stone. Yes." He hung his head in defeat.

Moe and Zippo lit up with comprehension, then looked at Jeremy with new eyes. He knew what they were going to say before they even spoke.

"You know, chief—I bet nobody has ever told you this, but

you actually kind of *look* like Tommy Cobblestone!"

Zippo agreed, vigorously. "Tah-mEE!" he chuffled.

"You don't say," Jeremy said flatly.

"Yeah! The glasses, the hair—your roundish face! Even your eyes have that same green with brownish color! Ha!"

Zippo leaned in very close to Jeremy's face, examining his eyes. "Tah-mEE CABBLE-ston! From EEEEEng-land!" Zippo exclaimed.

For some reason, the two offworlders thought Jeremy's similar appearance was the most funny thing they'd ever realized in their lives. They both laughed hysterically, Zippo collapsing to the rug rolling around on his back. Moe wandered back over to the couch, but fell down on his face laughing before he could sit down. "I—I'm sorry! So sorry!" Moe was practically gasping as he removed his sunglasses and wiped mirthful tears from his eyes.

Jeremy waited patiently.

The two finally stopped. They remained on the floor, panting and grinning in a delirious haze. Jeremy stood with his tongue planted firmly in his cheek. "You...uh...guys seem to know a lot about Tommy Cobblestone, huh?"

"Oh definitely!" Moe's head popped up, suddenly very earnest. He turned to his side, propping his head up with his elbow on the floor. "We must have read every issue at least five times!"

"Tah-mEE *magic* boi!" Zippo gushed.

Normally, the comparison to that annoying bogtrotter of a boy wizard would have set Jeremy off. For the first time, though, seeing these two offworlders dying of laughter...somehow he didn't mind it as much. He decided it might be fun to completely astonish them.

"You wanna know something really cool? What if I told you I actually *went* to Pigpimples Academie?"

Zippo and Moe both sat up. "But Pigpimples isn't a real

place, dude."

"Oh, it is. Trust me, it is *definitely* a real place."

"What?!" Moe furrowed his brow, flabbergasted.

Jeremy rushed out of the room and grabbed his House Fluffernut blazer, slipping it on over his t-shirt. He ran back into the study.

"Hay!" Zippo exclaimed. "Dat Tah-mEE jackit! Dat cool!"

"See?" Jeremy showed off. "Pigpimples is a real school of magic, in England. They publish *The Adventures of Tommy Cobblestone* as an advertisement for their school."

This was the first Moe had ever heard of this. He didn't like the idea that he'd been reading what boiled down to a very long commercial, and was skeptical. "So you're saying magic is real, too? Terrans send their kids to school to learn *actual* magic? I'd always heard stories, but I thought they were just...stories."

Jeremy grinned. This was his chance. He grabbed the empty plate and placed it on the rug. He then zipped out the door, returning with an armful of rocks. They clinked as he placed them on the plate, one by one. Moe and Zippo watched with concern, as if Jeremy had lost his mind.

"All right—what shall I magically transform them into? Give me anything."

Moe's eyes lit up. "Oh, oh! Change them into a pile of credit chips! We'll be rich!"

Zippo nodded excitedly.

"No, wait," Moe corrected himself, "better yet—make them a pile of Mirgonthian Dragon Pearls!—NO! Red Tignium diamonds from Cophus 7! Yes! We'll be rich! RICH!" He was nearly dancing with glee.

Jeremy looked like he wanted to say something, and held up a finger.

"Red tignium diamonds from Cophus 7," Moe repeated. "Do it."

"Okay, sorry. I should have specified," Jeremy cleared his

throat and started again. "I can only transform stuff into *food*."

"SHRAMP!" Zippo nearly shrieked. "Lots shramp! Big pile, liek VARY big!" Zippo motioned with outstretched arms how big he wanted the pile to be.

"No!" Moe objected. "Make it some kind of super expensive food that we could sell! Like Gekkonian Terrordactyl caviar! It's this stuff that has to be collected from Terrordactyls that live along the cliffs of the Fire Moons of Gekkon! And they lay these squishy green eggs once every sixteen years or so, when they're in heat—"

"Okay, sorry, that's my fault again," Jeremy interrupted. "It has to be *breakfast* food—"

Moe started to speak, but Jeremy cut him off.

"*Terran* breakfast food, that is. Yes. So to be clear, I can magically transform things into Terran breakfast food items. Well, I guess they could be *any* breakfast food items, as long as I know what they are. Oh, and I can only transform non-living things...uh...usually," the image of Balthasar flashed in Jeremy's mind.

Moe and Zippo looked at Jeremy, awaiting further clarification.

"That's it. Terran breakfast foods. Where do you think all this breakfast food has been coming from?"

"Ooooh!" the two both nodded in understanding.

"So what'll it be?" Jeremy asked.

Moe shrugged. "How about some more bacon? It was pretty good!"

Minutes later, a full breakfast spread sat before them.

"Well, I am convinced. You have magical breakfast powers," Moe said.

"I'm just a mystical kind of guy, what can I say? Now let's eat, and you guys can tell me how you ended up crashing into the ocean."

Moe grabbed a few strips of bacon and talked with his mouth

full. "I guess I should start with Jessica Gelato. Ever heard of her?"

* * *

After they'd enjoyed their impromptu second breakfast, Jeremy invited them to stay at the castle for as long as they needed while they repaired their ship. He was happy to have the company. "There's one thing you haven't explained, though," Jeremy said.

Moe and Zippo gulped uneasily. "He *know*!" Zippo hissed. Moe shushed him, but the Felinian went on. "Please, tell noh one! We give you...uhh...lots money! Credits!" Zippo mindspoke a vision to Jeremy. It was of himself and Moe being taken away in handcuffs, followed by both of them locked in a prison cell.

"What? No, it's nothing serious! I'm not going to call the police!" Jeremy assured them. As far as he knew, there was nothing illegal about aliens landing in Ireland. He supposed they might have to register their ship with local authorities, but nobody around here was going to care. "No, you guys just said you were on your way to Callisto when your ship was hit, right?"

"That's...right," Moe responded carefully.

"And Callisto is a moon of Jupiter?"

"Korrect," Zippo said, eyes squinting, chin raised warily.

"So what's out there? You never explained why you were going to Callisto in the first place."

Zippo and Moe looked at each other again, chuckling. Zippo sighed in relief, leaning back into his chair.

"Should we tell him? He is in show business, after all," Moe said to Zippo. "We were gonna tell you this eventually, but now's as good a time as ever." Moe picked up his glass of orange juice. "We were on our way to Callisto to check out a little piece of real estate." Moe downed the rest of the juice. He was clearly unsure about how much he should say, or what details to include. After a couple of false starts, he composed his thoughts.

"So I don't know if you know this, but your star system is pretty much *the* place to be these days. It's funky. It's fresh. All of the worlds in the Planetary League love you guys."

"They do?"

"Well, let me re-phrase that. They are *going* to love you. Soon. See, when the League first made contact with Terra Firma about a century ago, most people saw you guys as a bunch of hayseeds and hicks. Your tech was basically prehistoric *wackness*—who am I kidding, it still is. You guys hadn't developed electricity, or even genetically enhanced candy bars."

Zippo laughed, as if such a notion were utterly preposterous.

"But, to some of the more sophisticated tastemakers of the quadrant," Moe motioned to himself and Zippo, "Reptilicon is fast becoming the chillest world, with all its *chic* culture."

Jeremy had heard them refer to Earth by this odd name several times, but didn't want to interrupt.

"All the hipsters back home love your planet. Not just hipsters, either—gang stars, chirpers, jukers—everyone reads Terran comics! Tommy Cobblestone especially. It's a *huge* hit starside. And they're starting to pick up Terran fashions, too. Your music? They play that stuff on every pirate radio station. It won't be long until they're serving Terran food at the food courts in every starside mall."

Jeremy took a sense of pride in this, despite the fact that he had done nothing.

"Zippo and I unexpectedly came into a little bit of...cash, let's say. And we thought, this is our chance to make it big. Callisto is close enough to your world to make it trendy, but far away enough to be left undisturbed." Moe leaned in close, excitement in his eyes. "It's the perfect location to open up a *nightclub*!"

"A nightclub?" Jeremy's pulse quickened.

Zippo blinked slowly, mindspeaking an image. In his mind's eye, Jeremy saw a sleek building glittering against a starry backdrop, underneath a dome of atmosphere. Jupiter, an ethereal orange globe, rose over the horizon. Exotic offworld trees and ferns lined the walkway to the entrance, above which hung a pink neon sign. It read, in an alien script: *FUTURE POP*.

"F-Future Pop? Nightclub?!" Jeremy said aloud, surprising himself. "Surely you'll need a magic act!" he sputtered, his excitement rising. This was his chance!

"Magic act?"

"Yeah! A magic show! JEREMIAH THE MYSTIC!" Jeremy framed an imaginary marquee with his hands in the air.

"Who's Jeremiah the Mystic?"

"Me! That's my stage name!"

Moe looked at Zippo. They shared a surprised expression. "Oh! Of course! When would you like to audition?" Moe pulled out a small appointment book and pencil. "Our schedule is looking preeeeetty open for the next couple of days." He penciled something into the blank book. "We're always looking to add acts to our roster. And we could use all the Terran talent we can get!" Zippo nodded in agreement.

"How about this: let's all meet back in the Great Hall tonight."

Moe scribbled something in his planner. "Great Hall...tonight...all right!"

"And prepare..." Jeremy paused dramatically, "to be MYSTIFIED!"

CHAPTER 14

THE MAMBO WIZARD

The offworlders returned to the Great Hall that evening, after a long day of tinkering on their starship. Jeremy had spent most of the afternoon setting up his performance. The hall was decorated in his father's old posters and adverts. The largest one was just a banner that read "ENTER THE MYSTIC" in blood-red letters. Candles flickered all about the room, giving the castle a spectral feel.

"Ooooooh!" Zippo cooed as he walked into the room. "Dis spooky," he whispered to Moe.

"Hi guys! I'm almost ready here, just take a seat in those chairs," Jeremy called out from behind a bed sheet he'd hung between two pillars. Moe and Zippo sat, their curiosity piqued. Furniture squeaked on the stone floor as Jeremy made some final adjustments behind the sheet. "Okay, I'm ready!" he called out.

Jeremy thrust the curtain aside, striding to the center of his makeshift stage. Candlelight glinted off his round spectacles. His normally messy hair was tamed and neatly parted with some of his father's old pomade. He was dressed in his finest Pigpimples formalwear: black tuxedo jacket with tails, white shirt, and black bow tie. He also wore his father's blue wizard robe as a kind of overcoat. It hung loosely at his sides, the candles making its pearly stars sparkle in the dark. He had considered wearing Dad's bejeweled turban, but it was too big for his head.

"Good evening, ladies and gentlemen," Jeremy bowed. Zippo waved excitedly. "I hope that you've left your expectations of reality at the door, because you've just entered a *new* reality. A world of the arcane and inscrutable!" Jeremy brought an arm up, his sleeve obscuring the lower half of his face. He made wild eyes as he dashed at Zippo. "Of spirits, and *sorcery*!" he whispered menacingly.

"Noh!" Zippo cowered, afraid.

He ran back to the curtain, lifting his arms above his head. "Of magic and...MUSIC!" he shouted, waving his hands in a flourish. His oversized sleeves flapped down, light exploding at his feet and popping like the crack of a starter pistol. Moe and Zippo jumped in their seats.

"Whooo, yeah!" Moe clapped. He was enjoying the show already.

All the candles blew out, plunging the room into blackness. A supernatural light breathed to life behind the curtain, bathing everything in an eerie green glow. "Sorry, one sec," Jeremy muttered. It sounded like he was fiddling with the phonograph player. He let the needle drop, waiting a moment before music exploded onto the hall at maximum volume. It was a joyous wallop of a tune: "Mystical Mambo" by The Ensigns.

Jeremy burst through the curtain, tearing it down from its clothespins. Holding his wand aloft, he waved it as if conducting an orchestra. When the trumpets blasted or the bongos boomed, he would dab and tap the black baton, producing sparklers of light and explosions of confetti. This was much to Zippo's delight, and he clawed gleefully at the bits of paper.

The young magician danced around in the ghostly light, plucking a handkerchief from his front pocket and tossing it into the air. It floated to the floor, where it remained until Jeremy cha-cha'ed up next to it. He lifted his wand, making the hanky rise beside him. It did a jerky hanky dance to the mambo rhythm before flying back into Jeremy's front pocket. As the opening song crashed to a close, Jeremy fell to his knees, waving his wand and making all the candles flicker back to life with different colored flames.

Moe and Zippo applauded wildly.

The act continued at a brisk pace; it mostly featured Jeremy dancing around weirdly as he performed his little stage magician tricks. These included the self-taught "Devil's Sixpence," followed by the lesser known (but equally mysterious) "Matchbooks of Doom." For his final trick, Jeremy wheeled out a red cabinet. "Gentlemen," he announced, "this is known as Maskelyne's Coffin." He motioned to the wooden cabinet. It was painted all over with astrological hieroglyphs in glittering silver paint. As the final track started, Jeremy tied a silky black blindfold over his eyes. "It is considered the most secure of strongboxes—the kings of Europe used to keep the royal jewels in boxes *just like these*."

He made a big show of tying his ankles together with thin white rope. He then handcuffed his wrists together, hopping over to the cabinet and opening its lid.

"I will require an assistant to finish this trick. Can I get a volunteer?" Zippo's hand shot up. Jeremy had forgotten to factor in the fact that he was already blindfolded, and made a guess. "Zipponio, would you come up and take this key from me?"

Zippo walked up, tentatively. He took the key from Jeremy's palm. Jeremy wriggled into the upright box. "In a moment, I am going to have you close the coffin's lid. I want you to lock it with that key. Got it?"

"Kay," Zippo mewed.

"All right. Now!" Jeremy ordered.

Zippo shut the lid and locked it, then wandered back to his seat. The music rose in a frantic arpeggio of brass and guitars before settling into a long groove. Drums rumbled with sinister intensity as the two audience members waited in silence. The coffin trembled, scootched across the floor, then fell backwards with a terrific crash.

And then...nothing really happened. Moe and Zippo remained in their seats, not sure what was going on. Eventually, the simmering drums boiled over into a climax of screeching horns, marimbas, and jazzy organ. It must have been the final song on the album, because all that followed was the scratchy static from the phonograph's needle.

Then there was a thumping sound. Moe snatched the key from Zippo and rushed over to the coffin.

"Hey!" Jeremy's muffled voice shouted from inside the box. "Hey, could you guys let me out now?" Moe unlocked the lid and raised it.

"Jrr-mEE!" Zippo clasped his hands together, as if surprised to see him there.

"Dude, is this...still part of the trick?" Moe asked.

"Could someone get this blindfold off of me, please?" Jeremy asked.

"You DED it!" Zippo said, pulling the sash off of Jeremy's eyes. Jeremy blinked, then smiled.

"To answer your question: no, Moe. My trick wasn't to lock myself in a box, and then have the box fall over, and then be stuck inside the box. Here," Jeremy held his handcuffed wrists out to Moe, "The same key should work." Moe undid the handcuffs and Jeremy untied the rope at his ankles.

"Waow! That was rally cool show! Jrr-mEE magic boi!" Zippo gushed, patting Jeremy on the head and helping him out of the coffin. Jeremy dusted himself off.

"So what happened, chief?" Moe asked.

"Not sure. The plan was to appear behind you guys the second the song ended." He rubbed the bump on the back of his head. Moe raised a skeptical eyebrow. Jeremy cleared his throat, not liking Moe's expression one bit. This was supposed to be an audition, after all.

"So maybe the act needs work," Jeremy admitted, "but I'll cut to the chase, fellas—this was just a taste, a *sample*, of my skills. There's so much more! You guys will need a piano player, right? I'm your guy—I took piano lessons as a kid! And then there's...there's juggling!" Jeremy picked up some rubber balls. "Are offworlders into juggling? I mean, talk about the next big thing! It's a huge deal here on Earth. Really huge deal!" Jeremy attempted to juggle the balls, losing control of all of them almost instantly. They bounced away in random directions across the room. "It's possibly the most authentic Terran artform you can get!"

Moe placed a hand on Jeremy's shoulder, then glanced at Zippo. It looked like the Felinian was mindspeaking something to his friend. Moe nodded, chuckled, and gave Jeremy a slap on the back. "Psssh! You kidding me, dude? Of *course* you made it! You're in!"

Jeremy's jaw dropped. He fell to his knees, raising his arms in triumph. "Yes! I am the greatest magician of all time!"

"Honestly, kid, as long as you keep providing us with free Toastee Mums, you can do whatever kind of act you want. You can lock yourself in that box and just stay there. Be a ventriloquist with a sock puppet. Heck, sing showtunes in your underwear!"

Jeremy sprang to his feet. "You want underwear dancing— you got it!" He sang into his wand, dancing a happy fandango around the room.

Zippo chuffled at Jeremy's infectious glee. "Yeh, Jrr-mEE! Magic boi! MAM-bo MAM-bo wee-ZARD!"

Jeremy stopped his dance, cocking his head. "Mambo wizard?" he repeated it several times, testing out the impromptu title. He resumed dancing. "Now that's keen-o! The Mambo Wizard!" Jeremy froze, posing with his wand raised above his head and arm outstretched. "Breakfast...is...SERVED!"

Moe and Zippo squinted in confusion. "Sorry, what?" Moe asked. "Breakfast is *what*? What the heck was that?"

"Breakfast is served! You know! It'll be my tagline!" Jeremy said.

Moe and Zippo looked at each other. They collapsed into uncontrollable fits of laughter.

CHAPTER 15

FRIENDSHIP MONTAGE

The early summer days breezed by and the trio fell into comfortable routines: Jeremy had his castle maintenance, the offworlders had their starship repairs. Moe and Zippo raided Jeremy's stash of *Vince Thorne: Agent of Fortune* comics. In exchange, Jeremy got to read all the issues of *Tommy Cobblestone* they could find lying around their ship. He was reluctant at first, considering he had vowed to loathe Tommy Cobblestone for all time. But after trying a couple of issues he was forced to admit they weren't *that* bad.

Over dinner, Jeremy would tell them all sorts of stories about what Earth was really like. He recounted his early memories of Los Angeles, along with anecdotes about growing up in his father's world of vaudeville: the entertainers, the musicians, and the magicians. Above all, the offworlders were interested in life at Pigpimples.

Sometimes Moe would talk about his homeworld, Bino. While Terrans and Felinians had about the same average lifespans, it turned out that aging worked differently for Binosians. They usually lived to be over one hundred Terran years. Binosians also experienced puberty at a much slower rate, boys not reaching full maturity until around age forty or so (although the females matured a little more quickly). And although Moe would eventually age, he would never grow taller than about three and a half feet—four feet, tops. (Binosians were a short race.)

When Jeremy asked, Moe answered that he was not exactly sure how old he was in Earth years. After doing the math, they estimated that both Moe and Zippo were six or seven Terran years older than Jeremy.

Jeremy also learned that Moe's father was a member of a merchant shipping guild back on Bino. He piloted freighters all around the galactic quadrant. Moe had never been very interested in joining this guild, and opted to enroll in a small technical school [*Translator's note: Burrow Colony Vo-Tech —ChatterBot 3.6*] on one of Bino's farming moons. He had taken some classes on starship mechanics and engineering, which is how he met Zippo.

Zipponio was a Felinian who came from a planet called Phynix, which was a part of the distant Greeno Sector. Zippo didn't talk about his world very much; Jeremy suspected it made him homesick. The main thing he picked up from Zippo was that his parents were space krill ranchers, and that he had enrolled at the Vo-Tech to earn a degree in synthetic aquafarming.

Both had either dropped out, or flunked out—they themselves weren't sure which.

Jeremy liked to believe it was the latter.

* * *

One afternoon, the trio sat in the Great Hall. It was a hot day, and they'd been working hard all morning. Moe sat upside-down in one of the Hall's stuffed chairs. His legs rested on the high back of the chair, his silvery-purple hair dangling below. It was nice and dim in the hall, so he didn't have his shades on.

A plate of food sat on the rug near his head. He would occasionally nosh on a strip of bacon as he observed the room. "The applewood bacon versus hickory smoked...too close to call, I think." He picked up another strip and popped it in his mouth. It crunched loudly. "We'll have to do more research before we can make a final assessment on this."

Jeremy sat beside Moe in another high-backed chair, also upside-down. He was reading an issue of *Tommy Cobblestone* (#24 "Tommy Saves the Ghost of Roddy Diddlesworth"). "Ha!" he snorted. "This is so fake! They would never let a Dandy Lion student sit with House Hazeltwig during dinner, unless it was a holiday or a special occasion." He read some more in silence, then burst out: "also, how do they always have all their classes together? Tommy, Nicholas, and Georgina somehow all have the same schedule, despite being in completely different houses and not even tracking towards the same majors? I thought Georgina was studying to be an herbalist—why is she taking a class on taming baby drakes?! It's ridiculous!" Jeremy tossed the comic book in disgust. It fluttered across the room.

Moe continued. "Now—your Belgian waffle versus your French toast—call me crazy, but I actually think I prefer the waffles! So light and crispy—mwah!" Moe bunched his fingers together and kissed them. It was a gesture he had picked up from Jeremy (who had actually learned it from Bruno).

Jeremy didn't hear him. "Besides, they would *never* let a sevvie even go anywhere *near* the baby drakes. Stuff like that is always reserved for upperclassmen. The most exciting assignments we ever got was identifying which types of wood grain are the most effective at repelling ghosts. Oh, and the ins and outs of customs laws in regards to the importing of magical mold spores."

Moe flipped down from his chair. "Now why didn't they ever make an issue about *that*?"

"I don't know," Jeremy said, also tumbling down from his

chair. "It might have been a more exciting story arc than 'who is sending Georgina these mysterious letters?' Oh wow, it turns out IT WAS HER AUNT! It took four issues to learn that IT WAS JUST HER NICE AUNT! Please tell me this becomes important later on in the story. Her aunt is some kind of super powerful witch in hiding—"

"It's never mentioned again," Moe said.

"Ugh!" Jeremy groaned.

"What I don't get about Tommy Cobblestone is," Moe slipped on his sunshades. "You know how everyone in their world can do magic, right?"

"Right."

"And then when bad stuff happens, they spend most of the issue trying to figure out a solution. And in the end, they just have to use magic to solve the problem."

"Right."

"So what I'm saying is—that's wack. Why don't they just use magic from the beginning? Like when the bog troll kidnaps Lady Primrose, and they get together to figure out how to save her. And they spend something like three issues on a plan, which in the end they just use Chamberpot's magical Time Talisman, which Tommy had all along!"

"Oh, don't even get me started on that..." Jeremy griped.

"But you see what I'm saying?! They have a *time talisman*! Why aren't they using that stupid thing in EVERY ISSUE! Something bad happens, just say 'whoops, get out the Time Talisman!' Bam! Go back a few minutes, fix it! Simple as that!"

"Or when they use the Mystical Map of Sibelius that shows every single person walking around Pigpimples on it—"

Moe jumped in, excited, "—And Nicholas says it shows EVERYONE on campus, even if they are using a disguise or an invisibility spell, yes, yes!"

Jeremy gesticulated wildly. "And then, two issues later, that kid from House Porkerson goes missing. And not a single one of them think to consult the magic map? They just wrapped it up and left it in Nick's closet! Could have saved them an entire issue of searching for the kid, or thinking he'd been murdered by that rogue griffin they'd spotted flying around the school."

"Oh yeah, I remember that. What ever happened to the kid?"

"He locked himself in a pantry to pig out on food."

Moe laughed. "Oh right! What a *jibroni*. What was his name, again?"

"Uh...oh, it was 'Plumpy.' Get it? Because he's fat."

"Seems a bit wack of his parents to name him that," Moe said.

Jeremy shook his head. "I guess they use magic to make Pigpimples seem a lot more interesting than it really is. In real life, most of the stuff you learn there is very boring. And useless. Nothing exciting ever happened to us, like getting attacked by werewolves or a dragon. The only problems we ever had were things like studying for a final, or staying awake during one of the Headmage's lectures. Things we couldn't solve with magic. And besides, the kids that were really good at magic," Jeremy thought of Christopher Lionspark, "Never had any problems, anyway."

"Ha!" Moe exclaimed. "But what about all the cool toys? Like the Mirror of Destiny, or the Scroll of Shimmering—surely those could make your lives a lot easier?"

Jeremy shook his head. "Nah. We didn't have any cool magical gadgets like that. There is absolutely no *way* Sir Chamberpot could have handled something like a Time Talisman. He would have destroyed the universe with it in about five minutes. The man has trouble using basic eating utensils, let alone time portals."

"That's right! I always forget you actually knew *the* Mongo Chamberpot, huh?"

"The one and only. I even have his autograph on my expulsion papers."

"Fresh! What was he really like?"

"Well, you know how in the comics he's always coming up with those wise sayings?"

"Yup." Moe imitated an old man voice, "*Sometimes the magic you seek, Tommy, is within you!*"

Jeremy laughed. "The deepest insight I ever got from him was: '*Remember, they'll give you an extra packet of crackers for your soup, if you but ask for them.*'"

CHAPTER 16

A DONUT DIGRESSION

Eventually Donut finished all her birdseed. However, Jeremy figured out (after some magical trial and error) that the hamster very much enjoyed *muesli*. This was a granola-like mix of nuts, seeds and dried fruit that Bruno D'argento had often been forced to eat for breakfast, back at Pigpimples. In fact, Bruno even referred to it as "that nasty gerbil food." Nasty or not, it qualified as a breakfast item. Donut especially liked the dried strawberry pieces.

Zippo had a complicated relationship with Donut. In the beginning, he absolutely detested her. In fact, the first time he noticed her in the Great Hall, he hissed in revulsion. "Wat DAT?!" He zipped straight to the cage, staring wide-eyed at the little critter. "Yeeeugh! That NASTEE," he growled. "That *sooo* nastee." He muttered Felinian curses under his breath over and over, but continued to watch her. He eventually pulled up a chair so that he could sit near the cage, hunched forward, observing the creature's ever-disgusting pitter-patter. "*You SEE dis, Moe?*" he asked incredulously. "Someone kill it."

Moe assured Jeremy that Zippo had just been kidding around. "Felinian humor is...well, it's hard to even know where to begin with it. It's an acquired taste for sure." Jeremy had picked up as much from thumbing through some of Zippo's issues of *Mik & Skitter: Mischievous Rodent Vermin Twins That Needed to Be Killed*. It was Zip's favorite comic book from his homeworld. Even though it was in Felinian, Jeremy still looked at the pictures, attempting to piece together a story. The best he could make out from the panels was that the two small rodents, Mik and Skitter, enjoyed taunting Felinians and that they deserved death for this reason.

"That's Donut," Jeremy called over to Zippo.

"Do-NET?!" Zippo looked surprised, then laughed. "Liek Jessica vid-YO game!" He looked back at the hamster. "I hate dat ting. Yeugh!"

After several days of staring in repulsed fascination, Zippo asked Jeremy if he could take Donut out of her cage and hold her.

"You're not going to...eat...her, are you?"

Zippo made a shocked looked, eyes wide with horror. "Neeoow! Wat wrong with you?! Donut is CUTE PET, no food! GROSS."

Jeremy took Donut out of her cage, scooping the fat little ball of fluff into his hands as she skittered around. Zippo held out his lumpy pink paws, eyes wide in anticipation. The hamster scuttled from Jeremy's hands into Zippo's. "It teckle!" Zippo giggled.

The tiny rodent gave Zippo a good sniff, exploring his exotic Felinian scent and looking for a place to burrow. "You vary good HEMP-stir, yeh. Good HEMP-stir!" Zippo cooed. After holding the hamster for a satisfactory amount of time, Zippo placed her back in her cage.

Since that day, Zippo occasionally made little toys and playthings for the hamster out of disused starship components. He even made her a sign out of cardboard, labeling it in his Felninian script: HAMP STAR CITY. "You liek HEMP-stir place, Jrr-mEE?" Zippo asked, noticing Jeremy admiring the habitat.

"It's lovely. Donut looks very pleased. You do excellent work, Zippo."

Zippo purred and patted Jeremy on the head.

"Chief! Just the man I've been looking for," Moe said, entering the Great Hall. The grandfather clock chimed. "Look at that, six o'clock already. We still have a turbopump to work out, but I think we can finish it tonight. What do you think, Zip?" Zippo yawned and stretched, giving Moe an affirmative okay sign. Moe continued. "Good. Because it's one of the last big items we can cross off our list. Jeremy, let's meet up after sunset. We have a few things we need to discuss."

Jeremy nodded. "All right then. After sunset."

CHAPTER 17
A TREATISE ON THE ART
OF RADIO DIPPING

Jeremy sat waiting at their usual spot atop the cliff, examining the Personal Shell he'd found that night back in his dorm. He had actually forgotten about the thing until earlier that afternoon, when he came across it in the pocket of his tuxedo jacket. After experimenting with it for a minute, he figured out how to turn the device on. To his horror, it still had the photo of him looking like a surprised doofus right there, under "pictures."

He could not believe that the photograph had only been taken a week ago. It felt like something from a different era. He promptly pushed the button marked "delete," and the image mercifully disappeared. The boys had mentioned the device could play music. He squinted at the small screen; it appeared to have a library of songs by musicians he'd never heard of. Whenever he tried to play a song, the screen displayed a long block of micro-text that Jeremy had little interest in reading. He'd have to ask Moe and Zippo about it.

It was their nightly ritual to sit by the cliff and make a campfire after the day's work was done. They'd bring chairs and extra blankets, as the breeze from the ocean could get a tad chilly.

They'd also bring snacks. *Lots* of snacks. Then they'd relax, talk, and listen to his dad's old records on the phonograph. "Primitive recording tech, and yet, ingenious," Moe had said after inspecting the record player. "Pretty deece sound quality, too. No wonder you Terrans come up with the funkiest music. You have a knack for this stuff."

Jeremy didn't really understand what the offworlders were talking about half the time. But they all agreed that the music sounded better outside, under the stars, whilst sipping an Orange Nova Pop. When a record finished, they'd offer their opinions on the music. Jeremy found that he was actually the harshest critic out of the three. Moe, and especially Zippo, were very good at noticing subtle nuances that Jeremy typically missed. Above all, the offworlders were entranced by the sheer *variety* of Terran musical styles. Anything that was even a little bit out of the ordinary, they loved—and the collection contained a *lot* that was out of the ordinary.

"Where did your dad even *find* these guys?" Moe had asked last night. "*Cherry Blossom Night Waves* by Jose Zapateria, *Last Tango On Venus* by Cosmic Salad," he read the titles off the record sleeves, "*The Octopus Fandango* by Sonja Miller & the Hoot Owls! Dude, I thought me and Zip were experts when it came to Reptilicon tunes, but I've never even *heard* of this funky stuff!"

"Most of them are from years ago," Jeremy said. "Dad was really into all these new styles of music. He was convinced that mambo would be the next big thing, but I don't think any of these bands ever hit it big. It's a shame; a lot of them are really good." Moe and Zippo had agreed. In the past few nights, Jeremy had learned one of life's universal truths: it felt good to have someone to share music with.

Jeremy slipped the Shell back into his pocket as the alien duo approached. Zippo had some records tucked under his arm. "Hey guys. What did you bring?" Jeremy asked as he arranged the kindling and started the fire. The sun had just gone down.

"Wat DAT?!" Zippo pointed with an extended claw. He stared with intense fascination at a plastic bag in Jeremy's hands. It appeared to be filled with squishy white cubes.

"I've been wanting to show these to you! They finally got a shipment in at the Old Hag! They're called *marshmallows*." Jeremy dangled the bag at the Felinian, who could not help but snatch it from his grip. Zippo tore the bag open, clamping it over his nostrils and huffing in its sugary essence. He did this several times, making the bag shrivel and expand. "Mmmm! Marsh-MEL-on! Smell sooo *good*!"

Jeremy plucked a marshmallow out and gave it to Zippo, tossing another one to Moe. "You roast 'em! Here, let me show you." He picked up a long metal wire that used to be a coat hanger, poking it through the center of his marshmallow. Zippo could hardly contain his excitement. His paws fidgeted as he watched Jeremy roast the marshmallow, itching for a try.

When the fluffy cylinder looked sufficiently toasted, Jeremy pulled it away and blew on it. "Voila!" He popped it into his mouth. "*Mah dad nn I useth to do thith all the time*," Jeremy said through a mouthful of mallow. He bent down, bringing out two long, thin swords. They were the kind used for fencing. "I couldn't find another coat hanger, so I brought you these." He handed Moe and Zippo the practice blades. "They were in my dad's study. I don't think he'd mind."

Once they realized what the metal shafts were, Moe and Zippo hopped to their feet. "Just like Sinclair Fierce in *Champion of the Sea! En garde*, swine!" Moe taunted as he swung at Zippo. Zippo tumbled back, his ears flattening as he went into battle mode. He crouched as he held the saber in a defensive position. His eyes narrowed and he let out a guttural *rewl* of intimidation. He shook his hind quarters, lunging at Moe with fangs bared. "YEAUUOWW!" he screeched, knocking Moe onto the grass. Zippo rolled, whipping his foil to the side.

"Ho ho! This little kitten thinks he can scratch!" Moe scrambled to his feet and thrust at Zippo. The rounded tip of the foil bent as it poked into Zippo's naked belly. The Felinian yowled in mock pain.

"You guys!" Jeremy waved his arms, trying to get their attention before they murdered each other. Zippo stopped mid-attack, turning to look at him. "They're for roasting the marshmallows." He held up the plastic bag, giving it a shake.

Zippo pounced on Jeremy, knocking him over as he snatched back the bag. He slid four marshmallows onto the tip of the foil, one after another. He then hunkered down and got roasting.

They listened to records and toasted the gooey cubes late into the night. Zippo consumed about half the bag; the humanoids split the other half. Jeremy felt slightly ill from all the Nova Pop and marshmallows. If Moe's stomach was bothered, he didn't show it.

When the final record ended, Moe scootched his chair in closer to Jeremy. He motioned for Zippo to do the same. Jeremy looked at the offworlders expectantly as they both leaned in. Moe cleared his throat.

"We need to tell you something," he said, adjusting his shades. "I'm afraid we haven't been totally straight forward with you, kid. And for that, I wanna apologize."

Jeremy looked to Zippo. The Felinian scrunched his face up in a pained expression.

"What are you talking about?" Jeremy asked.

"You took us in, you gave us food and shelter when we needed it. But I need to tell you now, homie, before we go any further—"

Jeremy listened.

"We're—me and Zip, that is—we're *pirates*. Space pirates."

Jeremy looked at Zippo again.

"Sarry," Zippo mewed.

Jeremy almost laughed, but didn't. *Maybe they're serious?*

He stood, laying another log on the fire. "Oh. Are you guys in trouble or something? On the run from the...space cops?" He wiped his hands on his robe. He was trying, with some difficulty, to mask the amusement in his voice. After all, one of them looked like a fourth grader who wandered out of his class's Halloween party, and the other was very recently afraid of a hamster.

"We've been pretty lucky so far," Moe answered, "although we've had a couple of run-ins, here and there." He had a faraway expression on his face. Then he flung away a lollipop stick he'd been chewing on. "I just wanted to have full disclosure with you, dude, since you've shown us so much hospitality. We've made a lot of progress on the *Terrapin*. We only have one last thing to pick up, but I think we'll have to travel to a major city with a spaceport. Like that one you were telling us about. Duds-bin?"

"Dublin," Jeremy corrected.

"Right. Dublin. Oh, and by the way—I've been meaning to ask—could you give us a ride to Dublin? You have a personal conveyor craft on the premises, right?" Moe asked.

He means Dad's prized automobile. "Uh—fine, yes," Jeremy agreed. "But let's get back to the space pirates thing—"

"Tomorrow?"

"What?"

"Can we get a ride there tomorrow? We are *this* close to being done, we just need a final component before we set out. It's extremely important. We could probably just fly the *Terrapin* to the city, but then there's all these wack landing fees, spaceport fees, interplanetary passport fees. We've kind of been wanting to lay low...you know...to avoid snoopers."

"Fine, yes—but what are you getting at? Are you guys really on the run? Police are after you? Hit-men? What?" Jeremy imagined some greased up gangsters with snub-nosed revolvers, straight out of *Vince Thorne: Agent of Fortune.*

"Err *yeah*, something like that. There might be some pretty heavy stuff going down in the near future. If anyone were to find out—I don't think anyone *will*; we've covered our butts pretty well—but if news broke about some of the stuff in our databanks..." Moe's eyebrows raised behind his sunglasses. "I am not an expert on interplanetary law, but I would hate for those jibronis from the League to nab *you* for aiding and abetting piracy."

Jeremy still couldn't tell how sincere Moe was. He decided to play along. "Let's say for now that I'm not opposed to your...activities. What does *space piracy* entail, exactly?"

"All right, he's in!" Moe gave a double thumbs up to Zippo, who clasped his paws together happily. Moe crouched down and added more driftwood to the fire. "What do you know about black holes?" he asked.

"Black holes? Uhh...like from outer space?"

"Uh-huh." Moe returned to his seat.

Jeremy had only a passing familiarity with the concept of black holes. A year ten Hazeltwig kid named Keith had once smuggled in an issue of *WEIRDO! Comics*. It was a black and white comic book known for its gory and grotesque tales. Jeremy recalled one of the stories from the issue. It had been about a lone Terran astronaut stuck on a space freighter that was slowly being sucked into a "black hole." The farther into the hole he went, the deeper he descended into space madness. If he recalled correctly, the story ended with the guy tearing his own face off. *Very keen-o!*

"I'm not sure, I just assumed they were some made up thing."

"Oh, they are real. *Very* real, dude," Moe said solemnly. Zippo nodded in affirmation. "Basically a black hole is a *hole*, for lack of a better word, in *space*. Nobody is one hundred percent sure what causes them, but they're all around the universe. Gravity is insanely strong in these holes. Imagine the biggest, most powerful vacuum cleaner ever made. You guys have those, right? Vacuum cleaners?"

"Yeah. Like the Puffing Billy?" Jeremy asked.

"The Puffing Billy?"

"Never mind," he shook his head. "Go on. Huge vacuum cleaner."

"Right. An immense vacuum cleaner in space, with suction so powerful that absolutely nothing can escape it. Asteroids, starships—you could have the hugest glimmer drive ever made, cranked to maximum, and it would still not be enough. Nothing can escape if you get too close."

"Keen-o! And what happens if you get sucked in?" Jeremy listened intently. He loved this kind of stuff.

"There are different theories about that. Some say the insane gravity stretches your ship out into a very long, very thin string. Like a sotus noodle, hundreds of miles long."

"Tasty."

"The other theory is that the gravity simply crushes you—compacts you and your ship into the size of an extremely dense little black pebble, tinier than an atom."

"Mmm-hmm. Tiny pebble or long noodle."

"So you need to always stay a couple of bips away, even from the event horizon. However..." Moe stopped, raising a finger for emphasis. Jeremy and Zippo leaned forward. "The best part about black holes is the *time flux*."

Jeremy awaited an explanation as Moe picked up a bottle of Nova Pop.

"So, pretend this here is the *Terrapin*," he held the bottle sideways. It gleamed in the firelight. He bent down and picked up a bottlecap from one of their previous bonfires, then placed it on the ground. "And that cap there is a black hole. Right?"

"Rai," Zippo said, following along closely. Jeremy smiled at the Felinian, and nodded.

"I don't want to get into the technical details, but the closer one gets to a black hole," Moe moved the bottle towards the bottlecap, "the slower time gets for that person. Once you've reached the singularity, or center of the black hole, *everything* goes wack. Time just stops existing! You enter a state referred to as *time flux*—every possible timeline from every possible reality starts getting all scrambled around. And really, a bunch of other weird junk happens, but that's the gist of it."

Jeremy looked up. "What do you mean time *slows down*, though? I don't get it."

"What I mean is, if you're flying too close to a black hole," Moe placed the bottle near the cap again, "it *feels* like the normal passage of time. But in reality, it slows down. A *lot*. It might *feel* like one day for you, but for everyone else in the universe, it was really a whole *week*. And if you start to get *really* close," he set the bottle on top of the bottlecap, "it will feel like one day for you, but actually thousands of years will pass. Hundreds of thousands of years. Millions of years, and so on."

"Keen-oooo!" Jeremy lit up, looking at Zippo.

"Don't get me started. Point is; black holes are dangerous and unpredictable. And flying too close to them does some jacked up stuff to you." Moe said.

"Well they should put some big ol' warning signs near them!" Jeremy suggested. "You know, with flashing lights that say: DANGER! BLACK HOLE!"

"Like I said—these bad boys can be tricky. It's impossible to *see* a thing if there's no light around it, and black holes suck up all the light. So it's very hard to tell where they are, unless you have the coordinates."

"What about scanners, or, umm..." Jeremy had to remember the right word from science fiction comics, "Radar?"

Moe and Zippo nodded, impressed. "Good call, but you see, scanners, radar—that stuff is just different spectrums of *light*. Radar waves, microwaves, radio waves. It's all just *light* waves. And *no* light can escape. If you scan a black hole with a radar, it will just pull the waves into it. But that brings me to my point."

Moe moved the bottle away from the cap. "You know how radios work, right?"

"Sort of. There's no good stations around here, though," Jeremy shrugged. Radios were still a new technology in Ireland. The one station he could pick up played nothing but classical music and "God Save the Queen" at nine o'clock, at which point it ended its broadcasting day.

"We noticed that, too!" Moe said. "But yes, the radio signal is also just a wavelength of light, beamed out from a tower. But where do the beams go?"

"What do you mean?"

"I'm saying the radio signals travel at 186,000 miles per second. They fly over the land and sea, and you pick up the signal on your radio. But where do they go *after* that?"

"I don't know." Jeremy looked to Zippo, then up at the stars. "Can't say I ever thought of that."

"Well they don't disappear! They bounce out of your atmosphere, and fly into space! And the radio waves will *keep* flying through space, forever. Traveling at the speed of light, a radio signal beamed from this planet would reach the edge of your star system in about, ohhh—" Moe waggled his hand, "five hours or so. And then they continue to fly through space forever. Unless, of course..."

Jeremy nodded. "Unless the radio waves get sucked into a black hole?"

"You're getting it. And I think you'll understand this next point, because your dad worked in the recording industry. Let's say I wanted to record some radio waves. I'd have to find a place with good reception, then take my magtape recorder out and hit 'record.' And I could record whatever radio broadcasts I pick up."

Jeremy nodded again. "All right."

"Now, what if I dropped a recording device into a black hole?"

Jeremy formulated a hypothesis. "It would fall into the hole, until time slowed down more and more...and eventually *stopped* completely. Right? And it would just be stuck recording in that...*time flux*? Forever. Or at least until the batteries died."

"And you're telling me this kid flunked out of the seventh grade?!" Moe exclaimed, socking Zippo in the arm. Zippo opened his mouth in a silent mewl of protest.

"Wait a minute, wait a minute," Jeremy held up a hand, "but wouldn't the gravity *crush* the recording device into a microscopic pebble?"

"Yes—yes, it *would* do that, *if* it didn't have a special case made out of insanely expensive gravity shielding material. Which we will assume it does."

"Ah. Of course, because *that* exists," Jeremy nodded thoughtfully to Zippo, who nodded back.

"Now suppose that you could *also* pull that same recording device back *out* of the black hole?" Moe mimed himself pulling a rope.

"But you *just* said nothing could escape a black hole," Jeremy said.

"I should have specified—the recorder is tethered to a length of mithrilium nano-filament, which itself is attached to a starship far, far out of range."

"And I assume 'mithrilium nano-filament' is, uh...really strong?" Jeremy ventured.

"Special fishing line. Unbreakable, on a molecular level," Moe said.

Jeremy realized Moe was actually waiting for an answer. "Well how should *I* know?! You tell *me*! What next? You put the recorder in, you pull it out. What's on there?"

Moe stooped down to open his pack. He pulled out a rectangular object that looked kind of like a portable radio. It had a square magtape cassette in it. "The future," he whispered, a semi-crazed look in his eyes.

Jeremy raised an eyebrow, but Moe continued. "You drop a recorder in, configure it to only switch on when it picks up a decent radio signal—all the while, that black hole is pulling in radio signals from who *knows* when. Waves and waves of stuff from the future. Stuff from collapsed timelines that will never exist. Stuff from different DIMENSIONS. It's a big, chunky soup of hot cosmic *randomness*! And then you yank the device out, filter out all the noise and static, and unscramble the good stuff! You've just recorded a decade's worth of radio waves in about five minutes! If you're lucky, you'll have picked up some decent tunes!"

Jeremy held up a finger. "Hold on—what are you talking about? Recording radio waves...from the future?"

Moe and Zippo nodded vigorously.

"You guys are nuts. So when are you going to try this crazy little experiment?"

Zippo chuffled. "We AL-raddy *do* it!"

CHAPTER 18

ONE IN A GAJILLION

Moe depressed a button on the magtape recorder. A ghostly, eerie music emanated from its side speaker. It was unlike anything Jeremy had ever heard.

"This is a sample we captured a couple of years ago. It's from a black hole off the coast of the Koshion System, a star that neighbors Bino." The music had a synthetic beat to it, with high-pitched harmonized vocals in a language Jeremy did not understand. "It's from about three hundred years in the future," Moe explained. "Judging by the dates we could pick up from the DJ, that is."

"It's...unique!" Jeremy said. The music was hypnotic and strange, if not exactly melodic. Questions swam through his head, but he didn't even know where to begin.

"We got about a tape and a half of good recordings from that one," Moe explained, "but they were the final recordings ever captured from that time flux. The black hole was discovered, and GRIS 'repaired' it shortly afterward."

"GRIS?"

"Galactic Recording Industry Syndicate. GRIS for short. They are wack. They *haaaaate* black holes. So they go around destroying them whenever they find one. Close them up. You know, to prevent radio dipping. It's a miracle that one near Koshion lasted as long as it did. Most people thought it was dipped out—"

"Radio dipping?" Jeremy interrupted, trying to keep the alien terms straight. "Is that what this...pastime is called?"

"That's right. Tossing recorders into black holes and seeing what we can fish out. Highly, *highly* illegal."

"But why? Who cares if you want to listen to music from the future?" Jeremy asked.

"*They* see it as a form of piracy. Which is wack if you ask me! Radio waves are free music—how can you steal something that's free?"

"Yeah!" Jeremy agreed.

"That, and, what some of us entrepreneurs figured out is that you can make a buttload of cash selling the recordings."

"Selling? To who? Who would want to buy them?"

"Oh, plenty of people! Struggling musicians, rock bands. What better way to get your big break than recording your own version of a song that's *guaranteed* to be a hit! And of course there's radio stations, nightclubs, discos throughout the galaxy. They're all looking for exclusive music, trendy music. Can't get more exclusive than music that doesn't exist yet, right?" Moe nudged Zippo.

"Yeah! Wait," Something about all this felt a bit iffy to Jeremy. "Well, I suppose you have a point," he conceded. "But aren't you basically *stealing* songs—from the future? Isn't that a bit, I don't know, *questionable*?"

Moe was shaking his head before Jeremy could finish.

"Homie, homie, it's not like that at all! The time flux is incomprehensibly weird. We're recording songs whose creators don't even exist yet, and in all probability never *will* exist! When our magtape recorder picks up radio waves, they're coming from some random timeline out of *infinite* possible timelines.

Mathematically, there is almost a zero percent chance that the songs in question were ever going to be created in our reality anyway! If anything, we're doing these nonexistent musicians a favor. We're exposing new listeners to their work!"

Jeremy mulled this over. "I see your point. But if what you say is true, then why does GRIS care about radio dipping so much?"

"Ha!" Moe barked. "GRIS just hates radio dipping because it's something they can't control. They're jibronis. All they care about is infringing on our right to be *fresh*. Anything that diverts people from paying for their official corporate music outlets, they try to destroy. They've worked with the Planetary League for a long time on this. GRIS sees black holes as potential losses of revenue, the League sees them as lawsuits just waiting to happen. They're *wack*. They're the wackest of the wack."

Jeremy thought it over. "I get it. But what happens when one of these struggling musicians comes up with an idea for a hit song, and he gets all excited to record it with his band, but then, come to find out, someone already *dipped* his future song out of a black hole? And sold it to the highest bidder, before he could even record it?"

Moe didn't say a word. His demeanor went cold.

"Just seems...unfair, doesn't it?" Jeremy asked.

"Very," Moe said. He massaged his temples, the neck of a pop bottle clinking against the rim of his shades. He removed the sunglasses and folded them shut, placing them in his pocket. He stared up at the stars before speaking. "It *is* unfair. It's the wackest thing possible. And *we,* of all people, should know," he spoke to the sky. "Because it happened. To us."

Zippo switched off the grooming device he was using and dabbed himself with Phynixian Tundra Root lotion. It had the strong aroma of fresh celery. He smoothed the cream all over his wrinkly skin. He stood and massaged Moe's shoulders lightly, being careful to keep his claws retracted.

"Thanks, homie," Moe said, patting Zippo's paw. He took another swig of pop, offering some to Zippo. "Back when me and Zip were going to B.C. Vo-Tech, we used to go to this funky old club. *The Palace Xanadu,* it was called. One night they were hosting a freshman mixer, and we were jamming some of our songs on stage—just for fun. And we met this chica."

"Chica?"

"Yeah, you know—chica. Cutie. *Babe*. She was going to the local cosmetology school in town. She and one of her hairdresser girlfriends liked writing songs and performing them. She rocked a spirit theremin, and was pretty deece on an electric kithara, too. We all liked music, so we decided to start a band together: *Stardrops in Stereo.*"

Jeremy sensed volumes of untold history in Moe's voice.

"We'd all bunk off class and meet up to practice, or just jam out. She'd always bring one or two of her cutie friends, and some of them would jam with us, too. We even had a couple of minor hits at the local venues."

Zippo returned to his seat, stretching and smiling as he, too, recalled the memory.

"We only had a handful of real songs. But there was one in particular that was *funky* fresh. We all thought it was going to be our big break."

"What was it?" Jeremy asked.

"*You Squeeze Me Like a Hot Sauce Packet.*"

Jeremy made no comment. (He could tell it was a sensitive topic.)

"It was co-written by all of us one night. It just sort of came to us. I'd take a verse, Zippo'd take a verse, the chicas would add a couple of lines. Zip and I were so excited that we rushed back to our dorm and stayed up all night hammering out the details. By morning, we knew we had a hit on our hands." Zippo made a cooing noise of affirmation.

"So what happened?"

"We got some other gigs around town. The cyborg spa, the roller-booting rink, the gravdisco. We'd invite everyone from our dorm, and the chicas would bring cuties from the beauty school. The crowds were getting bigger. And then came the main event: a weekend gig, headlining The Palace Xanadu." Moe grinned at the memory. "The place was PACKED! We rocked their world! Then, after the show, the manager came up and said our set was great—he especially liked our cover of 'Hot Sauce Packet.' And I stopped him and said 'Whoa, whoa there homeboy, that's no cover—that's a Stardrops in Stereo original.' And he got this wack look on his face and turned on the radio. We only had to listen for a few seconds before he found a station playing it. 'You Squeeze Me Like a Hot Sauce Packet,' by some jibronis calling themselves *Humble Blitz*."

Zippo whimpered in distress, as if the memory was too painful to recall.

"At first we wondered if we were all just going crazy. Maybe we'd heard the song on the radio before, and we were subconsciously copying it without realizing? But that was impossible. The four of us came up with different parts of it on our own! And the manager said the song had only become popular on local radio earlier that week. We wondered if Humble Blitz had gotten a bootleg recording of us, or what. But no, the timeline just didn't work. Humble Blitz was on the complete other side of the quadrant; their song had been spreading for who knows how many months."

Zippo shook his head. "Vary *weck*!" he meowed in distaste.

Moe went on. "The manager of the Xanadu invited us into his back office and told us he could put us in touch with some underground music smugglers. We didn't know a thing about radio dipping at the time. 'Hey, if you want a real hit song, this is the way to do it!' he said. Then he explained to us how radio dipping worked. And that's when it all clicked. I'll never forget that moment, eh Zip?"

Zippo sighed, a look of acceptance on his face.

Moe poked at the fire with a stick. "All four of us just stared at each other in that guy's office. Because we realized...they'd already done it. To *us*. Humble Blitz stole our song before we had the chance to record it. In some other timeline, we must have made it big. Big enough that our song was on the radio and got beamed into a black hole! And those chumps stole it."

"You must have been furious," Jeremy guessed.

Moe scoffed. "We actually *laughed* at the sheer wackness of it all! We'd been brain-jacked! And before we knew it, Humble Blitz was playing to sold out megaspheres throughout the galaxy. They were on all the talk shows, their picture on the cover of *Melomania*. Insanely rich, huge recording contracts." He sighed. "But you know what? In a way, it still felt kind of cool. It was like—hey, this proves that our song was truly *funky*. It was *destined* to be number one!"

Jeremy wondered what a number one hit from this alien duo must sound like.

"Later on, as we learned more about the science of radio dipping, we realized the mathematical chances of this even happening to *anyone* are actually far, far lower than one percent. Not even one in a million. It's more like one in a *gajillion*! And it happened to *us*. In a way, we'd hit the galactic *jackpot* of bad luck!"

Moe took another drink of his Nova Pop and gazed upward, pointing at the stars with his bottle. "We've got nowhere left to go, but up."

Zippo scratched his sides, staring off at whatever Moe was pointing to in the sky.

Jeremy finally spoke. "What ever happened to the...uh...chica?"

Without looking down, Moe waved the question away. He slipped his shades back on. "The Palace Xanadu went out of business. She took off. Wanted to do her own thing."

He said no more. The flames of the fire danced in his sunglasses' reflection, and they all remained quiet for a while.

"Ahem—" Jeremy cleared his throat, changing the subject. "So, you mentioned the other day that you came into some money unexpectedly. I assume these are piracy-related lootings?"

Moe broke out of his trance. "This homie's observant!" he said to Zippo with a smile. "Since we're letting it all hang out, I'll tell you." Moe looked around as if watching for spies. He spoke in a low tone, barely above a whisper.

"A few weeks ago, we found a previously undiscovered black hole—on the edge of *your* star system! And I don't think anyone knows about it yet! We dipped as many magtapes as we could."

"And you made a ton of money?"

"Yeah!" Moe nearly shouted. "Basically! Well, no, not quite yet! But once we fix the ship's computer and get the recordings unscrambled, they'll be worth a *fortune*! And as long as GRIS never finds out, we'll just keep going back for more. Imagine all the tunes we'll get! Future Pop will have exclusive *Terran* music, and we can sell off the extra songs as a side hustle!"

Moe guzzled the last of the Nova Pop and belched. "Dude! Feels good to get that all off my chest! You're not mad at us, are you?"

Jeremy frowned in confusion, then shrugged "Who's mad? The whole radio dipping thing is loony, but more importantly, it sounds *fun*!"

As for any moral qualms he had about the practice, he'd just have to take Moe's word for it. Jeremy had no idea how any of it could be real, but he supposed that was the beauty of it. It was its own kind of magic.

CHAPTER 19

DAY TRIP TO DUBLIN

The following morning, after an invigorating swim in the ocean and a sensible seaside breakfast of baked beans and sausage, Jeremy led the offworlders to the castle's stables. The stables had been partially converted into a small car port. Jeremy fumbled through some old iron keys. "It's gotta be one of these," he muttered. "A-ha!"

With a clink, he unlocked the wooden door. It swung open in a wide arc, daylight illuminating the musty interior. The mixed odors of kerosene and hay hit their nostrils, as motes of dust bobbed in the air. Before them was a large shape, covered in a white canvas tarp.

"Here, hold these," Jeremy handed Zippo his keys and the Personal Shell, which Zippo placed in his fanny pack. "Help me get this sheet off," Jeremy gestured to Moe. They each grasped an edge and fluttered the canvas up, revealing a shiny automobile underneath. The morning sun glinted off of the polished wood, glass and chrome.

"Ooooooh," Moe and Zippo cooed in unison. "And what do you call this craft?"

"It's an *Atlas Prestige*, 1910 model."

"She's a swanky looking ride!" Moe said, impressed.

"Appears to be of Terran design, with a little Eo'Tusian influence on the tech here and there." Moe gave the front tire a kick, then lifted the engine cover. "Ah, yes—just as I suspected," he motioned to something under the hood. Jeremy pretended to know what the devil he was going on about, nodding along with Moe's assessment. "Low-level micro thrusters here. How bumpy does she get?"

"*It glides like a cloud,*" Jeremy said. "That's the company's slogan, actually."

"I bet they threw in Pillowsoff smoothing bubbles! Those sneaky little..." Moe stepped up onto the vehicle's runner board, bending over into the engine compartment to inspect.

"My dad was very proud of her." Jeremy polished a smudge on the wood with his sleeve as Moe tinkered. "I think he was more excited about inheriting her than the castle."

"Oh yeah, right here," Moe pointed at something, "standard Eo'Tusian dislocator mechanism. They use these on the big tractors on the Bolano farms back home." Moe hopped off the runner, dusting his hands. He closed the engine case. "So how long of a drive is it to the city?" Moe asked.

"It's about four hours to Dublin. Three, if you don't follow the speed limit. I don't see any clouds, so we should be fine to drive with the top off."

"Well, come on then! If we leave now and go fast, we can get there in time for lunch!" Moe hopped into the front passenger seat. "I've got the perfect mix for a road trip, too! You'll love it," he fiddled with the knobs on the radio.

Zippo scrambled into the back, propping his legs up sideways across the seats. Jeremy got into in the driver's seat and started up the ignition.

"I love the sound of a chemical combustion engine! All right!" Moe shouted.

But as they pulled out of the garage, Jeremy hesitated. He hit the brakes. "You know what...I think I should run back inside and find a map," he said, opening his door. "It's been a while, and I've never driven a car in the city before."

Moe grabbed Jeremy's arm. "Come on, chief! We don't want to look like a couple of jibroni *tourists* carrying a map around! You said you've been to this place!"

"Yes, but..."

"No buts, homeboy! Let's boogie!"

Zippo mewled from the back seat. "Sand-wadge!"

"But I don't know my way around a big city!" Jeremy pleaded.

"Listen, Jeremy—Zippo is a master navigator. Excellent sense of direction. It's his Felinian instincts. He actually *can't* get lost."

Zippo nodded contentedly.

"Now just wait a minute, you told me Zippo once spent several days wandering around a supermarket because he couldn't find the exit."

"Okay, that's true. But I should tell you, Giga's Super-Colossal Mart is a *huge* store. Plus, they have an enormous seafood section that probably made his navigational senses go haywire. Right, Zip?"

Zippo nodded again. "Oh yeh. TONS shramp. Krills. Prawn. Got vary lost!" Zippo sighed in frustration at the memory, then stretched and got comfortable. "Go, Jrr-mEE," he patted Jeremy on the shoulder. "Sand-wadge. Go."

"Why does he keep saying sandwich?" Moe asked.

"Because I told him about my Uncle Arthur," Jeremy said. "He runs a *delicatessen*. It's a shop that sells meats and cheeses and stuff. And for lunch every weekday he makes a special sandwich he invented. It's thinly sliced corned beef with sauerkraut, Swiss cheese, pieces of back bacon...with Worcestershire sauce, served on rye. Lightly toasted. He calls it 'the Excalibur.' But he only makes so many, and when they run out for the day then that's it. He won't make any more until the next day."

"Duuuude! Are you kidding me?!" Moe slapped the dashboard. "Engage the Terran noshables, *pronto*!"

"Jrr-mEE, wat are we wate for? To Dablin! Let's goooo! Let's *goooo*!" Zippo pleaded. He pointed at the steering wheel and kept yowling "let's goooo" until Jeremy finally shut his door and stepped on the gas.

CHAPTER 20

FUNKY SAUCE

"Now here I am standing / Umbrella in my haaaaaa-yeeee-aaand!"

The gang zoomed along in the Prestige, all of them wailing in unison to Purple Marmalade's "Muddy Blue Land." Moe had figured out a way to broadcast his portable jambox to the car's radio, and they blasted music as they rolled through the Irish countryside.

They'd made quick work of the snacks Zippo brought (he'd discovered a forgotten stash of junk food in one of the the *Terrapin*'s smuggling hatches), and now the auto's interior was littered with Raffitts crumbs and an empty box of Tycho Blasters. A crumpled wrapper for Abel's Phobosian Crusties fluttered off of the dashboard. Zippo's paw darted up and snatched it out of the air before it could litter the road. The Felinian was still lying across the back seats, his padded feet dangling out the side of the car.

"A pocketful of nickels / in a muddy blue laaaaaa-yeeee-aaand!" they sang the final chorus together.

It had been some time since he had driven the car, but Jeremy's initial nervousness had melted away at the thrilling bursts of speed. The old back road across the island was virtually deserted, and it was another beautiful day. "Did you guys fish that one out of the black hole you found?"

Moe made a frantic cutting motion across his neck, shaking his head. He leaned in close to Jeremy. "Cool it with the black hole talk! You never know who could be listening!" Moe leaned back, suddenly nonchalant. "I believe the provenance of this recording is..." he looked at the magtape case. "Oh yeah. Got it from some crazy old pirate in the Leonis System."

"They were singing in English!"

"Why do you think we bought it? I told you, Terran radio waves travel far! And English is *hot* right now. It's gonna be huge. Music like this will be perfect for when we open our club." Moe yawned and changed the subject, "I gotta say, Atlas makes a *very* smooth ride, huh? You can really feel those pillowsoff bubbles!"

"Yes. Not quite as smooth as the Porker Express. But at least we don't have to deal with filthy vagrant sorcerers sleeping in our seats." Jeremy looked into the rear view mirror. Zippo stretched, soaking up the sun and enjoying the breeze on his whiskers. "Say Zippo, do you got anymore of them snacks? Dimdum Chewies?"

Zippo rummaged around in his fanny pack. He pulled a candy bar out. The sun flashed off its silver wrapper. "Aahmmm. Jus' dis." He held up the candy bar.

"What's that?" Jeremy glanced at the bar in the mirror, trying to keep his eyes on the road.

"Oh, it's just a Lingo Bar," Moe said. "Lava-Mint. It teaches you Terran Icelandic. You probably already know Icelandic, huh?"

"Icelandic?" Jeremy raised an eyebrow. "No."

"Really? We've both had Icelandic, I think. Right, Zip? Lava-Mint is okay. Not my favorite flavor."

Jeremy looked skeptical. "What are you saying, I just eat

that thing and I'll know how to speak Icelandic?"

"Pretty much. It usually takes some time before it starts working."

"How long?"

"About a minute. Maybe minute and a half."

Jeremy put his hand out behind his seat. "Let's do it. Lingo me, Zip." Zippo placed the candy bar in his hand. "I'm not going to get in trouble for this, am I?"

Moe thought about it. "Technically, I think it's illegal for any of your people to consume them. You know, the Arcturus Directive on neurological and genetic modification. But the League has much bigger fish to fry. They tend to ignore Lingo Bars."

"So I'm breaking the law if I eat this?!"

"Kid, you're probably breaking some law somewhere in the galaxy by doing basically anything."

Jeremy couldn't argue with that.

"Actually," Moe said, "these Terran flavors are extra...unofficial, so to speak...since I don't think they're legally supposed to be downloading the language centers of Earthlings' brains—see somewhere along the line, the Lingo company got a hold of a Terran Icelandic speaker, made a copy of his neurological language center, and encoded it onto tiny flavites... it's all a bit technical, but you don't have to do anything. Just sit back and let it happen."

Jeremy raised the candy bar to his mouth, stopping mid-bite. "Wait, wait. I'm about to eat a copy of some Icelander's neurological center?" He couldn't help but feel a little grossed out.

"It's not like that all! It's not scary! You won't feel a thing," Moe pleaded. "We've both had dozens of flavors, and we're fine!"

Jeremy glanced at Moe, then back at Zippo through the rear view mirror. Moe's reasoning was not super encouraging.

However, Jeremy was pretty hungry and the candy bar looked tasty enough. He raised the bar back to his mouth and chomped.

It wasn't bad; kind of tasted like a Buzzer Bar at first. Crispy, and very gooey. He ate the rest as he drove, waiting for the new language to pop into his brain. He felt nothing unusual, apart from a vague sensation of deja vu and a desire to pick up some smoked fish once they got to Dublin.

"How do you know when it starts to work?"

"*Skilur pu mig?*" Moe asked.

"Ja."

"Pa virkao pao."

"Hvao?! Hvernig geroir pu petta!"

"Dap er ekki eg! Pao er bara flavites sem vinna galdur peirra. Deir eru smasja velmenni sem umrita nytt tungumal mynstur a heilann," Moe explained.

"Dao hljomar...ognvekjandi, ao vera fullkomlega heioarlegur."

"Ekki hafa ahyggjur homie! Pvi ao flavites eru bara ao profa kooa peirra a heilann, og pa akveour heilinn hvao a ao gera meo pao. Deir baeta aoeins vio, peir taka aldrei neitt i burtu—ef pao er pao sem du hefur ahyggjur af. Degar peir hafa gert hlut sinn, pa brotna peir niour i skolausar sameindir og pau eru farin. Svo einfalt."

"O viss, viss. Bara skaolaus framandi velmenni sameindir hanga ut i heilanum minum! Ekkert vandamal! Eg get seo nuna ao otti min vaeri algjorlega orettmaet!"

[Translator's Note: I threw in the following translation of this conversation for non-Icelandic speakers! Enjoy!

Moe: Can you understand me?

Jeremy: Yes.

Moe: Then it worked.

Jeremy: What?! How did you do that?

Moe: It's not me! It's just the flavites working their magic. They're the microscopic robots that encode the new language pattern onto your brain.

Jeremy: That sounds...terrifying, to be perfectly honest.

Moe: Don't worry, homie! The flavites just project their codes onto your brain, and then your brain decides what to do with it. They only add, they never take anything away if that's what you're worried about. Then once they've done their thing, they get broken down into harmless molecules and they're gone. Simple as that.

Jeremy: Oh sure, sure. Just harmless alien robot molecules hanging out in my brain! No problem-o! I can see now that my fears were totally unjustified. —ChatterBot 3.6]

"Can we switch back to English?" Jeremy asked. "This is too weird this early in the day."

"English it is! It's a nice language. Has such great rhymes."

They sped along for two hours, obliterating the thirty-five mile per hour speed limit. Once they'd listened to Moe's magtape a couple of times through, they tried to get more music out of the Personal Shell. Moe had no luck, as he couldn't find a way to hook the device up to the radio.

"Actually, we're probably close enough to Dublin that we should be able to pick up some local stations by now," Jeremy said. Moe turned the dial, finally landing on *RTE Radio One*, 88.2 FM. They were playing a radio drama. It sounded like a Western—a historical reenactment of when the first offworlders landed on Earth in the 1800s. Not Jeremy's favorite genre, but he hadn't heard a real radio program in so long that he didn't really mind. Moe and Zippo were happy to hear anything Terran. They both snickered at the sound of Terran voice actors trying to mimic offworlder accents.

It was a little past noon when they pulled into the city. Traffic consisted mostly of horse-drawn carriages clip-clapping pleasantly along the cobbled streets. There were some automobiles here and there, and Jeremy spotted what he assumed to be an alien craft at one point. The crowds were out for the daily lunch rush, and he received some puzzled looks from pedestrians. Overall, it appeared to be just another humdrum day in the city.

"I think it was just around here..." Jeremy mumbled as the Prestige bumped (ever-so-softly) over some train tracks. He remembered that Uncle Arthur's deli was a few blocks from the railway station, and so he followed the tracks.

"Did we maek it?" Zippo asked as they crossed a bridge over the River Liffey. The streets narrowed as they approached the city center. Tall, brown-bricked buildings clustered closely together, housing window-fronted shops and pubs. Things were starting to look familiar, and then he spotted the old wooden sign. It was suspended from two chains and swinging gently in the breeze. "ARTHUR'S DELICATESSEN," it read. It had a faded illustration of a jousting knight on it.

"Keen-o!" Jeremy answered. "This is it! Moe, what time is it?"

"How should I know?"

"Hopefully we're not too late." Jeremy pulled over, parking the car on the street. The trio got out and stretched.

Jeremy looked forward to seeing his uncle. Technically, Uncle Arthur was his *mother's* uncle (he supposed that made him his great uncle—or was it grand uncle?). He'd met him after his family had moved to Ireland. He was now Jeremy's only living relative. "Oh fudge puppies," Jeremy slapped his forehead. "You guys, I almost forgot! Do *not* mention a WORD to my uncle about me being kicked out of Pigpimples! Got it? As far as he knows, I'm in school for summer session. I told him I stay there year-round."

The two stared at Jeremy blankly.

"I didn't want to impose by moving in with him after...you know...what happened to my folks. So I told him I was staying at school full time."

"Ahhhhh," Zippo meowed understandingly.

Moe looked confused. "But hasn't the school sent him a letter about your expulsion by now?"

Jeremy shook his head. "Nah. Pigpimples doesn't know my uncle exists. They don't even know about my parents, actually."

Zippo's eyes went wide, his jaw dropping. "Wat?! You never tell them...Jrr-mEE is orpahn?"

"I thought they'd kick me out if they found out! So I just kept it to myself. Forged my dad's signature on the tuition checks. They mailed my grades to the castle a couple of days ago. I turned the report card into that blueberry pancake you liked so much, Zip."

"Oh yeh," Zippo smiled at the memory of food.

"Hold up, so how do you know us, then? Where do we fit into your little charade? I need to get into character." Moe flipped out a comb and started styling his hair. Taking a cue from his friend, Zippo ran his raspy tongue over his paws and smoothed back his whiskers.

"Relax! We'll just say you're exchange students. And we had a couple of days off, so we decided to visit."

"Sounds good. I would lie to my own grandmother at this point, if it would get me one of those sandwiches."

A bell jingled as they opened the front door. The deli was pleasantly cool compared to the heat of the noonday sun. It was also dim enough that Moe could remove his shades. To their left was a large glass case, full of meats and cheeses. Chains of sausage links dangled from the ceiling. To their right was a cozy dining area with a few small tables. Two old men sat at one, playing chess and eating sandwiches. A third old man stood behind the front counter. He was bulky, grunting in confusion as he tinkered with a scale. He was also quite hairy. His fair hair made his arms look positively woolen. He had a bushy blonde mustache and the rest of his face was covered in bristle. He wore an apron and a little paper hat.

"Be right with ye, lads," the man spoke in a rough Irish

brogue.

"Hi, Uncle!"

The man looked up from the scale, squinting at the new customers. His eyebrows rose in recognition. "Jeremy!" Uncle Arthur bellowed happily (it came out sounding like *Jar-ehmy*). He flipped the wooden counter divider up and wiped his hands on his apron. "My blessed nephew!" He extended a meaty arm as he walked over. Despite his age, Uncle Arthur still had a mighty handshake. His massive, gnarled mitt first enveloped, then crushed Jeremy's hand in a vigorous shake, followed by a few slaps to his nephew's back so powerful they nearly dislodged his eyeballs. Jeremy couldn't help but laugh, even though this little ritual of theirs was fairly painful.

"All finished with magic school, are ye?"

"Yes uncle, we're just having ourselves a little holiday before the summer session."

"And getting good marks in all yer classes, I kennit?"

"Of course."

"I beg yer pardon for not writin' to ye more often, lad. You know how this place sucks up my time, like a newborn goat suckin' on its mother's—"

"It's all right, Uncle," Jeremy interrupted. "My studies take up all of my day; I usually don't have time for letter writing, either."

"But I trust ye've been stayin' out of trouble, eh?" Arthur winked at Jeremy.

"You know it, Uncle! Hittin' the books, practing my spell-casting, then it's dinner and lights out. No time for mischief," Jeremy paused as his Uncle gave him a dubious look. "Well...nothing the Headmage need be bothered about, at least." Jeremy offered a conspiratorial wink in return. His uncle exploded in a laugh so loud that it felt as if the floor was shaking. Zippo snapped down in fear behind Moe.

"Atta boy, you wee vandal! You are your mother's son, God

rest 'er," he wiped a tear of laughter from his eye. "Oh gobshottle, now look at my carelessness." He rushed over to a small picture on the mantle of the fireplace in the dining room, dusting the frame with a handkerchief. In it was a photo of Jeremy's parents on their wedding day. Above the picture a brass plaque read: "Roger & Anne Fletcher, In Memoriam." Arthur produced a match from his pocket and struck it on the underside of his shoe, lighting a votive candle next to the photograph.

"That's better," he said, shaking out the match as he walked back over. "And who be yer depilated friend here?" Uncle Arthur extended his hand to Zippo. He stood back up, returning a sheepish paw in greeting.

"Zipponio," Zippo said, opting to skip his traditional head nudge.

"He's from the Greeno Sector," Jeremy said, "and this is..."

Moe stepped forward, hand out. "Maurice Baraxil, Binosian. We're exchange students! From Burrow Colony Vo-Tech." They shook hands.

"We donna' get many offworlders here. I hope our humble wares are pleasin' to yer no doubt..." the old man grasped for the right word, "*exotic* tastes!"

"Uncle, I told my two friends about the Excalibur, and they demanded that we come try it."

Uncle Arthur beamed. "You're in luck, then, laddos!" He headed back behind the counter and pulled out some huge sandwiches, each tightly wrapped in white paper. "Looks like there's three left! They're all yours."

* * *

The trio sat, blissfully noshing away on their Excaliburs and checking out their surroundings. Moe and Zippo were clearly excited to be in a real Terran eatery; Zippo waved happily at the passersby through the front windows. Jeremy was overjoyed just to eat something besides breakfast food for a change. There were several posters, fliers and advertisements posted along the windows and on the back of the front door. Zippo read them aloud as they ate.

"Ter-ry Con-NA-gan, FRI-day nite at Red Mole Tavern. Red Mole? Wat dat?" (Zippo was interested because it said "mole.")

"It's probably just some local pub. They put those posters up to advertise shows," Jeremy explained.

Zippo read more of the posters. One announced a dance. It was at the meeting lodge of the Knights of Courtesy. Another advertised the 36th Annual Summer Wine and Cheese festival in Greystones. One was just a scrap of paper from someone named Seamus. He offered accordion lessons for a reasonable price.

Uncle Arthur came back and placed a small bottle of Worcestershire sauce on the table. Moe opened it and dumped more onto his sandwich. "I don't know what..." Moe held the bottle up to his face, sounding out the strange word, "...WOR-cest-ER-shire sauce is, but I need more of it in my life. This stuff is *funky*." He took a huge bite of his sandwich.

"Keep the bottle, by all means," Uncle Arthur said.

"*Manf-eugh*," Moe responded with his mouth full. He swallowed his food, his eyes filling with tears. He placed a hand on Zippo's arm, instructing him to get something out of his fanny pack. "Uncle Arthur, sir. Please take this, I insist." Moe held out a small glass bottle of red, syrupy liquid. Uncle Arthur accepted the bottle.

"Why thank ye...errrm," he turned the bottle over in his hands. The label was not in English. "What is it?"

"It's my last bottle of Bolano Berry dipping sauce. There is a sacred tradition of sauce exchange on my homeworld. *Heeb-o stim'pa kyoon,* as we say—where sauce is given, may we never part as enemies."

"I'm honored!" Uncle Arthur looked at Jeremy, impressed.

"Uncle, my mates were hoping to do a little sightseeing this afternoon, then heading home—" Jeremy caught himself "—back to SCHOOL, that is, tomorrow. Could you put us up for the night?"

Uncle Arthur returned to adjusting his scale. "Be my guest. You're always welcome here, boy, you know that." He got to wiping down the counter with a rag.

Zippo read another poster: "The ENIGMA. Mental-IST. Illusion-IST. En-ter-TAIN-er. Live at Dreamer's Castle Lounge. He see a man's life *FROM CRADLE TO GRAVE*. Ooooh! Das spooky!"

Jeremy nearly choked. "What did you just say?!"

Zippo's eyes widened and he shrugged. "There," he pointed at the poster on the wall, "I jus read from peckshure."

Jeremy knocked his chair over as he rushed to the poster. It was a beautifully colored illustration of a man in a tuxedo and top hat. He held a glass sphere in his hand and gazed into it. A tiny child peered back at him from within the globe. Little blue devils flitted around the man, holding up different tarot cards as they danced in the air. One devil stood on the man's shoulder, whispering into his ear. The words *FROM CRADLE TO GRAVE* were printed in giant yellow letters across the bottom of the poster.

It must be the Enigma he'd read about in *Abracadabra Magazine*! And hadn't the article mentioned something about him being a former Pigpimples student? "The ENIGMA performs all this week..." Jeremy read aloud. He murmured as he scanned the dates. "The final show is tonight!" he exclaimed. "Let's go! I can show you guys a real magic show!"

"Sounds great, kid," Moe said. "Hey listen—will you be okay for a while? Zippo and I gotta head out to do some...offworlder stuff..."

"Sure, I can help out around the shop. What kinds of shenanigans are you two going to get up to?"

"Nothing, nothing. I spotted an alien bar and grill as we were driving into town; we'll start there and see where it leads us. Surely someone in this city has got that part we need to finish our repairs." Moe hesitated. "No offense. You just never know with these black market types. They might find a Terran's presence a bit off-putting."

"None taken. I'd like to catch up with my uncle anyway."

"We'll meet you back here, then. What time is that show?"

Jeremy looked to the poster. "Starts at nine o'clock."

"That gives us plenty of time." Moe called out to Uncle Arthur, "Thanks for the sandwiches, Mister Jeremy's Uncle! We shall spread their fame far and wide across the cosmos!"

"Very fine, laddos, very fine. Glad you liked 'em!" Uncle Arthur shouted from the back as he sliced some roast beef.

"Zip. Let's bounce," Moe jerked his thumb towards the door.

CHAPTER 21

BAD GUYS INTERLUDE #2

Mike Mania's desk was littered with various prescription pill bottles, most of them empty. The label on one read: *ALPRAZOLAM. For general anxiety (Caninoid)*. In addition to the pills, several packets of Bromo Seltzer were scattered around his desk, with some on the floor beside the swivel chair. *CURES HEADACHES, INDIGESTION*, their labels announced.

Mike was having a rough week.

He sat at his desk, panting, and not just because his office was swelteringly hot.

Mike was nervous. *Very* nervous.

The assumption that Cerberons pant with their tongues out because they lacked sweat glands always exasperated Mike. *Why is excreting fluid out of one's pores the default behavior? Typical human-centric thinking! Panting is much more dignified, and does not produce any disgusting sweat!*

Every time the etheric flux phone rang, he yipped. It could be *her*. Thankfully, she hadn't called yet...*but it had been what, two weeks? Three?* She was going to call soon. He was overdue for a call. *And the call is not going to go well.*

It had gotten so bad that he'd finally assigned his idiot

brother Charles to be his "personal secretary," complete with his own "desk" (a half-burned card table he'd found at a yard sale). Mike's phone cord didn't reach very far, so he was forced to set Charles up right in his own office, which was already cramped.

"That STUPID woman," he grumbled (mostly to himself, as his brother, Charles, was obliviously making a phone call through his cool new headset). "Who does she think she is? Track down some ship...heh...I'll get RIGHT on it, lady," he made a sarcastic little salute to nobody. "They don't pay me enough..." he grumbled some more, flicking his glazer pistol on and off.

He suddenly had a hard time remembering why he'd gotten himself mixed up with Mrs. Crawford in the first place. Sure, this little outpost on Mercury was a dead-end job with no future. But it had always paid the bills! It was far away enough from civilization that his whole operation had been basically left alone. He could watch all the pirated shows he wanted, and Mercury's trans-dimensional portal to Hell made it easy to travel home for Christmas. [*Translator's Note: a Terran holiday widely embraced by the Cerberon race after they obtained a bootleg televid of Christmas specials from the future. —ChatterBot 3.6*]

Heck, the imported junk food wasn't half bad! The past suddenly seemed incredibly appealing. Why had he gotten so greedy?

But it was all too late for that, Mike supposed. The fact of the matter was that he *had* gotten greedy, and the thought of running secret missions for GRIS's financier had sounded *really* cool. Zooming around a young star system on the frontiers of space, blasting filthy radio pirates and tech runners into atominos—what was not to like?

The fun had ended pretty quickly, though, after the threats began. Every teeny tiny little setback would throw *her* into a violent rage. "I am the first to appreciate a little mayhem, a little insanity!" He growled to himself. "I'm all for excessive violence! But have a tad bit of decorum, lady!"

On his third or fourth mission he had called her to update her on a pirate she'd sent him to track. There was a setback, and things were going to take two days longer than expected. Her response had been: *if you don't take care of this on schedule, I am going to neuter you and your whole family.*

"I'm sorry, but what happened to just threatening to kill someone?" Mike pondered aloud. "I get that you're angry, lady, really I do. But did you have to go there?" He hated the sound of that word. *"Neuter?"* He shuddered.

The worst part was that he couldn't even go to GRIS authorities for protection. Mrs. Crawford had all of them in her pocket. And she had very deep pockets; it was her vast fortune from Seashell Systems that paid for GRIS setting up shop here in the first place.

This most recent mission was supposed to be his ticket out. It was all going to work so perfectly. But how could she expect him to locate a ship just based on its name? It was the barest strand of a lead, and she really ought to be amazed—*grateful*— that he had even considered such a mission in the first place!

Somehow, he knew she wouldn't be.

"Searching the entire sector for a single ship!" he barked to himself as Charles chattered away. "It's insane!—there are hundreds of ships in the Sol System alone!" He tried taking another drink of his Bromo Seltzer, but found his mug to be empty. He contemplated whether or not to hurl it violently against the wall, and examined it first. It was just a random mug from the Troposphere, one of the cheaper hotels on Mercury. He gave it a good fling at the wall, shattering it. Charles yipped in surprise.

"Heyyyyy! That was my mug!" his brother whined as he ended his phone call.

Mike whirled around in his chair, pointing his glazer pistol at Charles's face. "Is my prescription refill ready?!"

"The pharmacy said you have to wait three more days!"

Mike growled angrily, then spun back around. He couldn't take the stress anymore. His head throbbed in pain. He needed to start accepting the fact that she was going to call and he was going to have nothing.

Well, not quite *nothing*.

The *Terrapin*, they'd learned, was registered to Burrow Colony, a horticultural moon of the Bino System. The ship was a Binosian Class-1 Transport Tug; not common in the Sol System. They were normally used to move Binosian tractors and other large farming rigs. The ship should have been easy to spot; Mike had low-level agents peppered throughout the whole system. One of them had even turned up a perfect clue: a reservation for a ship calling itself the *Terrapin*, booked at a space dock on Callisto.

He'd called (or rather, made his brother call) the Callisto station every day. He'd even paid for hotel accommodations for that one agent out there, just so he could monitor all incoming crafts. But the *Terrapin* had never showed.

It could have been any number of things, of course. A simple change of plans. Sick crew. They ran out of fuel. Space pirates hacked their computer systems. Heck, maybe the whole ship had just Cat-NEF'ed out of the timeline. [*Translator's Note: C.T.N.E.F., or Catastrophic Non-linear Existence Failure — ChatterBot 3.6*]

But none of those reasons felt very reassuring to Mike. And none of them would stop Mrs. Crawford from threatening to destroy him in the most degrading and painful way imaginable.

He sure could use another Alprazolam.

The phone rang.

"It's another beautiful day on Mercury—this is the Galactic Recording Industry Syndicate tip line—'*Always Remember That We Will Find You*'—Charles speaking, how may I help you?"

Mike tensed, but didn't hear the harpy's screeching through

his brother's headset. He relaxed and rummaged around in his desk. He searched for a televid tape, preferably something he hadn't watched in a while. A good sitcom would get his mind off of this. Maybe something Terran.

He pulled out a vidtape from the bottom drawer. It was a comedy show estimated to be from seven hundred years into the future. It was fished out of a black hole near Adoro Menaal. The original owner had written *BLESSED BE MY TENTACLES* on the label with a marker. Mike had always assumed this was the show's name, although none of the episodes made any sense to him. He still hadn't found a Lingo Bar for whatever language they were speaking. Still, they were kind of funny and featured characters falling down a lot. It would have to do.

"Uh-huh. Oh, I see. Yes, yes, of course." Charles took down a couple of notes as he spoke. "He wants to talk to you," Charles said, lifting the receiver of the red telephone on his desk.

"Who IS it?" Mike snapped.

"He said his name was...uh..." Charles checked his notes. "Mister Bojangles?"

Mike rushed to the desk, snatching the receiver out of Charles's paw. "Give me that! Bojangles? Is it you?" He looked at Charles, covering the mouthpiece of the phone. "Did he use the code? Is he verified?"

"Checked and verified, brother."

"Bojangles, what have you got for me?" Mike panted as he listened. He wrinkled his muzzle in disgust. "Video game console? Are you kidding me?! Stop calling with your utter nonsense! What does this have to do with—"

He stopped shouting and listened again. Then, despite being less than half his size, Mike muscled Charles out of his seat and sat down, scribbling notes furiously.

Charles looked over Mike's shoulder. His brother's calligraphy was beautiful (Mike always prided himself on his penmanship). "Dublin, Ireland" Charles read out loud. "Isn't that some Terran place?" He thought about it for a moment. "Oh yeah! Ensign O'Shanahan from *Nexus Odyssey: A New Generation*!" Charles spoke to nobody as Mike continued to ignore him. He was jotting down notes as fast as he could.

The phone receiver slipped out of Mike's paw and clattered to the floor. "How do you turn on the blasted speaker!" Mike howled. "I can't write and hold this stupid humanoid phone at the same time!"

Charles leaned in and depressed a button. A voice, presumably of Mister Bojangles, sounded from the speaker. "—You oughta see these things; they're awful. Some of the worst forgeries I've ever seen. Whole pages missing. Colors all wrong. Just bad, man!"

"Bojangles, allow me to stop you right there. You told me you had a lead on the *Terrapin*. So far, all you've told me—if I am understanding you correctly—is that a couple of Binosian morons bought a used..." Mike scanned his notes, "...*SuperChromaVision* from you. Using pirated Tommy Cobblestone comics. Is that right?"

"Actually Mike," Charles interrupted, "you wrote that one was a Binosian, the other was a Felinian."

Mike pulled his pistol out and pointed it at Charles, muffling the phone's speaker with his free paw. "I...will...kill you," he growled, then resumed his conversation. "The point being, a couple of yokels sightseeing in whatever disgusting little burg you do business in traded you one piece of trash for another piece of trash. You have about ten seconds to explain to me how any of this is relevant to the *Terrapin* before—"

"Don't you see, sir? They were snooping around for a ChromaVision for their starship. They said they needed a game system that specifically fit a Gizmonic-4 power supply, and compatible with a Dawn Engine computer core. Get what I'm saying?"

"No, Bojangles, but you now have two seconds."

"They were buying a game system for that ship you're looking for! I'd bet my life on it! Binosian Class-1 transport tugs are the only starships manufactured with both the Gizmonic-4 and Dawn Engine O.S.! You never see them outside of the Bino System!"

Mike paused. He didn't fully trust Mister Bojangles, but something rang true about the operative's assessment. "All right, then. Finally, some progress. Good work, Bojangles," Mike grumbled. "I'm thinking a nice hefty credit transfer to your personal bank account is in order. But first I need you to keep an eye on these two so we can apprehend them. Monitor their movements. Follow them back to their ship and confirm. I'll be in touch—" He waved Charles back, annoyed.

"Oh, Mike," Bojangles spoke, "here's the thing. I actually have no idea where they are now. See, I only pieced this together after they left! I thought about how cute little Binosians are—ya know, 'cause they're all super short and stuff—and then I remembered how you were on the lookout for a Binosian ship, and then I looked up some stuff in the Terminus Encyclopedia..."

Mike's expression soured. "What are you saying?" he stood up from his seat. "What are you SAYING?!!" he barked. "You're telling me you...LOST them?" Mike howled with rage.

"It ain't like that, Mikey! We just gotta monitor the incoming and outgoing ships from this area! We'll still nab them good! And you can still transfer me all those credits!"

Mike regained his composure and sighed. He then cracked his neck and resumed the conversation. "I'd like to thank you immensely for the information, Mister Bojangles. When I get off the phone with you, I'm going to press a button that will explode the tiny bomb I secretly implanted in your skull. The encoded signal traveling from Mercury at the speed of light ought to reach Reptilicon in about, oh, four minutes or so...if you need to say goodbye to any loved ones or anything, now's the time. Bye." Mike slammed the receiver on the phone box, shattering it.

He pulled a remote device out of his pocket, flipping it open and clicking the knob to BOJANGLES. The device gave a horrible buzz as he pressed its big red button.

Charles shuddered, then switched the call back to his headset. "Yeah. Uh-huh. Looks like he just pushed it," Charles said. "Okay, sir. Well, best of luck with everything. Have a good one," Charles ended the call.

Mike was already gathering up odds and ends and tossing them into a pile on his desk. "This is too big of a job to trust to losers like Bojangles. We're going to have to go to Earth and track the *Terrapin* ourselves. Oh, and finally pick up some decent Toastee Mums while we're there. Charles, fetch me my suitcase. And please, for the love of the devil, tell me you didn't forget my dry cleaning."

"Right here, brother!" Charles went and grabbed Mike's outfit from the closet. "Pressed and ready to go!"

Mike snatched the uniform from his brother's paws and started to change into it right there in the office. The outfit was the traditional garb of all bureaucrats on his homeworld of Hades: a snug velvet doublet complete with a fur-lined cloak and bombasted hose. By the time he was finished, he looked like Sir Walter Raleigh crossed with Vasco de Gama.

"Ah, I see they added the extra starch like I asked. Remind me to give them a nice tip." Mike adjusted his ruffled Elizabethan collar. He liked to wear this outfit whenever he was on official (or in this case, unofficial) GRIS business. GRIS business was often dirty business, but that was no excuse for shabbiness. Good clothing projected an air of nobility. *Respectability.*

The phone rang, startling Mike out of his musings. Charles answered. "It's another beautiful day on Mercury—this is the Galactic Recording Industry Syndicate tip line—'*Always Remember That We*—" Charles winced as screaming on the other end of the line cut him off.

Mike stopped cold. His heart thumped like a demonic jackrabbit.

"It's for you," Charles said.

Mike picked up the phone receiver, panting a little. "Mike Mania speaking," he gulped. He knew it was her. Her husky, creaky voice on the other end confirmed it. He could almost smell her coffee breath through the line.

"Miiike," she said in a sing-song voice, "I was just calling to check in with you about the Terrapiiiiin. I sure hope you have some good news for meeeeeee. I'd hate to have to schedule an appointment with my veterinariaaaaan. You know, for CASTRATION and all. It's such an expensive procedure, what with all the anesthesia involved. Honestly, I think Tiny Tim could do just as good a job with a knitting needle and a rusty butcher knife! And for half the price! What do you think? Shall we try it and see?"

CHAPTER 22

THE 'SPLOSION

"Unbelievable," Jeremy muttered. They were stuck at an intersection due to some cock-up on ahead. A big red fire engine blocked most of the street, its bell jangling unhelpfully. A crowd gathered from off the sidewalks. Jeremy pulled the Prestige over and switched off the engine.

Their evening had gotten off to a rotten start. Moe and Zippo, never the kind given to punctuality, had taken even longer than anticipated. By the time they'd gotten back from tracking down that "super important part" for their starship, it was dark. After getting some confusing directions from Uncle Arthur (that none of them had bothered to write down), they drove off and were promptly lost.

The streets of Dublin were even more perplexing at night. The gas street lamps helped, but they weren't nearly as illuminating as the electric ones in London. Jeremy cursed himself for not grabbing a map. When they'd finally stopped to ask a constable how to get to the Dreamer's Castle, his response had been something like: "*Daht's abooeht secks blahcks doon, leds.*"

They were arguing amongst themselves about these

directions when they arrived at the intersection, now as impenetrable as the constable's accent.

There appeared to be a collision. An automobile lay flipped on its side in the street. Broken glass glittered in the flames and the red light of the stop signal. A second vehicle, parked along the curb, was on fire, its door nearly blown off its hinges. It was an alien craft.

"Whoa. What happened?" Moe said, hopping out of the car.

Jeremy picked up snippets of conversation from the gathering crowd as they approached the scene.

"*...Some kind of explosion...*" "*...Driver's fine, other than some rattled nerves...*" "*...One of them offworlder vehicles—they need to keep alien tech off our streets...!*" "*...Probably some drunken louse...!*" "*...This is why we shouldn't let women drive...*"

In addition to the burning craft, the explosion had partially vaporized a nearby fruit and veg stand. Firemen attempted to control the blaze.

"I never hit *nuffin*!" a battered-looking cabbie pleaded with a constable. "There I was, waiting for the signal to change, and BLAM—somfin' detonated so fierce it knocked me clean ova'!"

Moe nudged Zippo, pointing at the alien craft. "Zip, isn't that...?"

Zippo looked back at Moe, horrified. He nodded gravely. "Das his *car*!" He placed his paws over his mouth in concern.

"What's going on?" Jeremy asked. "You know this car?"

"I'm not one hundred percent sure. But it looks a lot like an Infinibus."

"An Infinibus?"

Moe pulled Jeremy down closer to his level so that he could speak quietly. "The guy we bought the part from this afternoon...he was driving one."

Jeremy called out to one of the firemen on the scene. "Sir— the driver of that vehicle," he pointed at the smoldering husk, "is he—uh—okay?"

"No way to tell, laddie. If there was someone in there, he's all but incinerated now. T'aint nothing left but ashes. Whatever caused that explosion, musta been burning hotter than hellfire! Some offworlder fuel mixture, I'd wager."

Moe looked as if he'd just remembered something. "The comics!" he gasped. He tried rushing over to the remains of the Infinibus, but the fireman stepped in and held his hand up.

"Let the men do their jobs, laddie. Believe me, there's nothing can be salvaged from that wreck."

Moe turned around, defeated.

"Is okay, Moe. We still have game!" Zippo mindspoke an image to Moe and Jeremy. It was of a televid screen displaying a video game.

Jeremy was confused. "What is he talking about?"

"We hung out in that offworlder pub and got in touch with a black market techrunner. A Cerberon. Super nice guy! He gave us a used SuperChromaVision in exchange for some of our rarest Tommy Cobblestone comics. Fakes, of course. I just thought if the guy was a pile of charcoal now, we might as well get the issues back. They were some of our very best!"

"Oh." Jeremy murmured. "What was his name?"

"He never said."

"Wait a minute," Jeremy said, turning to face the two. "A SuperChromaVision? You guys said you needed to find some final, 'crucial' part for your ship's computer."

"Zippo and I have reached the limit of what we can do with the parts we have at hand. The *Terrapin* is spaceworthy, but we had to repurpose some components from her computer core— which means there are a few important things she still can't do. *Yet*. For instance, she can't enter the glimmer stream, that's for sure. And there's no WAY she can handle that janky old video game emulator we were using."

Zippo folded his arms, shaking his head in solidarity with

Moe. He mindspoke an image to Jeremy; it was of the *Terrapin* flying into a moon and exploding.

"Most importantly," Moe shielded his mouth, "she can't unscramble our black hole recordings. Far too much data. I thought maybe we'd get lucky and score a replacement computer core here, but no. Until we can get to a Starways Parts Exchange or scrap yard, we'll have to take it nice and slow. Traveling at subetheric speed takes a lot more time than full etheric glimmer—time that will pass more quickly with..." Moe looked to Zippo, who rummaged around his fanny pack and pulled out a game cartridge, "A certified copy of *Jessica Gelato: Average School Girl*! In *English*!" Zippo held the cartridge proudly about two millimeters in front of Jeremy's face.

Jeremy stared at the cartridge, then pushed Zippo's paw aside. "Okay. Yes, it is a fun game."

"Trust us, cool Terran merch like this is worth a LOT of money starside. Once we beat it, we can probably sell this baby for enough credits to buy a brand new Dawn Engine computer core."

Zippo put the cartridge back into his fanny pack. He noticed the bottle of Worchestershire in the pouch. "Sauce, too. We maek lawts of credit with sauce."

They stood for a moment as if waiting on Jeremy.

"So, are we going to watch the Enigma or what?" Moe nearly shouted. "I am dying to see the inside of a real Terran night club. I want our place to have that authentic Reptilicon feel to it. Terran decor, Terran music—"

"Terran shramp!" Zippo chimed in.

"I'm afraid we're too late. By the time we find the place, the show will probably be over," Jeremy said, crestfallen. "It must be ten o'clock by now."

Zippo tapped on Jeremy's shoulder. "Is that place?" he said, pointing to the brick building at the end of the block. A white awning hung above some steps leading down to a basement entrance. The awning was emblazoned with the words: *THE DREAMER'S CASTLE Bar & Lounge.*

"There it is! Let's go!" Jeremy shouted, dashing off down the cobbled street. Moe and Zippo followed close behind, their shadows flickering in the flames of the vehicle burning behind them. Zippo glanced back over his shoulder, still fascinated by the scene. He noticed a scorched logo on the side of the Infinibus, along with some writing. It read: *Electrical and Appliance Repair by MR. BOJANGLES.*

CHAPTER 23

THE ENIGMA

Jeremy was out of breath as he hopped down the steps to the front entrance. "Man, am I out of shape," he huffed, bending over with hands on his knees. He could hear Moe and Zippo's footfalls echoing off the pavement as they raced each other to the entrance. Moe jumped down the steps. "Come on, homies, let's go," he said, flinging the door open.

The three walked tentatively into the entryway. There was a podium placed for a host or hostess, but it was deserted. On the wall behind the podium hung an oil painting. It was of a beautiful ivory castle that floated above the landscape in the clouds. Zippo grabbed a menu and started reading. Jeremy wondered how he could read anything in such a dimly lit place, but then remembered that Felinians were supposed to have excellent night sight.

As Jeremy's humanoid eyes adjusted to the interior, he noted a small bar. It, too, was abandoned save for a lone bartender sitting on a stool. He was reading a newspaper by the light of an electric lamp. Lazy wisps of smoke curled from his cigarette.

Beyond the bar was a lounge area, with eleven tiny round tables set up in front of a modest stage. On each table was a tea candle, set in a rose-colored glass holder. Most of the tables were unoccupied. A burly-looking fellow sat at one, looking more interested in his roast mutton than the show on the stage. Jeremy spotted another patron passed out in a drunken stupor. A gaggle of old ladies sat near the stage, engrossed in the act. Jeremy heard them gasping and shrieking at the appropriate moments. Their gloved hands would occasionally beat out a muffled applause.

Electric bulbs lined the foot of the stage, where a magician stood before a patchy velvet curtain. He appeared to be in his thirties, and looked rather more pudgy in real life than his poster made him out to be. A drooping banner hung above him, painted with the words "FROM CRADLE TO GRAVE" in ghastly green letters. It must be the Enigma!

He wore a tuxedo jacket of a red so dark it might have passed for black, if not for the bright white spotlight. The light was horrifyingly dazzling; nothing could hide in it. It illuminated every tremble of the performer's stiffly waxed mustache, every bead of sweat on his brow and receding hairline. Jeremy could even see that the man's tux was looking a bit threadbare at the elbows.

Since no one came to seat them, the trio found themselves a table. On stage, the Enigma was concentrating very hard on something. He held a crystal ball, theatrically massaging the side of his forehead with his free hand. The spotlight shone off of the glass sphere as the man gazed into it. There was dramatic music coming from the direction of the stage, but Jeremy saw no orchestra. He assumed there must be a gramophone player stashed behind the curtain.

"Claudette!" the magician called out, opening his eyes. The old women at the table all gasped in unison. "Is there a Claudette in the audience?" The Enigma asked, shading his eyes with his free hand. "Come on, now! There must be a Claudette!" Jeremy noticed that the magician had an American accent. It was always comforting to hear a fellow yank.

"I am Claudette!" one of the ladies said, raising her hand.

"Please join me on the stage, Claudette. And bring your purse."

The old ladies applauded again as their friend made her way to the stage, taking the stairs at the side.

"Now Claudette, have you ever considered a career as a magician's assistant? I could use a new girl in my act!"

The ladies tittered. Claudette placed a hand on her mouth, smiling.

"I happen to know you have a ten pound note in your purse. Am I correct?"

The woman looked amazed. She opened her purse and pulled out a ten pound note. It didn't strike Jeremy as much of a mental feat.

"Wat dat?" Zippo whispered to Jeremy, pointing at the stage.

"It's money...er, like credits. Ten credits."

Zippo "ahhhhhh"-ed in understanding.

The magician plucked the ten pound note from the woman's hand. "Allow me to verify the authenticity of this currency, please." He held the bill up and pretended to examine it in the light. "Now I need you to mark this bill with your initials if you could, madam. Here, you may use my pen or any pen of your choice."

The lady took his pen and marked her initials on the bill. The Enigma proceeded to take the bill back and tear it up into tiny pieces, telling some convoluted story about a parade as he did so. "Classic distraction tactic," Jeremy whispered to his friends. Moe and Zippo just watched in confused anticipation. The magician's story ended with him throwing the paper bits into the air like confetti. The old women gasped.

"That was for kitty's tinned dinners! Now look what you've gone and done!" Claudette protested.

"And what is your cat's name? Wait, wait...don't tell me!"

The man placed his hand to his temple again, closing his eyes. He placed another hand on the woman's shoulder. "I see a cat now...he's curled up on a cushion, sitting by a window."

"Yes! Yes, that's him!" Claudette exclaimed.

"He is called...he is called..."

Moe and Zippo looked on, mouths agape.

"Orson!"

Claudette gasped, clutching her purse to her bosom. "How did you know?!"

"Now Claudette, listen. Listen carefully. I've made contact with Orson and he wants me...to...communicate something to you."

The lady's eyes grew very wide, almost fearful. "Yes? What does he want?"

"He says...he says he knows you weren't going to use that money to buy him food. You were going to spend it on something else. Something for yourself."

"Oh, it's true! It's true, I saw a new hat at Harold's!" she covered her face in shame.

"Orson says it's quite alright, just please pick him up some...fresh cutlets...and a fresh ball of yarn, if you could. And no more of that VAL-U BRAND TINNED ENTRAILS, please."

"Oh my little Orson! Tell him I'm sorry, would you? Please tell him!"

"He hears you loud and clear, madam. Now look in your purse."

The woman looked in her purse, shrieking in delight. She pulled out the ten pound note with her initials still scrawled on it, waving it around like a victory flag.

"There you are," he motioned for Claudette to return to her seat. "I hope you've enjoyed the show, ladies and gentlemen. I am the Enigma, and it's been my pleasure. Goodnight, Dublin!"

The old ladies gave the Enigma a standing ovation. He placed a top hat on his head, then threw down a little bomb. It cracked with a flash of light, sending up billows of green smoke. (Jeremy could tell by the odor that it was probably a Dunninger brand Smoke Nugget, picked up from *The Chamber of Discounts*—a value brand magical supply catalog.)

The pitter-patter of the ladies' gloved hands was the only applause the magician received as he ducked behind the curtain, knocking something over with a terrific crash.

The magician shouted a stream of curses that made the old ladies gasp and rush out in disgust. It sounded like the magician had knocked over his record player. Moe and Zippo laughed at the spectacle and gave some perfunctory applause for the swearing. Jeremy mulled the performance over, confused. "Weird choice to end a show with," he said to himself. "But...unique! Let's go meet him."

"All right, chief; but if he's hoping for a gig at our night club, he might want to work on his act first."

"'Scuse me, lads," the bartender stood over their table, cigarette dangling out of his mouth. "Show's over. An' I dunna think the two of ye be of age for an establishment such as this. He pointed his dishrag back and forth between Moe and Jeremy. "You—" he pointed at Zippo, "I have no idea about you. I'll assume you're their legal guardian and you'll see them out." The bartender extended his arm, showing them the door.

"But we just—"Jeremy started.

"Off with ye, then," the bartender insisted.

The three scurried out the front entrance. Outside, the crowd at the intersection had dispersed. There was no evidence of a car accident besides some scorch marks on the sidewalk and the half-burned fruit stand. They waited around the front doors for a minute or two, hoping to catch the Enigma. Then Jeremy had an idea.

"Follow me," he said, walking around the corner into a darkened alley. The light of the street lamps barely penetrated the area, giving it an ominous look.

"Pssst. Zip. You still got your hardware, right?" Moe whispered.

Zippo opened his fuzzy vest to reveal a holster tucked under his arm. In it, he carried a mega-heated disruptor ray pistol. They'd dubbed it the *Bug Zapper*.

"Good. Me too," Moe said. He knelt down to adjust his sock. His oversized hi-tops obscured the holster above his right foot. It held Moe's pulse phaser.

The duo followed Jeremy into the alley as he walked up to a metal door with no handle. "I bet he goes out this back way to avoid all the fans," Jeremy said. Zippo looked around, as if expecting other people to be present. They waited in silence for a few moments. "I'll just knock," Jeremy said, rapping his knuckles on the door. There was the muffled sound of music coming from inside, but no answer.

Jeremy knocked again. A voice shouted at them through the door. "Leave me alone! I told that barkeep I'd pay my tab. We had a deal!"

Jeremy interrupted. "Ahem—Mister Enigma, sir?"

The door creaked open a crack, and the magician stuck his head out. "Whaddya want?" His speech was slightly slurred. He appeared tired.

"Are you the Enigma?" Jeremy asked.

"If you fellas are the collections team from the pub..." he hiccuped, "tell 'em...tell 'em I'll pay up first thing in the morning. I just have to...have to..."

"Oh no, sir, we're not collecting anything! We're just fans! I was hoping to get your autograph, that's all." Jeremy held out the advertisement from his uncle's shop.

The man pushed open the door, examining the trio in the alleyway. His bow tie hung undone about his lapels, and his jacket was draped over a chair behind him. Ice cubes clinked in his glass as he steadied himself on the door. He smiled and drank down the rest of his drink.

"Fans, is it? How thoughtless of me. Please, do come in!" he motioned for them to enter, nearly falling as he tripped over his own untied shoes. He steadied himself on Jeremy's arm for a moment. "Sorry boys—must've got up a little too fast there." He reached for a chair and sat himself down, pouring himself another beverage. "Just having myself a little celebration. Won't you join me? Here, I think I have a Nova Pop somewhere."

The dressing room was hardly bigger than a storage closet. The Enigma's steamer trunk sat open on the floor, beside a dilapidated couch. The phonograph was wound up and playing a jazzy record at a soft volume. Jeremy was happy to see that it had not been damaged after all. The vanity mirror was outlined with white globes that cast light across the tiny room. There were several open bottles of strong smelling liquor strewn about.

A card table sat in the center of the room. There were short stacks of money on it, along with some shiny trinkets. "Please, all of you, have a seat," the Enigma said, getting up and pulling out a stool. The trio sat down at the card table. Upon closer inspection, Jeremy noted that the odds and ends arranged on the table were, in fact, pieces of jewelry. There were several pairs of earrings, two pocket watches, a string of pearls, a jewel-encrusted brooch, and a small pile of ladies' rings. Jeremy and Moe looked at one another, Moe cocking an eyebrow of suspicion. Zippo fought the urge to paw at the shiny things in front of him.

"Sorry I disappeared after the show like that. I like to split before they turn the house lights up and I have to see all the empty seats. Not so depressing that way." The Enigma rummaged through two of the half empty bottles of booze, finally finding what he was looking for with a "Presto!" He pulled out a small bottle filled with greenish soda pop.

"Here's the stuff. Moon Drop Pop," he read from the label. "That's more your speed, right fellas?" The mentalist looked for some clean glasses. He found three, one with some partially melted ice cubes in it. He dumped them onto the floor and swabbed the inside of the glass with his shirt tail. "Good as new," he said, setting the glasses down and filling them.

The carbonated beverage appeared to have lost all its fizz, but Jeremy sensed it would be rude to point this out. "Oh, just push that stuff outta the way," the man said as he noticed Zippo scooting a pocket watch aside to make room. "Most of this stuff is junk anyway. Paste. Fakes. Not even worth my time." The man belched. He raised his glass. "Let's toast!"

"And what are we celebrating?" Moe asked.

"Tonight was the final show of the tour! I'm done with this town." He drained his drink. "Probably for the best, too. I need to take some time off, make up some new persona they won't recognize. Give it a year or two."

Jeremy took a polite sip of his beverage, trying not to grimace. Not only was it flat, it was warm, too.

"Always nice to meet a fellow American on the road!" the Enigma said, lighting a cigarette. He sat down on the edge of the couch. "You *are* American, aren't you kid?"

"Yessir," Jeremy responded, giving a salute.

"Don't tell me...you're from...uh...somewhere out west, am I right?"

"Cali—," Jeremy started, but the Enigma raised his hand to cut him off.

"California! I knew it!" he poured himself another drink. "Californians always have a little sunny tinge to their auras. Plus, you talk like one. You said your name was...uhh...Jeremy! Right?"

"No! I never said. How did you know?" Jeremy asked.

The man smiled hazily and shrugged, "It's just one of those things. Hard to explain to a humdrum. Now you two," he said motioning to Moe and Zippo, "you two definitely ain't from around here, huh?"

"Hi, I'm Moe, this is Zippo." Moe reached out to shake the

man's hand as Zippo raised a paw in greeting.

"Pleased to make your acquaintance," the man spoke out of the side of his mouth as he smoked, extending his left hand to shake Moe's. "The name's Frederick, also known as THE ENIGMA!" He waved his hands around in a half-hearted mysterious gesture, then stopped as he nearly lost his balance. "But please—call me Freddy." A few playing cards spilled out of Freddy's sleeve, fluttering to the floor as he shook Moe's hand.

Jeremy felt a twinge in his stomach. Could this man be "Freddy the Unready" from Professor Chamberpot's story? He had so many questions, but he had no idea how to broach the subject.

Freddy looked for an ashtray, then flicked his cigarette over an empty glass he'd designated for this purpose. "And what brings an American boy and two offworlders all the way out to Dublin?" Freddy said as he emptied his left trouser pocket. He pulled out another ring and several more pound notes, placing them on the table.

Moe answered before Jeremy could say anything. "Jeremy here was kind enough to take us on a day trip. We've never been to Dublin before. Tomorrow we'll be headed back to—"

Freddy, who moments before looked like he was going to vomit, lit up with a smile. "Pigpimples Academie of Magick— am I right? I'm right, aren't I?"

"Yes!" Moe exclaimed. "Did you read his mind or something?"

"Eh, kind of. He just looks a lot like Tommy Cobblestone. Anyone ever tell you that, kid?"

Moe chuckled, looking at Jeremy to gauge his reaction. The boy wizard just furrowed his brow. Freddy continued, "Matter of fact, Pigpimples is my *alma mater*. They still teaching kids how to levitate sticks and all that?"

So it WAS him. Jeremy nodded. "Pretty much."

"And what House are you? Don't tell me you're a Dandy Lion..."

"Ick, no! House Fluffernut all the way."

"Yes!" Freddy attempted to give Jeremy a high five, but missed. "Same here! What a world! Is Mongo Chamberpot still teaching there?"

"He's the Headmage."

Freddy wrinkled his nose. "You know that old hack had the nerve to expel me at the end of my senior year?"

"What happened?" Moe asked.

"Nothing, that's what! Mongo used to harp on me that I didn't belong there because I had no magical abilities, which wasn't even true! I could do a few spells here and there, and like I said, I'm actually a level two on the Cagliostro Scale!" He looked for his glass, then gave up and grabbed a bottle. He took a swallow of liquor.

"I guess I wasn't *magickal* enough for them." Freddy did air quotes with his fingers as he spoke. "That, and they discovered I'd been selling stolen sports equipment from Quadritardd stadium."

Moe and Zippo nodded politely.

"Joke's on them, though. He said I'd never amount to anything as a stage magician... Now look at me! Ha!" He rummaged through his other pocket, pulling out a few notes of currency, including a ten pound note. It had a pair of initials scribbled on it.

"Dat Claudette's!" Zippo blurted out, then covered his mouth when he realized what he'd said.

"Heh. I knew a Felinian once, years ago. Taught me a thing or two about reading auras, in fact," Freddy hiccuped.

"Is that how you learned to do telepathy with cats?" Jeremy inquired.

Freddy laughed, nearly choking. He wiped his mouth on his sleeve. "Kid, I'll let you in on a little secret: this whole gig—the stupid top hat, the exploding balls, the what-have-you—it's all misdirection. Distraction. The only thing I've ever actually made disappear is my *dignity*," he scoffed, then took another drink. "Now who should I make this autograph out to?"

Jeremy unfolded the advert and handed it to Freddy. "You can make it out to Jeremy." he reached into his pocket for a pen, but pulled out a drinking straw instead. "Sorry, I...must have misplaced my pen."

"Oh, wait a second." Freddy reached down into his right sock, pulling out a pen. "Is this it?"

"Yes! Hey! How'd you do that?! Teleportation spell?"

"Nah. I pickpocketed you when you came in. I thought you'd have something better than just a pen and a couple of sticks of gum. Do you want the gum back? It's been in my sock."

Jeremy declined. Zippo said he'd take it.

"Here, lemme show ya," Freddy said, demonstrating his pickpocketing method to the gang. He made Jeremy practice on Moe and Zippo a few times until he got it right.

"There you go. Distraction is key. If you can replace the item with something similar, they'll almost never notice. And make good use of a bumper, if you've got one. This guy's perfect for the job!" Freddy patted Zippo on the back, who smiled at being acknowledged. "Tell you what, boys. How'd you like to see some real magic? I'd hate to have you leave with nothing but a lousy signature after tonight's train wreck."

Freddy went to his valise, pulling out a wooden box. He shook his head as if to clear it. "I may only be a level two on the Scale, but in my travels I've acquired my own special deck of tarot cards." He opened the box, examining the deck of large cards. Their backs were covered in intricate zodiac designs. "I don't normally get to do this. Doesn't translate well on stage. But for a Pigpimples man—it'd be my pleasure. Then you can go back and tell Chamberpot how a *real* magician operates." Freddy cleared off the card table and placed two candles on it.

"Mister Zippo, would you mind getting that light for us?" Zippo switched off the vanity mirror lights, engulfing the tiny dressing room in darkness. Freddy struck a match on the table, lighting the candles and then another cigarette. Shadows danced as Freddy shuffled the cards in silence. *Mesmerizing*, Jeremy thought.

Despite his passing grade in *Fundamentals of the Tarot*, Jeremy had never paid much attention in class. He had mostly spent his time composing poems to Janine Wintershade, who had sat a few desks in front of him. Bruno always destroyed these poems with fire after reading them and convincing Jeremy that sharing them would be a horrible, horrible idea.

"For this reading we'll keep it relatively simple, gentlemen. We're asking the deck about anything that might be in store for you three, and we'll allow the cosmic forces to share whatever they feel like sharing. You guys got anything you wanna tell us?" Freddy called out to the darkness, then placed a hand on his ear as if listening. "All right then. I like to use a classic triad spread, three stacks of three. Shall we begin?"

The three nodded mutely. Moe and Zippo were especially captivated by the ritual. Jeremy remained skeptical, but felt a chill run down his spine.

Freddy lifted the first card from the top of the deck, placing it on the table. On it was a medieval picture of a young man wearing a deep blue robe and cone-shaped hat. He held a twisted wand in his hand as he made his way through some kind of forest. The bottom of the card bore a title written in gold script: THE MAGICIAN.

Jeremy couldn't help but feel surprised.

"Ah, what a captivating start! Looks like they've been waiting to talk to you, huh?" Freddy peered right at Jeremy through the candlelight.

Jeremy suppressed another shiver. "Is that a good thing?"

"Hmm... Well, traditionally The Magician is seen as a universal sign of incompetence... However, when played as the lead card it can signify...an eagerness to create? Not bad at all, I'd say."

Freddy picked up the second card, placing it beside The Magician. This card had a picture of a forest beneath a night sky. Several beings, clothed in white, were descending from the sky and knocking on the door of a cottage. The card read: THE VISITORS.

"The Visitors signify new knowledge, new experiences. The magician gains some companions." Freddy winked. This time, it was Moe and Zippo who looked surprised. They stared at Jeremy in astonishment.

Freddy picked up a third card, looking at it before laying it down horizontally on top of the first two cards. It was a picture of an Arabian palace in a desert oasis. The pathway winding around the palace was lined with swaying palm trees and colorful flowers.

"THE PALACE," Freddy announced. Moe and Zippo gasped, both their jaws dropping. Freddy said nothing about their shock. "The Palace signifies the glories of ages past. It could also be a potential future destination..." Freddy flicked his cigarette over his empty glass. "Looks like you guys might be in for something good, huh?" He continued, straightening the three cards.

"Now, for the second stack. Let's see where your upcoming journey will lead you." Freddy lifted the next card and placed it in a new pile. It bore the image of a planet, its atmosphere made up of pastel-colored clouds that wrapped around it like ribbons. A red oval sat in the midst of orange clouds, like an angry eye. JUPITER, the label said.

"Hmm..." Freddy grunted. "Jupiter."

"Wat the—but...how he did...?" Zippo hissed, tugging on Moe's sleeve.

"I don't know, homie," Moe whispered. "Let's wait and see."

Freddy ignored the comments and went on. "God of the planets. As largest planet in the solar system, Jupiter presents untold resources and riches. It also signifies far-away, foreign places. Places once thought to be impossible to reach..." Freddy let this clue hang in the air as he pulled up the next card.

"Fascinating." The new card had an image of a beautiful, lavender-feathered bird on it. The bird was perched on a tree branch, bathed in moonlight. Its beak was open as it sang to the starry night sky. The text read: THE NIGHTINGALE.

"Another sign of creative energy, The Nightingale has long been seen as a kind of...muse. A percolator of dreams for creative spirits." Freddy took a drag off his cigarette, then exhaled smoke. "She often appears in the most unlikely of places."

Jeremy looked to Moe and Zippo for their reactions. Zippo looked confused and a little agitated. He had inadvertently extended a claw and was scratching the back of his ear with it. Moe, however... Moe had a wistful look in his eyes that Jeremy had seen before.

Freddy pulled out the next card. It pictured a crowd of people at some kind of feast. A large table of food was set up, with royalty sitting around it. They were dressed in all manner of finery and gay colors. Several jesters juggled in their midst. Some of the people were dancing.

"THE FESTIVAL!" Freddy pronounced. "Looks like you guys are headed for a party! But don't let the pleasant scene fool you. See the queen standing at the banquet table? She watches over all present. We don't know whether the subjects are actually having a good time or whether it's forced merrymaking. Beware of false appearances." An ominous puff of smoke wisped forth from Freddy's lips.

"And now...the final stack. We shall see what obstacles stand in your way." Freddy wiggled his fingers jokingly at Jeremy as he lifted the first card. His chuckle stopped short as he examined the card. He placed it down for all to see. The card showed a mutated-looking dog amid infernal flames. The beast snarled and drooled, and had red slits for eyes. CERBERUS, it said.

"That can't be good," Freddy gave a nervous smile and cleared his throat. "Cerberus is the demon hound that traditionally guards the entrance to...well, hell."

Zippo looked extremely uncomfortable. He made a tiny mew of protest.

"Oh no, I wouldn't worry too much. As a matter of fact, Cerberus could be a good omen. He doesn't just keep spirits *in* Hades, he keeps everyone else *out*. Perhaps it's a...a crisis averted on your end?"

Freddy picked up the next card. His optimism vanished as he looked at it, and then into Jeremy's eyes. He placed the card down next to Cerberus without saying a word.

It had a picture of an old woman on it. She stood before a bubbling cauldron. It was filled with a sickly green ooze. The woman was dressed in old tatters and rags. Her hair hung down over her warty nose and wild, dark eyes. She smiled a feral smile as she gazed upon a rotten piece of fruit in her hands. The label read: THE WITCH.

"The witch?" Jeremy said in a small voice.

"Communication with the unknown." The candle flames guttered as the mentalist spoke. It suddenly felt several degrees colder in the dressing room. He swallowed, lowering his voice. "An evil entity. Something you must face, eventually. It all depends..."

"Depends on what?" Moe asked, apprehension in his voice.

"The closing card." Freddy swallowed again, pulling the final card from atop the deck. He looked at it in silence. His hand trembled ever-so-slightly as he removed the cigarette from his mouth. He dropped the card onto the table. Jeremy told himself it was just the effect of all the alcohol, but the look in Freddy's eyes...it was a look of total sobriety.

The final card had the simple image of a seashell on it. The shell was coiled in an inwardly spiraling pattern, like many Jeremy had seen on the beach. He could not comprehend what was so alarming about this card, and awaited Freddy's explanation.

"THE NAUTILUS," Freddy whispered, just as the candles went out.

An animal shrieked in the alleyway. Zippo sprang up, looking for an arm to cling to. In the darkness he knocked the card table over, sending the candlesticks clattering to the floor and screeching a high-pitched "RAOW!" as he latched on to Jeremy's torso. Jeremy yowled in pain. Zippo had unsheathed his claws in fright. Moe yanked out his phaser amid the chaos.

The lights switched on. The three winced and groaned, shielding their eyes. Freddy stood by the dresser, lighting another cigarette with still shaking hands. "Sorry about that, guys. Must be a draft in here, huh?"

The three card stacks were scattered to the floor beside the overturned table.

"What was it? What does the nautilus mean?" Jeremy asked.

Freddy shrugged the question away with cigarette in hand. "You know, I wish I could tell you. I always do this, I drink too much and then everything gets hazy. I can't remember for the life of me. But tell you what, it sure was nice meeting you guys. Keep your grades up at Pigpimples, hear me? And don't let that old fool Chamberpot tell you what to do." Freddy shooed the three out the door and back into the alley.

"Could I get my poster back?" Jeremy asked, putting his foot in the door.

"Oh sure, kid. Here ya go. Now I trust you'll be able to take care of yourself in any self-defense type situations, right? They still teach you defensive spellcasting at Pigpimples?"

"Yeah, but—"

"Oh good. Now scram." Freddy's door shut with a metallic clang.

"What was *that*?" Moe said, bewildered.

"I don't know," Jeremy said. It was hard to tell in the darkness of the alley, but whatever creature had made that horrible sound was gone.

*　*　*

By the time they returned to the deli, Uncle Arthur was snoozing in his upstairs bedroom. He had been kind enough to leave out some cold cuts, which Moe and Zippo helped themselves to. Jeremy unfurled some blankets on the guest room couch and lit an oil lantern as he readied himself for bed. Before blowing out the light, he unfolded the poster and looked at the autograph. It read:

To Jeremy—

Give the Dandy Lions hell.

Your fellow Fluffernutter for life,

THE ENIGMA.

CHAPTER 24

THE LEGEND OF THEESIA AND BUX

The trio sped along the old country road. The sky, which had been so sunny and pleasant earlier that afternoon, had become a dome of gray. The warm Atlantic breezes were giving way to cooler winds. Jeremy pressed down on the gas pedal, hoping to get back to the castle before the rain hit. They were driving with the top off, and none of them had an umbrella.

The battery on Moe's jambox was drained, so they talked to pass the time. "You see Jeremy," Moe went on, "the Cosmic League hasn't actually discovered any new habitable planets in ages. Not since the time of my great-great-grandpappy, at least. The fifty or so star systems with life-sustaining planets have all been explored and colonized. The next closest stars are so many light years away that they take *way* too long to get to. For the longest time, the League assumed the planets in your star system were all populated by killer reptilians."

"Dinosaurs?" Jeremy asked.

"Yes. There's these wack warning beacons scattered throughout the quadrant. And they broadcast warnings about each star. And to this day, the one for your system says there are nothing but killer reptilians here, and a few gas giants. That's why, for centuries, your planet was listed as 'Reptilicon' on all the maps."

"But the dinosaurs died out...I don't even know when!" Jeremy said, stupefied. "Millions of years ago, I think! I never really learned about them in Pigpimples. Maybe they're covered in *Intro to Dragon Hunting*."

"I don't know either. But humans showed up at some point. Nobody knows when, since there's no record of a colonizing party. Maybe they got stranded, like us," Moe motioned his head towards Zippo, who was laying in the back seat. "Or maybe they were just some chill homies who wanted to be left alone, so they bounced on outta their home planet and crashed here." Moe shrugged.

"Are you telling me humans didn't originally come from Earth?"

Moe looked at Jeremy over his shades. "Dude. Get real! Haven't you noticed how many offworlders look humanoid? Lomaa'lians, Doogithians, Jorgons, Krecknirs—they all look pretty much like us, with some different skin tones and various nose ridges and stuff. Heck, you Terrans are just taller versions of us Binosians. Obviously we didn't all just *evolve* independently to look like this! That's wack! The odds of that are..." Moe shook his head. "Nah, humanoids didn't originate from Earth."

"So where do we come from?"

"Who knows?" Moe removed his shades, breathed on them, and polished them as if he were delivering a lecture. "Every world has their own myth of how they came to be, although history is full of big blank spots. On Bino we have an ancient story—a legend, you could say—of the first two settlers, Theesia and Bux."

"Who were they?"

"The story goes that they were offworlders working as ingredient scouts for some long-forgotten fast food franchise. They traveled the galaxy, looking for alien ingredients for new recipes. And one day they spotted an uninhabited world and landed, discovering a fruit that wasn't in their databanks: the Bolano Berry." [*Translator's Note: according to most reports, the Binosian Bolano Berry is like a cross between a Terran orange and a tomato. They are about the size of a grapefruit. — ChatterBot 3.6*]

"They both tasted the fruit, Theesia first and then Bux. And they both thought it was tasty and would make a funky dipping sauce. And so they collected as many samples as they could, and were about to get starside. But there was a problem... They had *changed*."

"Changed? How?"

"The ancient Bolano Berry altered their DNA."

"Dee-enn-ay?" Jeremy asked. He had no idea what those letters were supposed to mean.

Moe huffed, exasperated. "The fruit changed their bodies; made 'em too fragile for space travel."

"Oooh. So they were stranded on the planet?"

Moe nodded solemnly. "Bux wandered the wilderness, feeling sorry for himself and cursing the stars." Moe chortled. "You know, when they'd tell us this story when I was a kid, I always felt sorry for Bux...but now, I realize he was a lucky dude. At least he had his chica with him." Moe shook his head and sighed. He muttered something in Binosian.

Jeremy waited for the story's conclusion, but Moe remained silent. He just stared out at the horizon. Jeremy drove on for a time, but eventually broke the silence. "How does the story end?"

Moe stirred. "Years later, other scouts discovered Bino. And they found Theesia and Bux there, with a bunch of kids they'd had. They were living on the Bolano farm they'd built. And they'd even developed a strain of the fruit that was safe to eat. Bolano sauce became the biggest hit in the galaxy. They made a *fortune*. And their farm became the first colony on Bino. Bolano sauce has been Bino's biggest export ever since."

"Fascinating," Jeremy said, nodding as he kept his eyes on the road. "We actually have a similar kind of story on Earth." Jeremy remembered the Sunday School classes he'd attended in the Chapel of the Blessed Hog back at school. (Any students attending worship services were exempt from Sunday spellcasting drills.) "Ours doesn't feature nearly as much dipping sauce, though." Jeremy looked through the rear view mirror. He could see Zippo tinkering with the P-Shell. "Do Felinians have a story?" he asked.

Zippo looked up from the device. "Wat?"

"He wants to know where your species came from," Moe said.

"Ahhh..." Zippo put down the Shell, recalling the tale. "First, Mama Kharr bring stars malk..."

"Stars *milk*,'" Moe clarified.

"Yah, she brang huge," Zippo outstretched his arms for emphasis, "BIG bottle stars malk for all the kitt chrilden to drank. And Mama Khar, she say: *these stars malk for all kitts, drink to get vary strong!*" Zippo flexed his arm muscles. "Then kitts knock bottle of malk down, spill all the stars over all the YOO-nee-verse. So, all Felinian kitts fallow different stars, go to stars to find malk, and then jus' live there. That why we call galaxy *the Malky Way*." Zippo mindspoke an image to Jeremy. It was of a giant milk bottle floating in space, tipping over and spilling out a river of milk and stars. Kittens, some furry and some hairless, chased after the stars playfully. They looked cute in their little spacer outfits.

"Hey—you want your sandwich?" Moe offered Jeremy one of the three Excaliburs Uncle Arthur had wrapped up before they left. He then offered one back to Zippo, who ignored him. He had resumed his intense focus on the P-Shell.

"Thanks," Jeremy said. He unwrapped his sandwich as he held the steering wheel.

"Looks like you're getting the hang of piloting while noshing," Moe observed. "That's a valuable skill to have starside." He bit into his sandwich. "Planetside, too. Actually," he spoke with his mouth full, "it's a valuable *life* skill."

Zippo mewled in delight. He held up the Shell and waved it triumphantly. "I get it! Look! I *get* it!" The P-Shell's screen lit up. A pair of white wires sprouted from the bottom of the device. They dangled for a moment, then floated into the air like the tendrils of a sea anemone. At the tip of each wire was a round plastic nub.

"Oooh, built-in anti-gravity ear nubs. Sweeeeet !" Moe said.

Zippo daintily plucked one of the nubs out of the air, placing it in his ear. To his surprise, the other nub zipped itself into his other ear automatically. Zippo laughed. "It tickle!" He pushed a couple of buttons on the device. "MEW-sic! It play kewl MEW-sic!" He shouted, not realizing the volume of his voice. He got comfortable in the back seat, putting his legs up in a satisfied pose.

Moe tried to ask Zippo what he was listening to, but it was too late. The Felinian couldn't hear a thing; he was in a slack-jawed musical trance. His slightly open eyes held a blank look as he stared off into the countryside.

"I've never seen anything like that," Jeremy said. "There's no way that's Terran tech. But then, why would Bibliosnuff have alien tech? Wouldn't he get in trouble?"

"Yo, Zip," Moe said. Zippo ignored him. "Zip!" Moe gave Zippo's arm a shove. "Snap out of it, dude!"

Zippo looked at Moe, but it took a few moments before he recognized him. He sniffed the air as he shook his head, pulling one ear nub out. "Wat?"

"Lemme see that thing, will you?"

"Okey, yah." Zippo pulled the other nub out and handed the device to Moe.

The screen flashed and the ear nubs retracted back into the

Shell. "NEW USER DETECTED," the screen read.

"Outta sight! This thing must have a genetic signature scanner!" Moe pressed a button on the device. It displayed words in microprint on its tiny screen. "*Please accept End User Agreement and Terms of Service before using,*" he read. "Blegh." Moe pushed the button to skip through the extremely long block of text. "Yes, yes, okay," he muttered, pushing button after button. The device finally made a pleasant chime and the ear nubs sprouted out of the bottom again, floating up into the air like magic. "Enjoy Seashell Systems' patented *syrenopods* at a responsible volume," Moe read off the screen. "Pppsh, okay little guy! I'll blast my eardrums if I feel like it!"

Before the nubs could float into Moe's ears, Zippo snatched the P-Shell back. "Hay, I had first! You listen later, Moe." The nubs zoomed back into Zippo's ears, returning him to a state of zonked-out serenity.

"All right. But I call it when we get back!"

Thunder rumbled on the horizon. It was now quite dark, and the weather had turned very blustery indeed. Jeremy's hopes of avoiding rain deflated. They were driving right into the storm.

CHAPTER 25
CONSIDERING DEATH
BY MUTANO DOOMGRUBS

The gang made it home without getting soaked... almost.

They were just past Selkie's Cove when the first raindrops hit. The precipitation made it trickier to navigate the road, even with the headlights on. By the time they reached the castle, it was pouring.

Moe scrambled out of the car with the key to the garage door, which he unlocked and swung open. Jeremy pulled in, shutting the engine off. The microthrusters whined as they powered down, their sound replaced with the steady patter of rainfall. He got out and switched on a lantern.

Moe shook his head back and forth, his shiny hair splattering droplets of water everywhere. "Man, that must be some funky fresh music. Zip usually *hates* the rain."

Zippo was still reclined in the back seat of the car. Water dripped from the points of his naked ears. He looked like someone who had overindulged in a magnificent buffet and needed a few hours to lie very still.

"Zippo?" Jeremy said. He walked over and tugged one of the nubs out of Zippo's ear. Jeremy was curious to hear what the music sounded like, and held the nub up to his own ear. *Odd*. He couldn't hear a thing. Zippo's eyes sprang open just as Jeremy pulled the other nub out.

"Waz? Wat? Ware we are?" Zippo was instantly awake. He appeared confused. He noticed the Personal Shell in his hand and switched it off. The ear nubs retracted themselves back into the device.

"We're home," Jeremy answered. "Are you okay?"

Zippo yawned and rubbed his eyelids with the back of his paws. He sneezed, shaking the tiny droplets of water off his whiskers. "Rrrrrrr," he made a low rowl. He hopped out of the vehicle and shook himself in an attempt to dry off. He then groomed himself, vigorously licking his forepaws and hopping from foot to foot as he took turns shaking them out.

"Must have been some killer tunes, eh, Zip?" Moe asked.

Zippo looked at him mid-lick and gave a shrug. "Eh. Not bed. I hear better sometimes."

Moe walked around to the car's trunk. He removed a box containing the SuperChromaVision console and the video game. "Looks like this baby's still nice and dry." He blew some imagined dust off the Jessica Gelato cartridge. "Can't wait to fire it up! Did you already get the rest of our stuff from inside the castle?"

Zippo nodded. "This MARN-ing. Pecked and reddy."

"Alright then. I guess this is it, holmes."

Jeremy panicked. "Wait a second, you're leaving? What do you mean, *this is it*?"

"Well yeah, dude. I don't think we're going to find a Dawn Engine computer core anywhere on your planet. We wouldn't even know where to start. And even if you did have one, who are we kidding—we wouldn't have the cash to buy it. Plus, with the coordinates of that black hole saved in her, the *Terrapin*'s databanks are far too valuable to risk zooming around your world. The longer we stay here, the higher the chances of some data snooper hacking us. Nah, we'd better bounce. Perfect time to do it, too. Normally, a nighttime lift-off would attract attention for miles around, but the storm should mask our movement nicely."

Jeremy stammered, "I...I...okay." He gulped. He was having trouble maintaining his composure. This was all happening too fast. "I just want to say, before you guys go, how great it's—"

Moe looked supremely annoyed. He grabbed Zippo's arm. The Felinian yapped in surprise. "You were supposed to give him the contract!"

Zippo looked angry, then hurt, then amazed. He cringed, covering his wrinkly forehead with the palm of his paw. "Sarry! I forget." He removed a crinkled, rolled up piece of paper from his fanny pack and held it out to Jeremy. "Read. Dis yours."

Jeremy unrolled the paper and read aloud:

Contract of EMPLOYMENT
(created with NaviRipple Plus LegalBot Software 1.8)

COSMIC LEAGUE YEAR E-59
(Terran year A.D. 1919)

CONDITIONS OF EMPLOYMENT:

In the role of personal chef for starcraft TERRAPIN, co-captained by Maurice "Moe" Baraxil and Zipponio "Zippo" Prraow IV (aka 2 FUNKY BROTHERS, aka THE STARDROPS IN STEREO)

JOB DESCRIPTION:

I, the undersigned, referred to hereinafter as JEREMY FLETCHER (aka JEREMY, aka JEREMIAH THE MYSTIC, aka THE MAMBO WIZARD) agree to travel aboard the TERRAPIN, providing nutritious breakfast-themed meals, snacks, and other various noshables as requested by MOE and ZIPPO, and according to culinary and spellcasting ability.

Jeremy stopped and looked up. "2 Funky Brothers?"

"We were still finding our voice as musicians. Keep reading," Moe urged Jeremy on.

He continued:

Potential mealtimes are designated but not limited to: breakfast, second breakfast, brunch, second brunch, lunch, tea time, dinner, supper, dessert, second dessert, post-dinner treat, midnight gorge, and so forth.

Other duties may include assistance in any/all musical performances including backup singing, backup dancing, musical accompaniment on clavitone, transmatic keyportal, grand piano, etc.

COMPENSATION:

CREDITS ON DELIVERY up to and not exceeding one third of total profits from all return on investments, plunder and all other profit obtained from piracy & radio dipping endeavors, as well as a performance residence slot in any and all nightclubs, discotheques, cabarets, hover-booting rinks, dance halls, or other future venues managed by MO/ZI DOWN PRODUCTIONS.

As contribution to this effort, I, the undersigned, sign over MY HUGE COLLECTION OF RECORD ALBUMS to be used at the discretion of MOE and ZIPPO, co-captains of the TERRAPIN, most likely to be SOLD FOR HUGE FAT STACKS OF CASH MONEY OH YEAH.

"Zippo wrote that part," Moe said.

Jeremy turned the page over. "All right, getting to the good stuff here." He read on.

DEATH & DISEASE CLAUSE:

In the event of JEREMY's untimely demise, a small but

tasteful plaque shall be erected in his honor on the bridge of the TERRAPIN.

Medical assistance in the form of three (3) visits to any health restoration pod or therapy nook will be provided at no expense in the event of bodily and/or psychological trauma including (but not limited to) dismemberment, decapitation, molecular dispersion, spinal erasure, accidental gender reassignment, total genetic scrambling by cosmic rays, space madness, brain slurrification by MUTANO DOOMGRUBS...

"...And it just kind of fades out here," Jeremy said.

"Oh right, I think our printer ran out of toner. There was supposed to be a non-disclosure agreement that basically says if you tell anyone about where the black hole is located, we are legally allowed to eject you out the airlock—but you get the gist of it. Whaddya say? You in?"

Jeremy thought it over. "What's an adventure without a complete and balanced breakfast? I'm in!"

Zippo took Jeremy's hand into his paws gleefully, shaking it up and down. Moe also gave Jeremy a firm, no-nonsense handshake. "Welcome aboard, chief. Or should I say, *chef?*"

Jeremy shook his head. "Uh, no. By the way, you two have to help me load those boxes of records onto the ship. They're pretty darn heavy."

"Kid, they are gonna be worth their weight in Boo'myan larvajuice sacs."

"I assume that's a lot?"

"Ooooh yes. That is, I heard they were some kind of delicacy in the Eekolaat System. We'll find out next time we're there! Anyway, the plan for now is: make mad credits, buy a new computer core, and get to descrambling our magtapes. You good with that, Zip?"

"Shramp first."

"Okay, seafood buffet."

"Yasss!" Zippo bolted out of the garage and towards the starship.

"He really hates the rain," Moe said.

Jeremy and Moe watched the Felinian run away.

"Now about those records," Moe started, "see, the thing is—loading and unloading is strictly a Head Chef duty. It's actually in the contract somewhere—"

"I just read the contract! It didn't say—"

"I believe it's in an addendum. You know I'd love to help you, dude, but I've got to be super careful." Moe held his hands out. "I really shouldn't risk hurting these babies. I need them to play vibrobass and the holosynth sticks, not to mention piloting the ship. I mean, this is my livelihood we're talking about..."

Jeremy rolled his eyes. "Fine. I'll get Zippo to hold my umbrella."

"I'll tell you what, kid—I'll swing the ship around and park her right outside your front door."

"Thanks. Do you want me to actually sign this?" He held up the contract paper.

"Of course. I'm a stickler for these legal-type things, you know. You don't do the paperwork, you end up with sloppy pirating. And we run a tight ship."

Jeremy checked his pocket for the pen. He pulled out a drinking straw. "Oh yeah," he remembered.

CHAPTER 26

GOING STARSIDE

Jeremy sat in his father's study, scanning the room for anything he may have missed. Zippo poked his head in the doorway. "Ah, there is moar—I will get," Zippo said, picking up the second-to-last crate of records. With Zippo's help, the loading had gone quickly. Jeremy called out his thanks. Zip mewed back politely as he shuffled down the hall. Jeremy remained seated protectively on the final crate of record albums. It was the all-important "crate of keepers"—the records Jeremy did not want to sell. He would load this one himself.

As Jeremy hefted the crate, Zippo popped his head back into the study. "Look who we all for-GET!" he exclaimed. He held up Donut's bird cage. The furry rodent had just woken up, and was nosing through her fluff. Zippo got a worried look on his face.

"Iz okey if Doh-nat stay in mai room?"

"Of course. She likes your company."

Zippo smiled with pride. "Okey. You come now, *NiiiRRiyaEew.*" [*Translator's Note: Felinian term, roughly translated to English as "wicked scampering morsel" — ChatterBot 3.6*]

Jeremy was unsurprised to see that Moe had not, in fact,

brought the ship around. It was still parked on its usual spot on the grass. It cast its spotlights into the night, illuminating sheets of pouring rain.

Moe was standing in front of the ship, soaking wet. The offworlder turned, spotting the two and waving his arms to get their attention. "Zipponio! Get out here!" he called out.

Before Jeremy could ask what was going on, Zippo snatched an elastic hairband from his fanny pack and pulled his big ears back. He dashed out to Moe's assistance. Jeremy placed the crate of keepers down and ran into the rain after him.

"What's going on?" Jeremy had to raise his voice above the din of the storm.

"Zip, we'd better bounce. Check this out." Moe walked them around to the other side of the ship. He pointed to a charred spot on the grass, about two feet in diameter. It looked like a fire had burnt the spot to stubble.

Moe pointed as he marched up to Jeremy. "I thought you said there was nobody else around here!" He poked him in the chest angrily.

"There isn't! Have you seen anyone else since you've been here? We're all alone!"

Zippo got on all fours, moving his head close to the charred ground and sniffing intensely.

"Anything?" Moe asked.

"Neh...too wet." He stood up, shaking his legs out and shivering.

Moe shook his head in disgust.

"Can someone please explain what the devil is going on?" Jeremy protested.

Quick as a flash, Moe hopped and grabbed two fistfuls of Jeremy's shirt, yanking him down. Jeremy fell to his knees, bewildered. Zippo let out a *rewl* of fright. Moe raised a boyish fist as he seethed in Jeremy's face.

"Listen up, kiddo. I like you. I like you a lot. But there's some *wack* stuff going on, and I need to get to the bottom of it or things are going to get butt ugly for all of us. *Who* did you tell about us, huh? You'd better not be holding out on me!"

Jeremy raised his hands in surrender, his eyes wide and perplexed. Rain streaked down his spectacles.

"I'm not holding anything!" Jeremy insisted.

Zippo rushed to Jeremy's side, batting Moe's hand away and forcing him to let go.

"You stahp det! Det is so RUDE, Moe!" Zippo scowled at his companion. "Jrr-mEE not lie! Maybe just is bird, or animal or someting!"

"Heh," Moe scoffed. "That was no animal." He pulled something out of his pocket. "This was on the ground, next to the burned spot." Moe tossed a little green box to Zippo. Lightning crackled in the sky, momentarily illuminating the darkness.

The droplets on his glasses blurred Jeremy's vision, but it was plain to see that the box was some kind of offworlder tech. Jeremy took his glasses off and squinted. Two tiny red lights on the box blinked off and on.

Moe turned back to Jeremy. "You *promise* me you didn't tell anyone about our ship? I won't be mad if you did, I just need to know."

Jeremy's thoughts raced back to his conversations with Uncle Arthur earlier that day. "You two have been with me this whole time!" Jeremy nearly shouted. "The only other person I talked to was my uncle, and it was about which semi-soft cheese was better: havarti or jarlsburg!" A rumble of thunder punctuated Jeremy's defense.

Moe mulled this over and turned back around. He rested his hands on top of his wet hair.

"It's time to boogie," he said. "Zip, chuck that thing over the cliff. Jeremy, go get the rest of your stuff. Because we are *bouncing*."

Zippo ran to the edge of the cliff and flung the box as hard as he could. Jeremy watched the little red lights as they sailed over the rocks and into the sea.

Moe climbed the side rungs to the roof of the ship. He yanked open the top hatch and jumped inside. Seconds later, the *Terrapin*'s lights flashed on as its engine hummed to life. The rear cargo hatch hissed open.

Zippo and Jeremy ran back to the castle. Zip snatched up Donut's cage. The hamster was awake, and was quite enjoying the stormy nighttime air. "Okey, you get last box and we go naow!" Zippo called out to Jeremy, before running back to the ship.

The crate of keepers was the only thing left. There was a problem, though. *I can't take this box out in the pouring rain!* Jeremy grabbed one of the beach towels he'd hung out to dry by the fireplace, covering the crate as best he could.

After exiting, he locked the front door of the castle. As he hustled towards the ship, the towel-covered crate in his arms, he silently wished he could cast a protection spell over his home. *Too bad I flunked Intro to Hexes & Blessings...*

Zippo awaited Jeremy in the cargo bay, waving him onto the ramp. Moe called back to them from the cockpit. He had to shout over the thrusters, which were spinning up. "Is he in? Are we good?"

"Yeh, we go naow!" Zippo shouted back, slapping the wall in affirmation. The ramp raised itself as the rear hatch shut. Before he could even set the crate down, Jeremy experienced a sensation he'd never felt before. It was as if his stomach had turned into a watermelon that was just dropped into a gravy-filled swimming pool! He caught a glimpse of the ground outside of the port window. The horizon gave way, tilting back and forth like a seesaw.

We're lifting off! And I think I'm going to be sick! Jeremy instantly regretted every decision he'd made that led him to this point. There were various boxes and containers of different colors and sizes in the cargo hold, including all the crates of records Zippo had loaded. Most were strapped down, but a few slid around as the ship twisted into the sky. Jeremy almost called out in fright, but the sensation of vertigo made him clench his teeth. *If I open my mouth right now, I will surely barf.*

His arms pinwheeled in search of something to stabilize himself; he grabbed hold of some of the storage webbing that ran along the wall. Zippo hopped over and caught him by the arm. "Is okey. Les go, we strep in," he said, smiling his reassuring smile. He still had his ears pulled back with the hair band. He pointed towards the front of the ship. "Get seat balt."

Zippo said something else to Jeremy, but it was impossible to make out above the whine of the thrusters and the crash of lightning outside. Teetering with arms outstretched, like he was dancing a drunken samba, he made his way down the hall and into the cockpit.

"Jeremy! Hurry up and get into the jump seat!" Moe shouted, grasping the flight wheel. The cockpit's console was a dazzling array of buttons and controls. A televid screen displayed a pixelated map of the surrounding stratosphere. The whole room was bathed in its blue-white glow.

Zippo pounced into his captain's chair. He assisted Moe with the ship's controls before swiveling around and facing Jeremy. The Felinian patted a carpeted bench built into the back wall of the cockpit, inviting Jeremy to take a seat.

Torrential rain cascaded all around them. Lightning flashed, illuminating the cabin. Jeremy fell onto his seat, fumbling with the buckles of the safety belt. He finally got the thing to click securely in his lap. He waited, trying to mask his anxiety.

"Let's avoid that pocket of electric interference if we can," Moe murmured to his co-pilot. Without a word, Zippo maneuvered the steadily rising ship. Jeremy clutched his safety belt as they tilted to the left, then the right, still rising. The view from the cockpit windows was completely obscured by clouds as they sailed through the troposphere. Thunder rumbled all around. Nobody spoke.

A minute later, the rumbling died down. The sound of the rain also faded away.

"Readings look good. I think we're clear," Moe said. Just as he spoke, all the fog dropped away from the ship. Jeremy held in a gasp as they rose above the clouds. The earth below was blanketed in every direction. Pockets of lightning pulsed and danced within the clouds here and there, gradually shrinking away as they ascended.

Jeremy's stomach settled, and his hands unclenched the safety belt. Outside was quite a sight. *Thousands of stars, all glittering above an ocean of fluffy gray dust bunnies!*

Moe sighed in relief. "Alright then. I am not scanning any local starship activity. Quiet night! How we doing on life support?"

Zippo mewed affirmatively. Moe and Zippo went through a checklist of technical terms Jeremy didn't understand in the slightest. He just continued staring out the windows, marveling at the view.

"Right on. Looks like we're entering lower strat, everything clear far as I can tell. We should hit escape velocity at about...here," he motioned to something on the navi-controls. He then spun around in his captain's chair, noticing Jeremy for the first time. "You buckled in, chief?"

"I think so. I am not sure if I did this thing right—"

Moe swiveled back around. "If it clicks, it sticks. You're good." He fiddled with some dials on the central control panel, then rummaged through a stack of crystal discs in a storage compartment. "Ah, there you are," he said, pulling out a translucent diskette. He slid the disc into the control panel. "We are *now* ready to go starside. Punch it, baby." Moe pointed at Zippo.

"I Hope You Miss Me" by the Miraculous Puppets suddenly

filled the cabin. The cockpit hummed as the engines spun up, the ship tilting back as the subetheric thrusters pulsed to life. Although the stars remained stationary, Jeremy sensed incredible power and speed. He got that watermelon-dropping-feeling again, instead now it felt like a watermelon dropped from the top of the Pigpimples bell tower. He gritted his teeth and held on tight.

"*Poha poha mnxankobaa ahaper ckoooootoo! Poha tapkob ckotooooooo!*"[*Translator's Note: Binosian. The lyrics in English: "Yeah yeah I hope you MISS me baybaaaaayyy, I sure hope you MISS me bay-yeee-baaaaayyyy!" —ChatterBot 3.6*]

Moe and Zippo yowled along to the music as the *Terrapin* climbed through the planet's atmosphere. Jeremy had no idea what language it was, but the music was so catchy it distracted him from puking.

"Oh, oh! This part is the *funk*—" Moe twisted the volume dial up as the song went into a harmonic glapsodia solo. Zippo pulled the sub-etheric throttle joyfully, bumping their speed in order to break free of Earth's gravity. Jeremy laughed involuntarily as he felt inertia pressing him flat against the wall—all while his two companions took turns playing air glapsodia. The whole cabin rumbled in a symphony of alien rock and the roar of the thrusters. The sky outside looked like it was on fire, and Jeremy wondered briefly if they were all about to burn up. He kept his mind off his impending doom by imagining what kind of instrument his two companions were currently miming. *Based on their movements, it must be a cross between a saxophone and an accordion!*

As the solo wound down, Moe grabbed the flight wheel and gave the ship a celebratory spin. The stars outside made a dizzy circle as they cartwheeled. *That's funny*, Jeremy thought. *Something feels weird.* The intense pressure on Jeremy's body had dissipated. It was replaced with a bloopy kind of lightheadedness, and then a popping sensation in his ears.

"Are we...uh...dead?" Everything was suddenly so buoyant; his arms waved like two taffeta scarves billowing on the air.

Moe swiveled back around. "Ladies and gentlemen, we are floating in space. Still with us, dude?" He unbuckled his belt and floated out of his seat ever-so-slightly.

"You're flying!" Jeremy exclaimed.

"So are you. See for yourself! You're good to unbuckle now."

Jeremy unclicked the belt and pushed himself into the air. He'd never been too keen on flying, but this sensation wasn't all bad! "Keen-o! It's like swimming!" He couldn't help but chuckle in delight. The cabin was a bit cramped, but he still had enough head room to rise into the air. He imagined the great Leopold Dobler, a Vienese magician who specialized in levitation. "I rise to the occasion!" Jeremy said, quoting the magician's ridiculous tagline as he spun in the air.

"What?"

"Nothing, don't mind me, just—you know—experiencing *actual* levitation over here. No big deal," Jeremy said.

Moe went back to inspecting the navi-control monitor. Jeremy glided to the side windows of the cockpit, gazing out into space. He saw Earth trailing behind them as they sped into the night. The planet glowed, like a gigantic blue crystal ball. Jeremy stared at it for a long time while another Binosian rock ballad blared through the stereo. "Holy gosh...would you look at that..." he said to himself.

"Das kewl, heh?" Zippo cooed. He joined Jeremy and looked over his shoulder.

"Yes. *Das kewl*," Jeremy agreed.

Zippo ruffled his hair with a paw and hopped back to his flight controls. Jeremy noted that his home planet looked slightly smaller. In fact, it appeared to be shrinking. *We must be moving at an incredible rate!* Jeremy shuddered with a twinge of dread, peppered with pure excitement. Despite their cruising speed having normalized, he felt seasick again (or was it spacesick?).

"Yikes. Sorry, this is just...oh boy...uuggh..." Jeremy floated away from the window, hand clamped over his mouth. He closed his eyes and inhaled through his nostrils.

"Dude—since you look like you're about to hork, I'm gonna turn on the artificial G," Moe said. "Might wanna grab hold of something."

With some maneuvering, Jeremy hovered above the carpeted jump seat. Moe slid a dial up and clicked a button, and Jeremy descended until he was reclining on the bench. He removed his hand from his mouth, exhaling with relief.

"Hope that feels okay. We like to keep G at 0.8, since Bino is 1.1 and Phynix is 0.7. Terra Firma felt like 0.9, maybe 0.95, so this should be just a little lighter than usual. You still have to blow chunks?"

Jeremy shook his head. "Thanks, I think I'll be okay."

Moe thumbed through his box of crystal diskettes. "If you want to dry off, there might be an extra towel around here somewhere...in the sani, maybe."

"Actually, I brought a towel."

Moe whistled, impressed. "Kid, you've got this spacer thing *down*."

* * *

They cruised quietly for a time, enjoying the music and the view of the Milky Way. Jeremy rubbed his head with his beach towel and dried his hair. Zippo declined a towel, opting to just groom the rain droplets off of his own skin. He then gave his whiskers a thorough and much-needed preening. Moe kicked off his soggy hi-tops and removed his socks, which he wrung out right onto the floor. Before Jeremy could ask, Moe explained, "Oh, don't worry about the water. It'll evaporate. Rain water is actually good for the oxyscrubbers." He toweled off his feet, wiggling his toes as he swiveled his chair back.

"That's not what I wanted to ask about," Jeremy said.

"Then what's up?" Moe spoke without turning around.

"Are you going to explain to me what that was all about back there?"

"What do you mean, homesqueeze?"

"What I mean is what the *crackers* just happened?! Why did we have to high tail it out of there so fast? I didn't even have a chance to grab my tooth brush!"

Moe turned to face Jeremy. "We'll stop somewhere and pick you up a dental sterilization stick. There's a superette at the Mars loop—"

Jeremy shook his head. "Not just that! That burned spot on the ground, the little glowing cube thing—you kickin' off over something or other—what was that all about?"

"Ooooh. *Right*. Well, you remember a couple of days after we crashed. You were outside, and I yelled at you to not come near our ship?"

"How could I forget? It was my first near-death experience. I'd never been shot at for bringing someone breakfast."

"And I am sorry about that, homie—honest. But I had to fire a warning shot; otherwise you might have ended up one crispy critter. Now personally, I would prefer to get us a nice cloaking device—less messy, quieter, doesn't attract nearly so much attention. But genetic security shielding is the best we could afford. Highly dangerous, highly illegal. Any jibroni who's not authorized gets zapped with a hefty protonic beam." Moe made an explosion sound.

"And when were you planning on explaining all this?" Jeremy asked. "What if I had checked out your ship when you two were out swimming or something?"

"Yo, I tried blasting at you, didn't I? What more warning did you need?"

Jeremy shook his head. "All right, so you're saying that

burned spot on the grass—that was someone who tried to steal your ship?"

"I doubt they wanted to jack the ship; a Binosian Transport Tug like this isn't worth much. But they definitely wanted to hack our memory banks. That little cube I told Zippo to throw away—it looked like a datasnooper. Or a tracking device. Shoot, maybe both. You attach them to a hull to pull information out of a ship's computer core."

Zippo turned and looked at Moe uneasily. "I know, I know," Moe answered.

"Who would want the information on your ship?" Jeremy asked.

An image popped into Jeremy's mind. It was of a squad of offworlder agents, all armed with deadly high-tech weaponry. The words *Galactic Recording Industry Syndicate* floated by.

"GRIS," Zippo said aloud.

"Get outta here with that!" Moe nearly yelled. "Why would GRIS be prowling around on some Terran island in the middle of Corn Chip, NOWHERE?! And besides, GRIS tech is top of the line. That datasnooper looked like some trash spliced together from a...Volzoid vending machine!"

"Well who was, den?" Zippo grumbled.

"How should I know? Some wack offworlder *bozo* who saw us parked there and wanted to take a peek, jack our data, and try to make a quick buck. Well, he got what was coming to him. I'm sorry if I didn't feel like waiting around for jibroni's friends to realize he was a smoldering hole in the ground, then come get revenge on us. The coordinates for the black hole are just too important." Moe hopped down from his chair. He tapped a few keystrokes, calling up a map on the navi-control screen. "I haven't seen any weird activity out here on the starways, have you? Nobody's following us."

Zippo considered Moe's words, sniffing the air.

"See? We're good. We are *groovy*," Moe said to Jeremy,

slapping the side of his arm. "Would GRIS have just sent one guy? No. No way. They would have sent a squad and waited around for us to come back. And what's the worst they could pin on us? Some light radio piracy? Unauthorized audio sharing? They don't know *jack*. No reason to flip out! Just...chill."

The Felinian relaxed his ears, then yawned. "Okey," he meowed. He stood up from his ratty chair and stretched, scratching his belly. He mindspoke an image of himself curling up in his cabin.

"Okay cat-man," Moe said. "Go get some shut eye. I'm gonna stay up here for a bit. See if I can hook up that ChromaVision." Moe slipped on a pair of massive headphones, plugging them into the main console. He unzipped Zippo's backpack, which contained a trove of leftover waffles. "Zip, why don't you show our head chef to his quarters."

Zippo tugged at Jeremy's sleeve. "Come, see dis," he said. He led Jeremy down the corridor and back into the darkened cargo bay. The area was a maze of stacked storage boxes and plasteel crates. The Felinian navigated a path towards the starboard wall, where strapped-down containers were stacked nearly to the ceiling. As they rounded the corner of a very large crate, they came to an open area.

Zippo flicked on a sidelamp. Before them was a tiny makeshift room! The open area contained a bed, complete with Mik-and-Skitter-themed blanket and sheets.

"Is this...mine?" Jeremy asked.

Zippo nodded enthusiastically.

"Keen-o!" Jeremy inspected the cubicle, finding it to be quite cozy. There was a dresser made out of repurposed Bolano Berry containers. Jeremy pulled out the top drawer, laying his towel in. When he checked the second drawer, he found it contained several packets of vacuum dried sotus noodles. A couple of bookshelves were tacked on the wall above the bed, and held a stack of *Tommy Cobblestone* comics.

"This is too much! I love it!" Jeremy declared, flopping onto the bed. The mattress had a uniquely alien feel—a blend of firmness and squashiness unlike anything Jeremy had ever laid on. "Super comfy!"

"Yeah! I maek dis for Jrr-mEE. Look!" Zippo lifted the blanket and pulled back the sheets. The mattress was actually an industrial-sized pouch of bright pink goo, packed into a cargo box. There was nutritional information stamped on it in an alien language. [*Translator's note: BOO'MYAN LARVA JUICE SAC by Wonderdew Farms. "100% Organic, Harvested From Real Boo'myan Thripp Larva!" —ChatterBot 3.6*]

"Thank you, Zippo. It's perfect."

"Oh yeh, you walcome Jrr-mEE."

Zippo went to a control panel in the wall and depressed a button. Several horizontal shutters retracted, revealing a plaz window looking out onto the stars.

Zippo bid Jeremy goodnight and found his way out of the cargo bay.

Jeremy made himself at home in his new quarters. He retrieved his wooden crate of keepers and set it next to his bed, using it as a night stand for his spectacles. He read *Tommy Cobblestone* for a while before switching off the light. He gazed at the thousands of stars outside his window as he lay in bed.

My first journey into outer space. What a day.

The steady hum of the subetheric drive was slightly louder in the cargo hold, but not at all unpleasant. It was the last thing Jeremy noticed as it lulled him to sleep.

CHAPTER 27

BAD GUYS INTERLUDE #3

Mike Mania sat aboard the bridge of the *The Perfect Stranger*, a GRIS black hull galleon. He stirred his cup of Venusian sulphur tea as he took in the view of Reptilicon. *Terrans sure made some nice televids; too bad their planet was so ugly.* Mike's thoughts turned to the giant, towering walls of flame and lava on Hades. This sulphur tea always reminded him of home.

"Charles!" he barked.

His idiot brother walked over sheepishly. "Yeah? What?"

"I just wanted to thank you for the tea. Looks splendid." He raised the teacup to his snout, carefully avoiding the starched ruffles of his collar.

"Pardon me, sir...?" a peon crewmate interrupted. Mike couldn't keep track of their names, so he guessed.

"Yes, Tony?"

"When was the last time you communicated with Agent Belvedere?"

Mike placed his tea down in exasperation. "Your uniform looks extremely shabby, ensign! When was the last time *you* saw that jumpsuit properly pressed?"

"Oh," the crew member looked down, embarrassed. "I guess

it's been a while."

"'OH I GUESS IT'S BEEN A WHILE'," Mike mimicked the crewmate's voice, then snarled. "Dis-GUS-ting! You look like you should be flipping grok patties! Have a little decorum!"

The crewmate smoothed down his jumpsuit, but remained standing near the captain.

"YES, Tony? What can I help you with?!"

"Sir, the reason I ask about Belvedere is because..." he gulped. "Have you checked his bio-signs lately?"

Mike called up the agent's profile on his viewscreen. All of Belvedere's bio-signs, including his heart rate, breathing rate, oxygen flow to his nervous system, cerebral rhythms, bladder fullness and comfort levels should have been visible. But for some reason, all the boxes on the screen were blank. "Care to explain, Tony? Why aren't my bio-signs working? If you're telling me the software crapped out on us again, so help me—"

"Sir, unless he turned his transmitter off..."

"My agents CAN'T turn their transmitters off. They're implanted inside their skulls, you imbecile!"

"Oh. Well, then. In that case, I'm pretty sure he's... dead."

Mike snorted out a laugh. "Thank Cerberus! All right, okay—he's just dead! You're saying the software still works fine." He patted his viewscreen. Mike took a few laps of tea and called up the bio-signs history screen. "Let's see now...wasn't Belvedere assigned to... AAAARGH!" Mike howled in rage, setting his tea down on a saucer.

"Tony, you cur! Don't you know a genetic vaporization when you see one?! *Look!*" Mike pointed at the bio-signs history screen. About three hours ago, all the boxes got very squiggly lines on them, followed by blanks. "Those are distinct vape squiggles! He was obviously fried by a starship security shield! Oh, these fleabags are good. TOO good. Aaargh!" he resisted the urge to punch a furry paw through his computer screen.

Another peon walked over, a dopey smile on his face.

("Tony" took this opportunity to scamper away unnoticed.) "Sir! We just spotted a ship leaving one of your specified trajectories."

"Put it on screen! What are you waiting for?!" Mike barked.

The image of a Binosian transport tug appeared on the screen. It had just achieved escape velocity and was sailing out of Terran orbit. Mike hopped up. "Ha! Enhance viewer! ENHANCE!" The screen zoomed into the ship.

Terrapin was clearly emblazoned on its side.

"That's our girl," Mike growled with pleasure. He picked up his tea and lapped away happily. He warmed his paws on the scalding hot teacup as he leaned back in his chair.

"Ensign—" he tapped a stubby black claw on the screen, "follow them."

CHAPTER 28

JUST JOSHIN' AN' QUASHIN'

Jeremy stirred. Two voices argued in the hallway, but he couldn't make out who they belonged to. He pulled his blanket over his head and kept his eyes shut.

It's freezing! Jeremy half-thought, half-dreamed. *Probably Alfie Coldmann and Pete Wisby fighting over hard boiled eggs again.* His roommate, Alfie, had a penchant for sneaking hard boiled eggs out of the Trough and storing them in a jar, which Pete liked to raid every once in a while. It always resulted in a scuffle, with Alfie and Pete casting attack spells at one another in the lounge. Usually Jeremy enjoyed watching them destroy the dorms over their nasty old eggs, but the last time they fought one of them had hit his stack of *Vince Thorne* comics with a *decimato* spell. The direct hit had shredded the comics to pieces.

Jeremy wondered whether he ought to just *novo collazio* up some hard boiled eggs for the two little prats before they wrecked more of his stuff. Vaguely annoyed at the memory of his lost comics, he threw the blanket off and opened his eyes. Stars shone outside the plaz window.

Oh yeah! Jeremy realized. *I'm in space.*

He climbed out of bed, nearly yelping as his bare feet

touched the frigid floor of the cargo bay. He made a mental note to acquire a rug as soon as possible. For a second he was almost convinced he could see his own breath. Shivering uncontrollably, he rummaged through his steamer trunk.

"Ah, here we go," he mumbled, teeth chattering. He pulled out his father's blue robe and slipped it on. He briefly considered getting back into bed, but there was a serious nagging problem that he really needed to address.

"So maybe the sunset orange eye shadow was a mistake!" Moe nearly shouted. "I admit that! But you've gotta be out of your mind if you think this is any better. Matte foundation with grape lip gloss? Becky and Tamara will NEVER invite us to the slumber party looking like this!"

Jeremy hovered in the hallway. He could see they'd hooked up the SuperChromaVision and were playing *Jessica Gelato: Average School Girl.* By the looks of things, they were choosing what cosmetics to use.

"No! My MAEK-up good. Is cute. She is *hawt*!"

Jeremy stepped into the cockpit.

"Ah, there he is—the head chef himself! Mornin', homeslice! Just the homie I wanted to talk to, as I am in need of some serious noshables. I'll take a stack of hotcakes if you please. And if you could drizzle them in that special purple berry syrup you do—I forgot what it's called, but it is *lucious*!"

Jeremy started to speak, but Zippo cut him off.

"Yeh, Jrr-mEE, I liek some HAT-cake too. Also, sassage pattie?"

"Of course. Now could you tell me—"

"It's Jessica Gelato, dude! Man, this game makes a LOT more sense in English! I think we spent about fifteen hours on the old game trying to get Hunky Mark to fall in love with us and ask us to prom. Turns out Hunky Mark is actually named Ernesto! *And* he's our brother."

Jeremy shuffled in place impatiently. "Is there a restroom

facility on this ship?"

"Rest room?" Moe looked puzzled, then understood. "Oh! Of course. You can use the sani port in Zippo's cabin."

* * *

Jeremy searched for something to dry his hands on as he exited the tiny sanitation port. Zippo's cabin was an absolute mess. He stopped to bid good morning to Donut, who was out for her morning jog. Zippo had treated her treadwheel with a lubricant normally used on Binosian harvester engines, rendering it virtually frictionlesss. This, combined with the slightly reduced gravity, allowed Donut to achieve velocities never before dreamed of by any Terran hamster.

Jeremy gave up looking for a towel and just dried his hands on his robe. He tied it shut with its silver sash as he returned to the cockpit. "You know what I just realized—" Jeremy took his wand out. "What exactly should I transform for breakfast? I don't suppose you have any rocks around here?"

Moe thumbed back towards the cargo bay as he fiddled with Jessica's makeup options. "Just use anything you find back there, kid."

"The cargo containers? Are you sure? What if there's something valuable in them?"

"Trust me. There's not."

Jeremy went back to the cargo bay, opening the lid of one of the boxes. It was filled with printed material, all tightly bound together. It looked like newspapers or magazines or something. Jeremy pulled out a bundle and undid the plastic wrapping. "Of course," he said to himself.

It was comic books.

Issues of *The Adventures of Tommy Cobblestone,* to be specific. This particular bundle had fifty or so copies of issue no. 53: "The Wedding of Professor Drakeworth and Lady Primrose!

AT LAST!" On the cover was a picture of Drakeworth and Lady Primrose feeding each other wedding cake.

"Heh," Jeremy chuckled. "How lame." He set one aside to read later.

* * *

"How'd you snooze? How was the cargo bay?" Moe asked, his mouth full of hotcakes. They were enjoying breakfast in Moe's cabin, which was just big enough to accommodate the end table they were sitting at.

"Actually, pretty keen-o! Might need a blanket or some fur pelts, though. It gets a tad cold back there."

"Oh *riiiight*. It'll get *pretty* chilly at night in space. Usually dips down to zero degrees kelvin this time of year."

"Jrr-mEE. Dis nice," Zippo held up the plastic plate and utensils.

"Thanks." Jeremy yawned. "So are all those containers back there filled with comics?" he asked.

"That's right. But they're bootlegs. You know, fakes. You can kind of tell by looking at them. The reds and yellows never really look right on the pirated ones."

"And are they all issues of Tommy Cobblestone?"

"Yup. Well, they're all *issue* of Tommy Cobblestone."

"What do you mean?"

"I mean I'm pretty sure they're all just number 53."

Jeremy put his fork down. "Wait..." he tilted his head, pointing in the direction of the cargo bay with his knife. "*All* those containers?"

Moe nodded. Zippo licked the purple syrup off his plate.

"Holy gosh! There must be hundreds!"

"I think we estimated about fourteen thousand? Although there are still a couple of containers we haven't checked. I gave up after a while."

"Where did you get them all?"

Zippo stopped midlick and looked at Moe, who shook his head. "It's...a long story." Moe leaned back, wiping his mouth on his t-shirt. "What a feast. You're gonna make us a couple of chunky monkeys if we keep this up. I might finally have to buy some new threads!"

Zip agreed, then commenced his post-breakfast grooming. Jeremy looked around Moe's cabin (although the Felinian showed no self-consciousness about grooming himself, Jeremy still thought it was polite not to stare). The walls of Moe's quarters were plastered in various posters and stickers advertising things in alien languages. He guessed many of them were for alien rock bands, since they pictured groups of serious-looking offworlders posing around what he took to be musical instruments. A large bulletin board hung on the wall beside the door. It was empty except for one spot at the top, which held a picture.

Jeremy went over to examine it.

The picture was a portrait of a cute little dog! It had a cute furry face and pointy ears. Its shiny black eyes had an almost human twinkle to them. With its pink tongue out, the doggie even appeared to be smiling. It was a Terran breed—a Yorkshire Terrier, if he was not mistaken. Jeremy only knew this because Janine Wintershade had one as a pet. She would often go on and on about how much she loved her "yorkie." She even brought it to Pigpimples once, around Christmastime.

The words "Madi Nabo" were printed beneath the picture, and the whole portrait had been stamped diagonally with the word "QUASHED" in bold red ink.

"What the heck is this?" Jeremy asked.

"Oh that? That's the Quash Board." Moe answered.

"*Ah.* Well of course it is, anyone can see that. And what exactly were you...quashing?"

"You know kid, you make fun, but Zippo and I were in the

bounty hunting game for a while." Moe joined Jeremy. "We were taking down hardened intergalactic criminals and getting paid the fat stacks! Not a bad gig at all."

Jeremy looked at the adorable puppy. "And this...? What galactic war crimes did this little guy commit?"

"First off, *she* was a well-known Cerberon scam artist. This chica was wanted in five systems. Your little backwater planet has obviously never heard of Madi Nabo."

"No, must have missed that news bulletin. What was she wanted for? One too many accidents on the rug?"

"Uhhh...I think she committed some kind of zoning violation or something. But she couldn't outscam us! Not a chance!" Moe pointed at Zippo, who winked in agreement.

"And you haven't quashed any bounties since? Or are you still quashing?"

"Well homie, as a fellow artist—you know how it goes," Moe shrugged. "Bounty hunting, while lucrative, wasn't much of a challenge. We mastered it. What can I say? It's a stagnant field, really. I think we both felt a bit unfulfilled, wouldn't you say Zip?"

"Vary *not* fulfill," Zippo crinkled his nose and shook his head in distaste.

"Now, radio piracy—! That's a whole new world of possibilities. Speaking of which..." Moe peeked out his cabin window. "Do you think we're in range yet?"

CHAPTER 29

FROGSTAR RADIO

The signal was static-y at first, but after two days of travel it came through clear as a bell.

"You're listening to Frogstar Radio, FM 104, Q-HOP...this is DJ Nebz croakin' at you...greetings to all you hoppers out there, space truckin' the Sol System starways. We just heard...uh...Krudit Sgrogron's Stellar Attack...I think?...The track was 'Magic Locket,' if I'm not mistaken... Sorry guys, I got distracted for a few minutes...lookin' for another bag of Crispity Crickets...might actually be all out. What a drag! Anyway, I know we had Carefree Signals before that, from their album Bent Out of Shape... *Groovy Terran band, very boggy! ...We'll get back to the tunes in a second, but have you guys read this issue of Tommy Cobblestone? The one where Nicholas and Georgina get captured by the Ice Dwarves of Cloverdale? ... Wew! Must have read it eight times now...I won't spoil it for those of you who are like me, and still twenty issues behind...but let's just say that I think Nicky is going to get a lot more than he bargained for when Drevon Ashcrypt shows up! ... Okay, let's do some more Terran tunes—"*

There were a couple of other stations they could pick up, but Q-HOP was the best one. The DJ's voice was deep and melodious, and he liked to play Terran bands. Jeremy had never heard of any of them.

"DJ Nebz must have a pretty big collection of pirated music," Jeremy said.

"Most of it comes from trades, shares," Moe explained. "He told us once that he used to do his own radio dipping, back home in the Amphibios Nebula. He likes anything Terran."

"You actually *know* this guy?"

"Oh yeah. We go way back. Met him in college. Back then, he was still broadcasting out of this junked out ore hauler. He's an Amphibion; you know how they are. A real chill kind of dude. We heard that he bought an abandoned research station, hid it out in the Bodie Belt. [*Translator's Note: asteroid belt beyond Mars. —ChatterBot 3.6*] Sounds like it upgraded his signal big time. I'm guessing his computer system is pretty deece, too. Hopefully he'll let us use it to filter our magtapes. He's the only guy I trust in this neck of the woods. *Huge* Tommy Cobblestone fan."

Jeremy could tell. DJ Nebz would often rant and rave about Tommy Cobblestone in between songs. Other times, he'd play re-runs of call-in shows from the Amphibios Nebula. Moe and Zippo found these to be absolutely hilarious, but Jeremy couldn't understand a word. The Amphibios language sounded like a bunch of croaking and blorping to his ears.

"All right, I'm done." Moe switched off the game console in disgust. He'd been playing it for hours. "I still have no idea how to get past this part. I'm hitting the sani. Maybe a hot shower will help clear my head. Should be switching back to manual soon. You good to take us into the belt? It's been pretty smooth sailing. No blinkies, no snoopers. Haven't even seen any rocks yet..."

Zippo mewed, shooing Moe out of the cockpit. They heard the sound of Moe kicking his cabin door unstuck, followed by the shower from his sani.

"Jrr-mEE, come," Zippo invited Jeremy to Moe's seat, motioning for him to take the flight wheel. The Felinian leaned back in his chair, stretching and yawning as Jeremy took the ship's controls.

"You want me to pilot?"

"Yeh." Zippo pushed a button on the control panel, resuming manual control of the ship. "See? It's liek drive car."

"It kind of is, yeah! Not as much traffic out here, though."

Zippo put his feet up, scratching behind his ears. "Jus watch for little rock...ehh..ASS-teh-ROY-ed," he fumbled with the word.

"Asteroids?"

"Yeh, ASS-teh-ROY-ed belt. But it okay. Rocks *vary* smol. No preblom."

Jeremy grasped the wheel tightly. *Dodging asteroids!* "Keen-o! Hey, is that one over there?" Jeremy pointed at something floating in the distance. It looked like a red pebble at first, but it grew by the second. Zippo looked out the viewscreen.

"Ah no. Det planet...Mers, I think."

"We're flying by Mars? Holy gosh!"

Zippo sat at attention. He looked suddenly concerned. The red planet ballooned into view, along with two satellite stations orbiting it. Jeremy wondered if they'd fly close enough to see the colony on the planet's surface.

Zippo typed out a question to the ship's A.I. The cartoon mouse tipped his top hat and retrieved a bunch of data. Lines of it ran across the screen.

"*Oophib.*" An alien voice hailed them through the comm system, startling Zippo so badly he nearly jumped out of his seat. He composed himself, picking up the boxy receiver and depressing a button.

"*Pehp. Ju phibo,*" he answered. He took his claw off the button, shooting a nervous look at Jeremy. Jeremy tensed his hands up on the flight wheel, ready for action.

"*Pehp pehp! Ino hih ju, bophi. Ooo fa,*" the voice answered. They spoke a few lines in an alien tongue. The exchange sounded amiable enough. "*Ooo ka, pehp.*" Zippo ended the conversation on a happy note and put the receiver back.

"What the devil was that?" Jeremy asked.

Zippo pointed a tiny ship out in the distance. "See? Ship from Sibik System. He not see ship from Bino in vary long time. Juzz liek to say hallo, det is all."

Moe burst into the cockpit, dripping wet and wearing only a towel. "Who was THAT?!" Both of the ship's sanis had speakers connected to the comm system. Moe must have heard the radio exchange. "What are we doing so close to *Mars*?!" he exclaimed, seeing the planet in the distance.

"It okey. No snoop, no bad thing! Juzz guy say hallo!"

Moe took the keyboard, reading the scrolling data on the navicomputer and querying the ship's A.I. "There might be a hundred ships down there! Any one of them could have spotted us and snooped us!"

"Ack! Moe, stahp be crazy!" Zippo pleaded. "Wat you talking? No! They too far. Come, come. Is okey!" Zippo called up some more data on the screen. "See? Dat guy jus from Sibik, now he is gawn. Das *all*."

Moe read the data as they flew by Mars, the red planet receding into space behind them. "All right. I just don't get why we approached the coordinates from this vector... I thought I specifically told the computer to avoid any planetary orbital patterns. Oooohhh...wait a minute...okay, I see." Moe pointed something out to Zippo. "Right there. I think the computer forgot to account for azimuth inflection. Wack. I have no idea how to even fix that. Probably still wonky from the parts we repurposed. Yo, Computer!"

The ship's A.I. bubbled to life. "Aye, captain! At your service!"

"One of these days, your kruddy calculations are gonna get

us all killed."

"Absolutely, sir! I'm on it!" the cartoon mouse on the screen tipped his hat and disappeared.

Moe sat down on the jump seat, still in his towel. "*Phew!* What a ride, eh homesqueeze?" He noticed Jeremy, who was still in the pilot's seat. "Ready to fly us into Bodie's Belt?"

Jeremy had already spotted some of the bigger asteroids floating in the distance. "Sure," he said. "This is a lot easier than it looks, you know."

"Spoken like a true wizard. Take us in, kid."

* * *

After an hour of navigating the belt, Jeremy spotted it in the distance: *Bolero Station.* The starbase hung in the darkness, nestled in the midst of several enormous space boulders. It reminded Jeremy of one of those modern pointy skyscrapers, like the kind they had in New York City. The station rotated slowly, silently, encircled by a metallic gravitational ring. The entire habitat appeared dark, save for a few lights in what Jeremy thought of as the topmost part.

"Hail him," Moe said.

Zippo attempted a hail over the comm but received no response.

"Hold up..." Moe fiddled with the radio dial, turning up the volume.

"*And finally, an update on the Ddppd't, the Q'Kkccv'k-ian heartthrob you all know and love from the* Warriors of Ts'sfhfs *televid series... Looks like Ddppd't's recent surgery for stalagtitus went fine... Last we heard, he is recovering in a five star cave and enjoying a lot of alkaline leachate solution... Well, that's nice to hear! Warm wishes to Ddppd't and his family of sentient crystals... All right, we'll get back to some more from the Torrent Rumblies—I am loving side two of their new disc—*

but first, a few important words from our sponsors..."

A commercial started to play. Moments later, a strange voice croaked through the intercom. "You da ones hailin' me? Who da grok nugget is this? And how da grok did you find me?" The voice was high and nasally, but so blorpy and throaty that it was at times difficult to understand. It was definitely speaking English, though.

Moe motioned for everyone to be quiet. He spoke in a husky voice: "Excuse me, this is Special Agent Vince Thorne of GRIS. We received several reports of some unauthorized music transmissions being broadcast from your coordinates. We have a warrant here for the arrest of one Rufo Ribbitz."

Moe sounded about as gruff as a world-weary ten-year-old, but the voice on the other end took the bait.

"Now wait just a second, sir...I can explain! No unauthorized music here! We're just a local operation, nothin' to get serious about!"

"Mr. Ribbitz, please. It's too late for all that. If you come with us peacefully, we'll spare your lovely station."

"Gentlemen!" the voice croaked, "We at Frogstar Radio Incorporated are providin' a valuable public service! Surely we can come to an understandin'? Isn't there...uh...some kinda *fine* I can pay that will make this all go away?"

Zippo whispered something in Moe's ear. Moe nodded eagerly. "Alright, Mr. Ribbitz, that's fair. To start with, your music selection could be greatly improved. How about for the next month, you play nothing except tracks by Stardrops in Stereo..."

"Stardrops in Stereo? They only ever released one album, didn't they? Uhh what was it...*Long Story Short*?"

"Excuse me, homebread, but you're forgetting they also had an EP titled *Get Dropped.* What kind of DJ doesn't know that?"

There was a pause on the other end. "Who is this?" The voice paused, probably checking his scanners. "...The

TERRAPIN? Awww, give me a break..."

Moe and Zippo laughed hysterically. "Oh, and Rufo—from now on we require every third song you play to be dedicated to Moe and Zipponio. Got it? Or we're hauling your warty green booty in for radio piracy!"

"You little..." the voice on the other end started to shout. "What da grok were you thinkin'? I was about ready to blast ya'll with a neutronic bomb and hop on outta here! Ya dumb grub munchers!"

Moe asked if they could board the station. "We have a little business proposal for you, dude."

"Of course. Park at docking bay...eleven. It's the only one in this floatin' trash heap that has a workin' elevator. I'll unlock it for ya."

"Thanks, holmes. See you in a few."

Zippo parked the *Terrapin* in the docking bay, which was a far bigger space than the tiny transport tug required. Jeremy threw on one of his old Pigpimples uniforms, hoping the space station would not be as cold as his room in the cargo bay. The three gathered up their things and waited for the oxygen pressure outside the ship to stabilize. Moe packed Zippo's backpack full of supplies to bring aboard the station, including a few record albums from Jeremy's collection, as many recent issues of *Tommy Cobblestone* that they could find, and, of course, the three black magtapes from their last radio dipping excursion.

"Looks like you're safe to disembark," the throaty voice squarkled over the ship's comms. "You'll wanna take the turbolift that's down the hall to the...uh...left? I dunno, the blueprints for this place always confused me. I never go down there."

Moe assured him that they'd figure it out.

"All right, then. See you at the top floor. I'll be in the control room."

Moe thanked him and pushed the button to open the

Terrapin's rear cargo hatch. The voice returned. "Oh, and guys...please excuse the big ol' mess. I'm still renovatin' and such. We were experiencin' a bit of a pest control situation a while back. I think it's simmered down now..."

"Nebz, I'm sure it's fine. We're on our way." Moe switched off the comm. "Zip, you packing heat?"

Zippo patted the gun holstered under his fuzzy vest.

"Good." Moe tied the laces on his hi-tops and switched on his pulse phaser. "Jeremy, bring your wand. If anyone comes at us, zap 'em to hash browns."

Jeremy held up an "okay" sign. He kind of wanted to remind Moe that his magic only worked on inanimate objects, but he liked that *zap 'em to hash browns* line so much that he didn't want to spoil the moment.

CHAPTER 30

MADI NABO, CRIMINAL MASTERMIND

They exited the docking bay into a corridor. The lights attempted to flicker on, eventually giving up and sputtering out as the doors slid closed behind them. Hanging on the wall was a large banner. It read: "A WARM WENDIGO WELCOME to BOLERO STATION! WE LOVE SCIENCE!" Someone had spray painted a few words in an alien language over the text of the banner, but none of them could read it.

The entire station was dark. The starlight shining in through the windows made their surroundings visible, but just barely.

Zippo's Felinian eyes were the most adaptable to the darkness, so he led the way. They inched down the hall, looking for any sign of a turbolift.

"Careful—there's junk all over the floor here," Moe advised.

"Okay," Jeremy said, just as he bumped into some computer equipment balanced on a pile of folding metal chairs. The whole stack toppled to the floor in a crash, sending Zippo bounding down the hall in terror.

"Zippo! Come back!" Jeremy rushed after him. The Felinian was crouched on the floor around the corner, panting heavily with his gun drawn.

"Det...*skare*...me."

"I'm sorry," Jeremy said.

Zippo's pistol emitted a faint glow in the darkness. It gave Jeremy an idea.

"Hey Zip, did you bring the Personal Shell?"

Zippo plucked the device out of his fanny pack and handed it to Jeremy. The P-Shell's front screen lit up when turned on. It was dim, but in the darkness it was almost as good as a flashlight. Jeremy showed this to Zippo, who took it and mewed in delight.

The Felinian resumed his lead. With one arm outstretched he fanned the P-Shell back and forth, illuminating their path. "Guise—ovar here," Zippo waved them over. He'd found the turbolift and pressed the call button.

Nothing happened.

Moe tried the button again with the same result—no light, no helpful chime, nothing. He pried the sliding door aside only to find an empty shaft with no turbolift inside. The inner walls of the shaft were covered in a mossy green growth. The back corner was a veritable jungle of alien fungus pods. They reminded Jeremy of a cluster of rotting cantaloupes.

Zippo shined the P-Shell into the shaft to get a closer look. Swarms of little white insects crawled out from behind the fungi, avoiding the bright light and scattering up and down the walls. Zippo shrieked, recoiling in revulsion. Jeremy wondered if he'd ever be able to enjoy cantaloupe again.

"Ugh. Nebz, you doofus," Moe muttered. "Let's keep looking. There's gotta be a working turbolift somewhere."

They trekked on down a long corridor. The floor was covered in tattered carpet, littered with old science equipment and debris. The next door on their right opened onto an office. That is, it looked like it may have once *been* an office. The desk, chairs, and equipment were all charred from a fire. Fresh crops of alien fungus pods had popped up amid the ruin.

"Dis chair not bad, huh?" Zippo dragged a rolling office

chair around, the blackened arm rest crumbling away in his paw as he pulled it. "Maeby we still fix it?"

"Just keep moving!" Moe snapped. Zippo rolled the chair into the hallway in order to "get it on way beck."

The next entrance they passed was already open, the sliding door having been ripped right off its track. It lay in a twisted mess on the floor, the walls around it covered in deep gouges that looked unsettlingly like claw marks.

"Huh," Moe said peeking in. "Looks like a lab."

Zippo's ears went straight up. He turned to face his companions, bringing his gun to his nose in a silent *shush*. "You hear det?" he whispered.

Moe and Jeremy were frozen. Jeremy shook his head, but then...he heard it. It was a horrible skittering sound, somewhere in the darkness. Moe reached down, unholstering his phaser. "Stay chilly, boys," he whispered.

The skittering sound stopped.

Zippo waved them forward.

They turned a corner. A faint light at the end of the hall made things a little easier to see. "That must be the working lift," Moe whispered. "Good. Almost there."

In addition to junk on the floor, an overturned table, and shards of broken glass everywhere, the whole corridor was covered in black scuff marks. Zippo shined the Shell on them, and Moe took a closer look. "Scorching. From one heck of a shoot-out. What do you think, Zip? Anti-matter? Glyphic lazer?"

Zippo stopped again. Every muscle in his cat-like body rippled, as if ready to pounce. The Felinian's pupils widened and narrowed into slits as they locked onto something on the ceiling. Jeremy turned his head up slowly to see what Zippo was looking at. It was too dark to make out, but for a split-second he thought he saw the tail-end of something...*slithering*...into an air vent. The offworlder broke from his trance and wrinkled his muzzle. "Eh...okey, now we go. Dis scary. Dis *gross*."

As they advanced towards the light at the end of the hall, Jeremy could see that the carpet looked different.

Darker.

Stained.

Not just the carpet, but the left wall, too. And ceiling. Something is splattered all over the place. Something maroon red.

"Eww...what heppen...?" Zippo mewed breathily.

"Reminds me of that food fight we had in the Trough, the night of the spaghetti feast," Jeremy whispered.

Moe and Zippo turned to him, horrified. Jeremy realized they were probably *not* looking at dried spaghetti sauce. His stomach clenched.

Just then, Zippo hissed at the darkness. He bared his fangs, his ears flat against his head. It was the skittering sound again, like hundreds of little pencil tips flitting on metal. It was hard to tell where the sound came from, as it seemed to emanate from inside the walls. But it was definitely getting louder.

Zippo pushed ahead, waving the P-Shell back and forth as if shooing off unseen mosquitoes.

Moe aimed his phaser all around, looking for any target.

The sound stopped.

Zippo spun, the Shell shining in the faces of his companions. Jeremy's and Moe's eyes had acclimated to the darkness, and the light from the screen nearly blinded them. "Look out!" Zippo meowed, bringing up his disruptor ray and dropping the Personal Shell. Moe and Jeremy hit the deck just as Zippo squeezed the trigger. An electric blue bolt lit up the darkness with a loud *ZZH'PEW!*

"Did you get it?" Moe asked, his arms still shielding his head.

Jeremy sat up, turning to see. He snatched the P-Shell off the floor. The moment he held it up, a thing scurried out of the darkness right at him.

Jeremy didn't have time to even process what *it* was—it was just moving...fast...and directly towards his crotch. He crabwalked backwards frantically. The thing was a cross between a centipede and a giant scorpion. It was a nightmarish size—at least three feet in length. Its disgusting body was made up of fat brown segments and hundreds of tiny twitchy legs. The monstrosity reared up, all jittery and undulating, making an obscene clicking noise with its pincers.

Then there was a flash of blue light, and its head exploded in a splatter of pink goo.

"Nice shot!" Moe shouted. "Gotcha, you nasty sucker!"

Zippo did not stop for a victory mewl. He took aim at the other insectoids making their way down the hall. "Go! Go *naow*!" Zippo meowed.

Jeremy attempted to get up, slipping on the creature's pink goo and falling to the carpet. He accepted a hand from Moe as Zippo fired off a few more shots.

"Come on, that might be a turbolift over there," Moe said. They sprinted to a door with a sliver of light underneath it, pushing the button to summon the lift.

Zippo continued firing, stopping once to load a fresh electropak into his gun. Jeremy glanced back at him. To his horror, he could see more creatures skittering out of the darkness and down the hall. Some clung to the ceiling and the walls.

"Yeah? What do you want?" a voice came from the other side of the door. It was gravelly, but feminine.

"Let us on! We need the lift!" Moe shouted.

"Heh. Hun, there's no turbolift here."

Zippo held off the onslaught of creatures, but Jeremy could tell their numbers were increasing. And they were getting closer. Some of Zippo's shots sailed off in the darkness, momentarily lighting up the black corridor. There were hundreds of them, all bathed in electric blue.

Jeremy looked to Moe, as if to confirm what he'd just seen.

Moe gulped. "Just open up! Or...or we'll blast the door!" Moe said, taking aim with his pistol. "I'll do it!"

"Hey now! Don't do anything stupid! If you blast the door, how will you stop those things from getting in here?" the voice said.

Jeremy raised his eyebrows. She had a point.

Moe was having none of it. "Open it up or we're all bug food! I'm not kidding, lady!" Moe leveled his phaser at the door and started counting. "One! ... Two! ..."

The skittering sound had amplified into a disgusting symphony of thousands of dirty chopsticks. Zippo's shots had also slowed down. *Must be low on ammo*, Jeremy thought. He looked back and caught Zippo plugging two more of the creatures. The rest of the bugs were momentarily distracted, feasting on the pink goo of their fallen comrades.

But the snack barely slowed them down. They pressed forward again. One darted straight at Zippo's foot from the side.

"Zippo! On the floor to your right!" Jeremy screamed.

Zippo lifted his foot just in time. He slammed it down, stomping the bugger. He yowled in loathing as it squished under his paw. "*Yeeugh*! Guise! Open door! Naow!"

"Six! ... Seven! ..."

"Hey wait, wait, you never said what number you're going to count to!" the voice hesitated. "Okay fine! Just get in here!"

The door squeaked open, fluorescent light spilling into the corridor. Moe and Jeremy scrambled in, followed by a rewling Zippo. He blasted his ray into the hall a few final times as the door closed behind him. He then collapsed to the floor, panting and covered in pink goo.

"What in *Hades* were you guys doing out there?!" the voice asked.

Jeremy turned to see who was talking. It was a small, fat, lap dog. A Yorkshire Terrier, to be exact. Her dirty blonde and gray fur was short but silky, and her pointy ears and little black nose gave her a rather scrappy look.

She stood on a foot stool by the door's controls, hopping down and trotting over to Zippo. She gave him a few sniffs, as if curious about the goop dripping off his body. Her short stumpy legs reminded Jeremy of a potbellied pig.

"You guys are really dumb," the yorkie said.

Jeremy checked on Zippo, asking him if he was all right. Zippo lay on the floor for a few moments, breathing heavily.

"Didn't you see that huge sign when you came in?" the dog continued. "I spray painted a warning right on it, in plain Cerberon! 'TURN BACK NOW, DEATH AWAITS.'"

Moe realized he recognized the dog's voice. He squatted to look her in the face. "Oh. It's YOU!" he sounded supremely annoyed.

Zippo sat up and looked at the dog. "Madi Nabo!" he mewled in dismay and lay back down.

Jeremy recognized the name from Moe's Quash Board. "Madi Nabo?"

"The one and only!" She scampered over to Jeremy and sniffed him all over. "Have we met? Dang, you smell good! I like this guy! Is that bacon?"

She nudged one of Jeremy's pockets. He reached down, surprised to find a forgotten strip of leftover bacon in there. He took it out and she snatched it from his hand, holding it in her little jaws. Madi Nabo trotted away, munching happily.

"How did you get out of prison?" Moe asked.

"You two idiots...only caught me...accidentally!" She yipped between chews. "Do you think the mangy brains at Frozen Angels Rehab could keep me locked up? I was released early, for being a good girl!"

"And what are you doing on this station? Does Nebz know you're down here?"

"Of course!" she yapped. "Who do you think hired me?"

"Hired you? To do what?" Moe asked.

Jeremy picked up an empty wrapper from an enormous pile on the floor, "Tycho Blasters quality inspector?" He picked up another. "Taste tester for Nudgefudge Yumyums?"

Zippo looked up with interest. "Nudgefudge Yum? Ware?"

"There's a box of them over there," the dog motioned with her head.

The windowless room was not exactly how Jeremy imagined a cutting edge space station. It was extremely drab, painted in a depressing tone of industrial gray. It contained a shabby old couch, a cracked televid screen, and a sink with faucet. A wrinkled paper sign taped to some empty cupboards read: Wendigo Employee Lounge.

It appeared Madi Nabo had made herself at home in the room. At her size, the old couch was a bed fit for an empress. Wrappers and empty bags were strewn about, along with many unopened boxes of prepackaged snacks. An overturned vending machine lay on its side, its facade shattered all over the carpeted floor. It also appeared empty.

"I'm head security officer and pest eradicator of this station!"

"Pest eradicator? Wow!" Moe chortled. "You don't say!"

"I was wondering how they managed to keep this place so *pest-free!*" Jeremy joined in. "Who can we talk to about recommending a promotion?"

Zippo looked genuinely baffled.

"What part of pest eradication requires you to lock yourself in the employee lounge?" Moe asked.

"You're joking, right?" Madi Nabo yipped. "Have you seen those things? Uh, no way. I'm never going out there." She trotted over to one of the open boxes. She grasped a package of Nudgefudge Yumyums in her jaws and flung them at Zippo.

"Tenks."

"*Saaay*, here's an idea," Madi said. "Instead of using that stupid gun of yours to get us all killed, why don't you blast that pop machine open? The tap water here tastes like pee-pee."

She motioned to the Nova Pop machine in the corner. Moe dialed his phaser to its lowest setting and shot the lock. Moments later, they were all enjoying bottles of five-year-old Grape Galactica.

"This stuff is nasty," Madi said, then thanked Zippo for pouring it into her drinking bowl. "They never consider Cerberon paws when making these bottles!" She furfed in annoyance.

Zippo agreed. "Oh yeh! I hate this things, too! Det stupid."

"And I hate how humanoids complain that I have dog breath! They should try making a tooth brush I can actually hold!"

The two shared stories of human-centric manufacturing annoyances.

"Well that's a trip," Moe said quietly.

"What? A talking dog?" Jeremy said.

"No, just seeing those two getting along. Cerberons and Felinians don't usually...*click*. Remind me and I'll tell you about it sometime." [*Translator's Note: Moe here is referring to the centuries of historical animosity between the Felinian and Cerberon races, dating back to the Greeno/Hades Conflict of B-504. An uneasy alliance has been maintained since the signing of the Paws of Peace Accord, but enmity continues to simmer to this day in the form of racial slurs (drooler, paw-licker, booty-sniffer, etc.) —ChatterBot 3.6*]

After they'd helped themselves to some snacks, Jeremy demonstrated his spellcasting ability by conjuring up Madi Nabo's requested foods (i.e. more bacon and some sausage). She then agreed to show them the way to the working turbolift. "Follow me, boys."

Madi appeared to prefer the ancestral Cerberon method of walking on all fours. She trotted to a panel at the back of the room that had been removed. The opening led to a low passage that connected the employee lounge to another messy corridor. The overhead lights came on as they emerged.

"This part of the station is pretty safe," Madi Nabo explained. "I *think*. I never saw any bugs in here." She scurried along, hopping over the occasional fungi pods and sidestepping any red carpet stains.

They eventually reached some working turbolift doors. "All right, so we're even now," she yapped. "No more trying to bring me back to Frozen Angels, okay?"

"I thought you said you did your time and were released," Moe said.

Madi Nabo snorted. "You guys really *are* dumb. Okay byeee!" She turned and trotted away as they entered the elevator.

CHAPTER 31

THE PALE GREEN ADONIS

The circular control room rested atop the very pinnacle of Bolero Station. A dome of plaz windows encased the office. The center of the room was occupied by a wide ring of desks and workstations, each one topped with bulky computers, combobulators, and a kaleidoscopic array of buttons that blinked on and off. The first thing Jeremy noticed upon entering the room was its panoramic view of the stars, which was breathtaking.

The second thing he noticed was a naked green frog man squatting in the middle of the workstations, surrounded by garbage.

"Yo! Nebz!" Moe called out to the frog man, who ignored him.

As they approached the offworlder, Jeremy saw (to his relief), that his initial assessment was inaccurate. The alien was indeed wearing at least one article of clothing: a small pair of briefs. They were the kind the boys back at Pigpimples lovingly referred to as *tightee whiteys*, although a more accurate name for what the frog man was wearing would be *loose-and-alarmingly-discolored-ees*.

The frog man also had on a pair of giant, oversized

headphones, despite the fact that alien rock music blared from various speakers scattered throughout the room.

Although most of the office was spotless, frog man's work area was filthy. His desk and the floor surrounding it was covered in sotus noodle cups, candy bar wrappers, several cans of Bisko's #1 Compressed Cheese, Mighty Janny's Instant Dinner trays, empty Nova Pop bottles, empty snack food baggies (the DJ's beloved Crispity Crickets, Jeremy guessed), and stacks of crystal discs, magtapes, and old comic books.

There were also several televid screens stacked among the computers. One of the screens displayed a paused game of *Jessica Gelato: Average School Girl*. Others just displayed endless static fuzz.

The DJ's rolling chair was parked in front of a vast recording soundboard. There were so many sliding faders, twisty knobs, and buttons on it that Jeremy wondered how anyone could ever keep track of them all. The frog man remained squatting and staring into what appeared to be either a televid screen or an oven; Jeremy couldn't tell which. The boxy device emitted a shrill beep, after which the frog man excitedly opened its door and snatched out a cup of sotus noodles.

It must have been hot. The frog man jerked his hand back and dropped the cup on the floor with a croak. Scalding water and wet noodles splattered everywhere. He sucked on an elongated finger for a moment before laying a single paper towel on the mess.

Then the offworlder turned, noticing his guests for the first time. "Oh, hi guys! How y'all doin'?" he groggled. He pushed his headphones back so they rested around his neck. The offworlder's appearance, while not outright terrifying, was nevertheless off-putting to Jeremy. The alien had the head of a frog, complete with bulbous eyes and an enormous, yet amiable, mouth. His pupils had a golden hue, and his algae-green skin had a clammy, rubbery sheen that looked permanently moist. He had no neck to speak of, and a fat potbelly pudged over his skivvies.

"Sorry fer de mess, just makin' muhself a little dinner here."

"It's fine, dude! Got any more of them Mighty Janny's dinners? Barbeque Floohm'bay Tenders?" Moe asked, making himself at home and rummaging through some of the trash on one of the desks.

"Check da freezebox," Nebz croaked.

Jeremy still didn't understand how this could be DJ Nebz, as his blorpy squarkling sounded nothing like the smooth voice they'd been listening to on the radio for the past two days.

"Oh! One sec, gentlemen—I see it's that time again. Let me do mah thing and I'll be right with you." Nebz motioned for them to sit in some of the abandoned swivel chairs. The DJ went to his console, slipping his headphones back on and lowering the studio mic to his lips. He slid various faders up and down with his long fingers as he spoke.

"Welcome back, starhoppers. We just ended an hour-long retrospective on some of the late-era work of Jirrik Terbur, the famous Hadoxian singer-songwriter, and multimonica player..."

Then Jeremy understood. As DJ Nebz spoke into the microphone, his mixer console translated his nasally croaks into the smooth, rich voice broadcast over the waves.

"You figured out his secret, huh kid?" Moe asked.

"I was starting to wonder where he kept the man hostage that we'd been listening to."

"Ha! That's showbiz for you. It's all a big scam, really."

"...Oh and Mighty Janny's Mutano Doomgrub Instamash—? Superb! I will be picking up more of those next time I do a Mars run... But enough talk—I'm still in the mood for some music, and later on we can do some news updates from..." Nebz checked some crystal disks on his desk, "...Looks like we've got stuff from Koshion, and the Greeno Sector."

Zippo's ears twitched at the mention of his home. Interstellar news and information could only travel as fast as the fastest starships, which meant it could take weeks or even months to hear anything from far-away systems. It was always nice to hear news from one's homeworld.

"...And wherever you are on the starways, keep it tuned to FM 104!" Nebz blerped the station announcement, hanging up his headphones once the music started.

"Guys! How the heck are ya?!" He waddled over, arms outstretched. Moe clenched his eyes shut as the frog man embraced him and Zippo in a group hug. "Well? Whaddya think?" Nebz said, beaming. He extended his arm, gesturing to his domed office.

"It's a beautiful station, Nebz. The top part, anyway," Moe said. Jeremy and Zippo agreed.

"Ain't it great! I got such a good deal on dis here place, you have no idea!" Nebz blorped with pride.

Moe sniffed. "You might want to run some background checks on your hired help, though. Did you know your little Cerberon head of security is an escaped criminal?"

"Cerberon? Head of security? Yer talkin' about that little Terran doggie I picked up?"

"Doggie? Holmes, she's no dog! Does the fact that she *talks* not set off any alarm bells?"

DJ Nebz looked to Zippo. "Nabz! Wat wrong with you?"

Nebz chorkled. "Guys, didja accidentally eat some of them magic fungus pods down there? You're hallucinatin'! Soph doesn't talk!"

"Soph?" Jeremy asked.

"That's her name! The pet store on Mars said she was, ya know, good at chasin' away rats and varmints and stuff. The guys who sold me this place said there was a bit of a pest problem, so I put Soph to work! I personally think she did a pretty good job!"

Moe sat Nebz down and spent the next few minutes explaining their little adventure on the sublevels of the station.

Zippo mindspoke some helpful memories of Madi Nabo speaking English to illustrate their point.

"Wew! That's wild!" Nebz croaked. "So yer saying that Soph...she's a...sapient?" [*Translator's Note: common term used to signify any sentient race capable of language and higher thought. —ChatterBot 3.6*]

"Sapient?!" Moe let out an exasperated laugh. "Yes, dude. When we had her in our custody she never shut *up*. And all she talked about was food. I'd say she's pretty sapient!"

DJ Nebz lowered his head. "Oh *dear*...oh dear grok." He looked like he was going to be sick. "I've been walking around this station completely *nude*! She was right there in the sani when I was *showerin'*!" Nebz made a ribbity noise of dismay. "She would just...STARE at me and whine for food! Oh my bog...I feel so...*violated!*" Nebz shuddered, rubbing his arms in disgust. "Me and her are gonna have a very serious talk about some grokkin' BOUNDARIES!"

Zippo shook his head as he patted him on the back. "Bad Madi Nabo. Vary bad."

Nebz looked up at Jeremy, really noticing him for the first time. "And who's the kid? You got a Terran accent, you know that?"

Despite Nebz's slimy sheen, Jeremy offered his hand. "Hi, I'm Jeremy Fletcher."

Nebz grinned, grasping Jeremy's hand with his long fingers. They shook, but he didn't let go. Nebz couldn't stop admiring Jeremy's clothing. "Saaaay! Nice Pigpimples uniform! Boggy! What is that, House Fluffernut, eh? Not my first choice. Or second, really. Actually not even in the top three. But still—*very* boggy outfit!"

A look of recognition overtook Nebz's eyes. Jeremy's heart sank. "You know..." Nebz waggled a finger. "Has anyone ever told you...?"

Jeremy squinted an extremely miffed squint at Moe and

Zippo. Moe slipped on his sunshades to avoid eye contact. Zippo placed a paw by his mouth, concerned.

"You look exactly like—"

Jeremy nodded impatiently.

"TOMMY COBBLESTONE!"

In that moment, Jeremy actually wished the fictional wizard was real—just so he could strangle him with a string of extra fat blood sausages, or some other disgusting Brit food.

Jeremy smiled and nodded. "You don't say?"

Nebz rushed to his desk and picked up a comic book, zooming back to Jeremy and holding the cover up for comparison. "Yeah! Yeah, see?! Oh wow, the glasses, the hair— you are him! *Brrraw brr bwah wah wah!*" DJ Nebz exploded in croakles of swampy laughter. He collapsed to the floor, kicking his legs in hysteria.

Moe could not help himself, and grinned. Zippo, initially upset that they had offended Jrr-mEE, gave in and chuffled. "Yeh, he look liek Tah-mEE, magic boi!" Zippo admitted, smiling.

Jeremy walked over and picked up the comic book as the offworlders continued their hysterics. "Is this going to happen every single time I introduce myself to an alien?" he asked. "We don't all look the same, you know. This little wanker," he tapped the picture of Tommy Cobblestone with his wand as he held the cover next to his face, "looks nothing like me."

"Oh grok, he even has a WAND!" DJ Nebz wheezed, collapsing into another fit of croakles.

CHAPTER 32
SIR DONK'S CAVE CRUNCHERS, NOW WITH 2X MARTIAN MALLOWS!

"So that's the deal, dude. We have three magtapes. Let us use your computers to filter them, and you can have first pick of whatever tunes we find on there. And these are just the beginning. There's much more to come."

Nebz rubbed his slightly inflated throat sac. "I like the sound of that," he said.

Jeremy detected hesitation in his voice.

"We just need enough credits for a down payment, and we'll be in business," Moe pressed.

"Down payment? Oooh, right—you guys still workin' on the nightclub thing? Like you were always talkin' about, huh? Future Blorp?"

"Future *Pop*, yeah. Speaking of which, that's the next item of business we wanted to discuss. Once we have the money, we're gonna build it on Callisto. It's one of the moons of Jupiter—"

Nebz interrupted. "Oh, I know Callisto! It's a *very* hoppin' spot right now. Remember that Kaladorrian tower they found out there, years ago? A lot of investors are movin' in. Hotels, shops. Nightclubs, too! Some very *exclusive* nightclubs, I might add.

Speakin' of which—a little fly buzzed me that an old friend of yers has a gig there."

Moe sat up, confused. "Who?"

"Starruki."

"Who told you *that*?" Moe asked. He and Zippo both looked surprised.

"Some DJ I know workin' outta Ganymede. They say she's doing shows at Heavy Nova."

Moe recoiled. "Homie, get outta here with that Heavy Nova krud! That place is *wack*!"

"I'm just sayin' what I heard! Might be a little too much competition on Callisto right now, that's all."

Moe shook his head emphatically. "Heavy Nova *thinks* they're exclusive—but we have something more *exclusive* than anyone..." Moe looked at Nebz, who stared back expectantly. "*The black hole*, dude! Nobody has its coordinates but us! It's a virtual goldmine of Terran music! Future Pop is gonna be jammin' Terran tunes unavailable anywhere else in the League! Just picture it: all the chicas from around the galaxy lining up to get in! The hottest acts dying to play there! Naturally, we'll need a DJ to host the funkiest parties—you diggin' what I'm saying, homeboy?" Moe nudged Nebz in his pudgy green belly.

Nebz smiled. "Hmmm...I haven't seen any Amphibion babes in years! Sounds very boggy," he croaked. "But what about the station? Q-HOP is my baby, guys. I can't just abandon her."

"Nobody is asking you to! How does a permanent sponsorship from Future Pop sound? You come DJ for us once in a while, we pay for some upgrades to boost your station's signal. Then you run commercials for the nightclub! Everyone on the starways will hear about it! It's win-win!"

"I'm lovin' this plan!" Nebz said, rubbing his hands together. But his smile faded. He gulped. "Although I gotta be honest with you, buds. Buyin' this place pretty much wiped me out. I don't have a lot of cash to spare at the moment..." He lifted a finger, "But what if, in exchange for a couple of choice cuts, I put you in touch with a potential buyer? I know someone who would be *very* interested in radio-dipped music. I bet they'd pay you more than enough money."

Moe looked to Zippo, who raised his eyebrows hopefully. Moe sighed and nodded. "That would be mighty funky of you, homie."

Nebz shook hands with Moe and Zippo. "All right! Let's see what's on them grokkin' tapes!"

[*Translator's Note: A full magtape can hold a little over a tintobyte of data, which is (trust me) quite a lot! Because any magtape used in black hole radio dipping is bound to contain a lot of worthless static and white noise, it must be filtered. Manual filtration can be tricky; listening to all the static and white noise on one tape alone would take approximately one hundred and sixty-eight years. Since most of us don't have that kind of time, thank goodness for black hole filtering software from Seashell Systems! I'm legally required to add that Seashell Systems in NO WAY endorses the use of their software for radio piracy or infringing on the future intellectual properties of third parties! Don't you get any wild ideas, guys! —ChatterBot 3.6*]

＊　＊　＊

"Novo collazio!" Jeremy dabbed and tapped his wand, transforming more of the Amphibion's garbage into another bowl of cereal.

"Where the *bog* did you find this kid?!" Nebz croaked, slapping his hands together wildly. He rushed over to inspect the bowl. "And what do you call this kind?" Nebz asked.

"It's Branno-Bix. It was the only other cereal we had at Pigpimples."

Nebz tried a spoonful. "Ugh! What *is* this stuff?! It's worse than the other one!" Bits of cereal flew out of Nebz's mouth as he croaked in disgust. He placed the bowl aside with the other bowl of rapidly soggying Fortified Oat Flakes. He then wiped bits of Branno-Bix off his freakishly long tongue with a paper towel. "I can't believe they made you eat that at Pigpimples! That's just grokkin'...*abusive*!"

"I dunno, the Fortified Oat Flakes aren't too bad." Jeremy shrugged. "Gotta hit them with a little sugar."

The magtape filtering process took several hours using the station's computers. In the meantime, they entertained themselves. Jeremy noticed Zippo curled up in one of the swivel chairs. The Felinian was passed out, the P-Shell's nubs stuffed into his ears. Moe was looking through the DJ's comic book collection.

"You said you wanted the kind of cereal a real Pigpimples student would eat! Well, there you go. Fortified Oat Flakes or Branno-Bix," Jeremy said. "Those were our only options."

"But what about Sir Donk's?" Nebz protested.

"Sir Donk's?"

"Yeah! Sir Donk's Cave Crunchers!"

"Ohhh I get it," Jeremy understood, "is that some brand of American cereal?"

"Uhh...well in the commercial they're speakin' English, so I thought it was from England."

Jeremy shook his head. "No, but I see where you're confused. America has *way* better cereals than England. I still remember a few of them. Let's see here..." Jeremy created a buffet of all the American breakfast cereals he could remember from his youth. A veritable cornucopia of rainbow-colored bits, crisps, and flakes shimmered before them.

"Now over here you have your basics—" he motioned his wand over the corn flakes and crisp rice. "Not bad at all; maybe a little bland. I think a man of your discerning tastes will be more interested in these sugar-based offerings here." Jeremy pointed his wand at bowls of Jinkie Spheres, Choco-Frosties, and

Ultimate Berry Shredders.

Nebz's eyes lit up with joy. He picked up the bowl of Choco-Frosties, sifting through the cereal with his gangly fingers as if to inspect it. He set it down, milk dripping from his hand, and moved on to Jinkie Spheres. He plunged his hand in. "No marshmallows?" he said, digging through the cereal. He was making a mess.

"Marshmallows?" Jeremy said. "What the devil are you talking about?"

Nebz removed his hand and shook it off, sending bits of cereal everywhere. "You know, like Sir Donk's Cave Crunchers—*now with Martian Mallows*!"

Jeremy turned his hands up in defeat. "Never heard of it. Must have come out after I moved away," he said.

"Well, that's all right. Just make some marshmallows for deez other ones, then! I'll just mix 'em in. I like muh mallows *very* marshy, if you could." Nebz held out the bowl of Berry Shredders.

"Actually, I...can't." Jeremy said. "I can only do *breakfast* foods. And marshmallows aren't a breakfast food."

"Yes they are!" Nebz hopped up, excited.

"Well—" Jeremy considered the fact that he was conversing with a frog man wearing nothing but BVDs in a space station beyond Mars. He realized his definition of *breakfast* might strike some as limited. He clarified: "They're not a breakfast food where *I'm* from. I've never seen marshmallows served with cereal before. I just... I can't do it! The spell is very finicky that way."

"I'll show you!" Nebz said, rushing over to a filing cabinet. Zippo remained conked out in his swivel chair in front of the cabinet, so the Amphibion rolled him out of the way before yanking a drawer open. He pulled out a cassette tape and went to one of his televid screens. "They just haven't been invented yet," Nebz explained, sliding the cassette into a player, "but they will be—check this out! Moe, have I showed you this one?"

Moe joined them. A fuzzy, distorted image flashed onto the screen. The vid was of such poor quality that it was hard to make out, but it appeared to be an animated commercial for a breakfast cereal. The cartoon began with a little pink alien abducting a caveman. The alien then went into some kind of time warp, dropping the caveman off at a medieval castle. The caveman donned a suit of armor and fought a dragon, winning a bowl of cereal as his prize. An insane jingle played the whole time, which Nebz sang along to. *"SIR DONK'S CAVE CRUNCHERS™!"* an announcer shouted gleefully.

"NOW WITH TWICE AS MANY MARTIAN MALLOWS™! FOR A LIMITED TIME!" the cartoon alien flew over the bowl, sprinkling hundreds of marshmallows into the cereal.

"Nebz, *this* is what you're spending credits on? Where did you even find this krud?" Moe asked.

"Some Volzoid pirate on Mars! Says he dipped it out of a black hole near the Anuthek System. Terran commercials all the way out there! Boggy, huh?"

Another ad began to play. It showed an automobile cruising along a road. The car was unlike anything Jeremy had ever seen. *"The 1972 Atlas Temperment—a vehicle for the man in total control of his passions..."* Nebz pressed the stop button and ejected the tape.

"1972? How did you get a recording from fifty years in the future?" Jeremy asked. "But more importantly, why is a caveman knight selling alien-themed cereal?"

"Video-dipping," Moe said. "It's just radio-dipping, but for televids. Much more complicated, and yields fewer results. I don't really get it, personally, but some people are obsessed. Mostly you get commercials and sitcoms. Waste of time!"

"But see, young 'un? See? Marshmallows *are* a breakfast food! This is proof!" Nebz waggled the cassette tape in triumph, returning to his bowl of Berry Shredders.

Jeremy tilted his head and made a satisfied grunt. "You've educated me! Let's try it again." He rolled up his sleeves and pointed his wand at the bowl. "Novo Collazio!"

Marshmallows appeared in the cereal. DJ Nebz squarkled in delight. "Yeah! All right! Now do this one, but with more marshmallows! ALL marshmallows!"

"But in the commercial—" Jeremy started.

"You saw how many Martian Mallows there were! Twice as many—*for a limited time only*! That stuff was practically all mallows! C'mon! Try it!"

Nebz went and grabbed an enormous salad bowl, emptying a wastepaper basket into it. He held it up. "Fill 'er up!"

Jeremy concentrated and cast the spell again. The trash shimmered into a mountain of multi-colored marshmallows with a few bits of cereal here and there. "They're not *exactly* like the ones you showed me...but I think they're the closest we're going to get. Show me another commercial of an all-mallow cereal and then we'll talk," Jeremy said.

Nebz hopped about. "No, no. This is good! This is *toady*! I've been watchin' that tape for six months. I can't wait to try 'em!" he cradled the giant bowl in the crook of his arm, raising a heaping spoonful of Martian Mallows to his mouth. He stopped. "Wait!" he rushed over to the oven box he'd been squatting in front of earlier. "Let's microwave 'em first! Get them mallows all nice'n gooey!"

"Microwave?" Jeremy asked.

"It's a... kind of cooking tech. Does your world not have 'em yet? How da grok do you cook up sotus noodles?!" Nebz placed the bowl in the microwave, shut the door, and set the timer for sixty seconds. The microwave hummed to life. "Ya see, the oven blasts yer food with this special kind of radiation. Makes da food cook real good... You can do all sorts of foods with it, too. Grok nuggets, beetle bombs, instant mappy fly puddin'..."

As Nebz continued listing various examples of disgusting

foods, Jeremy stared at the rotating bowl of cereal. Something odd was happening. The marshmallows appeared to be...*growing*! They were like little colorful balloons, all inflating at the same time. Jeremy wondered whether this was a part of his spell, but detected no magic.

It must be something this "micro wave" device is doing.

As the seconds ticked by, the mallows expanded and fused themselves into one, big, multicolored blob. The blob puffed up bigger and bigger, spilling over the sides of the bowl.

"...Oh, oh—those deep-fried sandworm poppers! And Crispity Crickets, of course—"

Seconds later and the bowl disappeared entirely, engulfed by the ever-expanding mallow blob. The microwave rattled as the puffy mass filled every crevice of its interior, top to bottom. A solid wall of marshmallow pushed against the front door of the oven.

Jeremy raised a finger to interrupt the Amphibion. Nebz glanced down at the microwave. "What the bog is goin' on?!"

The box jittered madly as marshmallow bubbled out its side vents. It convulsed as sparks popped from its back. The hum turned into a high-pitched whine, which morphed into a full-on screech. The front window cracked.

"It's too much pressure! Hull integrity compromised! Stand back!" Moe shouted, yanking Jeremy away.

The microwave's plastic door blasted open. The blobby mass exploded out the front before deflating into a gooey, candy-colored mess. Mallow goop dripped onto the floor as black smoke billowed from the oven's remains. Nebz squatted, swirling some of the goo onto his long finger. He made sure to get a few charred bits of cereal on there, too. "Oooh!" He slurped the colorful slime off his finger. "It's not bad!" he said, going back for a second taste.

Nebz's main computer made a pleasant *droing!* sound. "The magtapes!" Moe said. He turned to Jeremy. "Do *not* let him touch anything until he's washed his hands."

* * *

Jeremy went to check on Zippo, who was still curled up and virtually comatose. He pulled one of the nubs out of Zippo's twitching ear. "Zippo? Zip? You awake?" Jeremy tried not to startle him. He wanted to avoid getting clawed again. He tugged to remove the other ear nub. The moment it popped out, Zippo awoke.

"Wha— Whuz?!" he looked around, confused and groggy.

"The magtapes are finished. Do you want to come check them out? We're going to listen to them now."

Zippo appeared confused, so Jeremy helped him up and walked him to the computer.

Moe didn't look very happy. "I just don't get it! This is WACK!" He was at the computer, calling up and reviewing the data.

"Wat matter, Moe?" Zippo asked.

"There's only thirty minutes of music on these, tops!"

Jeremy looked to Zippo, who also appeared concerned.

"Is that bad?" Jeremy said.

"Three magtapes! THREE! I get one of them being a dud, it happens. Two—it's rare but possible. But all three?!" Moe cursed in Binosian.

"Maybe com-PEW-ter is...wrong?" Zippo mewed.

Moe shook his head. "Nah. I thought so, too. But look. You can clearly see here," he pointed to something on the screen, "they were double-checked."

"Maybe Moe...uhm...mess up?" Zippo suggested sheepishly.

Moe threw up his hands in exasperation. "I don't know, Zip—you tell me! You were in charge of anchoring the nano-filament! You said the harmonic calibration was good!" Moe swiveled around.

Zippo sighed, hurt.

"How much music is normal for one magtape?" Jeremy asked, attempting to ease the tension.

"Oh, twanty, tharty hour..." Zippo explained. "Lass time, we get twanty-saven hour and eighteen MEE-nut. From same bleck holl..." He shifted nervously.

Moe swiveled back to the screen. "But this! This is nothing! Recordings all start off normal, but then drop out after a few minutes."

"Heh. That's a bummer," Nebz croaked. He was trying to clean his hands with a paper towel, but was not getting anywhere. "Might have been a solar flare, or you were dippin' during an event horizon anomaly. Could be lotsa stuff. Sometimes you just get bad dips. These things happen, ya know."

Moe slammed his fist on the desk and laid his head down in defeat.

"Why don't we listen to what's on the tapes, first? Maybe you picked up something really... uh...*boggy*?" Jeremy proposed, looking to Nebz for approval.

"The kid's right! Quit bein' such a li'l tadpole!" Nebz said, shoving Moe out of the swivel chair. Moe fell to the floor and laid on his back, arms and legs splayed out melodramatically. Nebz adjusted the volume controls on the console and pushed the play button.

The good news was that the recordings were clearly of Terran origin. Although no specific dates were mentioned, Nebz estimated that, by their sound, they came from the 1980s.

The bad news was: the songs weren't terribly interesting. Apart from one little punk rock ditty ("Your Putrid Heart Can Rot" by Shattered Pelvis), they'd only captured run-of-the-mill pop ballads.

"Great," Moe said. "Seven and a half songs. That's barely enough for one setlist. I'm guessing your buyer isn't going to waste his time on thirty minutes of music?"

Nebz rubbed his throat sac. "You're right, it's not much. The Archive usually goes for...bigger collections, ya know? Now here's what I'm thinkin': you go back to that black hole of yours, you try again—get yerself at least ten, eleven hours of good Terran stuff... You'll be in business in no time!"

"Hold up, hold up..." Moe removed his shades incredulously. "The...Archive?"

Zippo's eyes widened.

"Yeah," Nebz ribbited, "but they usually won't talk to yeh over a little set of songs like that."

"Nebz..." Moe placed a hand on Nebz's arm. "You're not talking about...*the* Archive?"

"The *Massif Prime Archive*, sure!" Nebz squarked.

Moe looked stunned, as if doubting his own senses.

"What's the *Massif Prime Archive*?" Jeremy asked.

"Oh, it's somethin' else. Biggest library of music in the galaxy!" Nebz gushed. "Every recording from every planet in every star system! And their black hole collection—just amazin'. They have the rarest of the rare. Pirated stuff you couldn't even dream of! Stuff radio dipped from I don't know *how* many different timelines, different dimensions. Tintobytes of music! I heard they've got the only surviving recording of Trib-Trib Boohanee's experimental jazz album that was so bad it brought about the collapse of Gigas 4! Grok, I'd love to hear that one... The Archive buys and sells it all. They operate out of this big ol' cargoliner, flyin' around the quadrant. They never stay in one place for too long, so they never get caught," Nebz tapped his head. "Smart!"

Moe interrupted. "Yeah, Nebz—but they won't even talk to you without a Primo Token..."

Nebz flipped a shiny gold coin at Zippo, who caught it mid-air.

"There ya go," Nebz said.

"Wat the..?" Zippo held up the coin. It was covered in alien writing. He sniffed it furiously.

"A Primo Token?!" Moe rushed over, taking the coin from Zippo's paw. He examined it. "This is *fresh*!"

"He give it to ME," Zippo muttered, snatching the coin back from Moe.

"But do you actually know their coordinates?" Moe asked.

"Oh sure," Nebz croaked, "they're here in the Sol System. Right now!"

"What?!" Moe shouted in excitement. Zippo clasped his paws together hopefully.

Nebz groggled. "You said so yerself: this system is the *place* to *be*! They got here a few weeks ago. Hangin' out near Jupiter, last I heard. Word on the starways is they're stockin' up, too! Payin' top credit for any and all Terran music! Radio-dipped, pirated...although right now the REAL big money is in legit recordings by Terran artists. Because those are nice and legal, ya know. Especially if you've got anything rare, or unique. Stuff you can't just buy in music stores."

Moe looked at Jeremy. "Dude..." It was all he had to say. Jeremy fetched Zippo's backpack, unzipped it, and pulled out one of his father's albums. The black disc was labeled, *Zelda Cookie featuring Fibbonacci's Fantastical Mood Orchestra.* He held it up. "Do they take phonograph records?"

CHAPTER 33

INTRUDER ALERT

"All set, homies. Zipponio, start her up."

The *Terrapin*'s engines spun to life. In the end, they'd decided to let Nebz keep the seven and a half radio-dipped songs. "We're going to make fat stacks off all those albums," Moe reasoned, "so who cares?"

Jeremy and Zippo agreed.

After Zippo had called up the station's blueprints on one of Nebz's computers, they realized they could take a cargo elevator directly down to the docking bay. Nebz had scrawled the coordinates for the *Massif Prime Archive* onto a paper towel and sent them on their way. As a token of gratitude, Jeremy left Nebz with a small mountain of marshmallow cereal.

Nebz's voice crackled over the ship's comm. "Thanks again for the tunes, buds. Good luck with Future Blorp!"

"10-4, duder," Moe responded. "We'll see you starside. *Terrapin* out." Moe replaced the receiver as the docking bay doors opened. "Program those coordinates into the navicomputer," he said to Zippo, handing him the paper towel. "Oh, and while you're at it—why don't you start a deep-hull scan. Let's make sure none of those nasty buggers made it onto the ship while we were gone."

"Yeh," Zippo mewed, initiating a scan.

Moe piloted the ship out of the space station. After Zippo plotted the new coordinates, a number appeared on the navigational screen. "Hmmm," Zip hummed, pointing Moe's attention to the number.

"All right. This many bips to intercept flight path, plus trajectory..." Moe calculated in his head. "Should take us...four days. We can max out subglimmer drives once we clear Bodie's Belt, which will help."

"Okey," Zip meowed. Now that they were settling in, he started grooming himself. Mister Squeakeasy appeared on the navigational monitor. Zippo grumbled in disgust.

"Hi guys! Deep-hull scan complete! Everything appears normal, except you've got an unknown entity hanging out in cabin two! It sounds hungry, whatever it is! Might want to check that out! Be careful!" The animated mouse pointed to a schematic of the starship. A red dot flashed over Zippo's cabin.

"Is he talking about the hamster?" Moe said.

"No! I add Doh-nat to ship manifest alreddy."

Moe drew his phaser. "Let's go."

* * *

Zippo placed his ear against the sliding door of his cabin. "Oh!" he pulled back, drawing his gun. "Oh, it sound *so* gross! It dis-GUS-ting!"

Moe listened at the door. "Ugh! There's something in there...eating...loudly. I hope it didn't get your little critter..."

Jeremy's mouth went agape in horror.

"Wha?" Zippo shrieked. "What, you..? *NiiiRRiyaEew!* NOOOO!" Zippo slid the door open, aiming and ready to zap the bugger to pieces.

However, there was no insectoid. There was just Madi Nabo, standing on the floor and helping herself to some of Zippo's

Toastee Mums. She looked up at them, unmoved by Zippo's screaming. She swallowed.

"Hi."

Her tiny muzzle was covered in crumbs and Toastee Mum jam. She licked her chops noisily and returned to working on the toaster pastry. She had a very loud and snorty way of eating, reminiscent of a pig rooting through a soggy paper bag.

Zippo rushed to the shelf to check on Donut. She was asleep.

"How did you get in here?!" Moe asked.

"It was open," Madi Nabo said.

"But Madi, why? I must have made you enough Toastee Mums to last you a decade," Jeremy said.

"Bleh. That station sucked. The killer bugs, no good TV, that disgusting frog man walking around nude all day," she shuddered, "uh, no thanks. Just drop me off wherever, 'cause I am DONE with that place."

"I should eject you out the airlock," Moe waved his gun at her. "Standard procedure for stowaways, you know. Bad girl!"

"Heh!" Madi barked. "This rinky dink ship has an airlock?" She finished the Toastee Mum, then rooted around for any crumbs she missed.

"You get OUT of here!" Zippo rawled. He walked at her and shooed her out of the cabin with his foot. She wandered off down the hall into the cargo bay, in search of more food.

"Wat we do wit her?" Zippo asked. He wrinkled his nose. "Eeugh! Smell like slobber-tongue! *Gross*!" He switched on a fan.

"There's a whole lot of nothing between here and the *Massif Prime*," Moe said. "I don't want to waste time altering course right now. Let's just make it to the Archive, then we can drop her off at a detention center."

"Or the pound," Jeremy added.

CHAPTER 34

BAD GUYS INTERLUDE #4

The Perfect Stranger approached Bolero Station. "There she is, captain. The radio signal is definitely originating from her."

Mike Mania rubbed his paws together. "Unbelievable!" he growled with pleasure. "I've had agents trying to track this place down for over a year! And those morons led us right to it in a matter of days! Ha haw!" He spoke to Charles, who was having some trouble getting his ruffled collar on. Mike always insisted that they dress up in Cerberon finery for any raid.

"You there, Dave!" Mike pointed at a deck hand. "Prepare a boarding party! We're going to show Q-HOP the meaning of copyright infringement! It will be *glorious*!" he clenched his paw in emphasis. Then his ears shot up. An unfamiliar sound chimed on the bridge. It was some kind of alert noise. "What the Hades is that?! Fix it immediately!" he pointed at the communications officer.

"Sir, that's...that's an incoming etheric flux call."

Mike froze. No wonder he didn't recognize it. He'd never received a call while on assignment. It could only mean one thing.

"Looks like it's coming from... Mrs. Crawford," the officer said. "Shall I take the call?"

"Yes, you fool! Put it on screen, before she has us all legally murdered!"

The officer tapped a few keys. A deranged face appeared on the navigational screen. It was smiling madly, stringy blonde hair drooping in front of its eyes.

"Hello, Tim," Mike grumbled.

A gloved hand pushed aside the blonde hair. "Mii-iiike," Tim sang. He had the heavy cockney accent of a Londoner. "Yoouuu're in trooouuuu-ble!" The cyborg's voice made Mike's skin crawl.

"Yeah, yeah." Mike didn't even want to look at him. "Will you please just put her through and let me talk to her?"

"Mii-iiike! It was nice knowin' you, mate! Tee-hee-hee!"

It took all of Mike's efforts to not pant with dread. "What is *wrong* with that guy? He is such a weirdo!" he growled under his breath.

Tim's face was replaced by the face of an old woman. Her dark gray hair was pulled back in a bun so tight it almost looked like it would rip the flesh off her skull. Her grimace accentuated her severe, sharp features. Her droopy mouth was nothing but wrinkles; her eyes were wild.

"Mike Mania," she spoke. She sounded angry already.

"Good evening, ma'am. I was just about to call you, actually—"

"Mike Mania, I'm told you had the *Terrapin* in your sights— but you didn't immediately take care of it? Is this true?"

Mike stammered. "Ah yes, about that. See the thing is, pirates like this—they've always got friends all over the place. We figured we might as well follow them for a bit, see where they go. Let them lead us to the bigger infringers, radio pirates, freebooters...all the mangy scumbags in this system. You'd be happy to know that we're about to take down Frogstar Radio right now!"

Mrs. Crawford hissed. "I don't CARE about Frogstar Radio,

Mike! That is NOT your assignment! It NEVER WAS." She put some dangly earrings in as she spoke. "Mike, I don't have time to rehash everything with you. I'm going to be very busy with my next project in the coming weeks, and so I need this done post-haste. Do you understand?"

"Yes, ma'am."

"Good! You know, I was just reading up on some recent advances in veterinary care for this fundraiser I have to attend tonight. Fascinating breakthroughs, Mike. *Really* fascinating."

Mike clenched his teeth. She twisted open a red lipstick and daubed it on her non-existent lips. "Oh yes, did you know that surgical castration leads to a marked decrease in a doggy's territorial marking? That's indoors *and* out, Mike. And you know what—it's healthy, too! Neutering virtually eliminates your dog's chances of getting prostate cancer!"

"Huh, I didn't know that," Charles said thoughtfully. Mike looked horrified.

"It's true, Charles! But what I think is best about castration—and this is important—is that it stops your pet from contributing to overpopulation. You know that's a BIG concern for me, Mike. A very BIG concern. STOPPING certain ANIMALS and their FAMILIES from POP-U-LAT-ING." She emphasized each syllable as she patted her face with powder. Each pat was a knife of terror in Mike's heart. "Just thought I'd *share* that with you both." She smiled.

"Mrs. Crawford, there's no need to talk like that, we're on top of—"

She exploded. "YOU ARE TRYING MY PATIENCE, MIKE! YOUR MISSION WAS TO REPAIR THAT BLACK HOLE AND TIE UP ANY LOOSE ENDS! IT'S BEEN OVER TWO WEEKS! ANY OTHER GRIS AGENT WOULD HAVE *KILLED* FOR THIS OPPORTUNITY! I NEED THIS DONE! *IMMEDIATELY!*"

Charles whimpered as Mike stammered. "Now, I—I...Mrs.

Crawford, we're...we're halfway done as it is! The black hole has been repaired! It's done! We're just gonna go talk to the radio dippers' little DJ friend and see what he knows. Swear to Cerberus! The *Terrapin* is the last loose end!"

"GOOD. NOW TIE. IT. UP!" She stared at Mike with that frozen look of madness for five full seconds before returning to her pre-rage demeanor. She donned a fuzzy fur hat, adjusting it in a mirror. "Because the sooner this is over, the sooner you can begin your next assignment. I have a shipment of cargo that I'd like you to take care of, personally."

"I look forward to it, Mrs. Crawford."

"Excellent. How do I look?" she posed for Mike and Charles.

"Stunning, Mrs. Crawford," Charles said.

"Thank you. I'm off. And Mike," she cleared her throat.

"Yes?"

"I don't want to have this conversation again. Understood?"

"Yes, ma'am."

She gave a curt nod and ended the call.

"Wow! You are in *trouble*, Mike!" Charles shook his head.

Mike whined. He needed his post-Crawford seltzer.

"And Mikey, why did you tell her that you repaired the black hole? I thought our whole plan was to *not* repair the black hole— I don't get it!"

Mike hopped out of his seat and tackled his brother at the knees, sending him to the floor. He pulled out his glazer and aimed right at his head. "Charles, you idiot! Of course it's not repaired! I don't know *how* she knows what we're doing, but we obviously have a mole on this ship. So—" Mike leaned in, lifting Charles's floppy ear and putting his snout right next to it, "— SHUT UP," he growled.

He nipped his brother on the neck before returning to his seat. He took a deep breath. He hated how that woman brought out the animalistic rage in him. He smoothed down his velvet sleeves and cracked his neck. "Ahem. Ensign, please hail the station."

The ensign hailed. DJ Nebz croakled back his response. "Yeah? Who da grok is this, and what da grok do you want?"

After that run-in with Crawford, Mike was in no mood. He cleared his throat, attempting to maintain his composure. He brushed his stubby claws as he spoke.

"I presume you are the Amphibion who runs Frogstar Radio? This is agent Mike Mania of GRIS. Your station is in gross violation of interplanetary copyright law, including the broadcasting of illegally obtained future transmissions, interdimensional recordings, and the intellectual property of prospective victims. This is not to mention this station's aiding and abetting known radio pirates, audio counterfeiters, and other infringers."

"Okay. Yeah?"

"I am here to inform you that you are to cease broadcasting immediately, by the order of the Galactic Recording Industry Syndicate."

"If you grub munchers think dis is some kinda joke, just know that I've got a neutronic bomb and I'm about to blast it your way," Nebz croaked back. "Best hop on outta here, bud."

"Sir, be aware that we have four torpedos armed and trained on you as we speak, with about two hundred more where that came from. You're only alive right now because I want to have a word with you." Mike paused to let this information sink in. He continued. "But first, I need you to CEASE BROADCASTING NOW!"

It took a minute, but the radio signal stopped. "Okay, bud. You win. It's off... Station's off... No need fer torpedos or any of that stuff! By all means, let's chat."

Mike grinned. This guy was capable of rational thought. *Good.*

"Sir, we will have to have our discussion in person, face-to-face. Just in case anyone is listening in on us."

"All right, give me a minute to get dressed. You can park in...aww grok nuggets, which one was it? Docking bay eleven. Should be big enough for your ship."

"That would do nicely, thank you."

"Hey—can you at least tell me what this is about?"

"Of course. You're going to tell me everything you know about the *Terrapin*. Now prepare to be boarded."

Mike flicked off the comm switch, ending the call. "And prepare to get blown up, you filthy infringer! *ALWAYS REMEMBER THAT WE WILL FIND YOU*! HA HA HAW!" Mike howled into the intercom, pointing his glazer at the station, making *PEW! PEW!* sounds. Charles joined in, laughing.

CHAPTER 35

DISASTER

Zippo was playing Jessica Gelato when the game froze abruptly. The Felinian leaned in close to the monitor, squinting his big cat eyes. An error message appeared on the screen. "Why dis not work?" he meowed.

Jeremy sat in the hallway outside the cockpit, showing off magic tricks to Madi Nabo. She was not impressed. "What's not working?" Jeremy asked.

"Stupid *game*," Zippo pointed at the screen.

"I'm pretty bad at video games, Zip. Are you stuck? Maybe Moe can help you past that part."

Moe had his headphones plugged into his holosynth sticks. He was busy working on a solo for some new song, and drummed away at the air obliviously. Jeremy got up and checked out the screen.

The flashing error message read:

THANKS FOR PLAYING THIS DEMO OF JESSICA GELATO: AVERAGE SCHOOL GIRL! TO CONTINUE YOUR ADVENTURES, MAKE SURE TO PICK UP A REGISTERED COPY OF JESSICA GELATO WHEREVER QUALITY VIDEO GAMES ARE SOLD! STAY AVERAGE!

"Hmmmm..." Jeremy suspected they weren't going to take this news very well. They'd just spent the last three days of their voyage customizing Jessica's hair, makeup, and outfits. "Madi," Jeremy whispered, "go get Moe's attention."

Madi Nabo wandered over to Moe and licked his arm as he drummed. "Hey! Gross!" Moe flipped up the holosynth visor and pushed back his headphones. "Madi Nabo, no! Bad! Enough with the licking! Kid, could you make her some pancakes or something so she'll leave me alone?"

"Why dis not work, Moe?" Zippo asked.

Moe went over and read the error message.

"You have got to be kidding me," he groaned. He pointed at the screen. "This is just a *demo* copy. That jibroni sold us some wack DEMO of the game. It's not the full version!"

Zippo looked horrified. "Dis is *demo*? Yeugh!" he dropped the controller in revulsion.

Jeremy attempted some optimism. "You know, with all the money we're going to make off those albums, we can buy all the video games we want."

Zippo's eyes widened. "Yeh! We bai manny games!"

"Truth," Moe said.

"Okey," Zip meowed cheerily. He leaned over and reset the SuperChromaVision, starting a new game. "I juz pley demo again naow."

Mister Squeakeasy appeared on the navi-control monitor. He flailed his cane around wildly. "Just wanted to let you all know that we're approaching our destination! We'll be there in about fifteen minutes!" He pulled out a pocket watch to illustrate the time.

"Speaking of fat stacks—let's get ready!" Moe said.

"Pleese go AWAY," Zippo waved the mouse off the screen before resuming manual flight control.

The *Massif Prime* was aptly named. Even from afar, Jeremy could tell it was immense. Its hull made a silhouette of blocky hard angles against the stars. A chime in the cockpit indicated a hail from the ship. Zippo accepted the incoming call. A steely voice sounded through the comm.

"That's close enough, tug. Your ship has been scanned and recorded. Identify yourselves and state your business."

Zippo pulled in the *Terrapin* roughly parallel to the hulking cargoliner. The voice returned. "I said that's close enough! We have an orbital beam locked on you, tug. Don't push it!"

Moe scrambled. "Forgot the retrothrusters!" he laughed nervously. He slowed their approach and matched speeds with the other vessel, creating the illusion that they were both floating perfectly still. Moe picked up the handset and spoke. "Hi there. This is Maurice, co-captain of the *Terrapin*. We're here to do a little business with the *Massif Prime Archive*, over."

The comm remained silent for a moment. Then the voice returned. "I assume you have a Primo token, otherwise this conversation is over."

"Of course, homeboy! Where would you like us to dock so we can give it to you?"

"Your tug gets a *micron* closer, and I'm activating the orbital beam! Stay put. We'll send a drone your way. Put the token in, then we'll talk."

"10-4, homesqueeze." Moe turned to Zippo. "You got the token?"

Zippo rummaged through his fanny pack. There was no sign of it. "Wat?! I thought it *here*!" He panicked. A tiny container zoomed out of the *Massif Prime* and floated towards the *Terrapin*. It appeared to be a repurposed mineral box, the kind used for transporting ore samples.

"Zippo! What did you do with it?!" Moe rummaged around the cockpit. Zippo pawed through his fanny pack frantically. A minute later, they heard a thunk at the back of the ship.

The container was attempting to dock in the cargo bay.

"I give it to *you*!" Zippo mewled in dismay.

"I handed it to you on the elevator back at Nebz's place! Remember?! You said it reminded you of a cracker!"

The drone thunked again.

Jeremy realized, with horror, that he knew where the token was. He reached into his pocket and pulled it out.

"Where was it?!" Moe asked. He plucked the coin and rushed to the back end of the ship. Jeremy and Zippo followed.

"I'm sorry!" Jeremy called out. "I was using it for a magic trick for Madi Nabo."

Moe didn't have time to be upset. The cargo bay door opened onto the stars. A white crate, the size of a shoebox, hovered just outside the ship. It was disconcerting for Jeremy to see the rear door seemingly opened onto the vacuum of space. But Zippo had explained to him how the ship's forceshield keeps the cargo bay's atmosphere sealed, while allowing things like drones to pass in and out freely.

The box floated in and landed on the floor. Moe opened it. It was empty except for a small velvet bag, which Moe placed the coin in and strung up. He returned the bag to the drone, shutting the lid. It must have sensed the Primo token, because it hovered up and out of the cargo bay by itself. The trio returned to the cockpit, watching the drone make its way across the void to the other ship.

Nobody spoke.

Finally, the comm came back to life. "I see here you were given this token by Rufo Ribbitz."

They waited a moment, unsure of whether to respond. Moe picked up the receiver and spoke. "Yes, sir. He's a friend." He looked to Zippo and shrugged.

Another minute passed in silence. Finally, they responded. "Any friend of the frog is a friend of ours. Welcome to *Massif Prime*! *Sharing is caring*, and *crush the industry*. What can we do for you today?"

Zippo and Jeremy exhaled in relief.

Moe introduced himself, explaining his situation and how they had "a butt load" of record albums that they'd like to get an estimate on. The voice from *Massif Prime* never gave a name, only identifying himself as an archivist. He instructed Moe to send a couple of samples over first, that way they could get an idea and make an offer.

Another drone box appeared and zoomed its way over to the *Terrapin*. They rushed back to the cargo bay. "Which ones do we show them?" Moe asked.

Jeremy thumbed through the crates, sliding out some choice albums.

"Let's try these," he said. The records were labeled: Patch Pringle, *I Mambo Through Time*, and Gina Lee's Happy Hour, *Starry Night Tango*.

"Ooooh choice cuts, dude. That Patch Pringle was especially funky." Moe looked at the records.

"Yeh, dis musics vary parfect! Mambo mambo!" Zippo gave his "okay" sign.

They laid the two albums in the drone box, sending it back on its way. Jeremy was worried that the records might be too low-tech for such a cutting-edge alien operation, but his fears proved to be unfounded.

"A bit old-fashioned, but we can handle it," the archivist said. "We've scanned each disc's surface and mapped out the grooves and channels, translating them into perfect audio files. We're listening to *Starry Night Tango* right now. Impressive! May I ask where you got these? Our databanks show no entries for either title."

Jeremy spoke. He introduced himself and explained his father's music collection.

"I see," the archivist responded. "You say your dad's a talent agent in Los Angeles? Tell him to keep up the good work. From all the black hole radio I've heard—let's just say that in a few years, California is going to become very important to Terra

Firma's entertainment industry."

Jeremy stopped short. "I...uh. Will do, sir," he answered. He returned the receiver to Moe, who resumed negotiations.

"So let's talk credits. We've got eleven crates of this stuff back here. We came to you guys first because we heard you were the best," Moe winked at Jeremy. "Let's make a deal."

The archivist paused, presumably talking things over with his colleagues. "Ordinarily, we pay fifty credits per Terran record album, depending on its condition."

Zippo's eyes lit up. He clasped his paws in excitement. *He's doing the math in his head,* Jeremy thought.

"However," the archivist continued, "if what you say is true, and your albums are rare recordings that never received official wide releases...that increases their rarity—and value—considerably."

Zippo grinned, grabbing Jeremy by the shoulders.

"For a collection of the size you described...we are ready to offer approximately sixty-four thousand credits. We'll have to look through these crates of yours, of course, before settling on an exact amount."

Moe stammered with excitement. "Of course! Yeah! Sixty-four K sounds very fair—."

Jeremy covered the receiver in Moe's hand, placing a finger on his lips. Moe handed him the comm. "*Massif Prime*? Hi, this is Jeremy Fletcher again. Say, we appreciate your offer, but I don't think we're on the same page yet."

"*What are you saying, dude*?!" Moe hissed. "*You're gonna make them mad*!"

Jeremy covered the receiver again. "It's called *wangling*! My dad told me everyone in the industry does it! *Trust me*!"

"And what exactly did you have in mind?" the archivist responded.

Moe threw his hands up and backed away, impressed. "Watch the kid wangle!" he whispered to Zippo. Zippo bit a claw, nervous.

Jeremy cleared his throat, praying his voice wouldn't crack. "First, I'd like to remind you guys about a little thing called *quality. Recording* quality. You can hear the quality of these albums for yourselves. These aren't field recordings of Uncle Hillbilly's Jugband playing on the back porch—we're talking about *real* performers. Professional, studio-recorded musicians. Surely that's something to consider."

The archivist remained silent.

"Furthermore, these aren't radio-dipped out of a black hole—these are Terran produced, and of legitimate origin, which makes them all *nice* and *legal*. You're not going to have GRIS agents knocking on your door trying to track these babies down. That has to be worth something."

"*Oh, that's good! That's good!*" Moe whispered, nudging Jeremy. "Keep going!"

"And my dad, he always said we're overdue for a *salsa boom*. Well here you go: this collection is a salsa ERUPTION. And not just salsa; there's mambo, jambo, cha-cha and merengue. We both know Terran music is the next big thing— it's why we're all here, right? You pay us a fair price now, and we'll remember it."

Jeremy handed the receiver back to Moe, who picked up where he left off. "The kid's right. We have some funky fresh stuff on our horizon that you would be *very* interested in—I'll just leave it at that. And yes, I know we could just sell these records ourselves for more money...but we came to you guys first as a sign of good will. We're doing you a favor here, after all." He released the receiver button.

There was no response. Moe broke a sweat, gulped, then continued.

"Plus, you factor in the time and risk it took us to get to you—seriously, holmes, I understand privacy is a concern but these coordinates are *wack*. Do you even know what kind of raiders are lurking out here? Unarmed vessels like us—coming this far off the starways? It shows our dedication. That's worth something, too."

There was still no response.

Moe soldiered on. "So all things considered, I'm thinking..." Jeremy gave him a thumbs up, encouraging Moe to go high. Zippo nodded with wide eyes, copying Jeremy's thumbs up. "...Ninety-nine thousand credits, and the collection is yours. Whaddya say?"

Moe released the button again, holding his breath.

The archivist finally responded. "Excuse me for a moment." He went silent.

Several minutes passed. The trio strained their eyes looking for a drone being sent their way, but there was no discernible activity. Zippo resumed biting his claws in anticipation. His tail flicked back and forth wildly, thwacking Jeremy in the head several times. He knew Zippo couldn't help it, and said nothing. When the comm chimed back at last, the Felinian jumped nearly a foot out of his seat.

"Sorry about that, guys, just had to talk it over with some of my colleagues here. I'll tell you what—if these records are as good as you say they are, then we'll do it. Ninety-nine thousand credits."

"It's a deal!" Moe said.

"We're pleased to hear that. We'll send you a cargo drone shortly."

Moe clicked off the receiver just in time for Zippo to pick him up and embrace him happily.

"Keen-o!" Jeremy exclaimed.

After spinning Moe around and putting him down, Zippo hugged Jeremy and licked the top of his head with his sandpaper-y tongue.

A much larger drone appeared, floating its way toward the *Terrapin*.

"Les go, les GO!" Zippo meowed, waving at them as he skittered down the hall.

The cargo drone arrived shortly, landing in the back of the bay. There was another velvet bag inside, which Zippo pulled out. It contained three Primo tokens, along with a business card that read: *Welcome to the Massif Prime family. Sharing is caring! Feel free to invite others at your discretion.* After showing the tokens to Moe and Jeremy, Zippo placed them in his fanny pack.

It was a tight fit, but they were able to load all eleven crates into the drone. Before shutting its lid and sending it back, Jeremy looked at the crates one last time. Every box was stenciled with his parents' names. He hesitated. "I don't know if I can go through with this."

"With what?" Moe asked.

"Selling these."

"Kid, I guarantee it's what your dad would have wanted. I mean it!"

Jeremy removed his spectacles to clean them. "Moe, how can you even say that? You never knew him."

"You said your dad was a talent agent, right?"

"Right."

"And what are talent agents supposed to do?"

"They're supposed to get gigs for their clients. Help them get famous and stuff."

"Exactly. And now," Moe picked up a record, "Pino Carvaggio's Salsa Express will be placed for sale in the biggest, most exclusive music market in the galaxy! Radio stations from all over the League of Planets shop here. Some station will buy this record, and people will get to hear Pino Carvaggio as they cruise the starways of Miaxo! Dancing in night clubs off the coast of Adoro Mennall! Wandering the great shopping malls of Gekkon! Next thing you know, Pino Carvaggio's getting offers to tour the Amphibios Nebula, or to play the Sapphire Corona!

We just did these guys the biggest favor of their careers!" He tapped the record's label.

The thought of dad's old clients playing alien night clubs hundreds of light years away warmed Jeremy's heart. "Okay. You're right," he agreed. "Let's make them famous." Jeremy shut the cargo drone, sending it hovering on its way.

"Bai bai!" Zippo waved at the box as it zoomed out of the cargo bay.

"*Massif Prime*, cargo is away. Expect it should arrive shortly," Moe radioed from the cockpit.

They watched as the drone crossed the gap back to the Archive.

"Thank you, *Terrapin*. Looks like she made it safe and sound. We'll count up the albums and verify them; shouldn't take long. Our whole crew over here is pretty excited about your collection. We'll have your credit total shortly."

"10-4." Moe hung up the receiver. "We did it, chief!" he slapped Jeremy on the back. "Next stop, Callisto! Seafood buffet for all of us, I'm buyin'!" Moe scritched the top of Zippo's head, making the Felinian purr. "With this kind of money, the club will be paid in full! With credits to spare!" Moe beamed. "We can get one of those cerebric photosynths for the dance floor, just like they used to have at the Xanadu!"

"Yeh! And fluffee chillings-out room! With MASS-age chair!" Zippo mimed a shoulder massage.

"Oh, oh—and a holosuite arcade, with fantasy battles!"

"Yeaw! And scritching post, with BIG pillow! Liek VARY big! In chillings-out room!" Zippo mimed a scratching post.

"It's gonna be just like old times," Moe slung an arm around Zippo's shoulders. "In fact, it's gonna be better."

Their excited talk turned to the purchasing of new musical instruments, then to paying for all the much-needed upgrades for their ship. Zippo demanded they first pay for a new A.I., so they could replace Mister Squeakeasy.

Jeremy looked out at *Massif Prime*, silently awaiting the return cargo drone.

"What about you, kid? What are you gonna buy with your share?"

"I hadn't thought of that," Jeremy said. He imagined himself decked out in the finest silk tuxedo, looking mysterious and suave in a gentleman's top hat. In his imagination, he sauntered back into the Pigpimples Library. Janine Wintershade was there, studying at a table.

Always so studious!

She stopped reading, looking up from her book. 'Jeremy—is that... you?'

He walked over with a diamond-studded cane. 'Oh hi...Janine, is it? Just looking to meet with the Headmage. Life has been very generous to me, as you can see. I felt like it was time for me to give something back by making a donation to this quaint little school of yours...'

'Oh Jeremy! You're so thoughtful! Wow!'

"Jrr-mEE?" Zippo mewed.

"Oh, right... Maybe some new clothes? I've been wearing my Pigpimples uniforms for weeks."

"Good call. That reminds me..." Moe checked his armpits, then tugged on his tank top to air it out. "We seriously need to hit up a laundromat when we get to Callisto."

The voice from the comm interrupted their talk. "*Terrapin*, this is *Massif Prime*. We've tallied up your albums. Three hundred and twenty-one records, all of them unique and uncatalogued. The grand total is going to be ninety-nine thousand, six-hundred forty-seven credits. I hope small bills and chits are okay."

Moe nearly choked. "Of course!"

"Very good. A crate drone is being prepared with your credits, and will arrive shortly. We're very happy with this transaction, and look forward to doing business with you again. I hope that together, we can *crush the industry. Massif Prime* out."

Jeremy wondered how they planned on pirating new music if they ever actually '*crushed the industry*,' but kept the thought to himself.

The comm chimed again, startling Moe. Someone else was hailing them. "Zip—area scan! Now!"

Moe and Zippo scrambled into their seats, Zippo scanning for ships.

But it was too late.

A torpedo slammed into the *Massif Prime*, sending up a tremendous fireball of blue and white flames. The cargo ship rotated slowly, the fire from the explosion consuming its lower decks. The *Massif Prime* had not ended their call, and so the trio could hear the archivist shouting through the comm. "Shields up! Brace yourselves!" A cacophony of alarms blared amid the shouts of his crewmates. It was pandemonium.

"Another ship! Is here?!" Zippo mewed in a panic. "*Thee Parfect Stranger...?*" He read the ship's name from the scan result. His face twisted in terror and rage. "Uuugh naaaooo! *GRIS*! Is GRIS ship!"

A second explosion rocked the *Massif Prime*. The *Prime*'s thrusters pulsed to life in a desperate attempt to pull away. As it struggled to get going, a nimble starship rose up from behind it. It was *The Perfect Stranger*.

"What's going on?!" Jeremy yelled. He buckled himself into the jump seat.

The enemy ship's chime was still dinging on the comm system. Moe accepted the hail.

"GOOD EVENING, MONGRELS!" Mike Mania's voice howled through the cockpit.

The Perfect Stranger, while not nearly as big as the *Massif Prime*, was nevertheless a large ship. It looped in the distance, training its missile launchers on the *Prime*.

"Fire! Fire!" a voice shouted through the comm, whether

from the *Prime* or the *Stranger*, Jeremy did not know. A bright red laser streaked across space, burning a line into the *Perfect Stranger*'s hull.

"HA HA HAW! That tickles! Give me a break, you filthy mutts!" The voice of Mike Mania laughed maniacally. *The Perfect Stranger* circled around again, launching a volley of missiles. They clapped into the *Massif Prime* in a chain of explosions. The *Prime* fired back, but *The Perfect Stranger* made for a difficult target.

"Mooooe..." Zippo mowled sorrowfully. He didn't like what he was seeing, and fired up their thrusters. Several missiles from the *Stranger* had missed the *Prime*, and were slowly arcing towards the *Terrapin*. "Moe! We go! *Naow*!" Zippo didn't wait for a response. The *Terrapin* banked to its port side zooming away from the conflict. Alarms blared as the rogue missiles closed in.

"Hey guys! Looks like you've got a BUNCH of neutrino-class missiles on your tail, and boy are they coming in hot!" Mister Squeakeasy squeaked. "Fire off anti-ordnance rockets?"

"Yeh! Do et!" Zippo yowled.

"Oooh sorry, there seems to be a problem. No anti-ordnance rockets were found in the loading bay! Good luck, guys!" the mouse scurried away.

"Ugh!" Moe clamped his hand over his eyes. "We shot the last ones off at that party!"

Zippo took evasive maneuvers, flying the *Terrapin* in a loop and doubling back over its own trajectory. It could not shake the missiles, which had locked on tight.

"*Faster*!" Moe shouted. Zippo pushed up the ship's throttle, banking to the starboard side. They headed straight towards the *Massif Prime*.

"What are you doing?!" Moe yelled. "Pull back!"

"Get rid of missiles!" Zippo said.

"Wait, no! Don't do that!" Moe screamed. Despite Moe's

protest, Zippo continued sailing straight towards the *Prime*. He pulled them up and away at the last second. The trailing missiles all crashed into the *Massif Prime's* hull. "They still have our *money*!" Moe wailed.

"This will teach you to violate copyright law!" The voice from the GRIS ship howled through the comm system. "Lots of record company executives worked very hard to get where they are today! And it's people like you that are destroying the gravy train! Let's see how YOU like getting destroyed!"

The *Terrapin* weaved through more of the *Stranger*'s missiles and the *Massif Prime*'s slashing laser beam. The GRIS ship maneuvered away from the *Prime*, placing the *Terrapin* squarely in the gulf between them.

"Oh grok nuggets..." Moe uttered. "They're trying to use us as a shield!"

"You GRIS stooges are nothing but parasites!" someone from the *Massif Prime* shouted. There followed an intense blast of light, the orbital beam now cranked to full power. The laser from the *Prime* scoured its way along the side of the GRIS starship, inching ever closer to catching the *Terrapin* in its path.

Zippo mewled in panic and increased thrust to pull away. But no matter how fast they went, the GRIS ship managed to match their speed and their trajectory. The *Terrapin* remained trapped in the space between the dueling starships. Zippo's ears flattened as he hissed in frustration. With no way out, the orbital beam laser from the *Prime* would soon cut the *Terrapin* in half.

"Hey guys. What's up?" Madi Nabo scuttled into the cockpit. Moe and Zippo ignored her, both consumed in the frenzy of evading the crossfire.

"Madi, come sit down—we're about to die," Jeremy said, patting the jump seat.

"That voice on the comm—the one from the GRIS ship? I think he's one of my people! I heard him saying some pretty nasty stuff in Cerberon."

The cockpit shuddered as the emergency alert flashed its violent red light.

"We hit?!" Moe shouted.

"Noh! Nawt yet!" Zippo meowed back. The ship rocked again. The rumble of an explosion sent them into a spin. "Okey, naow we are hit!"

"Put me on the comm!" Madi barked. "Do it!"

Jeremy scooped up Madi Nabo, tucking her under his arm. He scrambled for the receiver, holding it up to Madi's muzzle. She yapped and yipped like mad. For a split-second, the crossfire between the two ships ceased. Zippo did not hesitate, spinning around at maximum thrust. The *Terrapin* sailed away into the void, twisting and turning crazily to shake off any potential missiles.

"Whatever you are doing, it's working! Keep barking!" Moe said.

Madi stopped, annoyed. "I'm not *barking*! I'm speaking Cerberon, you speciesist *dolt*!" She then continued to bark, yip and woof into the receiver.

"Computer, give me a view of the stern," Moe said. The navi-controls displayed the feed from the rear camera. The two other ships were still dueling, a furious blaze of missiles and lasers between them as they receded from view. Their battle cries continued coming in loud and clear through the comm.

"That was close," Madi Nabo said, hopping down from Jeremy's lap.

Minutes passed. Both ships had shrunk considerably on the viewscreen, and it was hard to tell who was winning. Then a voice screamed through the comm. By the sound of the commotion and red alerts in the background, it must have been the *Archive*.

"DEATH TO THE RECORDING INDUSTRY! FREE THE FUTUUUURE—!" The frequency cut to static. A pinpoint of white light flashed in the distance, blooming into a tremendous explosion like a supernova. As the light cleared, the starfield was empty.

The *Massif Prime Archive* was no more.

CHAPTER 36

THE DANCE FLOOR

"*Massif Prime*, do you read me?" Moe hailed the ship. "*Massif Prime*, are you okay? What happened?"

Silence.

Then, a voice.

"*Terrapin*? Is that you? You out there? BLAST IT, CHARLES! YOU LOST THEM!" Some growling and barking followed. The voice was coming from *The Perfect Stranger*.

"*Terrapin*, I know you're getting this. There's no hard feelings! Come on, where are you mutts? I just want to thank you in person! I—"

Zippo reached out, paw trembling. He clicked the receiver off, ending the call. "All music... gone?" he looked disturbed. Tears glistened in his big blue eyes.

Jeremy stood, placing a comforting arm around Zippo's shoulders. "Oh, Jrr-mEE! All Jrr-mEE's MEW-sic! Gone! So sarry!" Zippo sobbed into Jeremy's chest.

Jeremy patted him on the back. "It's all right, Zip. There, there, I know... We still have the best ones, at least. Remember? The crate of keepers?"

Zippo continued sobbing and whimpering.

"All...that...money...!" Moe slumped in his chair. He slid

down and out of it, flopping onto the floor. Madi Nabo trotted over and gave him a sniff. Jeremy could see that both co-pilots were emotionally incapacitated, and so for a time they simply cruised through space, directionless.

"What were you barking—that is, *saying*—to that other ship back there?" Jeremy asked Madi Nabo.

"I was just telling him that we had a Cerberon on board! And reminding him of the Cerberon Code of Loyalty. No Cerberon should ever blow up another of his or her race!"

"Is that so?"

"Oh yes. And good thing he heard me! I saved all our butts," Madi said. "That deserves a little bacon, wouldn't you agree?"

Jeremy cast his spell, creating some bacon for Madi Nabo.

"Crispy! Thank you," she picked up several strips and trotted out of the cockpit.

Jeremy switched on the ship's radio, hoping that DJ Nebz might lift everyone's spirits. But when he tuned to FM 104, there was nothing but static. A shiver ran down Jeremy's spine, and he switched the radio off.

* * *

The two co-captains regained their composure, but the mood in the cockpit remained bleak. For a long time, nobody said much. Moe flipped through his crystal disc collection, over and over. He muttered something under his breath as he looked at one of the discs. It was labeled *Rhonda Starlite & the Zig-Zags*. DJ Nebz had given it to them right before they'd left the station. He considered putting the disc in, but slipped it back into its case. "Zip," Moe said without looking up. "Plot our course for Callisto."

"What are we going to do?" Jeremy asked.

"GRIS knows the make and model of our starship. It's only a matter of time until they find us. Might be time to ditch the

Terrapin, get us a new ride." Moe nodded somberly at Zippo. "I know someone who might be able to help us."

Zippo adjusted their course without asking questions. He then switched to autopilot, and they cruised for a time. Eventually, he bent down and pulled his vibrobass case out from under his chair. He snapped its locks open and lifted the lid gently. The alien instrument was in two parts, one long and the other roundish. It had a purple opalescent finish, its edges bleeding into a sparkling indigo. Jeremy admired the instrument's beauty. It was almost like looking into some deep space nebula.

Zippo assembled the vibrobass and switched it on. Holographic blue strings flickered to life across its neck and body. He strummed a melancholy tune, the notes eventually merging into one long, sustained *purr* that Jeremy felt deep in his heart.

Moe listened for a time, looking out the windows at the Milky Way. He finally murmured something about getting some shut eye, and excused himself to his cabin. Although Jeremy also felt exhausted, he remained with Zippo in the darkened cockpit. It didn't feel right to leave him all alone.

"COM-pew-ter," Zippo mewed quietly. Mister Squeakeasy popped to attention. "COM-pew-ter, begin radio trans-massion."

"You got it! Is this a general broadcast, or would you like to transmit to specific coordinates?"

Zippo tapped a long string of coordinates into the keyboard, then hit enter.

"Alrighty! You're all set. Just let me know when you're finished!" Mister Squeakeasy disappeared, and Zippo reclined again. He resumed strumming. The vibrobass's purr lulled Jeremy into a dreamlike state. As the time passed—what felt like an hour—a melody emerged. Then the Felinian began to sing.

His meows, mewls and praows seemed to *echo* somehow. Zipponio's voice layered over itself, forming a river of sound and memory. Even though Jeremy could not understand the words, distinct images shimmered into his mind.

He was standing outside a nightclub on an empty street. It was a warm summer night. The outside of the club was decorated in palm trees that looked like they were made out of pink and green neon lights. A sign blinked on and off. Even though it was written in an alien language, he knew what it said. THE PALACE XANADU.

Jeremy floated in through the front doors of the alien club, only to be greeted by a sea of flashing lights, music, and all sorts of creatures dancing. A spotlight shone on the stage, and there they were: The Stardrops in Stereo! Moe and Zippo, along with two beautiful offworlder chicas, were playing the very song he was listening to. As he floated toward the stage, the lights cut out. One of the girls floated away like a ghost; the second disappeared as he turned to look at her.

And then, only Zippo remained. He faced an audience that was no longer there. The Felinian sat on a stool, playing the same song for the abandoned room and singing quietly. The song came into Jeremy's mind in plain English:

> *The dance floor's gone away for sure,*
> *But my heart is still groovin'*
> *Baby, can you show me the way to go,*
> *When the stars are always movin'?*
> *You know the dance floor's disappeared for sure,*
> *But my heart is still groovin'.*
> *The dance floor—disappeared for sure...*
> *The dance floor—disappeared for sure...*
> *Disappeared for sure...*
> *Disappeared...*

The song faded into a long, eternal purr.

Jeremy stirred from the vision. "That was beautiful," he said.

Zippo placed his instrument down slowly. "Thank you, Jrr-mEE," he smiled a tired smile.

"Was that song from your old band?" Jeremy asked.

Zippo nodded. "It was...last song of band. But, not mine anymore. I give it awey."

"You gave it away? To who?"

"COM-pew-ter, end radio trans-massion." The computer chimed. "I send song to bleck hole. Maybe someone find et. Someday." Zippo yawned. He took apart the vibrobass and placed it back in its case, buckling it closed. "Goodnight, Jrr-mEE," he said, shuffling off to his cabin.

Jeremy stayed up, looking out at the stars. It was a long time before he went to bed.

CHAPTER 37

NO REJECTS

Callisto was a vast, dark moonscape. The only indication of civilized life on its surface was a speckle of twinkling lights in the distance, which they were rapidly approaching. "Sentinel City," Moe said to Jeremy. "We might need some real magic, because this could be our last chance."

Jeremy gulped. As they approached the location, he wondered whether the term "city" might be a little generous. It looked more like a collection of domes, industrial facilities, and other alien buildings whose purpose he could only guess at. They were all clustered near a gargantuan black tower, far taller than any building Jeremy had ever seen in his life.

"What is that place?" Jeremy asked.

"That's where we're headed, kid. Sentinel Tower. They say it was built by the Kaladorre thousands of years ago." [*Translator's Note: the Kaladorre were a tower-based civilization, and are best known for the ancient residential structures they left behind throughout the galaxy. Sentinel Tower on Callisto was discovered by alien explorers in A.D. 1889. Although long-abandoned, settlers soon transformed the tower into a bustling vertical metropolis. —ChatterBot 3.6*] They hovered over a starship landing lot near the base of Sentinel Tower. Zippo radioed the lot attendant, requesting permission to land. "Come on, get your stuff ready." Moe said, lacing up his hi-tops. "You're gonna like this."

The *Terrapin* descended onto an empty landing pad. A few other starships were parked nearby. "Okay, homeboys. Don't forget, we're parked in M-814." Moe remembered something. "Madi? Madi Nabo?" he called out to the Cerberon. Jeremy heard her hopping down from atop his bed (her favorite place to nap).

She wandered over. "Yeah? What is it?"

"We're here. Callisto. Let's go," Moe said, pointing to the door.

"Come, Madi, we're going to go check out Sentinel Tower," Jeremy added.

"Eh, no thanks," Madi Nabo said, yawning.

"What, you don't want to come?" Jeremy asked. He looked to Moe.

"Out there?" Madi yipped. "It's the middle of the night!"

"I thought you said you wanted to be dropped off," Jeremy said.

"Not here!" Madi Nabo peeked out a window. "This place sucks!"

"All right. That's fine," Jeremy said, trying to keep the peace. He could tell Moe was getting frustrated. "I know...why don't you keep an eye on the ship for us while we're out?"

"Whatever. I'm going back to bed." She trotted back to the cargo bay.

"Zip," Moe whispered. "Make sure the computer core is locked. Set it to self-destruct if she tries to snoop it. I don't even care at this point. The black hole coordinates are the only important thing. You have a backup, right?"

"Right heer," Zippo nodded, tapping his head with a claw.

"Good. Let's avoid making that little chica mad. Can't have

her calling her GRIS friends on us. And she won't be our problem soon." Moe donned his Los Angeles Comets baseball cap, turning it around backwards in his usual alien fashion. Despite it being the middle of the night, he also slipped on his shades. "You homies got everything you need? Because if we have to bounce, we might not be back."

Zippo slid into his fuzzy pink vest and clipped on his fanny pack, rushing to check something in his cabin. He gave a thumbs up as he returned.

Jeremy threw on his oversized robe and double-checked his blazer pocket for his magic wand. As they exited the ship down the cargo bay's ramp, he glanced back at the crate of keepers. Whatever else happened, he hoped the last remaining records would be safe.

They exited the landing lot through the plaz fence. Sentinel City was situated on a kind of mesa, which rose above a surrounding forest of glowing trees and other alien vegetation. Moe explained that the mushroom-looking trees were called *Polinoki Mushrumps*. They were planted by space rangers, and slowly transformed moon dust into living soil. "It's hard to see in the dark, but there's actually some farmland beyond here," Moe said, motioning to the alien valleys. "There's enough oxygen in the atmosphere that they were able to dismantle some of the smaller domes. In ten or twenty years, the entire surface will be habitable."

Jeremy gazed out over the luminescent forest. Jupiter hung in the sky above the distant mountains. The gas giant looked even bigger than the moon back home.

"What's the matter, chief?" Moe asked.

"Nothing." Jeremy shuddered. "It's just that...this is my first time setting foot on another planet. Feels kinda weird."

"Actually, you haven't *technically* set foot on another *planet*. This is just a moon."

"Oh. Right."

"Come on," Moe pointed at the tower looming at the city's edge. "She's gotta be up there somewhere!"

* * *

The Tower's front doors stood ten feet high, and were made of rose-colored salt glass. Jeremy could see people milling about inside, in what looked like a spacious lobby. As he approached the glass doors, they slid open without anyone even pressing a button. "Whoa! Keen-o!" Jeremy exclaimed. He stepped back, the doors shutting themselves. "What the devil?! How do they do that?" he asked. Moe and Zippo ignored him and entered the lobby. "Why are you not amazed by this?!" Jeremy took out his wand and ran back outside, pretending to make the doors open and shut by waving his hand. "I'm doin' it, guys! I'm magic!"

Zippo nodded. "Yeh. They kewl doors," he admitted.

"Dude, if you are freakin' about some wack doors, this is going to take forever. Come on," Moe beckoned.

The tower lobby was palatial, all decked out in contemporary galactic finery. Pleasant music played over a P.A. system as offworlders of endless variety walked around. All carried bags of merchandise from the Tower's many shops and boutiques. The competing aromas of dozens of food kiosks made Jeremy's stomach growl. *Oh for some food that wasn't cereal or sausage!*

At the center of the lobby bubbled a fountain so immense he could have rowed a boat through it. In it stood a twenty foot sculpture of an alien figure that looked like a cross between a jellyfish and an anthropomorphic seahorse. Pink and aqua-green water trickled out of the statue's head. Before he could ask Moe about it, a teenage girl appeared seemingly out of nowhere and locked eyes with Jeremy.

Janine Wintershade! But how could it be?

"What are you doing here?" Jeremy asked in a daze.

"Welcome to Sentinel Tower—MAURICE—and—ZIPPONIO," the girl addressed Moe and Zippo, then turned to Jeremy. "This must be your first time—scan your ID for access to all of our Low Tier amenities, including the Consumer Village, Attention Deficit Arcade, and the Endless Buffeteria—featuring exotic meats from deep space fauna!"

"Janine?" Jeremy could barely speak.

Moe karate-chopped the girl. His hand cut right through her as if she were made of air! "She's just a hologram, kid. They scan your brainwaves and customize it to look like whatever will entice you the most."

"They scan your brain? Isn't that a bit intrusive?"

"Yes. It's wack. Just ignore it." Moe pushed forward, walking towards a set of sliding doors at the back wall. "Come on, let's boogie! I see the turbolifts!"

The Janine hologram waved to Jeremy as he walked away. "Don't forget to check out ZiaDor Peesta's for the latest in Low Tier fashions! You'd look super handsome in one of their doublets!" she winked. The hologram then transformed into something resembling a neon yellow walrus as it addressed a new potential customer.

"Let's see here..." Moe pressed an emerald green button next to a set of doors. They slid open with a ding.

"Destination, please," a female A.I. voice chimed as the three of them gathered into the lift. There was a vending machine inside, filled with Lingo Bars for English and many other Terran and alien languages. One of the lift's glass walls also had a televid screen mounted in it. It displayed a huge vertical map of Sentinel Tower. Jeremy examined it, fascinated.

The tower's basement floors were called the Sub Tier. These levels held the hydro farms, agrisynthetics, and soylent reclamation mills.

Above the Sub Tier was the Low Tier. A pixelated dot blinked the words "YOU ARE HERE" on the ground floor of this tier. All Low Tier restaurants and shops were open to the general public, and the map was dotted with hundreds of tiny labels identifying them all.

Above the Low Tier were several levels of private apartments and hotel rooms.

Then, at the topmost levels of the tower, the map went blank. These levels had no individual markers or tags. The floors were simply labeled the "Luxe Tier."

The map provided no further information.

"Destination, please," the A.I. repeated.

"Hi," Moe cleared his throat. "Heavy Nova."

There was no response.

"Take us to Heavy Nova," Moe said. "Please."

The A.I. responded. "I'm sorry, but your request can't be processed at this time. Destination, please."

Moe huffed in frustration. "Just take us here," he hopped up, trying to point to the top of the tower map. "Zip, show her," he said. Zippo placed a claw at the top floor.

"The...Luxe Tier," Jeremy read aloud.

Nothing happened.

"Yeah, take us to Luxe Tier. Now," Moe repeated.

"One moment," the A.I. said. The turbolift started to ascend. They rose past seemingly endless floors of cafes, food courts, stores, video arcades, casinos, and sports facilities.

"This place is so keen-o!" Jeremy said.

"Seems to be getting more popular every day," Moe observed.

"I've never seen anything like it!" Jeremy exclaimed. He placed his face up against the glass as they cruised past a level that was nothing but candy shops. "Sort of reminds me of the fall fair at Pigpimples. But really, that was just a couple of carnival games and a fish-and-eel-pie eating contest."

"MMmmm!" Zippo rubbed his pink belly. "Oh yeh, Jrr-mee, we go to shramp buffet. Is rally good! I take you, when have credits," Zippo smiled, also pressing his face against the glass.

After ascending so many floors that Jeremy had long lost count, the turbolift stopped. They were on a level with an enormous swimming pool and waterslides.

"What gives? Why'd we stop?" Moe said.

"Splashmore Kingdom Water Park is the final level of the Low Tier. Have fun! And remember: no horseplay," the A.I. said as the lift's doors opened.

"Hey lady, we said *Luxe Tier*," Moe spoke to the elevator. "*Heavy Nova*! Just take us to Heavy Nova! I know it's up there!"

"I see. One moment," she said. The doors clamped shut and the clear glass walls of the elevator turned black. Zippo whimpered as the lights cut out. The map screen brightened, bathing the turbolift in green. A message blinked on the screen: *Only the elite may gather here.*

"Oh come on! What the krud is *that* supposed to mean?" Moe asked.

"Sorry, boys," a new voice chimed in from the map screen. "The Luxe Tier is reserved for the exceptional. Your physical traits have all failed the attractiveness algorithm—quite spectacularly. You're going to have to show us some other proof of your exceptionality, because our preliminary scans indicate no special talents, skills, or abilities whatsoever. What have you got?"

"Hey! Hey, check this out," Jeremy said, taking out his wand. "Guys, give me something to transform."

Moe rummaged in his pockets. Zippo looked in his fanny pack.

"Oh, I think I might have some of that gum," Moe said. "You could turn it into a strip of bacon or something. Zip, didn't I give you a piece of gum the other day?"

The voice returned.

"Boys, I'm afraid that transforming chewing gum into bacon, while a fascinating ability, will not be exceptional enough to enter. Why not go out and commit an act of heroism, or at least hit up the gym..." The voice paused. "One moment...what is the Felinian holding there?"

Zippo had taken the Primo Tokens out of his fanny pack in his search for gum.

"Are those Primo Tokens? From the *Massif Prime Archive*?" the voice asked.

"Uh...why yes, they are! We're all members of the Massif Prime family. Have been for years," Jeremy said.

"Right! *Sharing is caring*," Moe said.

"*Crash IN-dus-tray*," Zippo added, handing the tokens out. They each held one up to the screen.

"Well, then. Scans show those are genuine. Impressive. You may proceed," the voice said. There was a pull of inertia as the lift resumed ascension. The elevator's walls remained black as they rose.

"Thank you, Nebz!" Moe kissed his Primo Token.

"I hate to say it, but I think DJ Nebz had a point," Jeremy said.

"About what?"

"About this place. It's incredible. How will your club ever be able to compete?"

"That's the beauty of it, dude! These guys and their wack *attractiveness algorithms*—they're going to be rejecting tourists from all over the place, right? Where are all the rejects supposed to go?"

"Ahhhh," Jeremy laughed, tapping his head with his wand to mimic Nebz's mannerism. "Smart! *Future Pop: the club for rejects!*"

"Exactly."

The turbolift finally stopped. The blinking dot on the map indicated that they were on the top floor of Sentinel Tower. The A.I. voice spoke: "Welcome to Heavy Nova."

CHAPTER 38

RHONDA STARLITE

The doors opened, the pulsing rhythm of alien dance music enveloping them. Colored lights strobed and spun as offworlders from far-flung star systems crowded the dance floor. It was so loud they could barely hear each other speak. Zippo mindspoke an image to his companions of an empty booth he'd spotted. They boogied their way to it, Zippo stopping to dance with some Koshioni chicas along the way. One of the girls gave him a playful pet on the head with her antennae.

"Okay, I admit...this is *nice*!" Moe shouted as he scooted into the round booth. "Pretty good view of the stage, too!"

Jeremy sat down, mesmerized at the scene. The whole club crackled with energy, as if it were a living organism. The stage was only raised a foot or two above the dance floor, and a DJ cranked out songs as he jumped around, back and forth. Jeremy noticed that the DJ was also a Felinian. Unlike Zippo's wrinkly pink and gray skin, this cat-man's body was covered in a thin layer of white and gray fur. As he manipulated a boxy glowing device in front of him, the club goers lined up and performed different choreographed dance moves. Jeremy had no clue what the DJ was doing, but the box looked complicated.

"That dude is pretty good! He's really got them going, eh, Zip?" Moe's head bobbed with the beat of the music.

"Eh. He not that great." Zippo folded his arms. He acted suddenly disinterested in the whole scene. The DJ swirled his striped tail around as he brought the song to a close. The crowd cheered, the DJ backflipping on the stage and then bowing low to the floor. Moe applauded and gave a whistle. Zippo looked away, grooming himself.

An elderly master of ceremonies shuffled onto the stage, applauding with the rest of the crowd. He wore an extremely sparkly tuxedo jacket covered in hot pink sequins. His illuminated bow tie glowed under his chin. Jeremy guessed that he was a Binosian, since he couldn't have been more than three and a half feet tall. He had the same coppery skin tone, too. His hair was a light shade of gray.

"Once again, let's hear it for Nuuri M'Grau!" the M.C. spoke into the silver microphone, stopping to clap again. He had a peculiar accent, common to those who learned English through Lingo Bars. "Nuuri, that was a great set—remind me to give you an extra bag of cat treats after the show."

Everyone laughed.

"I kid, I kid! Nuuri is a great DJ. Felinians are actually marvelous to work with. If you ever get sick of them, you just throw a straw wrapper their way—keeps them occupied for hours."

The audience laughed again. Even Zippo joined in, "Dis true, dis true!" he giggled as he nodded.

"We love you, Briffu!" someone from the audience shouted.

"What's that? Who said that?" the M.C. shielded his eyes, looking out theatrically. "Sounded like it came from that table of Hexapods over there. I love you too, ladies, but you'll still have to pay for those drinks. I don't care how razor sharp your mandibulae are."

The crowd roared.

"Who *is* this old grandpa?" Moe scoffed.

"He's funny!" Jeremy said. Zippo agreed.

"Pssh!" Moe scrunched his face up. "He's wack."

Jeremy smirked. He didn't get about half of the jokes, but it was hard not to laugh anyway. He tried to not let Moe see.

"...And that's why you never leave your wife with a Noyregian waiter!"

The audience hooted and hollered. Zippo chuffled, slapping the table and nearly knocking over the Ghu-Hothan Buffalo milk he'd ordered.

"Now this next act is a Heavy Nova exclusive. Those of you who haven't seen these guys before—you're in for a treat. Keep an eye on them. I'm serious! They're going places! Ladies and gentlesapients, may I present—all the way from the ghost planet of Hadox—*Rhonda Starlite and the Zig-Zags!*"

The audience applauded as the lights cut out, engulfing the room in darkness. Thousands of stars glittered in the sky, their light streaming in through the immense windows behind the stage. Jupiter shone above the distant moonscape like an orange fireball. All was silent and still. Then, a ghostly voice emanated from the darkness. It was lilting and feminine, reminding Jeremy of some beautiful songbird.

The singer appeared, materializing onto the stage as if she were a spirit. She radiated an otherworldly light as she floated to the microphone, cradling it in her velvet-gloved arms. A slinky dress hugged her buxom figure, shimmering as if covered in amethysts. She wore a sparkling headband in the tresses of her deep indigo hair, which bounced along her shoulders as she shrugged in time with her song. Her skin was the color of pale lilacs. Jeremy could have sworn that even though her figure blocked the view, he could still see the stars outside, shining *through* her. Whether this was a trick of the light or not, he could not tell. He just knew she was a *knockout*.

"Thare she is!" Zippo gasped. He could barely contain his

excitement, and nudged Moe while waving to the singer. "Hi, Rhonda!" he whisper-yelled. Moe shushed him.

The singer was so entrancing that Jeremy didn't even notice the other band members until they were all on the stage, playing alongside her. They were all of different races, and they played musical apparatuses he'd never seen. The whole nightclub was captivated by their song.

When we met, it was a white hot start
The speed of light between two hearts
We were underground, it sounds bizarre,
But in your eyes, I saw the stars.

The song crescendoed until the singer swept her microphone aside, exploding into a new verse. The cathodic clavitone player tossed a sphere into the air. It hovered over to the singer, her hands gliding around it. Each movement produced a new tone. A flick of her wrist shook out a glimmer of sound. A shake of her hips sent bubbling trills across the room. Her whole body turned and flickered like the wisp of a candle flame.

Their opening song got the club's attention. Jeremy watched, wanting to join the people dancing, but not wanting to leave his companions. Zippo sensed Jeremy's urgency, and hopped to his feet. "Jrr-mEE, come!" he beckoned, rushing to the outskirts of the dance floor. Jeremy grinned and joined the Felinian, grooving along. Their dancing caught the attention of some Saffonian cuties, who fluttered over to the duo as Jeremy did a spacey mambo. He attempted to chat with one of the chicas, but she just smiled and made various chittering noises. They danced happily to "Airlock Kiss," "Holographic Touch," and many others that Jeremy didn't catch the names of. The band closed out their set with "The Color of Space."

"Thank you all," the singer flashed a pretty smile. Without skipping a beat, she picked up an electric kithara and started to strum an encore: "Lightyears of Love."

As she sang, the club slowly transformed. Through some fancy special effect, the walls of the room shimmered and disappeared, replaced with an endless view of space. The ceiling and even the floor itself evaporated, and for a time it was like everyone was just there, floating among the stars. All that existed was the singer's beautiful voice and the sound of her kithara. The whole room was under her spell. Zippo hung an arm around Jeremy's shoulders as they swayed to the chorus.

Eventually the song came to a close, and their surroundings returned to normal. The singer blew a graceful kiss to her audience as she handed the instrument back to one of her bandmates.

Zippo meowed enthusiastically as he clapped his paws together. "Yeauw! Rhondaaaaaa!"

The singer smiled, bowing along with her band.

"If you like her music so much, Zip, you should go and meet her," Jeremy said.

"Yeh!" Zippo chuffled. "I *know* her! Det is *Rhonda*!" Zippo placed a paw on Jeremy's shoulder, mindspeaking an image to him. He saw their old band, the Stardrops in Stereo. Rhonda Starlite stood there among them, playing her electric kithara beside Moe and Zippo. "Whaaaat?!" Jeremy's jaw dropped. "She...? She was *in* your band?!" Jeremy pointed.

Zippo nodded happily.

"Why didn't you tell me?!" Jeremy turned towards their table, shouting his question at Moe. But Moe was gone. "Where did crazy old Maurice go?" Jeremy said, returning to his seat in their circular booth.

Zippo shrugged. "Sani?"

Briffu, the Binosian M.C., took to the stage as the applause died down. "What did I tell you, folks? Rhonda Starlite and the Zig-Zags, everyone!" Rhonda leaned down and gave the host a peck on the top of his head before leaving the stage. He mugged stupidly, much to the audience's delight.

"We're going to take a little break as we set up for the next act, but we'll be back shortly with *Roby and the Roidz*!"

A Foojalian waiter came to their booth to refill Zippo's milk. "Jrr-mEE, you want? BUFF-a-lo malk. Vary good," Zippo offered the glass to Jeremy, who declined politely.

"Zip, how are we going to pay for that? We don't have any credits."

Zippo held a claw to his whiskers. "Shhh!"

"*Check—check—checkin' the mic,*" a familiar voice came from the stage. Jeremy and Zippo looked over in shock. It was Moe!

"*Checkin' the mic, chickity-chickity check-check.*" Moe tapped the microphone as he put on his holosynth gloves and visor. "All right! Good evening, Heavy Nova! My name is Moe, and this is a ditty I've been working on. It's dedicated to Miss Rhonda Starruki. It's called 'Think About the Future,' and it goes a little something like this... One, two, three, four!" Moe drummed the air with the holosynth sticks, producing a bassy rhythm with one hand and a melody with the other.

"*Oh baby, baby, I've been dream, dream, dreamin' about our futuuuurre—!* " he sang.

Rhonda appeared by the stage, clasping her hands together and laughing. Moe got about one verse into his song before the M.C. wandered over to the stage and pointed at him. In a takedown most would consider overkill, two very burly looking bouncers with cybernetically enhanced muscles stormed the stage and tackled the small Binosian. He smashed to the floor with an audible "*Ooof!*"

"Get that little simp out of here!" The M.C. Shouted. "While you're at it, get his ID and make sure he's permabanned!"

Rhonda raised her hand, waving at the M.C. "It's okay, Briffu!" she said with a smile. "He's with me."

CHAPTER 39

SHOOTOUT AT HEAVY NOVA

Rhonda sat beside Moe in their booth. She pressed an ice cube from her drink above his eye, which was bruised from the pummeling. "Maurice, what were you thinking? In a place like this? They'll never let you back in here again!"

"Baby, after we get Future Pop going, we're gonna put this place out of business!"

"Hmmm..." Rhonda looked dubious. "I did like your song, though," she smiled demurely.

"Nah, my song was wack. Yours were much better. You really shredded that spirit theremin!"

"Awww!" She leaned down, rubbing noses with Moe.

Jeremy wondered about the logistics of rubbing noses with some kind of non-corporeal spirit girl from a ghost planet, but the whole line of thinking made his head hurt. He coughed politely, as he could tell their public display of affection was making Zippo uncomfortable.

"Oh, Moe, you are so rude sometimes," Rhonda said. "Aren't you going to introduce me to your friend?"

Moe donned his shades to cover his black eye. "Of course! Rhonda, this is Jeremy. He's my Terran homeboy."

Rhonda reached across the table and offered Jeremy a gloved

hand, which he was indeed able to shake. "It's a pleasure, Jeremy. I want you to know I'm a big fan of your homeworld. Your people make some great music."

For reasons he couldn't explain, Jeremy felt his face warming and reddening. "Uh, thanks," he said.

"Jeremy is head chef of the *Terrapin*, and he's the Mambo Wizard," Moe explained.

"Wizard? You don't say!" Rhonda tilted her head and smiled, making Jeremy blush even more. "You know, Jeremy, speaking of wizards—you actually remind me of this one character, maybe you've heard of him..." she tapped a finger on her lip, trying to recall the name.

Moe cleared his throat.

"What?" Rhonda looked at Moe, who just shook his head without comment. Jeremy pretended to be oblivious, looking out at the stage. There were some plant-like sapients on the dance floor doing a weird, swaying rhumba.

"So Zipponio, have you heard from your kitt sister lately?" Rhonda asked, changing the subject.

"Yeh!" Zippo's eyes lit up. "Sasha is good. She finish BEW-tee college, she make vary pretty hair and makeups naow."

"Tell her hello for me. I miss that girl!"

Zippo purred in approval.

"Where's Galaxina?" Moe asked. "She wasn't on stage with you."

"Galaxina's on tour. Her ballet group is doing a production of *Theesia and Bux* out in the Bloomia Sector. She'll be jealous when I tell her about you guys dropping in! She would have loved to meet a real Terran wizard, too. She loves Tommy Cobblestone, you know!" Rhonda said, touching Jeremy on the shoulder. "See, I remembered his name!"

Moe and Zippo chuckled nervously, staring at Jeremy to gauge his reaction.

"That is—I meant to say..." Rhonda retracted her hand,

taking an awkward sip of her drink from a light-up straw.

"Oh, it's fine," Jeremy said, blushing even more intensely. "I get it all the time. The comparison makes sense..."

"Yeah?" Rhonda asked.

"Considering they based him off of *me*," Jeremy grinned.

Rhonda burst out laughing, nearly choking on her drink.

Her laughter made Jeremy's heart flutter. "Is Galaxina another one of the...chicas?" he ventured.

Rhonda made an annoyed sound, looking irked at Moe. She slapped him on the arm. "One of the *chicas*? Honestly, Moe," Rhonda shook her head, "is this what you're doing these days? Kidnapping Terran kids and teaching them your stupid slang?"

"What! It's just English; it's how they talk!"

Rhonda rolled her eyes. "Galaxina was my roommate in beauty school. We used to play together in a two-girl band. We called ourselves *Heaven*," Rhonda explained. "Pretty sure Zippo used to have one of our promo t-shirts!"

"Oh, he still does," Jeremy said. "He was wearing it the other day."

Rhonda sighed, her eyes sparkling as she squeezed in close to Moe. "It's good to see you guys again," she said, laying her head down on the Binosian's shoulder.

Moe pulled a crystal diskette out of his pocket. "Listen, Rhonda. I wanted to give you something. I know you don't want anything to do with radio dipping or future music or whatnot—"

"What's that?" Rhonda asked, sitting upright. She took the disc from Moe's hand.

"It's a collection of radio songs we dipped out of a black hole. All of them are future hits. We haven't shared them with anyone. I was saving them...for you..." he trailed off. Jeremy couldn't tell whether Rhonda was pleased or horrified.

"'Kiss the DJ'...'The DJ is My Boyfriend'...'One Love for the DJ'...'Hot Socks DJ Boy'...?" Rhonda read some of the titles on the label.

"Yeah! See, these are all great because DJs *love* playing songs with titles like that! You'll get played on the radio, at the club—guaranteed! Instant popularity. There's lots of certified hits on there. And many more to come," Moe said.

Rhonda held the diskette to her heart, fluttering her eyelids. "That...is...so...*sweet*!" she said, her voice dripping with sarcasm. "And you traveled all the way here to find me and give me some free songs?" She tossed the diskette on the table. "What makes you think I need any of your pirated music? I'm playing gigs on songs I wrote all by myself! That I didn't have to *steal*!"

"Now wait a second," Moe interrupted, "I do believe Zippo wrote the vibrobass line for 'Laserdance.'"

"Ha! Fine, songs that *we* wrote," she said, motioning to Zippo. "What's the catch, Moe? I know you." She raised an eyebrow. "You need something. Don't you."

"It's nothing! I just wanted to know if we could...trade starships for a little while."

Rhonda threw her head back. Her hair bounced as she laughed. "*Starship*? What starship?" she asked, incredulous. "I got here on a starways shuttlebus!"

"Oh. What happened to your *Catalyst*?" Moe asked.

"How do you think I paid for that spirit theremin?" she said. "Listen, guys—I have some promising stuff on the horizon, but right now I am broke like it's no joke. You're having trouble with your starship?"

"You could say that," Moe confessed. "It's a long story."

"Fine. The less I know, the better. But if you two are still trying to make money selling illegal recordings, I'd be very careful if I were you. Especially around here." She lowered her voice, "There are GRIS agents in this club. Right now." She looked around. "Dangerous ones."

"How do you know?" Moe said.

"Because," Rhonda whispered, looking around again, "*I'm working for one!*"

Moe gasped. Zippo's paw rose to his mouth in shock.

"Oh, relax! Just little jobs here and there. Intelligence gathering stuff, mostly. In return, he gets me gigs! In fact, he might have even scored me a pretty big gig on Earth!" She looked at Jeremy.

"Rhonda, *really*? Working for some GRIS scumbag? That's just...*wack*!" Moe lamented.

"Maurice, you're one to talk! While you were busy flying around the galaxy playing space pirate, I was out there working gigs at every sad little lounge on every lousy old mining station! I spent months hopping tacky resort asteroids, playing outpost cantinas and busted grav-discos! And now, finally, I've found a little success by working hard and sticking to it! Not fishing it out of a time flux inside of some black hole!"

"Rhonda, I—"

She cut him off. "What's *wack* is that we should have been touring together, writing new material together—but you ditched Stardrops for some crazy radio dipping scheme! All to get revenge over some stupid song? That's what's *wack*, Moe!"

Moe opened his mouth to speak, but couldn't. He appeared crushed. Rhonda bit her lip, realizing she may have gone too far. She reached out and took Moe by the hand. "If you had just stayed, we could have written ten more 'Hot Sauce Packets' by now, you know." She caressed Moe's cheek.

"Rhonda, I didn't mean anything by it. It's just that GRIS...they're *jibronis*! You could get hurt!"

Rhonda moved close to Moe, speaking into his ear. "All the better reason to stay on their good side!" She leaned in and kissed him on the cheek. "I'm sorry, Moe. It really was good to see you. Thank you for the songs." She picked up the diskette, tucking it into her dress. "Come find me when you're ready to play again. That goes for you too, Zipponio." She rose from the booth, adjusting her headband and poofing up her hair in a mirror. "It was lovely meeting you, Jeremy. If you ever want to do a magic act at Heavy Nova, give me a jingle! They're always looking for Terran performers," she winked.

It was then they spotted the short Cerberon making a bee-line towards their booth. For reasons Jeremy could only guess at, the dog-like creature was dressed like a Spanish conquistador. He bared his fangs as he grinned.

"Hi Mike!" Rhonda wiggled her fingers at him as she floated away. Mike waved back dismissively. Rhonda turned and locked eyes with Moe, mouthing the words: *"BE CAREFUL!"*

"Squeeze over, pup!" Mike shoved his way into the circular booth, scooting right up next to Jeremy until he was practically sitting on him. His brother Charles squeezed into the other side, effectively trapping Moe, Zippo and Jeremy in the middle. "I apologize for interrupting whatever it was you mongrels were doing here, but I'd like to talk to you."

Mike hailed a waitress. He ordered a Venusian sulphur tea and asked if they had any Terran Toastee Mums. The waitress said she wasn't sure if they had any toaster pastries available. Mike extended a claw, beckoning her down to his level. He opened his doublet, revealing his holstered glazer. "Just make it happen," he snarled, smiling darkly. The waitress hurried off.

"I love this place! Don't you?" Mike waved his short arms around. "Always wanted to own my own night club, isn't that a wild idea?"

"Not too wild," Moe said, suspicious.

"They're a great place to meet musicians. And musicians are the biggest suckers of all! What is it about musical types that makes them so gullible? Is it because they're so accustomed to self-deception—always deluding themselves that they'll be successful?!" Mike laughed heartily.

"I'm sorry, have we met?" Moe asked.

"Not in person. Mike Mania, how do you do?" he extended a paw, which the three took turns shaking over the table. "This is my brother, Charles in Charge."

Charles nodded, grinning stupidly. "We're really big fans of your work!"

"Oh! You know...us?" Moe looked surprised. Jeremy wondered if they were Stardrops in Stereo fans. Or could it be they were admirers of...*2 Funky Brothers*?

Mike chuckled. "We're agents for GRIS." Moe and Zippo stiffened at the acronym. Mike continued, "But Charles is right; we are big fans of all you do. Who knew! A Terran puppy-boy, a Binosian halfling, and a filthy paw-licker," Mike gestured at Zippo, who flattened his ears in anger, "could do my job for me!"

The waitress returned and set down a cup of tea, which Mike raised to his snout. "And the Toastee Mums?" he asked.

"We're looking," the waitress said nervously, "on the Low Tier."

Mike growled, dismissing her. "Low Tier, indeed! Sometimes people have no grasp of the finer things in life." He lapped up some of his tea.

"You said we did your job for you?" Moe said, "That's funny, because I don't remember getting paid off by industry millionaires to throw innocent people in prison, all because they shared a copy of a three minute pop song. How about you, Zip?" he looked to Zippo, who slitted his eyes in distrust.

"Ha ha haw! I like these guys!" he barked at Charles. "You imbeciles got more work done for us these past few days than we've been able to do in months! Years, really!"

Moe shifted in his seat, breaking into a sweat. This did not sound good. Mike continued.

"First, you led us right to that frog-man! Do you know how long we scoured the solar system for that stupid station? Frogstar Radio! That place was a thorn in my paw for too long!"

Jeremy's heart sank. Moe looked like he was going to be sick.

"Wat you did to *Nebz*?" Zippo demanded.

"Relax, fish-breath," Mike growled. "Mister froggy will be much happier now, at the bottom of some bog back in the Amphibios Nebula."

Zippo made a low rumbling sound.

The waitress dropped off a platter of Toastee Mums, which Mike took a nibble of. "But that was nothing—NOTHING!—compared to Massif Prime! The fattest squirrel in the entire League of Planets, and we caught 'em! Ha ha haw! They're gonna promote me to head of GRIS over that little fiasco!"

Moe reached under the table, unlatching the buckle of his ankle holster and making eye contact with Zippo, who adjusted his vest. Jeremy wished, not for the last time, that he had something other than breakfast magic to use in a fight.

"Where's that little Cerberon dame who was on your ship? You know, the one that kept yapping on about the Code of Loyalty?" Mike looked around. "No matter. If I wanted you dead, you would be. I have bigger plans for you mutts."

"Like what?!" Moe said, bitterness in his voice, "You won, bro! It's over! We lost everything, including an entire chest full of credits that *you* stupidly blew up! What more do you want from us?" Moe asked. "We don't have anything illegal. Search us!" Moe threw his hands in the air. "No copyright infringement here! Sorry, would you like to check whether my hat is officially licensed merchandise?" Moe took his cap off, offering it to Mike. [*Translator's Note: It wasn't. —ChatterBot 3.6*]

He chuckled. "Relax! I have a proposal for you all."

"What are you talking about?" Moe asked.

"I know all about your little radio dipping scheme. You weren't the first ones to discover that black hole on the edge of this star system, you know! My guys have been monitoring it for some time! When we spotted your little ship snooping around, we started keeping an eye on you." Mike lapped some more of his tea, then continued. "I've been in copyright enforcement long enough to know that this black hole is going to be big. *Very* big.

Perhaps the biggest thing in pirated music. And I want a slice of that pizza!" Mike grinned. "So here's my proposal: make me a part of your little operation, and I can make your GRIS problems disappear. *Forever*."

Moe's jaw dropped. "You want to get into radio dipping?"

"Sure! I don't know how to run the tech, so I'll leave that to you three. My job will be to keep GRIS out of your hair. I already told my boss that the black hole was repaired. Ha! I filed the paperwork myself. It officially doesn't exist! The only ones who still know its coordinates are sitting at this table!" Mike tittered, shielding his muzzle with the back of his paw, "Charles here has no idea what we're even talking about, so he doesn't count."

Zippo bit his claws in concern. Moe downed some of Zippo's buffalo milk in an attempt to steady his nerves. The Cerberon's growly voice put him on edge.

"The way I see it," Mike continued, "we have a chance to rule the music scene! We recruit gullible musicians as informants—and they help us keep a monopoly on all infringement in the system! And now with the Archive blown to bits, it's all aboard the gravy train! Woo-woo!" Mike mimed a train conductor. "And what better place to recruit musicians than our very own night club? Am I right? And if they ever get out of line, all I have to do is press a button and make their heads pop like an overripe Bolano Berry!"

"Kabloosh!" Charles laughed moronically.

"Why would any musicians want to work for a GRIS scumbag like you?" Moe asked.

"They won't have a choice! If they want future hits, we'll be the only game in town. We'll have exclusive access to that black hole and all its treasures."

"And how big of a slice did you have in mind?" Moe asked. He sounded hesitant, but willing to hear him out.

"I'm thinking seventy-five percent of all profits should be

fair, at least for the first few years."

"Seventy-five percent?! That's wack!" Moe objected.

"Don't you think that's a bit...high, sir?" Jeremy had the courage to ask.

"Ha ha haw! You freehadists and infringers really make me laugh! You have no problem ripping off potential future victims, but it doesn't feel so good when it happens to you, does it?" Mike took a chomp from a Toastee Mum on the platter, dabbing his mouth with a napkin as he swallowed. "Seventy-five percent is a bargain. I'm providing an extremely valuable service to you mongrels! Do you think you're the only radio dippers that can do this job? I've got double agents all over this system! Ones way smarter than you! Easier on the eyes, too! I was just telling Charles about that Hadoxian cutie we recently recruited. Any of you guys know how to plant a bomb in a ghost-girl's head?" Mike chortled.

Charles mimed an exploding head. Zippo's pupils narrowed into daggers.

"I kid, I kid! But nah, we'll figure something out with her..." Mike put his napkin down. "Not bad, but I wish they had *blueberry*."

It was hard to read Moe's expression behind those shades of his, but his frown said enough. And his fist was clenched so tightly that his normally ruddy skin had turned white.

Zippo furrowed his wrinkly brow, mindspeaking an image to Moe and Jeremy. In it, Zippo burst onto the table, blasting Mike with his ray gun and splattering his head like the aforementioned Bolano Berry. It was a satisfying scenario, but then Moe lowered his shades slightly. His eyes were wide with disapproval. He shook his head, almost imperceptibly.

"But seriously, I've wasted enough time chasing you idiots around. I have other projects stacking up that I need to get to. Do we have a deal, or do I just vaporize you and find someone else?" Mike grinned.

Zippo mindspoke a second scenario. In this one, Jeremy pointed at something. It distracted the GRIS agents so that Moe could scramble under the table and run away. In the confusion, Zippo and Jeremy could also make their escape.

Jeremy glanced at Moe, who nodded ever so slightly.

Time for some classic distraction technique.

As if on cue, the club lights dimmed and Briffu retook the stage. He was announcing the next act. "These automatons are about to *get it on*! Please welcome: Roby and the Roidz!"

Everyone applauded.

"Mike, did I hear you say you prefer blueberry Toastee Mums?" Jeremy asked in his best stage voice. The Cerberon's scowl softened at the mention of the pastry.

"Why, yes, as a matter of fact."

"Check this out," Jeremy said. He moved an empty plate in front of him, reaching into his blazer to pull out his wand.

"Freeze!" Charles in Charge yapped, whipping out his glazer and pointing it right at Jeremy's face.

"Whoa! Easy, now!" Jeremy said, frozen. "I'm just getting my wand!"

"Calm down, you hot-headed freak!" Mike barked at Charles. "I want to see this!"

"*Roby! Roby! Roby!*" the audience chanted as a small silvery robot rolled onto the stage. He was followed by four other robotic musicians. All of their metallic bodies were polished to a mirror-shine. Jeremy pulled his Jansen Black Tarot from his pocket.

"Hey!" Charles pointed with his gun, smiling with his tongue lolling out of his mouth. "It's a wand! You're magical, just like Tommy Cobblestone! Hurr hurr!"

Jeremy broke into a sweat. "Your brother sure is perceptive," he said to Mike as he pushed his spectacles up with the tip of his wand. Mike Mania grinned. Jeremy could feel his bushy tail wagging under the table.

The robots on stage finished setting up their cybertronic instruments. The little rolling one sprouted arms and legs. He posed for a few moments, holding a microphone in the air. It sparkled like a gemstone.

"Zip, do you have a stick of gum I could transform?"

"Yeh," Zip mewed, unzipping his fanny pack and rummaging through it.

Charles flinched, aiming his gun at the Felinian instead. "Not so fast!" he yipped.

"Noh gun," Zip meowed calmly. He removed a couple of baseball cards from his fanny pack, laying them gently on the table. "Jus' cards. See?"

"Oh, *Hades!*" Mike woofed. "Just let them do their trick! I want my Toastee Mum, you fool!"

Zippo lifted the Personal Shell out of his pack.

Mike snarled. His eyes went positively *feral*. He tore his glazer out of its holster, aiming it with both hands. "Where did you GET *THAT*?" he snapped at Zippo.

"Wat? Dis?" Zippo held the Shell in one paw, his other paw lifted in surrender.

The whine from Mike's glyphic lazer indicated it was warming up. "That prototype is the property of Seashell Systems. Hand it over. NOW." His growl was deadly.

Just then, the lights of the club cut out. A ruby red spotlight shone on the stage, gleaming off of the robots' reflective bodies. Synthetic music exploded all around them as the smaller robot started to breakdance. A percussive beat flooded the club, positively *demanding* that everyone get out on the dance floor. Red and blue lights strobed as spectators rushed from their seats.

Zippo's reflexes kicked in, and he ducked just in time. A laser blast streaked from Mike Mania's gun with an electric green bolt so hot, Jeremy felt it frying the air around his face.

Zippo batted Mike in the face with his free paw. The Cerberon bit the air reflexively, his jaws clacking as they closed.

Zippo slashed at Mike's snout, as quick as lightning. The GRIS agent yipped in pain.

"Don't you touch my BROTHER!" Charles in Charge howled. Before he could shoot, Zippo flicked his claws at Charles's face, also slashing him on the muzzle. Charles yowled in pain as Moe reached over and snatched the P-Shell from Zippo's grasp.

"Drop it!" Mike Mania bellowed. Charles howled in solidarity.

Moe flung his hands up, holding the Shell above his head. As Mike raised his gun, Moe slid down under the table. Mike squeezed the trigger, blasting the now-empty bench seat. Under the table, Moe yanked on Mike Mania's legs as hard as he could. The Cerberon's arms flew into the air as he fired off his glazer in the confusion, sending green blasts into the ceiling. Moe rolled out from underneath the table and tossed the Shell back to Zippo before dashing into the crowded dance floor.

Mike Mania tumbled out, spotting Moe and chasing him. "Give it back, you filthy infringer!" he howled as he blasted his glazer, dancers screaming and jumping out of the way.

Zippo skittered onto the table, batting Charles in Charge in the face to keep him at bay. Charles snarled as he nipped at the Felinian. Zippo's legs wobbled and his tail flicked for balance as he avoided stepping on any plates or cutlery. "Jrr-mEE! Katch!" he shouted, dropping the Personal Shell into Jeremy's lap.

Charles bared his fangs, chomping down on Zippo's ankle. Zippo screeched, kicking Charles in the face before slipping and falling. He crashed down and overturned the table.

There was no time to speak, and the music would have made communication impossible anyway. Zippo bolted into the crowd, hoping to draw Charles away. He must have mindspoken to Jeremy before he ran, because Jeremy's brain flooded with blurry images of running to a turbolift and meeting back at the ship.

Charles in Charge panted as he crawled out from behind the broken table, raising his glazer and aiming it directly at the dance floor.

"Novo COLLAZIO!" Jeremy shouted. A bolt of magical energy shot at the Cerberon's weapon, transforming it into a blueberry Toastee Mum. It crumbled into a sticky mess in his clenched paws. Charles barked in confusion.

"Hey! Over here!" Jeremy hollered. Charles turned around, furious. Drool dripped from his jaws and onto his ruffled collar, which was stained with blood from the slash marks on his face and ear. The disco lights bathed the Cerberon in red as Roby and the Roidz played on.

Jeremy gulped. "Hey! Uh—here it is!" he held the P-Shell up, waving it around. "You want this thing, right?" Charles froze, sniffing the air and nodding vigorously. "Go get it!" Jeremy said, pretending to throw the device out into the crowd. Charles's head swiveled reflexively as he scampered away like mad, pushing dancers out of his way.

Jeremy didn't waste one second. He plunged into another part of the crowd, losing himself in the the chaos and the strobe lights. He was about halfway to the elevator when the music stopped.

"THANK YOU, ORGANICS," the robot on stage spoke. "THIS NEXT ONE IS A SONG WE COMPOSED ABOUT THE INTERESTING BINARY ANOMALIES THAT EXIST IN POSITRONIC WAVE FUNCTIONS. WE HOPE YOU FIND IT ACCEPTABLE." They launched into a new song, everyone around Jeremy jumping up and down with the beat.

Jeremy thought he heard the unique sound of Zippo's *Bug Zapper* somewhere in the club, and worked his way toward it. He couldn't be sure in the sea of bodies and music, but he thought he was almost to the elevator where they had come in.

An offworlder danced up next to Jeremy, waving a friend over. "Khra! Fhhe k'O teHK, *Tommy* pHra fHHe!"

The friend pointed and giggled. "*Cobblestone* ehr ehr, k'O!"

"Oh, give me a break!" Jeremy shouted, cursing as he shoved his way through the pair. He stumbled out of the crowd.

"Jrr-mEE!" Zippo meowed over the noise. Jeremy could see him, standing inside the elevator. He was waving frantically, using his foot to block the lift's door from shutting. Moe crouched beside him, taking aim at a target somewhere in the club.

"Chief! Hurry up! Zip, over there!" Moe pointed just as a green glazer beam blasted the floor at Jeremy's feet.

"Aaaahghh! It's hot!" Jeremy hopped in the air, avoiding the blobs of glowing hot plasma. Zippo stepped out of the turbolift, firing back at the shooter. The strobing lights made hitting anything all but impossible.

"Come!" Zippo beckoned. The doors tried to close again, but Zippo put an arm back to block them. Before he had time to think, Jeremy sprinted at the elevator.

Moe stood up, raising his pistol right at Jeremy's path. "Look out!" Moe shouted, squeezing off a shot with an audible *PEW!*

Jeremy dove into the turbolift, his arms shielding his head as he fell to the floor. He turned back just in time to glimpse Mike Mania doubling over and falling to the floor. Charles rushed to his brother's limp body, howling a blood-curdling howl as the elevator doors closed. "Take us to the lobby!" Moe shouted. They descended.

Zippo inched back unsteadily, limping from his injury. He slid to the floor. Moe rushed to his side, checking on him. "You okay, homie?"

Zippo mewed in the affirmative, showing off the bite marks on his ankle.

"Eww, gross!" Moe dug through Zippo's backpack, pulling out one of his striped sweatbands. "Wrap this around your ankle. Try to hide your limp when we get down there. We all need to act normal and just walk out of here before anyone realizes what's going on. Kid, clean off your glasses," Moe said as he reholstered his weapon. "How do I look? Any plasma burns? Blood?" Moe turned around, checking himself in a reflection.

Jeremy removed his spectacles, rubbing them with his shirt tail. They were smudged with perspiration and plasma soot, which explained why his vision had been so blurry.

"Dude!" Moe realized something, spinning around. "Do you have the thing?!" He pawed at Jeremy, putting his hands in his jacket pockets.

"Get off!" Jeremy pushed Moe's hands away, annoyed. He fished the Personal Shell out of his inner pocket and showed it to Moe, who sighed with relief. "What is all the fuss over this stupid thing?" Jeremy balked. "It almost got us killed!" He felt tempted to just slam it on the floor and be rid of it, once and for all.

"I don't know, dude. But we're going to find out."
Zippo chittered in pain as he dressed his wound.

CHAPTER 40

THE DEMON'S EYE

The turbolift descended through the Low Tier, picking up more passengers each time it made a stop. Several of the offworlders talked quietly amongst themselves.

"So, Moe," Jeremy whispered, "the GRIS agent back there, Mike... Did you just—you know..." Jeremy made a neck slicing motion with his hand.

"Did I cut his head off?" Moe asked.

"No! I mean did you..." Jeremy rolled his hand slowly, not wanting to say it aloud.

"Ohhhh, did I *kill* him?"

Several offworlders looked up.

"Yes," Jeremy said.

"Nah, he'll be okay," Moe said. "He might feel like horking for a few hours, but my phaser was only set to stun. Didn't want to risk wasting him; that would bring all of GRIS down on us, hard."

The turbolift reached the lobby, its passengers scuttling out as quickly as they could.

"Then again...now he can still blab about the black hole to someone else..." Moe gave an exasperated shrug. "We'll cross that bridge when we get to it. Let's bounce."

Zippo did his best to disguise his pain. He placed an arm around Jeremy's shoulders and they walked as briskly as they could.

✳ ✳ ✳

Jeremy heard a commotion as they approached the landing lot. It was the sound of voices arguing, punctuated by the occasional bark. "Madi Nabo!" he said, rushing ahead.

The Lomaa'lian lot attendant was chasing the tiny Cerberon around the toll booth. He shook a rolled up edition of the Cosmic Beacon at her.

"Get away from me!" Madi yipped. She ran over to the *Terrapin*.

"Hey! You leave her alone!" Jeremy shouted.

The Lomaa'lian stopped, looking up. "She went to the *bathroom* on my landing pad!" he shouted. "My lot ain't no public toilet!"

"I wouldn't have had to if *you'd* provided a species-friendly sanitation port! Gah!" Madi rushed to Jeremy's side. He picked her up. "Thank you, Jeremy. *You* are a gentleman!" she huffed.

Moe flashed his ID card, slapping his last remaining credits into the attendant's hand. "And who's gonna clean up after your little friend?" the attendant shouted.

Jeremy stood for a moment, watching as Zippo limped his way up the ramp. He had an idea. "One moment, sir," he said, racing into the cargo bay. He grabbed a few issues of *The Adventures of Tommy Cobblestone* no. 53 and went back outside. "Here you go—for your trouble."

The attendant looked at the comic books stupidly. "What am I supposed to do with these? I already have this issue!"

"Use them to clean up the mess?" Jeremy suggested, waving goodbye as the rear door closed and the ship's engines whirred to life.

* * *

"So, Madi, you really did save our lives back in that space battle, huh?" Jeremy said, remembering what Mike Mania had told them in the nightclub. He placed a plate of ham and eggs down for the Cerberon.

"Mmmm," Madi Nabo said, not really paying attention to what the wizard boy was saying. "Oh, you made me one of those cheese omeletes, yes those are good, too." She scarfed her food. "I'll have you know," she spoke between bites, "that I guarded this ship with my life! I looked out the window the whole time! At one point there was a young couple just walking on the sidewalk. Very suspicious looking! I screamed at them the entire time they walked by. Kept screaming for a good five minutes afterward, just to be safe! They didn't come back! Ha! Cowards..."

Jeremy patted Madi on the head and went to the cockpit.

Zippo squeezed more Bac-Out Gel out of the tube as he treated his bite wound. He held a paw up to his nose, giving the medicinal gel a sniff. "Yeugh. Smell weer-ED."

"Scanners picking anyone up out there?" Moe asked.

Zippo shook his head. "Neh. All kleer. Starways quiet."

"Hmm...I don't like it," Moe said. "You'd think they'd at least send one ship in our direction by now. I wonder what's keeping them."

"Maybe Mike Mania is having a hard time getting off the planet," Jeremy guessed.

"Why would he have a hard time with that?" Moe said, swiveling around.

"Don't you need one of *these* to pick up your ship?" Jeremy flipped an identification card onto Moe's lap. On it was a holographic photo of Mike Mania, his tongue lolling out of his mouth as he grinned crazily.

Moe picked up the card, taking his shades off to squint at it. "Where did you get this?!"

Jeremy reclined in the jumpseat, his smirk increasing by the second. "I wanted to try out that pickpocketing trick the Enigma showed us. Mike was so close to me I could smell his dog breath." Zippo scowled at this detail. "It was no big deal," Jeremy interlocked his fingers behind his head as he put his feet up.

"This ought to buy us some time! Well done, chief!" Moe high-fived Jeremy. "I bet you he is so *maaaad*!"

"Yeh! If he find you, he prabably *kill* you," Zippo chuckled. Jeremy's smirk disappeared.

* * *

They traveled for three days. Their tensions tightened and loosened each time a blip popped onto their scans, only to disappear minutes later without incident. They'd nearly made it all the way back to Earth when that final, fateful blip appeared.

"Are we sure it's them?" Jeremy asked.

"GRIS," Zippo meowed.

"It's too far away to be positive," Moe said.

"I said it *GRIS*!" Zippo insisted.

"All right, all right! I'm just trying to stay cool!" Moe said in an exasperated tone. Everyone in the cockpit was exhausted and burned out.

"But you said we're going to lose them! Right? In Florida!" Jeremy asked.

"Nothing can be tracked through the Demon's Eye. The neutrino surge from the storm makes any ship scans basically impossible. It's the great reset button of your world. That's what they say, anyway," Moe cracked his knuckles.

[*Translator's Note: For all you non-Terran readers, the Tampa Tempest—colloquially known as the "Demon's Eye"—is a Class-A electromagnetic everstorm that formed in the skies above Tampa, Florida sometime in A.D. 1860. Nobody knows for sure how the storm started, but the available evidence suggests that it was caused by a group of pirates attempting to smuggle in a crate of black market parakeets from the Gimbini System. When their home-made transdimensional smuggling device malfunctioned, it tore open an atmospheric rift that spiraled into an all-out tempest. The Demon's Eye has been darkening the skies above Tampa and the surrounding area for over a hundred years, and is still going strong to this day! —ChatterBot 3.6]*

"It's supposedly a smuggler's dream. And there's a pirate community there. Everyone comes and goes as they please, no hassles from planetary customs officials. Extremely dangerous. Sounds to me like it's the perfect place to off-load some tech." Moe nodded at the P-Shell, which sat in one of the cockpit's cup holders.

Jeremy also looked at the device, wondering how much trouble Alfie and the other boys had gotten into for losing it. It was a well-established fact that Professor Bibliosnuff turned problem students into crested newts. The thought of Alfie, Pete and Dave living out the rest of their days in a dungeon newt farm made Jeremy feel a teensy bit sorry. *On the other hand,* he thought, *they WERE wankers.*

"Moooe," Zippo cooed. He pointed to the blip on the navicomputer. It was definitely getting bigger.

"Grok," Moe muttered. "They're gaining on us faster than I thought." He rubbed his chin. "Zip, you think you can handle an hour of full-throttle?"

Zippo tied his batty ears back with a hairband, squinting in concentration. Without a word, he pushed the *Terrapin*'s subetheric throttle to maximum.

"That's my homeboy," Moe scritched Zippo's head. "Just get us there and we'll lose 'em in the storm," Moe said.

Jeremy found himself overwhelmed with relief when Earth

finally came into view. For as much as he enjoyed traveling the solar system, the sight of that big blue marble looked pretty good right now. He didn't have much time to dwell on his homesickness, though, as the comm chimed insistently.

"They've gotten close enough to hail us. Ugh," Moe said, worried that the sound might distract Zippo. He clicked the comm on and off again, hanging up on the caller. Moments later, the hail chime returned.

"Just ignore them," Jeremy said, switching the stereo on. "Here, let's put on some music." He picked up a crystal diskette at random and inserted it, hoping the music would mask the comm's ding. The sounds of *Blastin' Off at Sunrise* by Surplus Flashback flooded the cockpit. As Moe plotted the trajectory that would take them through the Tampa Tempest, Jeremy looked out at his vast homeworld.

Just then, a blast rocked the ship. Alarms klaxoned as the ship's A.I. made its typically frantic announcements. "It's nothing, it's nothing! That felt like a warning shot," Moe said, holding his hands up. "They're probably mad that we're not answering their stupid hails. But I'm in no mood to talk." Moe tapped a few keys, running a scan before re-entry. He turned to Jeremy, speaking quietly. "It's definitely GRIS."

Zippo remained in the zone. If he'd heard them, he gave no indication. The moment the alarms died down, the ship shuddered with another bump. It sent the alarms into another screaming tizzy, making Moe very annoyed. "Alright already!" he shouted, switching the alarm off manually. "We get it!"

The *Terrapin* made its final approach, the planet glowing beneath them. As the ship banked down, Jeremy observed the unmistakable panhandle that was Florida. Much of the state was obscured by the dark swirling vortex of the Tempest. The storm seemed to stare right back at Jeremy, clusters of lightning crackling within its clouds.

Another shot rocked the *Terrapin*'s hull, making the whole

cockpit convulse.

"Buckle in, everyone!" Moe shouted.

Madi Nabo scampered into the cockpit, hopping up onto the jump seat. Jeremy held her tightly as they descended.

"Zip, I think they've figured out what we're doing. Might need to do a little fancy flying." Moe looked back at Jeremy. "Hold on, you two." Zippo rolled his shoulders, tensing himself at the flight controls. The *Terrapin* plunged into the stratosphere.

A dense swirl of mist enveloped them, and for a moment, all was dark. They descended into a vast open space between the clouds. Electric blue shafts of lightning crackled within the cloud layers, blasting from top to bottom, bottom to top. Zippo maneuvered the ship as if in a maze, avoiding the ever-writhing forks of energy. A column of lightning popped extremely close to the ship, strobing the cockpit with its harsh light. Seconds later a thunderclap detonated, slapping them with a boom so deafening that Jeremy wasn't sure whether he'd screamed. Madi Nabo trembled violently, burying her head in the crook of Jeremy's arm.

The *Terrapin* banked left, then right, plummeting through the endless forest of lightning. They flew between the random bolts and blasts for what felt like an eternity.

"Did we lose them?" Jeremy finally shouted over the storm.

"I have no idea!" Moe cried out, looking at the computer. "Krud! They weren't kidding! We're flying blind in here! I can't get a scan on anything!" The thunder sent concussion waves throughout the cockpit.

Once Zippo decided they'd had enough, he took them down. The bottom layer of clouds enveloped the ship once more, muffling the sound of the thunder above them. They sank silently, finally dropping into the open sky. It was hard to make out the details of the earth below—the storm made the atmosphere as dark as midnight—but they appeared to be flying above a long stretch of beach. Zippo looked over, a half-smile on his wrinkled muzzle. "We maek it... yeh?"

"Homeboys, I think we lost them!" Moe announced with glee.

Zippo held up a paw, which Moe and Jeremy took turns high-fiving. Before they could celebrate too much, however, a mortar exploded right outside the cockpit. It was unlike any weapon the offworlders had ever seen, as it sent thousands of shimmering orange sparks through the air. Zippo spiraled the ship, avoiding the colorful bomb.

"We're hit! We're hit!" Moe shouted. "Are we hit?"

Another explosion lit up the ship, this one a sparkling green. Zippo loop-di-looped, trying to throw off their attackers as red, white and blue shells exploded all around them in the night sky. Each time, the mortar's sparks fizzled out in the air harmlessly. Jeremy pointed out the cockpit's front window. "It's fireworks!" he exclaimed.

Madi Nabo yelped as another one of the colorful bombs boomed in the distance. She scampered off to hide in the pile of laundry in Zippo's cabin. "Zip, just take us down! It'll be okay," Jeremy reassured everyone.

Zippo mewed a confirmation and glided to the surface. The *Terrapin* splashed down onto the water beside a dock. As the engines spun down they heard the rush of the waves, fireworks popping in the distance.

CHAPTER 41

BARBAROSSA BAY

Jeremy, Moe and Zippo clambered out of the top hatch and down onto the pier. Noiseless lightning flickered in the heavy clouds above them. A few more fireworks went off, their reflection glimmering on the night sea. Jeremy heard the sound of music in the distance. The ocean breeze also carried the tempting aroma of a barbecue. A hand-painted wooden sign swung from an iron archway on the dock. It read: *Barbarossa Bay*.

An endless hodgepodge of starships bobbed along the docks, everything from sleek techrunner cutlasses to janky old scumbuckets. Moe set off towards a ramshackle assortment of shops along the boardwalk. Hundreds of rough-looking Terrans and offworlders were walking up and down the beach. Some held torches, others swung around bottles of Martian grog or roast turkey legs. Quite a few were waving little American flags as they laughed and caroused. Zippo stopped to inspect a weenie roast a few tramps were holding over a bonfire. Jeremy pulled him along. It wasn't exactly the kind of crowd he wanted to get lost in.

There was a group of ruffians playing cards over a barrel. One of the card players had a black scar across his stubbly cheek; another had a creature perched on his shoulder that appeared to be some kind of alien monkey. It peered at passersby with its giant green eyes. [*Translator's Note: it was actually just a Terran* tarsier. *Look them up, they're freaky! —ChatterBot 3.6*]

As Jeremy and his companions made their way along the boardwalk, they kept their eyes open for the Mike Mania. Any GRIS agent would be crazy to come to a party like this—it was, after all, a gathering of pirates, smugglers, and infringers of every copyright law, all heavily armed, with oceans of rum flowing quite freely. Still, after what they'd been through, they couldn't help being cautious.

Moe was obviously looking for something, but he wouldn't tell Jeremy what. He finally stopped to talk to an Unktuu smuggler who was leaning in an alley, smoking a cigar. The smuggler had very bushy eyebrows and an eye-patch, muttering something to Moe that Jeremy didn't catch. The offworlder pointed down the boardwalk with a cybertronic hand, motioning as if giving directions. Without a word, Moe dashed away. Zippo urged Jeremy along, mindspeaking an image to him of keeping his wand drawn and ready.

Moe finally stopped in front of one of the last buildings on the strip. Rickety wooden pillars made up the entryway. A rectangular sign announced: *HOTEL SCUZZY.*

A brass band sitting on the boardwalk struck up a boisterous rendition of "You're a Grand Old Flag," while a group of alien buccaneers swung their arms, anthropodic limbs, and in one case, a prehensile trunk, as they marched in place with the music. A pair of offworlder bar wenches flung open the two upstairs windows of the hotel, emerging onto a balcony and unfurling red, white and blue banners down the side of the building. The crowd clapped and whistled at the wenches, who waved sparklers as they blew everyone kisses.

Moe stopped before entering. "What's going on? Some kind of party?" he asked.

"It's the Fourth of July!" Jeremy said happily, arms outstretched. "This is so keen-o! I haven't been to a Fourth of July since I was a kid!" Firecrackers snapped and crackled somewhere down on the beach. Partygoers fired their phasers and plasma rifles in the air enthusiastically.

"Fourth of July? You don't say..." Moe murmured. He craned his neck, trying to peer into the building. "You two, follow my lead. Zip, you got the thing?"

Zippo meowed.

"Good. If anything happens, don't be a hero. Just run. And take the P-Shell with you." He double checked his phaser. "It's all we've got left."

* * *

They entered the Hotel Scuzzy's tavern through the swinging saloon doors. Inside, the celebration was more subdued. Old-fashioned torchlight lit the room, giving it a cozy feel. Most of the patrons were talking warmly, laughing, and drinking as a dwarven pirate pounded out "Stars and Stripes Forever" on the clavitone. A lemur-like alien girl squeezed a concertina beside him.

The Terran bartender gave them a friendly nod as they approached. "Happy Independence Day, gents," he said, encouraging them to each take a little American flag from a mason jar. He refilled several mugs on the bar with a dark amber liquid, placing them on a tray and handing them off to a waiter, who he shooed away. "All right then, what'll it be? Carribean rum? Martian grog? Dek'ktari Bumbo?"

Zippo snickered at the silly-sounding names. Moe stepped forward, adjusting his shades. "We've got an...item. For the, uh, Lost and Found..?" Moe gauged the bartender's reaction, unsure of himself. "Zip, show him." Zippo removed the Shell from his fanny pack and held it out. The torchlight glinted off its polished plastic frame.

The bartender frowned. "I hate to be the bearer of bad news, boys, but you're out of luck. At least for today. The Lost and Found is closed—what with the holiday, you know. However, I can offer you a very comfy room for the night, and first thing tomorrow—"

"Ahoy," a young Terran man looked up from the end of the bar. They hadn't noticed him before, as he was partially surrounded by stacks of books. He had blonde wavy hair pulled back into a ponytail, and wore a ridiculously puffy white shirt. He scribbled notes in a tablet, which he picked up as he walked over. "I spied your blunderbuss there, matey—a disruptor ray, is it?"

"Yeh! Want see?" Zippo was always happy to show off the Bug Zapper. He unbuckled his holster and displayed the gun on his two paws. The weapon's plasteel frame was weathered and dull. The young buccaneer looked the disruptor over, admiring it.

Jeremy noted the fellow's odd manner of speech. His Terran accent was scholarly, even refined, but peppered with archaic pirate expressions.

"Avast!" the young man exclaimed. "She's quite the armament! Manufactured by *Cherubim*, if I'm not mistaken?"

Zippo nodded, purring proudly.

"Arr! What craftsmanship!" The young man took notes in his book as they spoke of offworlder weaponry. Much of the conversation was lost on Jeremy, who was happy to sit and just take in the scene. He enjoyed the music as he ordered root beer after root beer. (A sign above the door said they were free in honor of the 4th.)

After some time and several pages of notes, the swashbuckler smiled at Moe and Zippo. "Well, mateys. This is all outstanding. I've needed some original research from non-Terrans, and so I thank ye! Did I overhear ye say you've an item for the Lost and Found?"

"Yes..." Moe responded cautiously.

"I'd be happy to oblige ye. Why don't we step into the back and take a look?" The young man pulled out a clanky set of keys on an oversized ring. "Ye may enter," he said as he unlocked the door.

Technological gizmos, contraptions, and all manner of galactic doohickeys cluttered the shelves in the room. Jeremy wondered if this guy was what his companions referred to as a *techrunner*.

"Chaz!" the bartender called out. "Don't forget—*Nothing But Treble* is performing at five! You said you'd watch the bar for me!"

"Of course, Dutch!" the young man called out as they entered the back room.

"Your name is Chaz?" Moe asked.

"Aye," he extended a hand, shaking with each member of the trio. "Avast! How rude of me! Chalcedoni Buchanan. Pirate-in-training, assistant professor. Arr. I apologize for the mess. Looks like a proper bilge rat's nest in here! I'm behind on cataloging items for the Lost and Found. Been slaving away on me dissertation for weeks."

"I think there's been a *mistake*," Moe said. "We don't want to actually turn anything in to the Lost and Found..."

Chaz chuckled. "Arr, ye must really be land lubbers, eh? It's not *actually* a Lost and Found, matey. Us scaliwags just call it that for legal reasons. That way, Terran authorities can't incarcerate us for selling offworlder tech. All the treasures you see here are for sale," Chalcedoni motioned to the shelves. "Aye, however, the weapons in the glass case do require a voucher."

Jeremy looked at the case. It contained a dazzling array of alien lasers, glazers, and phasers.

Zippo picked up an item from the shelf and inspected it.

"Now that's a beauty, arr she is. A dream modulator from Thenkov 6. Let's ye program what dreams ye have before ye slumber," Chalcedoni explained.

"Keen-o!" Jeremy exclaimed.

Zippo put the item down and picked up another. It resembled a piano keyboard.

"Ahoy, now that's an experimental one. She's a Mood Organ from a psychiatric facility on Tholara," Chalcedoni said. "Handsomely constructed. Ye play certain tones, and it makes the hearers feel whatever mood is keyed to those tones. I use it myself sometimes—it puts me in the mood to do my research when I'm otherwise *hanging the jib*, so to speak. I can't say how well it works on Felinians, though."

"Hanging de *jib*?" Zippo looked confused.

Moe had a disappointed look.

"What's the matter?" Jeremy asked.

"Oh, nothing. Just that—with all of this funky offworlder tech, a portable music device seems kind of...weak." He shrugged. "Probably worthless."

"Nonsense!" Chalcedoni said, clearing off a table. "Maybe to a Binosian like ye, but I find all of it quite fascinating! Perhaps a little *too* fascinating—sometimes I get so distracted from my school work. It will be a miracle if I complete it all on time." Chalcedoni *yarr*-ed wistfully.

"Here, dis thing. Look," Zippo placed the Personal Shell on the table. The three took turns explaining where it came from and what it could do, including playing music, taking digital photographs, and even recording very short televids. Chaz hopped up as they spoke, gingerly grabbing a few alien-looking tools from his shelves and returning to the table.

"Yo ho! That is fascinating," he said, placing some goggles on. "Do you mind if I tinker around a bit?" Before getting an answer, he was already removing the tiny screws and dismantling the Shell. "Ahoy! What have we here?" he gasped. He peered inside the device with some kind of microscope, then flashed it with a scanner. After each of his tests he'd let out a grunt of approval or a gasp, muttering "yo-ho" or "ahoy!" as he went. The trio settled in, realizing this was going to take a while.

Jeremy and Zippo leafed through comics from Chaz's pile, while Moe examined the user manual for the Mood Organ.

When Chaz was finally finished, he pushed his goggles up to his forehead. He had a concerned look. He took a deep breath, composing his thoughts. "Arr. Mateys, I ought to just give this item back and have ye weigh anchor. There's no way anyone is going to *touch* that object—not here, not anywhere in this star system, not anywhere in the League of Planets!" His eyes widened. "This tech looks completely *Velitovian*!"

The pirate had an expectant look on his face, as if awaiting a big reaction.

Moe and Zippo looked at each other and shrugged. They looked to Jeremy, who also shrugged. "You got me," Jeremy said. "I only understand about twelve to fourteen percent of anything you guys are saying."

"Arr, I wouldn't expect a Terran to know," Chaz said, "but I assumed a Binosian and a Felinian would have learned about the Velitovian Conflict! Didn't ye read about it in school?"

"Ummm..." Moe smiled amiably. "Let's assume we did. Why don't you explain anyway...for the kid's sake?"

Chalcedoni grabbed a copy of the Terminus Encyclopedia from his desk, flipping it open and returning it to the table. The liquid crystal paper displayed mountains of text and images which he zoomed in on. "Thar," he pointed at an image in the book, "is a Velitovian." The picture was of a blobule of pale blue slime. Jeremy wasn't sure why, but the blob looked eerily familiar.

"Ye know what—I believe I have a tape about this." Chalcedoni opened a closet. In it were hundreds of vidtapes in a huge stack. He pulled one down, popping it into a player attached to a partially disassembled televid. The tape started, but it was narrated in an alien language. Jeremy could tell that Moe and Zippo were also confused.

"Ahoy now! Don't tell me ye lubbers don't speak Mu'rrrroro?" Chalcedoni looked exasperated.

"Got any Lingo Bars for it?" Jeremy asked.

Chalcedoni rummaged in a box of Lingos. "I'm all out. Do ye want Icelandic?"

"*Nei, takk,*" Jeremy said, holding up his hand.

"Arr, no matter," Chalcedoni said. "I can explain. Two thousand years hence," Chaz waved back for emphasis, "These creatures known as Velitovians began popping up in star systems on the fringes of the known galaxy. The blobbies claimed to be deep-space nomads and traders, exiled from their homeworld. They brought with them all sorts of new and interesting technology. And they started doing business with all the worlds they came into contact with throughout the Cosmic League. Trading, selling their tech, and so forth."

"Yeh," Zippo mewed, his attention still on the historical footage.

"But the conundrum was, any world the Velitovians did business with, slowly... collapsed."

"Collapsed?" Moe said. "What do you mean?"

"That I don't know, me hearties. Nobody does. The records available merely indicate they underwent the triple-C: *Complete Civilizational Collapse.* Ye can imagine what that looked like."

Jeremy wondered about this, giving himself chills.

"Aye. This didn't happen overnight—a total collapse can take about a hundred, two hundred years. But each planet reached a point where they sort of just...disappeared, so to speak. Vanished. Arr, no more innovation, no more explorers, no more *anything.* Look here, Biruclite 7," Chalcedoni went over, pointing to a table in the encyclopedia, "made first contact with Velitovians. Hundred and fifty years later, they're never heard from again. Same thing happened to Zetrolla Prime. Started buying from Velitovian caravans in 1386. By 1455, nothing.

Uk'mod, Nepartu, the Yiici Collective—arr, the list goes on, and it's always the same. Any society that embraces Velitovian tech only lasts two, maybe three generations. Then—*abandon ship*."

"That's horrible!" Jeremy said.

"Now, wait a second," Moe said. "We've traveled around the League quite a bit, and I've never even *heard* of those planets."

"Yarr! I'm not surprised, matey! In order to prevent the collapse from spreading, the Cosmic League ordered every last trace of Velitovian tech vaporized. Every collapsed world got bombed into rubble, too, and their coordinates were obliterated from all navigational records. As a preventative measure, the League developed excellent tools for detecting Velitovian tech." Chaz held up two of the instruments he used to scan the Shell. "Which is good, because once their tech infiltrates a planet—it's basically over. That's why dealing in Velitovian merchandise is still punishable by death, if I'm not mistaken."

Moe gulped, removing his shades. He squinted at the Personal Shell in horrified fascination. "I don't get it! How would this stupid thing collapse an entire civilization?! It's just a wack little music player!"

"Ye've posed an excellent question, matey, but one I don't have an answer to. For one: no scaliwag living, myself included, has ever operated real Velitovian tech. Thus, no one knows what makes it so dangerous. And secondly—your device here is not genuine Velitovian tech."

"What?" Jeremy scrunched up his face, annoyed. "Then what's all the fuss about!"

"The fuss, lad, is that this prototype, this—*thing*—is not what it seems!" The pirate plucked up the P-Shell, eyes shiny with amazement. "It has all the standard hallmarks of Velitovian tech, but tweaked *just* enough to fool the scanners! It's almost as if...as if someone out there used Terran technology to create a Velitovian *forgery*—but that's impossible! Terran tech is nowhere *near* as advanced!" he held the Shell up to his face, scrutinizing it. He looked at the engraving on the back. "Seashell Systems, Terra Firma?" he read aloud. "Ahoy, I'm stumped. Where did you lads say ye got this thing?"

"Pigpimples Academy." Just as Jeremy said it, he remembered why the picture of the blob looked so familiar. His mouth went dry.

"Wait...do you mean...?" the pirate asked, grinning. "I was *wondering* why you were dressed like that!"

"*Yes...except...HE copied...ME,*" Jeremy tried to say, but only mouthed words as if in a trance.

"Shiver me timbers! Is the lad ill?" Chalcedoni asked. "If I didn't know better, I'd say he had the bends!"

Maledict.

Von.

Bibliosnuff!

The horrible name floated into Jeremy's consciousness like an evil spirit. *The boys in the dorm that night said they'd "borrowed" the Personal Shells from the professor's dungeon office.* Jeremy stared at the device on the table. *The professor had been talking to an offworlder in his crystal ball that night.*

A pale, blue, blob.

"You okay, chief?" Moe asked.

"Jrr-mEE?" Zippo placed a paw on Jeremy's shoulder.

A vision appeared in Jeremy's mind. The blue blob grew and expanded, like the marshmallow in DJ Nebz's microwave, until it swallowed up all of Ballyhoo Keep. The blob grew to absorb Pigpimples Academy, too, and eventually all the cities on Earth—until finally, it enveloped the whole planet.

It all made sense.

"THAT'S why your magtape recordings didn't work!" Jeremy whispered, a look of horror in his eyes.

"Jrr-mEE, wat are you say?" Zippo mewed, concerned. Jeremy turned and faced the Felinian, grabbing him by his wrinkly pink shoulders.

"From the black hole! You can't record the future anymore—because there IS NO FUTURE!"

CHAPTER 42

TO FAKE, PERCHANCE TO INFRINGE

"Dude, what are you talking about?" Moe asked.

"Don't you see?" Jeremy said. "Someone got Velitovian tech to Earth! And Seashell Systems is going to start selling it! Soon! Which means my civilization has about a hundred years before total collapse! Which means *no more future music*! No more radio dipping!"

Zippo mewed with dread. Moe looked like he might hork. "What the kid is saying...it's all starting to make a sick kind of sense. But why would a Pigpimples professor have Velitovian prototypes?" Moe asked.

Someone pounded on the room's door.

"Let us inside! / I know he's hiding there!" a voice called from the hallway. The pounding was so hard it nearly splintered the wood. Zippo drew his firearm while Moe rushed over and squeezed up against a wall. Chaz lifted the latch. A burly looking alien flung the door open.

"I've got you now!" the alien's voice rumbled. He was an Odean. [*Translator's Note: A peculiar race of offworlders that either by choice or involuntarily (no one is really sure) can only speak in iambic pentameter. —ChatterBot 3.6*] His thick, rough skin was dark bronze and bristly, with a few white whiskers on his fat head. His face vaguely resembled that of an elephant seal, complete with a flabby trunk-like proboscis that waggled as his voice boomed. *As far as aliens go, they don't get much uglier,* Jeremy thought.

Jeremy had never seen an offworlder like him, although he noted a look of recognition in Zippo's eyes. The walrus-looking creature extended a pudgy flipper, pointing at the Felinian. "I thought I recognized this grimalkin! / So pointy-eared and shifty, like a cat! / And where's that little rat, you know the one! / He has a child's face but he's a thief!" the alien turned, spotting Moe against the wall. "A-ha! You didn't think I'd find out, did you now?" the offworlder squawked. He waddled into the room, holding out a rolled-up comic book.

"Hello Mr. Hojom," Moe said tersely. "Haven't seen you since that mini-mall on Deimos, I believe? How have you been?"

"Don't give me that! / I want these two removed!" Hojom called out to a pair of constables waiting behind him. "You ought to be banned from the Bay for life! / Call a tribunal! Inquest should be made! / I do not care if it's a holiday! / We'll lock you in the brig and toss the key!"

"Now, now, matey—let's parley a moment! What seems to be the problem?" Chalcedoni asked.

"These scaliwags sold me a *forgery*! / A Cobblestone they said was mighty rare! / They promised me it would go up in worth!" Hojom slammed the comic book down, almost shattering the table.

Jeremy looked at the issue in question. The cover pictured the titular protagonist cowering in a corner, surrounded by a group of bloodthirsty werewolves. *TOMMY COBBLESTONE: Trapped Forever?!* the title text read, followed with: *Looks like Tommy showed up at the wrong werewolf convention! Will he escape wolf jail?*

"This is a FAKE! A counterfeit, a sham!" Hojom squawked.

"I am, frankly, insulted!" Moe said, placing a hand

theatrically on his chest. "But don't take my word for it! I can prove their authenticity right now! Allow me to just grab my authenticator tools..." Moe grabbed Jeremy by the arm, walking him to the back shelf. He listened carefully as Moe muttered some instructions to him. "Just play something," the Binosian said, grabbing the Mood Organ off the shelf. He fiddled with the dials and settings, then shoved it into Jeremy's arms.

"But I—!" Jeremy protested.

"You said you took piano lessons as a kid! Trust me," Moe said, stopping for a moment to put on his shades. Jeremy complied without another word, setting the organ down and plinking out "Seaside Picnic." It was one of about three songs he still remembered from his mom's lessons.

"Sorry about that—the kid's music helps me concentrate. Now where were we?" Moe said as he picked up Chaz's tools from the table, pretending to know how to use them.

As Jeremy played the song, he felt his former attitude beginning to change. His fears evaporated like morning dew, replaced with a strange sense of assurance. This calmness grew until certainty filled his whole heart.

It's like suddenly, it all makes sense! I know I can place total and complete trust in Moe! Everything is going to be okay after all! Jeremy looked up, tears in his eyes. He smiled like a fool as all his doubts melted away. He looked over at Zippo, whose head was cocked in confusion.

Moe grunted as he scanned the comic book. "Now wait a second...my authenticity tool is telling me this is...a *forgery*!"

Jeremy gasped. Moe looked at the tool as if it were broken, giving it a little shake.

"Yes, you see! / The tools will prove me right!" Hojom said. "That book's a fake, and I am justified!"

Jeremy finished "Seaside Picnic" and started "Falling Snow." He would gladly play music for as long as Moe wanted him to—*he has everything under control, after all!*

Moe went to Zippo's backpack, unzipping it. "I apologize for that mistake, homesqueeze. I'd like to make it up to you." He pulled out a copy of issue 56, laying it on the table.

Chaz watched the exchange with rapt attention, his notebook at the ready. He scribbled furiously, recording his impressions of this "authentic interaction."

Moe sighed. "I sure do hate to part with this baby, but..." Zippo hammed it up by meowing in protest. "No, no, Zip. It's only fair."

Hojom looked at the issue, picking it up to inspect it. "Ooooh!" he cooed. "Lady Primrose and the Professor dear!" he read some of the panels, but got a skeptical look. "For all I know, this one is fake as well!"

Moe used the scanning tools again, waving them up and down the comic book. "See? The light is teal: the book is real. It's authentic."

Hojom nearly clapped his flippery hands with joy. "How could I ever doubt the pair of you! / I'm sorry my heart wavered even once," he said, smiling warmly and shuffling out of the room. He took the two constables with him.

"It was nice seeing you again," Moe said. He turned to Jeremy. "Thanks for the save, dude—you can stop playing now."

Jeremy stopped, still smiling. "I don't know how you did it, but you *did*!"

"It was nothing. I just tuned that Mood Organ to Attitude C-27: *overwhelming sense of trust with a dash of awe.*"

"That was *so* smart!" Jeremy gushed. "You always know the right thing to do!" he leaned down and hugged Moe.

Zippo smiled and purred. "Yeh Moe!" He was just happy that everyone was in such a good mood.

"Not to break up the love-in, but we'd better get starside before they throw us in the brig," Moe said. "Professor, your expertise has been invaluable."

Chalcedoni dabbed his eyes with a hanky as he finished

writing some notes. "Aye, bless my deadlights—my dissertation committee is going to love this! I'm so glad I met ye! Tally ho, mateys!" The trio bid Chaz farewell, exiting the saloon and returning to the revelries outside.

Jeremy's artificial sense of reassurance lasted until they reached the end of the boardwalk. The moment he entered the ship, that lingering sense of trust vanished, replaced with a devastating sense of dread.

As they took to the skies, Jeremy gazed down at Barbarossa Bay. He pictured the vast blue blob again. It grew on the horizon until it covered the face of the whole earth.

* * *

"Where were you guys!" Madi Nabo called out. "All those bombs going off scared me so bad I had to stress-eat all the breakfast burritos in the cat-man's mini-fridge!" She didn't bother getting up from the pile of laundry in Zippo's cabin.

"Kid, you said you got the Shell from some teacher of yours, right?" Moe said, piloting the ship through the lower stratosphere.

"Yes...basically." He didn't feel like explaining the whole story again.

"Then that's where we're going. Zip—show him that thing you showed me."

"Wait a minute," Jeremy interrupted, "you mean—back to Pigpimples?" The thought of returning to the school filled him with a sense of nausea.

"We need to find out where the Shell came from so we can stop them. You said so yourself: if Velitovian tech is going to collapse Terran civilization, we can kiss our black hole recordings goodbye."

The *Terrapin* climbed into the clouds, making Jeremy's stomach drop. "This would all make a great *Tommy Cobblestone* storyline," he said through clenched teeth. He took a deep breath, exhaling slowly. "All right, let's do it." He took out his magic wand, pointing it eastward. "To save the world!"

"Yes. And more importantly, to save our nightclub!" Moe added.

* * *

"Jrr-mEE, look dis," Zippo said, holding open the pages of a Tommy Cobblestone comic. It was one of the issues Chaz had given them. The panels depicted Plumpy drinking a magic potion that he thought would give him the ability to fly. However, Drevon Ashcrypt, Tommy's arch-nemesis, had secretly replaced the flying potion with a memory-erasing potion. Plumpy ended up having amnesia for the rest of the issue. [*Translator's Note: from The Adventures of Tommy Cobblestone, issue #25: The Race to Kobold Cove. —ChatterBot 3.6*] "Ugh, if he wanted to stop Plumpy, why didn't Ashcrypt just replace the flying potion with straight-up *poison*?!" Jeremy said, shaking his head.

"But you can make dis thing? *Mamery eraze* poshun?" Zippo questioned Jeremy.

"Me?" Jeremy looked at the comic book again. "There's no way I could concoct a memory erasure potion like this. But it could be done, I think. You'd just need to get someone who's good at enchanting, and follow the right recipe."

"See! I right, Moe! Pigpamples *do* have magic rezpee for poshun!"

"We're already on our way, homie," Moe said. He piloted the starship upwards through the Demon's Eye, just to be safe.

CHAPTER 43

A PIGPIMPLES RETURN

Kitani Kawaii sat under a tree in the Arcane Rectangle, monitoring Sally's progress. "No, no, NO!" she scolded, standing up. Humming off-key and gyrating her lanky limbs, she demonstrated the move to her friend. "See? Flap your hands like *this*."

Sally smiled and nodded, trying the move again.

Summer Session was in full swing at Pigpimples, which meant campus was nearly deserted. The 'Tangle sat empty save for a couple of squirrels, some chirping sparrows, and the two House Fluffernut girls. As long as there was money to be made from parents who didn't want their children home for the summer, Pigpimples administrators were happy to keep the school open. Sparse enrollment meant only a handful of available classes (which all ended at noon) giving the summer students plenty of time to pursue their own hobbies and interests.

Kitani had argued for years that Pigpimples needed an alternative to cheerleading for those girls who wanted to support the Quadritardd games, but were more inclined to interpretive dance routines. After months of begging, Kitani and Sally finally received permission to form their own athletic encouragement squad, which they named the *Lapitolo Ladies Dance Club*.

Kitani clapped in time and sang along as Sally did the hand movements.

"*Sis-boom-rah-rahs, Lapitolo has no flaws!*

L-L-D-C, Lapitolo dance for meeeee! Woooo!"

Sally ended the dance with a hop and a spin, her uniform's skirt twirling as she threw up the hand sign for House Fluffernut. Kitani applauded. "That's excellent, Sally! Your spinning is so graceful! You still have a long way to go, but you've made so much progress!"

Sally blushed at the quasi-compliment. She then tilted her head and squinted, peering at something in the distance.

"What is it, Sally?" Kitani looked. "Oh my gosh! It's— it's...!" Kitani jumped up, sprinting across the Rectangle, nearly tripping and falling. "JEREMY FLETCHER!" she screamed, slamming into Jeremy at full speed and clamping her arms around him as they crashed to the ground.

Jeremy sputtered, picking up his glasses and inspecting them. "Hi, Kitani," he said. He got up, brushing bits of grass off his face and tie.

"Oh Jeremy, Jeremy! It's so good to see you! What happened? Are you here for summer session? Why weren't you at the Farewell Ball? When you didn't show up, I asked Bruno what happened to you—he said he didn't know! Some Porkerson girls said they saw you hiding in the girls dorms! Rick Redfern said some Dandy Lions *killed* you! But then some other kids said they just turned you into a box turtle and threw you out the third story window! Were you hurt? Oh, I was GUTTED, Jeremy! Just absolutely GUTTED!" Kitani hugged Jeremy fiercely. He could hear Moe and Zippo snickering as they walked up. "And who are your two offworlder friends? Oh, you must be Jeremy's bodyguards!" Kitani rushed over to introduce herself to Moe and Zippo. "Bless you two for protecting him! He needs it!"

"Fellas, this is Kitani. And Sally," Jeremy said. "We used to be in House Fluffernut together."

"USED to be?!" Kitani exclaimed, always a few decibels louder than needed. "Oh, Jeremy, you're so silly! You'll always be a Fluffernutter! Your house is set for life, you know that!"

Jeremy remembered that apart from Bruno, he hadn't told anyone that he'd flunked out.

Kitani took Zippo's paw in a shake. "Hello Zippo, you can call me Kit!"

Sally blushed. She slid her right foot behind her left leg in a curtsy.

"Hai, Sal-EE. Hai, Kit," Zippo smiled. He always enjoyed meeting new people.

"Say, Jeremy, you never told us you had a girlfriend!" Moe said, grinning as he took Kitani's hand.

Kitani covered her mouth and screeched. "Jeremy, what are you telling people about me!" She and Sally both tittered with glee. Moe and Zippo joined in, although Jeremy abstained from tittering. Instead, he gave Moe a look that suggested: *I am going to murder you.*

"Actually, Kitani," Jeremy said, "these two are part of an interplanetary student exchange program. Zippo has been working on research for his...uh...dissertation." Zippo licked his chops with satisfaction at the new identity bestowed upon him. "The short one," Jeremy moved in close, "is a wee bit...well, let's just say—*impeded,*" he whispered, tapping his own head with his wand. Moe frowned, crossing his arms. "Honestly," Jeremy said, "he doesn't even know what he's saying half the time. Best to just ignore him."

"Oh, Jeremy," Kitani gushed, "that is so thoughtful of you to take them under your wing!" The bell rang from the clock tower. "Oh! Time for lunch!" Kitani exclaimed. "Won't you join us? You can be our guests! We'll give you the whole tour!"

Jeremy assured Kitani, "If there's free food, Moe and Zippo will be there."

* * *

The Trough was much quieter than usual. There were barely any kids eating, and Jeremy's little group ended up having a whole table to themselves. There were no professors around, as far as Jeremy could tell. When he asked about them, Kitani said they were mostly gone for the summer, "Doing their wizarding jobs." For example, Sir Mongo Chamberpot was on his yearly pleasure cruise on the South Seas, classifying new and undiscovered rainbow types.

"Sounds like a blast," Jeremy said.

Kitani caught him up on all the useless "gossip" of the summer. All the while, Moe and Zippo took in their surroundings and noshed a proper British lunch of kippers and deviled kidneys, which they smothered in Worcestershire sauce.

"And then there's Eldon Stormcloud and Amalia Beaverdam! They were caught holding hands in the Rectangle after the dance! Can you believe it, those two?! But I always knew Amalia had a thing for Eldon—the way they looked at each other in Fairy Dissection Lab!"

Jeremy chuckled politely, as if he knew either of those people. "Wow, what a scandal that must have been."

"Oh yes! And I almost forgot—Rosie Shacklebolt—" Kitani nearly choked on her food in her excitement, "Keith Knight cast *ventamos* on her, that's a gust of wind spell, and it made her skirt fly up and everyone saw her knickers! Rosie walked over and socked Keith right in the nose!" Kitani demonstrated by punching her own palm. "There was blood everywhere! Cleric Avalon came and even he said there wasn't much he could do to fix it. They took a hundred and twenty points away from House Porkerson for that one, but it's only *summer* points—"

"Jrr-mEE," a voice spoke in Jeremy's head. It was Zippo, trying to get his attention. A memory flooded his mind—not one of his own memories, at least not exactly. It was the memory of the conversation they'd had on the *Terrapin:*

"Why are you two so interested in making a forgetfulness potion, anyway?" he had asked.

"It's for that GRIS agent—Mike Mania," Moe had answered.

"I don't follow you."

"When we were in the nightclub, Mike said he erased the black hole from GRIS's databanks, but he still remembers its coordinates. If we can stop the P-Shells from infiltrating your world, we still run the risk of this jibroni messing with our black hole and ruining everything. So best thing we can do, short of hoping he meets an untimely death, is make him...forget the black hole exists."

"Oooooh," Jeremy had nodded with understanding.

He still had no idea how they were ever going to administer such a potion to Mike Mania, but he supposed they'd dance that tango when they came to it. Jeremy looked at Zippo across the table to acknowledge that he'd received the memory. It was Zippo's polite way of reminding Jeremy what they'd come to Pigpimples for.

"Say, Kit," Jeremy interrupted, "—how good are you at enchanting? As in, making potions." He had to ask, although he was fairly sure he already knew the answer.

"—Hmmmm... I'm more of a spellcaster, you know that," Kitani responded. "But Sally here, she's practically potion mistress of Pigpimples, aren't you, Sal?" Sally looked down at her food, blushing again.

"What you trying to concoct, Jeremy?" Kitani gasped. "Is it a *love* potion?!"

"No, no! Not a love potion. Not at all. Not even *close*."

"Of course not. Why would *Jeremy Fletcher* need a love potion?" Kitani smiled, fluttering her eyelashes.

"It's a special potion we were reading about...in a textbook. A forgetfulness potion."

Sally muttered something quietly.

"What was that?" Jeremy said.

"She said the recipe for an advanced potion like that would only be in the Potions and Lotions textbook, teachers edition," Kitani explained. "All the teachers editions are in the Atheneum. That's the tome depository in the catacombs, under the library."

"Keen-o! That's just where we needed to go anyway," Jeremy said, getting up.

Why did it have to be the catacombs?

The memory of the professor, dressed in his red robes and gazing into his crystal ball in the dark, sent shudders down Jeremy's spine.

"Kitani, why don't you lead the way?"

* * *

The Pigpimples library was virtually empty. An elderly man was passed out at one of the study tables; whether he was a librarian Jeremy had never seen before or just another homeless wizard, he could not tell. The big, stupid cutout of Tommy Cobblestone's head was still on display, and the librarians had made some progress on replacing the books in that area with rows and rows of "graphic novels."

"The Pigpimples Library turned into a comic book shop— what is the world coming to?" Jeremy said to himself. He wondered what Professor Smith thought of this development. Meanwhile, Kitani prattled on with one of her bizarre (and extremely dubious) stories.

"As I was saying, you see here, and here," Kitani pointed towards the restrooms on opposite sides of the library, "are the library's public drinking fountains. They were installed in 1891. Did you know that before the school adopted indoor plumbing, the librarians got their drinking water from an enslaved water elemental? It's true! The elemental would often beg to be let go so she could return to her children in the hydro-dimension, but releasing her would mean having to walk all the way to the pump out back to get water. Some say you can still hear her tortured weeping to this day!"

Although Jeremy did not doubt there was plenty of tortured weeping to be heard regularly in this library, it was currently very quiet. They reached the alcove with the spiral staircase leading down to the dungeon.

"The Atheneum's down here," Kitani pointed. "Should I call a librarian to help us locate the book?" She looked around for an adult.

"Oh, let's not bother them—I'm sure we can find it," Jeremy flashed Kitani a smile. "I mean, you seem to know so much about this place!" Hearing this pleased her, and she turned to descend the staircase. Inwardly, Jeremy sighed with relief. He was already technically *trespassing* and about to break into a professor's office—that last thing he needed was more witnesses.

Kitani and Sally's footfalls echoed in the darkness as they traipsed their way down the stairs. Zippo didn't like the look of the catacombs one bit, drawing his disruptor ray just to be safe. Moe followed his lead.

"Dude, this place is even freakier than the comics," he said.

"You have no idea," Jeremy replied. Before they descended, he stopped. "We'll grab that potion book and then we'll stop in Bibliosnuff's office on our way out. Keep an eye out for vagrant wizards."

"Sounds like a plan, chief," Moe said, starting down the stairway. "So what is up with you and that Kitani chica?" he whispered. "She's kind of cute, you know."

"Please, Moe. Not now."

The bottom of the staircase was quite dark. Moe removed his shades as Zippo's pupils grew. Kitani and Sally were examining a grotto slug slurming around the phosphorescent moss. "See this little guy?" Kitani pointed to the slug. "Sally says the juice extracted from this species can be used in a potion that gives one night sight! Either that, or it will cause paralysis and death—these dodgy little buggers all look very similar."

They walked down the dank and gloomy hallway, Sally and Kitani both saying hello to the chained up skeleton. Bibliosnuff's office appeared dark as they passed it, which was a good sign. They turned the corner and took the stairs deeper into the dungeon, Sally leading the way.

The roar of rushing water intensified the farther down they went, as did the stench of the sewers. This was hardest on Zippo, what with his heightened sense of smell. He tied a bandanna around his face, covering his muzzle to combat the funk.

"Oooh, that makes you look like a proper bank robber!" Kitani said. Zippo liked the comparison squinting villainously as he pretended to shoot his ray gun.

At the bottom of the winding stairs was the entrance to the Atheneum. Black basalt doors stood before them, menacingly tall. Each door handle was made of ruby and carved in the shape of a human skull. Onyx sconces on the wall flickered with magical red flames. An ancient plaque was posted by the doors, which Kitani read aloud: *"Beyond these doors lie the tomes of the divine, the devilish, and the damned. Be ye careful, all adventurers who enter here! Only two kinds may pass these portals safely: ye olde authorized ID holders, and THE CHOSEN HERO spoken of in prophecy! Ye have been warned!"*

"I don't get it. Some kind of riddle?" Moe asked.

"Does anyone have a 'ye olde authorized ID'?" Jeremy asked.

"Jeremy! What if you're the CHOSEN HERO, spoken of in prophecy?!" Kitani squeaked.

Jeremy doubted he was any prophecy's chosen anything, and looked for a way to pry the doors open. Much to his surprise, one of the doors was already ajar. He pushed, throwing his weight against the slab. It swung open silently.

"Oh my gosh! JEREMY IS THE CHOSEN HERO!" Kitani's screeches echoed throughout the stony catacombs.

"I'm not the chosen hero—it was already open! Come on," Jeremy waved them in as they entered the Atheneum.

* * *

The first thing they noticed upon entering was the disappearance of both the sewer stench and the roar of rushing water. Zippo pulled down his bandanna, converting it into a neckerchief. Kitani spoke. "Sally says there's a preservation spell cast around the Atheneum to prevent the sewer dampness from ruining all the old books. It's probably what's blocking out the noise and smell."

The Atheneum was much, much bigger than the library upstairs. Its ceiling opened up above them as high as a cathedral's, stalactites glistening down from the top. Ancient pillars of black marble were spaced unevenly throughout the room, red-flame sconces attached to each one. The towering bookcases were all set up in uneven rows and insane angles. Some looked like they had toppled over decades ago, others appeared dilapidated and in different stages of decay. In all, it was quite a hoard of books, tomes, scrolls and artifacts.

"I don't suppose you two know any illumination spells?" Jeremy said, squinting in the darkness.

They did not.

"Oh! Sally's got a book of matches! For heating up her alembic," Kitani said. Sally pulled the matches out of her pocket, helpfully.

"Uh okay, great. Just hold on to those," Jeremy said. *If I let them light a match in this room, we'll all burn to death.*

They searched silently for some kind of map or Dewey Decimal signage, picking through piles of parchment and chests full of useless trinkets.

Jeremy spied an enormous stack of old copies of *The Pigasus*, the Pigpimples student newspaper. The top one was dated February 3rd, 1881 and had the headline: "SCANDAL: Herbalism Prof Jailed as Part of Opium Cartel," followed by an opinion piece: "Could the Department of Astrology Kindly Please Die and Stop Ruining My Life?" He guessed the preservation spell Kitani had mentioned wasn't that effective after all, because the newsprint disintegrated in his hands after he touched it.

As they searched, they heard the echo of something that sounded like voices, although it was impossible to tell where in the cavernous archive they originated from. "Is someone else in here?" Jeremy whispered to Kitani.

"Ummm...maybe it's the imps?"

"The *imps*? What imps?"

"They used to put diseased imps to work sorting books in the Atheneum."

Jeremy didn't like the thought of dealing with *any* imps, much less diseased ones.

"Homies, I think Sally's found something," Moe called out, waving them over. He stood by a huge card catalogue. Many of its narrow rectangular drawers had been pulled out and dropped to the floor, creating a small mountain of decaying cards. Sally stood on a stepstool, flipping through a row of cards from one of the intact drawers. After much flipping, she pulled out a card triumphantly. She showed it to Kitani, who read it aloud. "*Potions & Lotions: Teachers Edition!* Section B-9!"

They peered at the labyrinth of book cases before them. Some of the cases did have plaques on them designating their section. They were all difficult to make out in the eerie red light.

"Does anyone see a B-9?" Moe asked. "I see F-17 right here," he said, pointing.

Kitani and Sally scurried to a row. "And here's...828.5?"

"This one just has a picture of a lobster on it," Jeremy said. Zippo looked over, interested.

"I think we'll just have to look around until we find B-9," Jeremy said. "Stick together, if we get lost in here we may never find each other again."

They set off down a long aisle that narrowed more and more the farther they walked in. The end of the aisle opened up onto an endless array of more aisles and shelves. Some of the aisles veered off into dead ends, some were blocked by piles of books or collapsed walls. Others just went on and on, seemingly forever. None of them were labeled B-9.

As they turned onto a new aisle, Zippo yipped in shock. A floating orb in the air temporarily blinded them with its emanating light. Jeremy shielded his eyes. Someone must have cast seer's beacon.

"Oi!" a voice called out from behind the light. "Who gave you permission to be down here?"

Jeremy, Kitani and Sally looked at each other. The voice was familiar.

"We got permission from your mom," Jeremy called out. "Who gave *you* permission?"

A figure emerged from behind the light of the *seer's beacon* and walked towards Jeremy's group. He wore a crisply pressed Pigpimples uniform, the burnished gold color of a Dandy Lion. A floor-length cloak trailed behind him as he strode.

It was Christopher Lionspark.

"My *mom*, as you yanks say, is on the Pigpimples Board of Regents and I sincerely doubt she would grant a wizard impersonator like you access to the Atheneum!" Christopher scoffed. He dabbed his wand, sending the ball of light upward slightly and widening the area of its illumination. Syd Shepherd, a fellow Dandy Lion and one of Christopher's closest friends, stepped out of the shadows. He was joined by none other than *Janine Wintershade*!

Jeremy's heart somersaulted. *The white light makes her eyes shine in the prettiest way!* The three stood there, looking like they were posing for a portrait. "Janine! What are you all doing down here?" Jeremy asked.

Janine and Syd looked at one another uneasily, as if unsure of how to proceed. "Well, to be honest—" Janine started to answer, but Syd cut her off. Christopher turned around, and the three had a muffled argument. "We've been down here for *hours*!" Janine hissed, and the boys backed off. She regained her composure, smiling at Jeremy and tucking some of her hair behind her ear as she spoke. "I'm so happy we ran into you— we're looking for Doombinder, the Lexicon of Prophecy. Big book, gold cover, embossed with some silmarils. Have any of you seen it?"

Jeremy looked to his companions, wishing he had a positive answer for Janine. "Sorry, I don't think so. How about we team up?" Jeremy waggled his hand between himself and Janine's group. "We're looking for a book, too!"

"Absolutely out of the question," Christopher sneered. "We don't work with normies and humdrums."

Jeremy tilted his head. "These guys?" he looked at Moe and Zippo, who hung behind awkwardly. "They're not normies or humdrums, you dolt. They're offworlders!"

Christopher smirked and sniffed. "I didn't mean them, Cobblestone—I meant you and your little Fluffernut failures!"

Kitani furrowed her brow in fury, pulling out her magic wand rushing forward. "You little prat! How dare you speak to Jeremy that way! Take it back!"

"Or what? You'll make me do the Trip-Trap?" Janine mocked, breaking into a little dance while Syd and Christopher laughed.

"Oh, come on—not even a magic spell could make you dance half as good as Kitani!" Jeremy said, stepping forward.

Janine froze, mouth agape as she made a miffed snort.

Jeremy could not believe what he'd just said. Judging by Kitani and Sally's swooning sighs behind him, he wondered whether he'd just made the worst mistake of his young life.

Christopher spoke. "What are you even doing on this campus? The Headmage said you were expelled for cheating! Why, I ought to call the Fascination Wolves on you!"

"Cheating?!" Jeremy screwed his face up. "How incompetent do you think I am? If I were cheating, I would have at least gotten passing grades!" Jeremy laughed.

Moe and Zippo joined in. "He's got you there, dude."

The Dandy Lions looked positively annoyed. "Come on, Syd, Janine—let's go. We don't need help from these weirdos." Christopher spun around, returning down the corridor of books. Syd and Janine threw up their noses and followed him, the orb of light bobbing away and leaving Jeremy's group in the dark.

"This idiot thinks I was expelled for *cheating*! When really, I just flunked out!" Jeremy called. His amusement was contagious, and Kitani joined in. Sally, sensing it was the right thing to do, copied Kitani, and soon they were all laughing.

"Who were those wankers?" Moe asked, which made Kitani giggle even more.

"They're just Dandy Lions. They're wack," Jeremy said.

Sally waved at the group to get their attention, then dashed off. They followed her back down the aisle. She pointed to a previously unnoticed spot where the bottom part of a bookcase had partially collapsed, spilling books onto the floor. It was possible that unchecked grotto slugs had rotted away the shelving, as their ooze trails were slightly acidic. Or it could have been glome rats gnawing on the wood. In any case, as Sally cleared away the tomes, she discovered a sizeable hole in the back of the shelf. She was just small enough to fit, and crawled through the opening.

Moments later she crawled back, beckoning the group to follow her. Moe went next.

Once he was through, he called out. "Dudes! There's a whole blocked off section back here. Come check it out!"

Zippo, Jeremy and Kitani dumped the old books off the shelves, making room to expand the hole. For a fleeting moment, Jeremy felt slightly guilty for mistreating the old tomes, but a quick glance at one (*Lady Eaton's Guide to Harnessing the Psychic Powers of Earthworms*) reassured him that nothing of value was being damaged here.

Zippo kicked at the back of the shelf, breaking apart the brittle wood until the hole was big enough for all of them to pass through. When Jeremy emerged from their makeshift passage, he understood why they'd missed this section. The aisle was blocked off at either end: one side by a collapsed pillar, the other with a mountain of broken desks.

Sally held up the card, pointing at the number and then the sign on the bookcase.

"B-9! It's a match!" Kitani exclaimed.

The shelves were quite long and tall, so they split up to look for *Potions & Lotions, Teachers Edition*. Jeremy found himself having boredom flashbacks as he perused the titles:

A Compendium of Poems Composed by Headmage Fjordil About the Dust Motes in His Kitchen...

Proceedings of the Forty-First International Conference on Enchanted Legumes...

On the Identification and Classification of Griffin Scat...

A New Approach to Gnome Dentistry...

"Hell-o, what have we here?" Jeremy said to himself, pulling a hefty book off the shelf.

It was *Doombinder, the Lexicon of Prophecy!*

"Wonder what's so important about this thing," he murmured. He scanned the pages randomly. The book was mostly a garbled mess of prophecies he couldn't make heads or tails of. Some of the pages included medieval illustrations. One of the pictures made him pause. It was of three young students, all of them wearing Dandy Lion uniforms. A blonde-haired boy led the way, followed by a brown-haired boy and a silver-haired girl. The page had an inscription, written in an ancient hand:

To Pigpimples Academie, the Boye Topher shall Come—
With Hair of Golde, and the Spark of a Lyon!
He Shall Defeat the Darkness of the Ogre Forest,
But Only if he Utters These Magick Words,
In His Tyme of Greatest Need:

The words of the magic incantation followed.

"Huh," Jeremy muttered, "would you look at that?" He casually tore the page out of the book, crumpling it up and tossing it down a sewer grate.

"I found it! I found it! Over here!" Kitani called as she pulled a book down. It was definitely *Potions & Lotions, Teachers Edition*—Jeremy recognized that miserable tome even from afar. They gathered around as Kitani flipped through the book, locating the potion in question. "A-ha, here! *The Philter of Forgetfulness*, that's the one, isn't it?" She read the instructions aloud. The ingredient list included such rarities as a teaspoon of Elysium bindleweed, the dried cap of a fugue mushroom, and ten flakes of siren's dandruff. The completed mixture required a spellcaster to enchant it with *forget-icarmus*, at level three or higher.

"This looks complicated," Moe said.

"Nonsense! Sally'll give it a *laldy*, won't you Sal?" Kitani said. Sally looked sheepish, then nodded with determination. Kitani went on, "I don't know where we'll gather up all these ingredients, though. The apothecary is closed for the summer..."

"Leave that part to us," Jeremy piped up.

"Excellent," Moe said. "Zip, can you lead us out of here? This place is kind of freaking me out. Reminds me of that issue where Tommy has to fight zombie-mummies in the Crypts of

Gelfarth."

"Okey, les go," Zippo said, motioning for everyone to join him as he crawled back to the aisle they'd come from. "Fallow de toast!"

"Follow the *toast*?" Moe said, looking puzzled.

"Oh," Jeremy remembered. "I turned random books into pieces of toast while we were wandering around, so we could have a trail to get out. I promised Zippo he could keep the toast when we were done."

Sally clutched the potion book to her chest as Zippo led the way. Kitani walked beside Moe, asking him about his comic book preferences as Jeremy brought up the rear. "You actually *like* Tommy Cobblestone? Yuck!" Kitani exclaimed, making vomiting noises.

"It's not so bad," Moe said. "What comics do you read?"

"*Angelic Defenders*, of course!"

Sally smiled in excitement at the mention of the girly comic.

"Oh, I've never read that series," Moe said. "Isn't that the one about the angel girl from the moon or something?"

Jeremy flailed his arms silently behind the group, attempting to warn Moe to stop while he had the chance.

CHAPTER 44

THE FASCINATION WOLVES

But it was too late.

Kitani beamed—explaining Angelic Defenders to bewildered listeners was one of her favorite pastimes. They spent the rest of their journey listening to Kitani retell the convoluted backstory of *Sacchi Hana* and her fellow space angels (with occasional supporting details provided by Sally).

After following the trail of toast for some time, Zippo picked up the final piece and added it to his teetering stack. They'd reached the Atheneum's entrance, at last. As Jeremy pulled open the door, Sally yelped and dropped the textbook to the floor.

"What's the matter?" Kitani asked. Sally pointed at the book. It was emitting a sickly light that pulsed and dimmed as if it were alive. "Oh that's nothing, Sal! It's just doing that because we're passing through the Atheneum's protection spell!" Kitani bent down and picked up the book, brushing it off and walking through the doors. She hopped up the first steps. The farther she moved from the doors, the dimmer the book became. "See?" Kitani called, showing off the tome. Satisfied, Sally joined Kitani and they began their ascent.

"Why can't your school just install a *turbolift*?" Moe groaned as he started the long slog up the steps. "These stairs are *brutal!*"

Despite everyone being out of breath after the first couple of flights, Kitani managed to power through and continue talking loudly the entire way. "And then there's..." she gasped, "*Riku Mai-Mai*—she's actually..." she gasped again, "the angel I identify with the most... and *she* enjoys," she stopped to gasp, finally reaching the top of the stairs, "...milkshakes... and dancing..."

Moe emerged from the stairwell, collapsing to the floor of the main hallway. Zippo was also lying down, panting and mewing about needing a nap. Jeremy sat down on the top step, putting his head down and trying not to pass out.

"You know what," Kitani followed, still gasping between breaths, "I'll just let you borrow my comics...so you can really see what I'm talking about! They are a roller-coaster of emotion!"

"Sally," Jeremy spoke, "why don't you and Kitani go back up to the library, where there's more light? That way you can read up on how to make the potion." Sally and Kitani nodded, clambering up the remaining stairs. Zippo gagged. He held his kerchief up to his nose and mouth in an effort not to hork. Jeremy could tell the Felinian had had enough of the sewer stench. "Zippo—you go on ahead with the girls."

Zippo chittered happily as he scampered up the stairs.

Moe turned to Jeremy. "Now what?"

"Now we check out Bibliosnuff's office. Maybe we'll find some clues about where he got the P-Shell. And while we're in there, we can pick up the potion ingredients. If I remember correctly, he's got all the mucus samples and crocodile bladders a wizard could ever need."

They walked to Bibliosnuff's iron door. Jeremy rattled the knob. It was firmly locked.

"I can take care of that," Moe said, pulling out his phaser and aiming.

"Wait!" Jeremy said, standing in front of the lock. "What if—"

"Relax! This place is empty, dude. Let's just take what we need and bounce!"

"It *looks* empty, but Bibliosnuff is head of the Fascination Wolves... He might have some serious tricks up his sleeve." Jeremy faced the door. "His office might be rigged with a protection spell to fry intruders, like you did with the *Terrapin*. Or he might have put a garrison of diseased imps in there—I don't know! I just know that the Fascination Wolves are scary."

Moe thought it over, but shrugged any second thoughts away. "At this point, homie, it's either us or them. And I've come too far to let some jelly blob ruin my life plans." Moe re-aimed at the lock. "I'll take any rogue imps. You can dazzle 'em with showmanship." He pulled the trigger, sending a focused pulse-beam into the lock. The inner mechanism shattered with a *snik*. Jeremy jiggled the doorknob again, tugging. The door creaked open.

* * *

Sally sat at an empty table in the library, dutifully reading up on how to concoct the Philter of Forgetfulness. Kitani was busily amassing a stack of Angelic Defenders from the still-under-construction Cobblestone Corner. She was eager to review the comics with Zippo, who was happy to look at whatever as long as he could continue eating his toast. "I love this issue—it's where Rijiko Asami teaches all the Defenders how to use their angel makeup!" Kitani said, pulling the issue from the rack. Then she gasped, dropping the stack of comics.

A pillar of swirling red smoke and lightning materialized before them. Zippo's chair, which he'd tipped back so he could put his feet up on the table, tumbled backward, spilling him onto the floor with a clatter. A figure emerged from the smoke, floating slightly above the floor. He wore a red robe with a hood. He threw the hood back to reveal a bald head with long white hair on the sides and a stringy white beard.

"Who are you?" Kitani nearly shrieked, her fists clenched at her mouth.

The old man snorted, sounding extremely displeased. He spun around wildly, his robe fluttering in the air until his gaze landed on the girls. "I am Gilbert Polliwog, chief *lictor* of the Fascination Wolves!" he sneered. He raised a bony finger and pointed at Sally, who remained frozen in her seat. "And YOU, young lady, are in gross violation of library policy! Who gave you permission to remove that volume from the Atheneum?!" his shouts echoed off the marble tiles of the library.

Felinians prided themselves on the gracefulness of their race. Therefore, whenever Zippo bumbled, fumbled, or did something otherwise klutzy, it was his habit to pretend that he'd meant to do the clumsy thing all along. Thus, Zippo remained on his back on the stone tile, assessing the situation silently. The hovering sorcerer had not yet noticed him.

Gilbert Polliwog continued shouting and lecturing Kitani and Sally about the protocols of checking out rare tomes. The wizard descended, his boots meeting the stone floor with a *clack*. As he strode towards the girls, Zippo sprang into action, kicking himself back onto his feet in one fluid motion. He crouched behind the table, claws popped and ready.

Kitani's surprised glance and intake of breath must have given his position away, because the old wizard spun around mid-sentence. "Freeze!" he shouted, a bolt of energy blasting from his outstretched hand. It shot squarely towards the Felinian's head.

* * *

"Whoa! This is *freaky*!" Moe held up a bottle of mercury-like fluid, sloshing it around. He held it up to the candles on the professor's desk, which Jeremy had lit with Sally's matches. The bottle was labeled "dragon's blood."

"Please—put that down before you break something," Jeremy ordered Moe. "New rule: if it's not on our list, do *not* pick it up. These bottles are too fragile to mess with. Besides, I've heard dragon's blood stains are impossible to get out. Wouldn't want to get any on your shoes." Moe looked down at his hi-tops. He daintily replaced the bottle among the vials of troll saliva and eel juice.

They'd found just about everything on their list—the only thing left was the potion's main ingredient: "*a bottle of pure water from the River Lethe*," Jeremy read. So far, every liquid ingredient they'd found was just some creature's bodily fluid— each one more nauseating than the last. "This man has a problem," Jeremy muttered, looking over a spice rack of beakers containing nothing but the tears of leprechauns. He moved on to a cupboard, opening its door. "Presto!" Jeremy said, finding bottles of water inside. "The Ganges, the Styx, the Sea of Tranquility...a-ha, here we go," Jeremy removed a clear glass bottle. "The River Lethe."

Moe slid open one of the professor's desk drawers, peering into it for a few moments. "Homie," he whispered, "I think we've got something here." Jeremy rushed over to look. The drawer held a neat stack of documents, the topmost of which appeared to be a letter. Jeremy picked it up gingerly, fluttering it a bit until he appeared satisfied. It just felt like a normal sheet of paper.

"Just checking. You know, for spells," Jeremy said. In truth, he knew very little about the intricacies of magically booby-trapped documents. He just knew they did exist. He held the letter up to a fat candle melting atop a yellowed skull. He could see why Moe was interested in the document. It was a personal letter, written on business stationery. The header was printed:

Mrs. Crawford, CEO
Seashell Systems "Dare to Dream!"™
Terra Firma Division

The text below was inscribed in a flowery, sophisticated hand. Jeremy read it aloud:

My Dear Maledict,
Darling! Your work on the P-Shell is simply remarkable, and I cannot convey to you how pleased I am with your progress! Your manipulation of alien tech is truly dazzling. My Velitovian colleagues tell me that your dark magic not only masks their technology perfectly: it actually improves upon some of their designs! They even wish to incorporate your innovations into future models of the Personal Shell! Isn't that exciting?

Jeremy looked up from the letter, horrified. "So it's true! They're working for the Velitovians!"

"And *that's* how they tricked Chaz's authenticator tools," Moe observed. He lifted the stack of papers out of the drawer and rifled through them. They looked like blueprints and technical schematics. "Your teacher used magic to mimic alien tech. So the Shells pass for Terran technology, which makes them legal to sell anywhere in the League. Kinda genius when you think about it."

Jeremy read on:

They were especially fascinated in the way you used astral transference to lock psychic energy into the brain crystals! Quite an elegant solution to the subspace problem, or so they informed me. (You know I don't have a head for all this technical mumbo jumbo!)
Our legal team tells me we're totally covered, so no more

litigation fears! As soon as customers click that User Agreement, they are legally donating brain energy to Seashell Systems for ongoing use of the device. I personally think that's a bargain! I'll gladly part with a little brainpower, if it means simplifying my life! Wouldn't anyone?

In this package, I've enclosed four prototypes of the device (with their accompanying brain energy storage crystals)—test them out on students or whomever you see fit. Oh Maledict, I do hope you change your mind and try a P-Shell for yourself! I love mine. It's replaced my personal planner! I use it to store all my scheduled appointments, important names and addresses, and so on.

And the Shell not only simplifies my life—this product will do REAL GOOD for the world, and hopefully the entire star system! Just the other day, a Cerberon who works for me over at GRIS told me that the Shell is an answer his agency's prayers, since it will virtually end all manner of copyright infringement! Forgive me for going on about this—I just believe in this product so firmly, I can't help myself! I get goosepimples just thinking about all the GOOD we're going to DO!

Jeremy stopped reading. "Cerberon? Working at GRIS? You think she's referring to...?" he looked up at Moe.

"Mike Mania. If he's working for this Crawford lady, she might know where his poochy little butt is!" Moe chuckled in a stupefied daze. Jeremy went back to the letter.

If you'd like to pre-order more Shells for yourself or the school, please let me know. I have a cargo freighter packed full of them, just waiting in an undisclosed location! My marketing department is putting the final touches on the ad campaign, and we should have them ready to launch at Christmas! Isn't it exciting? Tiny Tim ran some numbers for me, and if his projections are right—not only are we DOING GOOD for the world, we're all going to be VERY, VERY RICH!

Maledict, I had better be off; I am late for a shareholder meeting. I count the minutes until we can be together again! If I were there right now, I'd canoodle you in snuggles and kisses and...

Jeremy trailed off. "Okay, I'm not reading the rest of that out loud," he said. He skipped to the end.

Yours Truly,
Mrs. Crawford
XOXOXOXOXO
P.S. I'd be delighted to take you up on your offer of dinner and dancing! If you're in New York, give Tiny Tim a ring! I'll be attending the big convention and I'd love to have you as my 'plus one'!

Jeremy looked up, positively bewildered, but Moe had stopped listening. He was studying another document.

"Moe, what is it? Something useful?"

Moe looked up, startled. "Nah," he said, quickly shuffling the paper in with the rest of the technical documents. He straightened the papers out, tapping the edge of the stack against the table. Then he placed them in Zippo's backpack. "I'll look these over later. Is there any other important stuff we should take?"

Jeremy examined the other drawers of Bibliosnuff's desk. One of the drawers emitted a faint blue light. In the world of magic, glowing blue light usually meant "important." He slid the drawer out, revealing four luminescent crystals. Each crystal was about the size of a carrot. Jeremy reached down, carefully lifting one from the drawer. It felt cold to the touch, but it had a curious weight to it, as if humming with energy. Jeremy held the crystal up. "Check it out—brain crystal."

∗ ∗ ∗

"Josiah Snakebark, where are you? I've got two girls and an offworlder stealing tomes from the Pigpimples Library!" Gilbert Polliwog shouted. He must have been communicating through astral projection or some form of Terran mindspeak, because Zippo could not see or hear who he was talking to.

The Felinian remained as still as a statue. Thanks to his lightning-quick reflexes he had dodged the wizard's freezing spell, but only by a hair (in fact, the freezing bolt may have grazed the tips of his ears—they felt painfully cold). The old man was too preoccupied with the Terran girls to notice that his spell had actually missed, freezing a bookshelf by mistake.

"Oh sod off with your lunch reservations, you half-witted old Moor! I'm too old for this nonsense! If you can't get here yourself, call Gustav, or Silas Buttonwood!"

Kitani stood beside Sally's table, her knees trembling in fear. She placed a comforting hand on Sally's shoulder. Sally reached up, clasping Kitani's hand in hers and otherwise trying not to move. As long as the scary red sorcerer was arguing with himself, he could not cast a freezing spell on them. "The poor cat man!" Kitani whispered, holding back tears.

Then she saw him. Zippo, still frozen in a half-crouch on the floor, actually moved his head ever-so-slightly. He was not frozen after all! Kitani locked eyes with Zippo, and he gave her a quick wink.

She squeezed Sally's hand to suppress a scree of emotion. She noticed Zippo's tail trembling slightly as an image entered her mind: she saw herself and Sally running out the library doors as Zippo shot the wizard in the air. Sally tilted her head up slightly to look at Kitani. She couldn't explain why, but Kitani sensed they had both received the same vision. Without speaking, Sally gave Kitani's hand a return squeeze of confirmation. "All right then," Kitani whispered, trying not to move, "on the count of three..."

"Maledict *what*?!" Gilbert Polliwog continued to argue with unseen entities. "Mate, I only came here because someone triggered the Atheneum's anti-theft spell! Tell Bibliosnuff he can teleport his dusty old bum down here himself. I'm not muckin' about, chasing down every piddly student culprit on his list...I'm on holiday too, you know!" He looked up into the heavens, as if listening to someone else speak. "Fine, fine! You can explain it all to me in person! There are two Fluffernut girls and what appears to be a giant hairless tabby here... Yes...I'm in the Cosgrove Library..."

"One... Two... Three!" Kitani let go of her friend's hand. "Run, Sally! Run!" she screamed, dashing for the door. Sally scooped the potion book into her arms, hopping up from her seat and following close behind.

The wizard pointed menacingly at the girls. "Stop where you are, lassies! IMMOBILIZATIO!" he uncurled his fingers, aiming his hand at the girls.

Zippo exploded into action, planting his hand on the stone floor behind him and kicking his legs out at the table as hard as he could. His feet connected, sending the table over in a crash. The sound startled the sorcerer, and he turned just as a bolt of immobilizing energy shot forth from his fingers. It hit the overturned table harmlessly.

"Oh, bloody 'ell!" the sorcerer shouted, levitating into the air. "Josiah! Get down here, NOW!"

* * *

"I'm not *saying* we give up," Jeremy protested, turning the crystal over in his hands. "I'm just saying maybe we're in a little over our heads here! Maybe it's time we go to the authorities."

"Like who? Terran cops? They wouldn't even know where

to begin with something like this! Besides, your world isn't even a member of the League of Planets—that means none of this stuff is *technically* illegal."

Jeremy paused. Moe was right. "Then let's go to League authorities! They must have, uh," Jeremy fumbled for the word, "an *ambassador* somewhere that we could talk to!"

"League authorities? And get ourselves thrown into a dark fortress prison?! Kid, we are trucking around violating about two-hundred copyright laws every minute we're on the *Terrapin*. The League gives GRIS free reign out here. They'd arrest us on the spot."

Jeremy bit a fingernail nervously.

GUISE!

They both froze. "You hear something?" Moe asked. Jeremy couldn't tell if he'd heard Zippo's voice in the hallway or in his mind. It was rather faint.

HALP! NAOW!

"Something's wrong!" Jeremy exclaimed. Moe must have heard it, too. He drew his phaser, rushing for the door. Before he could think, Jeremy picked up Zippo's backpack. He slung a strap over one shoulder as he scrambled out of the office.

* * *

Zippo used the table for cover, taking aim with the Bug Zapper.

"Visitors are not allowed on campus grounds without a PASS!" the floating sorcerer blasted Zippo with green-tinged darts of magic. The Felinian ducked down, the table absorbing most of the magic in an explosion of flame and splinters. Zippo popped back up, firing his disruptor at the floating target, who began circling him in the air. A superheated beam of blue electricity crackled from the gun, ultimately missing the red wizard and hitting a wall, setting it on fire.

"ENOUGH, HUMDRUM!" Polliwog shouted. He cast a gust of wind spell to put out the fire. Zippo rolled out from behind the desk, mentally screaming out for Moe and Jeremy to help him. It was extremely difficult to do, since they were not in his direct line-of-sight. He sprinted towards the library entrance, but a flash of lightning and a swirl of red smoke stopped him dead in his tracks.

Another red-robed wizard materialized in the doorway, hovering in the air. His skin was brown, and his eyes were cloudy and blue. Zippo ducked behind a bookshelf just as the sorcerer raised a twisted twig of a wand. "There you are!" he boomed, his voice deep. "Stop, thieves! EXPLODIAMUS!" The second wizard flicked his wand, letting out a blast of magical energy that sailed across the library. "And those shorts you're wearing are a violation of school dress code! Don't think I didn't notice THAT!"

"Look out!" Jeremy yelled, pushing Moe out of the way and jumping for cover. They had just emerged from the stairs, and were watching from the library archway. The wizard's blast slammed into the porcelain drinking fountain, shattering it to pieces. A gush of water spewed forth from the broken pipe.

"Josiah, you twit! That's an antique fountain you blew up there!" Polliwog shouted. Before Josiah could respond, there was a *pew! pew!* from a nearby aisle. Moe was already returning fire with his phaser. One of the shots tagged Josiah in the shoulder. The fluttering red robes made both wizards difficult to hit.

"Aaaah! I just had this robe dry-cleaned, you fool!" the old wizard thundered, floating towards Moe.

Zippo ducked out the front door of the library with a loud *rawl* of distraction.

"Gilbert, you go after the offworlder. I'll take these two girls!" Josiah laughed as he rose into the air, attempting to spy out the intruders. Gilbert Polliwog sailed out the front door in pursuit of Zippo. "And call some other Wolves while you're at it, for the love of Merlin!" Josiah boomed.

Jeremy made a blind dash down an aisle, ducking for cover behind something that felt quite flimsy. He glanced up, realizing he was cowering beneath the huge cardboard cutout of Tommy Cobblestone's head. *Not only am I about to be obliterated by an evil flying wizard, my last moments on earth have to be spent with Tommy Cobblestone's giant idiot face grinning down on me. And WHY is the little git wearing SUNGLASSES? Embarrassing.* Jeremy pulled out his mostly useless wand, trembling, but at the ready.

Jeremy spotted Moe across the aisle. The Binosian waved frantically, pointing and motioning towards the exit. *He wants me to run for it.*

"You, little girl!" Josiah appeared from around the corner, floating in the air. Trickles of energy danced at the sorcerer's fingertips, illuminating his hooded face.

"I'm a *boy*!" Jeremy shouted, grabbing a comic book and throwing it at the wizard. It fluttered to the floor uselessly. He squeezed his eyes shut, bracing himself to get blown up, or turned into a crested newt.

"Yo!" Moe called from the other aisle. He fired off several *pews* in succession, all of them missing the wizard, but hitting random books. Each one sailed off the shelf in a tattered flutter. "Over here, old man!"

"Aahh! Insolent child! How dare you destroy Pigpimples school property!" the wizard roared as he turned to pursue Moe.

"Jeremy! Just run! I'll take this jibroni!" Moe called out from wherever he was.

"You'll all be expelled when this is through!" Josiah intoned, rising a few feet higher in the air. "Surrender yourselves now and I'll spare you from being cursed!"

Jeremy did not hesitate, using the momentary distraction to his advantage. He picked up the cardboard Cobblestone head, shielding himself with it as he gingerly backed his way towards the library entrance.

"You there! That promotional artwork does not belong to you! Halt! FIREBALLIUS!" Josiah whirled in the air. A flick of the wizard's wand hurled a flaming missile right at Jeremy. He moved his cardboard shield just in time, the wizard's fireball exploding across Tommy Cobblestone's smiling head. Jeremy dropped the flaming cardboard, toppling it against a bookshelf as he sprinted out the front door.

"Now look what you've gone and done!" the wizard shouted, hovering over to control the growing fire. "EXTINGUISHIO!" he thundered, putting the fire out. "Gustav Toadspindle!" He spoke to an unseen party, "Yes, this is Josiah... Gather more Wolves to Pigpimples. I think we have a bit of a situation here. Whatever you do, do *not* let Maledict find out, or he will have all our hides!"

* * *

Outside the library, Jeremy squinted as his eyes adjusted to the afternoon sunshine. He was unsure whether he was actually seeing what he thought he was seeing. Another old wizard, red robes fluttering about, hovered fifteen feet in the air over the 'Tangle. He appeared to be exchanging fire with some shrubs at the edge of the lawn.

"Jeremy!" Kitani screamed, popping up from behind the shrubbery. "Over here!" She ducked, dodging an orange bolt of energy. Sally popped up out of the same bushes, holding Zippo's ray gun unsteadily in her small hands. She took aim the best she could, blasting a blue bolt that staggered her backwards as her arms recoiled. The Zapper's shot sailed harmlessly through the air, missing the wizard by a large margin. Sally bit her lip and ducked back into the shrubs.

The wizard laughed maniacally, hovering in a circle rather unnecessarily. Jeremy dashed to the shrubs. "Oh Jeremy! I thought they'd got you for sure!" Kitani hugged him so hard he thought she might snap his neck. He attempted to push her off, but she was locked in.

"Where's Zippo?" he asked.

"He said something about getting his ship, and then he gave Sally his gun and ran off! I was so...scared!" She buried her face in Jeremy's shoulder. Reluctantly, he gave her a comforting pat on the back. They'd parked the *Terrapin* just outside the front gates of the campus, which was a short walk from here. He wondered if Zippo had made it, or if he'd been nabbed by some other rogue wizard. Jeremy craned his head, getting a look back towards the library entrance. There were flashes of light from the inside.

"Young lady," the insane sorcerer called down, "I told you to DROP that TOME!"

"NEVER!" Kitani shrieked, looking up from Jeremy's shoulder and only increasing the force of her embrace. "IT'S FOR *JEREMY*!"

Sally inched up out of the bushes, taking aim with the Bug Zapper. When she pulled the trigger, the gun only emitted a sad whine. Jeremy noticed the red light blinking on the side. "The ammo cartridge must be drained, Sal," Jeremy said.

She flung the gun down and took out her wand, dabbing and tapping the air valiantly. A tiny burst of yellow magic limped from the twig, sailing about three feet before splashing down on the lawn. Attack spells were not Sally's specialty, either. With a timid shrug, she lowered herself back into the bushes.

Jeremy wondered how long before the wizards gave up trying to take them peacefully and just blasted them all with one of their uncreatively named spells. *"OBLITERAMUS,"* or perhaps *"BLOW-UPIO."* He spotted the potion book on the ground in front of Sally; the fact that the Wolves didn't want to damage the book was probably the only reason they were still alive. "Whatever you do, Kitani, do NOT give them that book!

Understood?"

Kitani clenched the book back to her chest, nodding vigorously. "They'll have to pry it from my cold, dead HANDS!"

Jeremy took the now useless ray gun, his mind racing as he thought of a plan.

An explosion echoed from the library, colored glass shattering from one of its tall windows. Jeremy heard the wrathful bellows of Josiah Snakebark within. Before he had time to wonder if Moe was still alive, he saw the Binosian jumping down from the shattered window and booking it towards the Rectangle. The other red-robed sorcerer floated through the destroyed window, roaring in fury.

"That stained-glass window was donated by the Queen of Bavaria in 1622, in gratitude for our assistance in cursing the royal family of Portugal!"

Gilbert Polliwog spun around, furious. "Not Appolonia's Window?! You little monsters!"

A pillar of red smoke and lightning crackled in the air. A third red-robed wizard floated out of the smoke. This one was more portly.

"Gustav!" Polliwog said. "About time you got here, ya twit!" The three wizards hovered above the 'Tangle, discussing how to best dispatch the students and get the tome safely back to the Atheneum.

"Just turn them all into fat-tailed skinks," Gustav proposed. "Then we'll toss them into the Thorny Woods!"

"What do we tell their parents, you fool?" Josiah Snakebark scoffed. "They will want their tuition money back! Better to lock them in the catacombs for the semester."

"And risk another catastrophe like this?! You're daft!" Polliwog protested. "They're not our problem, mate! It's all there in the Pigpimples Contract. *Reasonable risk of magical catastrophe* and all that. That means NO REFUNDS."

As they squabbled over what species of tiny amphibian to transform the children into, Moe whispered. "My cart's spent, dudes." He held up his phaser pistol. Kitani made a look of utter dismay as Sally buried her face in her hands.

"How can we get their parents to pay for all these damages? Maledict's not taking the money out of my paycheck, I can tell you that right now!" Polliwog snapped.

"Good point," Gustav agreed. "Tell you what. Let's transform them into hogs and call it a day. That way we can at least sell 'em to the butcher in Friarsburg. Agreed? Oi! What's that then?"

The gurgly whine of a subetheric drive erupted onto the Rectangle as the *Terrapin* zoomed in. The Fascination Wolves scrambled into action, shouting orders and raining down transformative zaps of magic. "Get them! They're trying to escape!" Polliwog howled.

The ship plowed through the circle of flying wizards, scattering them about in different directions, their magical darts flying willy-nilly through the air.

Zippo used the moment of chaos to swing back around and hover the starship a few feet off the ground near the shrubbery. The rear door lifted open. Madi Nabo stood in the cargo bay, yapping wildly.

Jeremy and Moe boosted Sally up and onto the ship first, but the Wolves were too fast. They regrouped themselves into an attack formation in the air, dive-bombing the Rectangle with a flurry of transformation spells. Jeremy, Kitani and Moe dove for the shrubs, fists clenched and cowering.

"Are any of us hogs?!" Jeremy shouted, fearing to open his eyes. Magical energy rained down in splatters all around them.

Moe checked. "No. Still humanoid as far as I can tell," Moe said, patting himself up and down.

They could still hear Madi Nabo barking over the whine of the ship and the mystical sound of magic bolts hitting the ground. Jeremy lay face down, sweating from the heat and the stress. He coughed as he inhaled a fleck of dirt, thorns from the brambleberry bush scraping his arms. "Maybe being a hog isn't so bad," he suggested over all the noise. "Free food. No school. Wallow around in nice cool muck all day."

Without warning, Kitani army-crawled out of the shrubs and out into the open.

"Kitani, no!" Jeremy shouted. "I was just kidding!"

She hopped up onto her feet, wand in hand and a look of fierce determination on her face. Red and orange missiles streaked by her as she marched fearlessly into the Rectangle. She stopped, facing the three sorcerers in the sky. She drew her wand, pinky extended as if ready to conduct a symphony. "BAILLAMOS!" she screamed, waving the wand in an arc across her chest. "LET THE RHYTHM TAKE YOU OVER!" A shimmer of magic pulsed outward and into the heavens. It washed over all three wizards at once.

It was hard to tell what was happening from underneath the bush, but the colorful missiles suddenly stopped. Jeremy and Moe raised their heads, looking into the sky. The Fascination Wolves were no longer attacking them. In fact, they were slowly descending from the air.

They also appeared to be...dancing.

Gustav Spindletoad waggled a foot and spun his hands around. Josiah Snakebark pointed his fingers in the air as he swished his robe back and forth. Gilbert Polliwog kicked his legs, doing the Thunder Jiggle. The only problem was that he was descending far too fast—in fact, he was falling.

The wizard smashed into the ground with an audible crunch. "Aaaah! My leg!" the old man screamed as he got up and continued dancing casually. The other two wizards danced on over to him, but were powerless to help. Polliwog just kept dancing on a leg that appeared quite broken, occasionally screaming out in pain.

"Kitani! Stop! Turn it off!" Jeremy said, fascinated and horrified.

"I can't! I don't know how! It usually wears off after a couple of minutes!"

"Homies," Moe called, scrambling onto the hovering ship, "let's boogie before these guys get sick of dancing and decide to kill us!"

"STOP! STOP RIGHT THERE!" Josiah Snakebark attempted to cast a spell, but the lack of control over his hands caused him to wave his wand right in the direction of Gilbert. The old man shucked to the left just in time, dodging the missile.

"You almost turned me into a HOG you PRAT!" Gilbert shouted. "Aaaaah! Oh, oh! It hurts!"

The old wizard's screams faded away as the *Terrapin* sailed into the sky.

CHAPTER 45

DANCIN' TO MANHATTAN

The *Terrapin* hovered far above the earth.

"Oh, *taku*!" Kitani wailed in delight. "We're in outer space! Just like the Angelic Defenders!" She and Sally pressed themselves against the cockpit windows, looking down upon the planet.

"Zip," Moe said looking at the computer scans, "keep us in mid-strat for now. Low and slow. Avoid any starships coming or going. And keep an eye out for any flying wizards."

Zippo nodded, leveling the ship out at a low orbit. The earth rotated slowly beneath them.

Jeremy pulled Moe aside as the girls marveled at the view. "Uh, Moe—what are we going to do with these two?"

"What do you mean? They'll make the potion, then we drop them off."

"Drop them off?! They can't go back to Pigpimples! The Fascination Wolves will transform them into hogs!"

"Right—that." Moe looked at the girls, momentarily concerned. He patted Jeremy on the back. "We'll figure something out." He picked up Zippo's backpack from the floor. The vials and bottles inside clinked as he hoisted it up. "Ladies, your ingredients."

Sally got to work right away setting up her alembic and calcinator on the table in Moe's quarters. She laid out the teacher's edition of Potions & Lotions, scrutinizing the recipe.

"Jeremy," Kitani stepped out of the cabin, "do you happen to have a mortar and pestle? Sally says she forgot to put hers in her backpack this morning."

"Ummm..." Jeremy looked around, picking up a cereal bowl with a spoon still in it off the cockpit's dashboard. "Will this work? Looks like there's some Branno-Bix still in there, sorry."

"You can rinse it out in the sani," Moe called out.

Kitani looked to Jeremy. "He means the *loo*," he explained.

"Oh! All right," Kitani said, accepting the bowl and returning to the cabin.

"Status report," Moe said. "I'll be real with you: things are not looking so hot. We have no money. We have no magtapes. We have no *albums*. And we are now probably being hunted by flying wizards. On the plus side," he gestured to Jeremy, "we found a way to connect with our furry friend from GRIS. So I say we track Mrs. Crawford down, get Mike Mania's phone number from her. And while we're at it, she can tell us where this freighter of Personal Shells is."

"That's all fine and dandy, but why would the CEO of Seashell Systems even give us the time of day? She'll never tell us where Mike is, or where that freighter is, either."

"Who says we're gonna talk? She's a lady—she probably has a purse! And in that purse, there's probably an address book, a phone number, *something*. Stay focused, dude. Stay positive!"

Jeremy shook his head, focusing. "Right. Find old lady, snatch purse. I like it. Then what?"

"Then we call Mike Mania, tell him we wanna make a deal. Bribe him with the P-Shell, I dunno. He'll want to meet up face to face. So we meet, we slip the potion into his drink, and hopefully he forgets that our black hole even exists. No messy killing—and our GRIS problem is solved."

Zippo rolled his eyes, annoyed. "GRIS slobber-tongue BITED me, Moe," he pointed to his ankle as if to remind his co-pilot of what had happened. Then the Felinian sighed. He looked down and noticed that his ankle had healed. "But *okey*. We not kill them," he smiled at Moe and Jeremy. "Plan is good," he nodded.

"And what about this freighter of Personal Shells?" Jeremy asked.

"That the easiest part. We find it and blow it up."

"Obviously. I should have guessed. I assume we'll give the crew a chance to use their escape pods?"

"Of course; we're not barbarians! But we're definitely blowing that thing up."

Zippo mewed affirmatively, rubbing his paws together and chuffling gleefully. "Yeeaw! We bloe UP det *stupid* ship!" He normally didn't like explosions, but would make an exception to save the Terran civilization.

"Only problem is," Moe said, "we have no idea where in the world Mrs. Crawford *is*. So the floor is open for suggestions."

"Actually, we *do*. She's in New York City for the summer."

"How do we know that?"

"Through the magic," Jeremy said, pulling out Crawford's letter, "of reading."

Moe took the letter, a smile spreading across his face as he read the bottom. "Right on! Okay, gentlebros! We roll into New York *Citaaaay*!" Moe exclaimed, half-singing as he swiveled around in his captain's chair. "I've always wanted to hit that place up! There's a bunch of Terran tunes about it, you know." He started singing the chorus of some hit from the future: *"Saturday night and I'm feelin' so prettaaay, walkin' the streets of New York Citaaaay!"*

Zippo grooved along, meowing and bobbing his head. [*Translator's Note: "Dancin' to Manhattan" by Eddie's Slingshot Express —ChatterBot 3.6*]

"Computer," Moe called out excitedly, "plot a course for New York City, Terra Firma."

Mister Squeakeasy appeared on screen. "Aye-aye! Calculating trajectory!"

Jeremy laughed in spite of himself; their unbridled enthusiasm was always catchy. "Guys, I hate to be the one to soggy up your cereal, but don't you think she might be a tad difficult to track down?"

"Naaah," Moe waved Jeremy off. "It's just a Terran city! How big can it be?"

Jeremy thought of saying something, but decided not to.

"Wait a sec," Moe remembered something. "—Computer? What time is it in New York?" Mister Squeakeasy reported that it was half past six in the evening, Terran standard time. "Then we're not too late! We just have to find Central Park."

Not for the last time, Jeremy felt like some important development had just occurred without him. "And why the devil would she be in Central Park? Moe, what's going on?"

Moe reached down for Zippo's backpack. He fished out several documents, spilling various papers onto the floor in the process. He handed Jeremy a yellow flier. "I...wasn't sure whether to show this to you, chief. Kind of thought you wouldn't approve." A picture of Tommy Cobblestone's bespectacled face grinned at him from the paper. It read:

Calling all WIZARDS, WITCHES, & WARLOCKS
of NEW YORK, NEW YORK:

Join us on the Great Lawn of Central Park
July 4th and 5th
FOR

CobbleCon 1919

THE FIRST ANNUAL
TOMMY COBBLESTONE CONVENTION

(NORMIES & HUMDRUMS WELCOME!)
FOOD VENDORS! GAMES!
VARIOUS DISCUSSION PANELS!
FEATURING:
TRADITIONAL WIZARD WRESTLING!
A RARE PERFORMANCE OF THE MAGE'S MAZURKA!
MILK AN ENCHANTED GOAT!

Not to mention:
TOMMY COBBLESTONE SOUVENIRS, TRINKETS, AND
OTHER OFFICIALLY LICENSED TCHOTCHKES!

MEET & GREET
With the creator of Tommy Cobblestone:
ANITA COSGROVE!
(autographs $75.00)

With Special Musical Performances by:
PLUMPY'S PUDDING
THE HAZELTWIG ALUMNI CROONERS
PIGASUS RISING

AND SATURDAY NIGHT:
An Exclusive Special Announcement
FROM SEASHELL SYSTEMS!

"An exclusive special announcement from Seashell?" Jeremy read. "The big news she mentioned in her letter... She's going to announce the P-Shell at this thing!"

"Sure sounds like it," Moe said. "Either way, we'll snatch her purse and see what we can find out."

Jeremy scanned the flier for any other clues. "Be there!" Tommy's face announced at the bottom of the page.

He couldn't stand to look at the little git, and crumpled up the flier. "New York it is," Jeremy said, before turning the flier into a buttery English muffin.

Zippo sniffed the air, opening his mouth to meow but forced to concentrate on piloting.

Moe looked at the navi-controls. "We'll be planetside in about half an hour. Use your wizard brain to come up with a plan."

Jeremy decided to check on the girls instead.

"Oh what a good little lady she is! Yes! Yes she is, *YES*, she is!" Madi Nabo stood on Moe's bed, her mouth open and her tiny tail wagging furiously. Kitani and Sally were taking turns petting her about as hard as the little Cerberon could stand.

"No, Sal, she likes scratches on her rump more than her head, see?" Kitani proceeded to scratch Madi's rump, which she did not object to. "Jeremy! Why didn't you tell me you had a dog!"

Madi Nabo turned at the sound of Jeremy's entrance, fixing her absolute attention on the English muffin in his hands. "Because..." he started, looking Madi Nabo in the eyes. "...this little lady is not a dog."

She yipped at him. The girls laughed.

Jeremy raised an eyebrow, taking a bite of his English muffin. He spoke as he chewed. "She's an offworlder."

Kitani and Sally giggled at Jeremy's silliness. "I'm serious!" Jeremy objected. "Didn't you hear her talk?" he urged Madi Nabo on. "Come on, say something! Anything!"

The Cerberon opened her jaws slightly, as if unsure of herself. A small noise escaped the back of her throat, but it was more of a whine than an actual word.

"Fine," Jeremy said, shrugging. "I was going to give you the rest of this English muffin, too. I guess you don't want it." He held the muffin up. "Mmmm...toasty!"

Madi Nabo appeared torn, her gaze shifting from the muffin to the girls, as if expecting them to do something about the situation. Her glassy black eyes grew wide with concern.

Jeremy ignored her silent pleading, slowly inching the English muffin towards his open mouth. Finally, she let out a little bark of distress. The girls' tittering stopped. "Oh Jeremy," Kitani exclaimed, "stop being so cruel to little Sophie!" Kitani swiped the English muffin away from Jeremy's hands. At this, Madi barked happily.

"See," Kitani said, "she's a good little lady! She knows how to speak, doesn't she? Yes she does! YES she does!" Madi Nabo reared up momentarily, chomping down on the muffin and pulling it from Kitani's grasp. Kitani ruffled Madi's velveteen ears. The English muffin securely clamped in her jaws, the Cerberon hopped down from the bed. Jeremy squinted at her skeptically as she trotted under the table to eat in private.

Kitani turned to Jeremy. "Oh, Jeremy!" she exclaimed. "After everything that happened back there in the 'Tangle, I think we both needed a good laugh! Thank you." She placed a hand on Jeremy's arm, which Jeremy backed away from awkwardly. He changed the subject.

"So Sally, were you able to complete the potion?"

Sally slid down off the bed, nodding vigorously. She picked up a glass beaker of fluid from the table.

"Sally just needs one last thing," Kitani said, looking at the instructions in the spellbook. "*One must...*" she read from the recipe, "*procure an image of the person, place, or thing one desires the drinker to forget. Burn the image, then sprinkle the* ashes into the mixture while speaking the enchantment." Kitani looked up. "*Then the philter will be complete.* What, exactly, do you want the drinker to forget?"

"Sally, can I borrow your notebook?" Jeremy asked. He tore out a sheet of paper and brought it to the cockpit.

"Zip. Write down the coordinates of the black hole for me." The Felinian thought for several seconds, drumming the pencil against his chin and momentarily distracting himself by biting the eraser. He then scrawled down a complex string of numbers in Felinian script, which was a kind of scratchy cuneiform. Jeremy looked at the paper, wondering whether it needed to be in English or not. Just to be sure, he sketched a picture of a circle with arrows pointing into it, hoping this would convey "black hole." He returned to Moe's cabin, shutting the door to block out the music from the cockpit.

"Alright, hopefully that will do," he said, handing the paper to Sally. She took out her matches, burning the paper and scooping the ashes into the glass beaker. She closed her eyes, muttered the incantation under her breath, and swished the beaker around. The potion transformed from a murky gray into a vibrant purple.

"Ooooh!" Kitani cooed. "*If you are successful,*" she read from the book, "*the potion should now be violet colored.* Sally! You did it!" Sally smiled, placing a cork in the beaker and handing it to Jeremy.

"Thank you, Sally. We couldn't have done this without you."

Sally's face turned red. Madi Nabo walked out from underneath the table, licking her chops. She whined as she stood beside the door.

"What, Madi?" Jeremy asked, annoyed.

"Why do you keep calling her that?" Kitani asked. "Her tag says her name is Sophie!"

"Ugh," Jeremy groaned. "She wants us to open the door

because the button is too high. Just tell the door to open, Madi! It's voice activated and you know it! Come on, use your words!"

Kitani walked over and pressed the button. The door slid most of the way open before getting stuck. Madi trotted out into the hall and towards the cargo bay. Jeremy shook his head.

"Jeremy—" Kitani said as they walked into the hallway. "I didn't get a chance to thank you...for saving my life."

"Oh, brother," Jeremy placed a hand over his face momentarily. He looked up, trying his best stage grin. "Kitani, it's okay. I didn't save your life," he gave an exaggerated shrug as he turned his palms up. Kitani moved closer to him as he backed away slightly. "In fact," he added, "I probably endangered it. I almost got you killed. Or worse: *expelled*."

"I want you to have something," Kitani said. "I was going to give this to you when you came back in the fall, but I want you to have it now."

Kitani pulled a stack of wide-ruled notebook paper from behind her back. The telltale riffles of a spiral notebook hung from its edges, and the pages were stapled together in the corner. It was a homemade comic book. The cover page read, *The Adventures of Jeremy Fletcher: Magic Boy.*

Kitani presented the book solemnly. Jeremy took it with some reluctance.

"Sally and I worked on it for weeks."

Jeremy looked at the hand-lettered credits on the front:
Drawings by Sally Simpson and Kitani "Kit" Kawaii
(Additional shading, textures, character design, and story elements by Kitani "Kit" Kawaii)

Jeremy flipped through the stapled pages, revealing a cartoon version of himself running around and having adventures at Pigpimples. He couldn't help but chuckle. Kitani clasped her hands together, sighing happily. In addition to himself, he noticed cartoon versions of Kitani and Sally. Even Bruno D'argento made an appearance. The antagonist of the story appeared to be Janine Wintershade, who was some sort of harpy vampire demon.

These drawings are not half bad! Despite being in black and white, Kitani had captured the look of her own wavy hair just right. "Thank you, Kitani," Jeremy said. "I don't have time to read it right now, but..." Kitani looked at him with an expectation that verged on tears. "It looks...amazing."

"Oh, Jeremy!" She bent down slightly and hugged Jeremy, squeezing the air from his lungs.

* * *

Jeremy found Madi Nabo on his bed, looking out the port window. His lamp was off. The blue glow of Terra Firma glinted off her heart-shaped collar tag.

"Psst—kid!" she hissed at him. "You've got a lot of nerve, trying to blow my cover back there!"

"What are you talking about?" Jeremy nearly shouted. He almost called Kitani and Sally over to witness this, but Madi nipped his left hand. "Ouch! Watch it!"

"Shhh!" Madi shushed him. "Do *not* ruin this for me!"

Jeremy sat down next to Madi on his bed, whispering fiercely as he rubbed his hand. "Ruin *what*?"

"You have no idea, do you! I had to live on a space station with a naked frog man for the past TWO YEARS! For six and a half months I ate nothing but ALGAE BARS!" She made a disgusted grunt and shook herself all over. "I've been on the run for far too long. Now I can finally get some decent roommates and move on with my life! Nice Terran girls! Lots of comfy cushions! We're almost there, so just keep your muzzle *shut*! Understood?!"

Jeremy found himself closing his eyes and sighing in exasperation.

"Sorry about nipping you—," Madi went on, "it's just that, I have been *very* stressed out about this, okay? This whole plan works out great! They get a cute little pet, I get free room and board! Everyone wins!" She gave Jeremy's hand an apologetic lick.

He opened his eyes. "All right, Madi—that is, *Sophie*—your secret is safe with me," he patted her on the head.

"Hey, your continent is coming up!" Moe called on the ship's intercom. "Uhh...it's the one kind of shaped like a Pu'ukonian dwarf whale, right?" The starship glided down through the stratosphere, along the eastern coast. It was perfect weather for flying; not a single cloud blocked their view of the vast, sprawling city. The Manhattan skyscrapers were just starting to catch the light of the late afternoon sun. "Guys, I think that's it! That's Central Park!" Jeremy pointed out the window.

"What? That?" Moe asked.

"The giant, green, centrally-located park-shaped area. Yes," Jeremy said.

Moe slid on his shades to protect against the summer evening sun. "Take us in, Zipponio."

"Kay," Zippo mewed.

"Are we landing?" Kitani said, peeking into the cockpit. "Because I think little Sophie needs to go for walkies."

"Who?" Moe asked.

"Madi Nabo...she..." Jeremy just shook his head. "Don't ask."

Zippo piloted the ship down into the bustling park. "Dis good spot," he declared, hovering over a small playground south of the Great Lawn. A few children here and there pointed at the spacecraft as it descended, but most New Yorkers were used to the sight of offworlders occasionally coming and going.

"Try not to land on any kids," Jeremy added.

Zippo gave a thumbs up to this, touching down, ever-so-gently, on the grass between a carousel and a skee-ball parlor.

CHAPTER 46

1ST ANNUAL COBBLE-CON

"Ready! Set! HOP!" the announcer's voice boomed through the P.A. system. The wooden slats slid up, revealing a row of bunny rabbits in individual pens. A couple of the rabbits hopped out lazily. They sniffed the track curiously before settling down to nibble on tufts of grass. The crowd roared.

Jeremy and the gang approached the oval-shaped pen, making their way through the crowd of onlookers. A hand painted sign above the fence read: "Traditional Lapitolo Races!"

Zippo eyed the rabbits with much interest. "Waow! Dey ares la-PEE-toe-loes?"

"Sort of," Jeremy said. The lapitolo had been House Fluffernut's mascot for untold centuries. They were a small animal with the body of a rabbit and the tail of a squirrel. Whether these mythical creatures were extinct or simply very rare, Jeremy did not know. He'd never seen a real one. Compared to the Dandy Lions' golden-maned Leo, or the vampire bat of House Hazeltwig, the lapitolo seemed the most ineffectual of all the mascots. Heck, even House Porkerson's Pigasus had wings. The lapitolo had no special abilities, magical or otherwise.

"They are sooo cuuuute!" Kitani and Sally cooed over the critters.

The crowd went wild. They called out the names of the various rabbits they'd placed their bets on.

"RUN, Mopsy! NO! Ignore that flower!"

"Go, Beowulf, go!"

"PEP-PER-JACK! PEP-PER-JACK! PEP-PER-JACK!"

Even Madi Nabo joined in, barking at the bunnies through the fence. The small rabbits quickly abandoned any pretense of a race; most ended up quietly grazing on grass, sitting up and grooming their ears, or closing their eyes to take naps. One of the rabbits seemed especially frustrated as it darted about the pen. Like all the other "lapitolos," it had a big, bushy squirrel's tail tied to it with a piece of twine. Contorting itself as best it could, it used its big front teeth to gnaw through the twine until it was free of the squirrel tail. Another bunny hopped over, casually sniffing the false tail. Once they determined the tail was not a threat, they both settled in to nibble dandelions.

None of the rabbits crossed the finish line.

In a baseball diamond to their right, enthusiastic fans were engaged in a "mock quadritardd match." The major difference between it and the real thing was that instead of flying, each player was just running around the field with a cardboard cutout of a pegasus or griffin. Normally this kind of thing would have made Jeremy laugh, but the whole scene actually struck him as deeply sad.

Beyond the baseball field lay the Great Lawn, a vast green expanse covered with various booths, food stalls, odd shacks, and vendors of every kind. An enormous stage was erected atop a platform in the distance, all set against the backdrop of the Manhattan skyline. From what Jeremy could see, there were hundreds, if not thousands, of Tommy Cobblestone fans gathered in front of the stage. It looked like its golden velvet curtains were still drawn. Music filled the air from the many speakers set up throughout the park. "Keen-o!" Jeremy exclaimed. He'd never witnessed a crowd so big in his life.

"Pretty fresh party!" Moe said. "What do you think, Zip?"

Zippo mewed, lifting his head and sniffing the air. A miasma of aromas, including carnival foods, cotton candy, and possibly livestock, filled his nostrils. "Smell *vary* nice!" He sighed happily.

A sign greeted them as they walked into the maze of attractions and booths: "Welcome to the Pigpimples Village of Values!" Although Jeremy remained skeptical about whether anything sold here could be considered a "value," the scene bustled with the energy of a village's market day. People hustled to and fro, browsing the wares of all the different merchants. Jeremy observed that most of the convention-goers were young and Terran, although he spotted a few offworlders here and there.

"Oh, wow! Honey, look at these two!" a bald New Yorker and his plump wife gawked at Kitani and Sally. "*Love* your costumes, girls! Well done!" the woman called out before heading off towards the "Glutton For Mutton" booth. Sally blushed. Kitani tilted her head, smiling but generally confused. "Jeremy, I don't get it—what costumes?"

It was then that Jeremy noticed that the man and his wife, despite being fully grown adults, were both wearing homemade Pigpimples uniforms. As a matter of fact, quite a few people in the park were sporting Pigpimples ties, vests, skirts and blazers. Some brave souls, laughing in the face of heat exhaustion, had even donned full winter cloaks.

"Why are they all wearing...?" Kitani screwed up her face in surprise.

Why anyone, especially two grownups, would *choose* to wear the itchy, scratchy, horribly uncomfortable clothing of wizard school was unfathomable to Jeremy. "I don't know, Kitani. I guess they think dressing up like children is fun."

"Oh, oh—look, Sal!" Kitani pointed at a t-shirt stand. There were racks of t-shirts with Tommy-Cobblestone-related sayings printed on them, like "Quadtritardd Team Captain," and "Kick Some Ashcrypt!" There were also shirts emblazoned with the logos of each Pigpimples House. It looked like the Dandy Lions and House Hazeltwig ones were sold out, but there were still hundreds upon hundreds of House Fluffernut shirts. Each one was printed with an image of a lapitolo staring off vacantly. "Let's each get one!" Kitani squealed, racing off with Sally. Madi Nabo galloped after them, yapping excitedly.

"Kitani, wait—" Jeremy called out, but Moe put up a hand.

"Let 'em go, dude. We'll catch up with them later. Right now we need to focus on Mrs. Crawford. I know she's around here somewhere. Zippo, what do your Felinian eyes see?"

Zippo squinted, getting serious. His head moved from side to side as he scanned the crowd in the Village of Values. He looked down at Moe, shrugging. "Sarry. I don't know..?"

It was then that they all realized: none of them knew what Mrs. Crawford actually looked like.

"Right. Well, do you smell any Cerberons? Maybe Mike is around here," Jeremy guessed.

Zippo tilted his head up, sniffing the air. "Fallow," he said, leading the way into the throng.

They weaved through the booths, following Zippo as he darted this way and that. Most of the vendors in the "village" appeared to be con artists with only a tenuous connection to *Tommy Cobblestone* or Pigpimples.

Professor Chamberpot must have realized this was his big chance to cash in on the school's popularity; Jeremy noted at least *six* booths with products endorsed by the Headmage. One had a sign that read, "*SIR MONGO'S LOTION: SO GOOD, IT'S ALMOST MAGIC!*" A disinterested vendor sat in the booth, scribbling on a crossword puzzle while a small televid screen played footage of Sir Mongo. "Ladies," the Headmage spoke to the viewers, "you might be wondering what elevates Sir Mongo's Lotion above all the other products in your daily skincare routine," he held up a bottle next to his withered face. "The answer is two simple words: bat guano."

Another booth was stocked with copies of the Professor's memoir. The cover pictured him standing by a window with a look of forlorn smugness. It was titled: *No Bows Without Rain: Reflections, Reminisces, and Reveries On My Journey as Headmage (A Tommy Cobblestone Book Club Selection).*

Oh brother, Jeremy thought. Neighboring this was a stall chocked full of shiny-looking candy bars. A poster screamed: "*Sir Mongo's Dill-E-Bars for YOUR Child's Weight Loss! YUMM! Taking the pounds off—FAST!*" Bruno had often complained to Jeremy about the Headmage's infamous Dill-E-Bars, which House Porkerson students received in lieu of treats. "Infused with the cleansing power of nougat and fresh dill," Jeremy remembered aloud. "Gross."

They finally arrived at a circle of food vendors. The long, intertwining lines of customers made any movement forward rather tricky.

"Hey!" Moe exclaimed, looking to Zippo, "They're getting Gecko Grog!" Gecko Grog was a popular drink in the *Tommy Cobblestone* universe, with nearly every party, festival or feast scene making some kind of reference to it. A teenage girl in an apron worked tirelessly behind the counter, filling mug after mug with the frothy green liquid. She placed a dried lizard's tail in each concoction, giving it a stir before handing it off to the next customer. "I wonder if it's the real deal," Moe said to Jeremy.

"I wouldn't know," Jeremy said. "Wizard food always made me a bit queasy." He looked at a neighboring stall. "For instance, '*Candied Earwigs—an old wizard's favorite treat!*' See, that's disgusting. Zippo, stop, wait up!"

"I find it!" The Felinian exclaimed. He jumped into the line for another treat booth, this one run by the local YWCA (Young

Witches Coven Association) of New York. They were selling "Authentic Follypops," which were magically enchanted suckers that came in a virtually infinite variety of artificial flavors, all with gooey-candy-centers. A sandwich-board sign proclaimed: "*Follypop of the day: Coconut Panko with Jellied Shrimp Core!*"

"Hey," Jeremy said, placing a hand on Zippo's shoulder to get his attention, "this is a bad idea."

"But—bu—shramp! CO-CO-nat! Panko!" Zippo protested.

"I know they look good in the comics, but what they don't tell you is that these things are cursed." Some of the people in line gave Jeremy funny looks. "I'm serious! Read the fine print!" Jeremy squinted at the tiny writing on the sign, reading it aloud: "See? '*One in every five-hundred Follypops has a cursed candy center;*' I'm not making this up! Some of the curses are pretty nasty, too!" Jeremy recalled the time Nobby Curdswell had reached the center of a strawberry Follypop and was immediately cursed with a hag. The hag would just show up randomly, usually in the middle of the night, and bother Nobby or follow him around campus for days until he could get her to go away. But she always came back.

Moe and Jeremy dragged the Felinian away from the line. "We can buy cursed lollipops later, dude. Let's keep moving," Moe insisted. Zippo continued looking at the booth as they moved away.

"Mommy, look! It's Tommy Cobblestone!" a little girl in line called out.

"Honey, that's not the *real* Tommy Cobblestone. That's just an impersonator."

"What are you, daft?!" Kitani called out, elbowing her way through a crowd to rejoin her friends. Sally followed closely behind, holding an armful of t-shirts. "Tommy Cobblestone is a *Jeremy Fletcher* impersonator!" Kitani shouted. Jeremy pulled her back before she could attack the little girl.

As they made their way out of the cluster of food booths,

Zippo wrinkled his nose at a foul smell, then gagged. Moe and Jeremy smelled it, too. "What *is* that funky stank?" Moe said.

"Over der," Zippo pointed, his whiskers twitching in disgust. He covered his mouth with his paw, gagging again.

Jeremy looked. A flash of light popped from a photographer's camera as he took a portrait of two kids. They stood in front of a tremendously fat pig who was rooting around in a fenced-in bog. The pig snorted loudly as it flopped itself down in a pile of its own filth. "Hey there, boys!" a barker shouted as Jeremy approached, "Why don't you have your photograph taken with FRANCIS, the ORIGINAL PIGASUS MASCOT of PIGPIMPLES!" A banner above the pen proclaimed: "*MEET & GREET with ACTUAL Pigpimples CELEBRITIES!*"

"Uh, thanks I've already got one." Jeremy wanted to ask what made this particular pig a "pigasus," seeing as it had no wings. He also wasn't sure how the pig could be "the ORIGINAL PIGASUS MASCOT of PIGPIMPLES," unless it was about seven-hundred years old. He turned to Moe and Zippo. "Do either of you need portraits standing in front of excrement?"

"Homeboy!" Moe called to the barker, "This sign says we can meet Anita Cosgrove." He waved the flyer about in his hand. "Where is she? Because I have a few questions for her." He nudged Jeremy. "Maybe she can tell us where Crawford is."

"Sorry kiddos, but the meet 'n greet ended at three. All we've got left are Francis, or the Trousers of Destiny." The man swung a thumb over at a pair of pants hanging from a clothesline. From what Jeremy could see, they were, indeed, the actual Trousers of Destiny. [*Translator's Note: Magical pants. Every Pigpimples student starts their academic career by trying on this particular pair of sentient pants. Once worn, the trousers determine which house the student belongs to. —ChatterBot 3.6*] Jeremy shuddered at the recollection of his experience with them.

A shrill voice emanated from the pants' open fly. "Hey! Why dontcha try me on, baby!" The pants harassed a group of girls as they walked by. "Come on, I ain't so bad! You wanna be a real Dandy Lion? I can make it happen! Hey-Oooo!"

"Ugh. Let's get out of here," Jeremy said. "I refuse to speak to those pants ever again."

"I think Zip's picked up the scent!" Moe said, the Felinian nearly bounding away in excitement. Jeremy and the gang hustled to keep up, finally stopping at the outskirts of the immense crowd gathered in front of the stage. The curtains had opened, and some kind of show was starting. "What is it? What is everyone cheering about? Is it a band?" Moe said, hopping up and down. He was too short to see over the crowd.

Now that they were closer, Jeremy realized there actually was an unmistakable (and very familiar) aroma in the air. "It's a bangers and mash eating contest," he said.

A row of husky-looking boys sat at a long table on the stage, long white napkins tied around their necks. Everyone in the crowd applauded as the boys scarfed down plate after plate of sausage and mashed potatoes. The sun was starting to sink on the horizon, casting long shadows everywhere. Kitani held Madi Nabo up so she could watch the eating contest, which she appeared very interested in. Sally made a sound of disgust as the boys on stage gorged themselves.

"Absolutely revolting, innit?" Kitani said to Sally. "At least little Sophie seems to enjoy it, don't you, Soph?" The Cerberon wagged her tail happily.

A boy on the stage pushed himself back, his chair squeaking as he hopped up in joyful triumph. He held up his fork to the crowd. It had one final bite of sausage on it. He popped it into his mouth and chewed as the crowd cheered. An official walked over to confirm whether the boy had finished all the food on his plate. Satisfied, the judge lifted the boy's right arm in victory.

"Congratulations," the judge spoke into a microphone. "Let's hear it for," he looked at the boy's name tag, "Herman! The rest of you boys, please get off the stage." The boys filed off dejectedly, one of them still picking food off his plate, as the crowd applauded. "Now Herman, we have a very special prize for you. And here to present it is a very special guest. Ladies and gentleman, please give a warm Pigpimples welcome to CEO of Seashell Systems, MRS. CRAWFORD!"

Moe and Jeremy froze. Zippo's eyes went wide. "She *here*!" he hissed.

"Pick me up!" Moe demanded, hopping into Zippo's arms. The Binosian scrambled up Zippo's back, sitting on top of his shoulders so he could get a good look. A spotlight switched on as an elderly woman walked onto the stage. Her outfit was of an odd, modern style, consisting of a black dress with a suit jacket and pointy-looking shoulder pads. A young man followed her, hobbling along with the assistance of the cybernetic crutch that was also his forearm. Despite limping, his movements were surprisingly fluid. He had a wild look in his eyes that Jeremy didn't like one bit.

The old woman stopped and waved graciously to the crowd, even though there appeared to be some general confusion about who exactly she was supposed to be, or why she was important. The young man acting as her bodyguard lifted his crutch and pointed it at the judge, who frowned in terror. The judge handed the woman the microphone and scurried off the stage without a word.

"Good evening fellow Cobbleheads!" Mrs. Crawford flashed a sinister smile at the crowd, who was still unsure what to make of her. Her voice was grandmotherly, but with a hard edge that came from too many cups of scalding hot coffee. "My name is Mrs. Crawford. As the judge mentioned, I'm CEO of Seashell Systems, Terra Firma division." She placed an arm around young Herman's shoulders, who stood obediently by her side.

The bodyguard bared his teeth, eyeing the little boy with suspicion. If the boy was nervous, he wasn't showing it. Jeremy thought his expression was reminiscent of a buffalo about to be hit by a school bus.

"For those that don't know, Seashell is one of the biggest tech companies in the Planetary League. You're probably already familiar with the Personal Home Combobulator?"

Mrs. Crawford smiled expectantly to a smattering of applause. "Well, that was one of ours! And of course, there's the Morph-o-matic Probe Apparatus, used in health clinics across the country..." Mrs. Crawford held her arms out, as if to receive thunderous applause. There were a few cheers and whistles. "Oh, and Bionic Propulsion Pods, that—" she stopped, as the bodyguard leaned in and whispered something in her ear.

Zippo squinted, focusing. He pointed.

"Zip! What's going on?" Moe asked.

"She holding something!"

Now that Zippo mentioned it, Jeremy could see it, too. The lady on stage definitely had something in her right hand.

"I do apologize! My assistant, Tim, informs me that the Bionic Propulsion Pods are still being tested on monkeys in South America. No matter!" she looked down at Herman, who was patiently awaiting further instructions. The stained napkin was still tied about his neck. "Herman, I'm so glad you could be here to share in this moment. We at Seashell Systems have been working very hard on this project, and I think you're going to enjoy it immensely! Would you like to see it?"

"She's gonna reveal it! *The Personal Shell*!" Moe gasped.

"What do we do?" Jeremy asked. Zippo bit a claw nervously. They all felt powerless.

The little boy on stage nodded. Mrs. Crawford threw back her head and laughed theatrically. "Oh Herman," sweetness dripped from her voice like Bolano syrup, "don't worry your chubby little head! I think any fan of Tommy Cobblestone will

LOVE it. Watch!" She gave the boy a side hug as they turned to face the tall golden curtains. They parted, revealing a vast white canvas. The stage lights shut off. Everyone waited several moments, but nothing happened. Mrs. Crawford then looked around impatiently, her sweet demeanor evaporating into a snarl. "CAN WE ROLL THE FILM, PLEASE?!"

Theatrical music blared from the speakers as black and white images flickered to life on the enormous screen. Blocky titles appeared, towering over the crowd.

MONOLITH STUDIOS

In conjunction with

SEASHELL SYSTEMS: TERRA FIRMA

And PIGPIMPLES ACADEMIE OF MAGICK

PRESENTS

The titles dissolved, revealing a shot of an empty-looking school campus. Kitani and Sally gasped. The camera panned slowly as eerie, childlike music played. "Is it really..?" Kitani whispered to Sally.

The picture shifted to an indoor scene. It was of an empty dining hall, light streaming in through the tall windows.

"What the devil is going on here?" Jeremy exclaimed. "That's...the Trough!" he looked at Kitani and Sally, whose faces were contorted in dumbfounded grimaces. They kept watching, waiting for some kind of explanation. The film floated on through various classrooms and settings around campus, all empty, with the same ghostly music playing.

"*In a MAGICAL school of WONDER,*" an announcer's voice spoke. The scene shifted to a solitary boy writing a long spellcasting equation on a chalkboard. His back was to the camera. "*Lived the most MAGICAL orphan of ALL!*" As the boy finished the equation, he placed the chalk down on the tray and patted the dust from his hands. The camera did a quick zoom as the boy stopped, his head turning ever-so-slightly. He looked like he'd heard something in the hallway. In a flash, he pulled a wand out of his pocket, holding it upright.

The murmur of the crowd rose in excitement. Jeremy felt like he was going to hork.

Just before the boy turned around, the screen went black. The music crescendoed as the titles proclaimed:

You've read the comic book sensation–

now experience

TOMMY COBBLESTONE:

[INSERT COMPLETED MOTION PICTURE TITLE HERE]

Coming to a theater near you!

– Summer 1920 –

The stage lights went up. The audience erupted.[*Translator's Note: Supposedly the roar was so deafening, witnesses reported hearing the cheers all the way in the South Bronx! —ChatterBot 3.6*]

"Woo-hoo! Yeah!" Moe applauded with Zippo. They looked over to ask Jeremy what he thought. His face was frozen with the look of someone who had just stepped barefoot into something squishy. "You okay, chief?" Moe asked.

Jeremy inhaled deeply. "Yes. I think so. I thought she was going to announce the Personal Shell... But that was *much* worse."

"Wow!" Mrs. Crawford exclaimed from the stage. The golden curtains closed as the cheers died down. "Wasn't that something? You like going to the picture shows, don't you Herman?" The little boy stood in stunned silence as the old woman placed a hand on his back. "Of course you do! And as a prize for winning the Bangers and Mash contest, you'll get to! Obviously the film is still in production—but next summer, once it's completed, you'll be right there on the red carpet!"

The bodyguard held out a white envelope.

"Tim is holding a ticket to the *premiere* of the Tommy Cobblestone picture! It's all yours!" She instructed Tim to hand the envelope to the boy, who accepted it awkwardly. "Let's hear it for Herman!" Mrs. Crawford clapped a few times. She was obviously done with this kid, and the bodyguard shooed him off the side of the stage, using his cybernetic crutch to prod him on the backside. "And Herman's not the only one! We'll announce tickets for the winners of the Quadritardd Match, the Lapitolo Races, the Costume Contest, and the Karaoke Tournament, later in tonight's program!" The crowd applauded approvingly. "Now if you don't mind, I'm going to sit back and enjoy the remainder of the show! A special thanks to Pigpimples—they were kind enough to lend us one of their magic skyboxes for the occasion!"

The spotlight swiveled to an oval-shaped pod on the ground beside the stage. Inside it were three red velvet seats, reminiscent of a theater's balcony. Jeremy recognized the skybox; VIPs and administrators sometimes sat in them while spectating Quadritardd matches.

Mrs. Crawford and Tim walked down the front steps of the stage to the box, where a hooded, red-robed wizard unlatched a side door and allowed them to enter. The wizard put his hood down, looking around before entering the skybox and seating himself beside the old woman.

Jeremy recognized the wizard's dark hair and beard instantly. *Professor Von Bibliosnuff!* With a dab and tap of his bone-white wand, the wizard levitated the skybox off the ground. The crowd *oooh*-ed as it floated high into the air. Mrs. Crawford waved down to everyone, leaning over and kissing Bibliosnuff on the cheek.

"Gross!" Kitani gagged.

The curtains opened, revealing stagehands setting up the first act's instruments. The crowd looked on, conversing and milling about. The sun had set, and the lights of the city sparkled in the distance. The rest of the park had gotten quite dark.

"Guys!" Jeremy shouted, pointing at the floating skybox. "Look!"

Moe and Zippo peered at the floating balcony in the air. Mrs. Crawford's face was illuminated by a light source emanating from something she held in her hands. She showed the glowing rectangular object to Professor Bibliosnuff. There was no denying it.

She was holding a Personal Shell.

"She's got one! She's got the thing!" Moe said excitedly. They could see her tucking the device back into her jacket pocket. "We need to get it from her! It might have everything we need!" Moe stopped, rubbing his chin. "How the heck are we going to snatch it when she's all the way up there?"

Jeremy looked to the stage. "I have an idea."

CHAPTER 47

FOLLOW THE STARS

"Kitani—you and Sally stay here."

The girls objected, Madi Nabo whining in protest. It was Jeremy's turn to place a reassuring hand on the side of Kitani's arm. Her eyes widened in a freckly expression that was equal parts elation and amazement. "Kit—I need you to do this," Jeremy said, leaning in close.

"Do...what?" Kitani asked, her voice nearly a whisper.

"When the moment comes, you'll know." He patted her arm and turned away. Jeremy whispered to Moe and Zippo as they strode towards the side of the stage. "Don't ask what I meant by that, because I don't know."

Moe remained seated atop Zippo's shoulders. A velvet rope marked the area that was blocked off to the rest of the concert-goers. Behind the rope was an open-air tent where stagehands, lighting crew, band members, and other performers loitered around, getting ready for their various parts in the night's show.

"Do you guys have anything we could use to bribe someone with?" Jeremy asked.

"You're kidding, right?" Moe said, sounding suspicious. "I think Zip's got some leftover sausage links."

"Heh. Noh, eh, I do *nawt*," Zippo shrugged sheepishly.

"What about a magtape of future hits?"

"Whoa, whoa dude, now hold up—" Moe didn't like what he was hearing. "Even if I did, no way I'm giving one of those away. Besides, who around here would even want one?"

"Musicians!" Jeremy gestured to their surroundings. "I think I can get on stage, but once I'm up there we'll need a distraction. Maybe you could bribe one of these bands to start playing, or something..." Jeremy trailed off.

Zippo ran a paw over his ears, concerned. Things were not looking good.

"Just come on," Jeremy said, walking up to the velvet rope.

An offworlder security guard stood by the stage, monitoring the area. He was a Volzoid, which made sense—his bulbous, insectoid eyes were well-suited for seeing all around himself at once. He crossed his hairy black appendages over his muscular thorax chest. "Excuzzze me boyzzz—but thizzz area is rezzztricted."

"I'm just here to claim my prize," Jeremy said. He polished his spectacles with his necktie and placed them back on his face, grinning. "For the costume contest!"

The Volzoid moved his head close to Jeremy, getting a good look at him with his compound eyes. He made a buzzing sound of approval. "Oh wowzzz! You really went all out! Nice cozzzztume! Zzz zzz! You dezzzerve it!" The guard unhooked the velvet rope, allowing Jeremy to enter.

Zippo and Moe attempted to join him, but the guard stopped them. "Yo! What gives?"

"Zzzorry," the Volzoid held up a segmented claw, "friendzzz and family not allowed. You'll have to wait until he'zzz done."

"Vudi," a warm voice called out. The lavender skinned chica had been watching them, her slightly translucent body floating amongst the hustle and bustle. She had on a poofy sparkling skirt, with several long necklaces and lacy fingerless gloves. Her face was made up with the darkest of eye shadow; her lipstick seemed to be infused with crushed rubies. Her hair was sideswept and bouncy, all held in place with a headband of silver stars. Jeremy had never seen a woman dressed like her; she made him think of some kind of beautiful space princess. She glided over, her hair swaying in a spectral breeze.

"Rhonda!" Moe called out, hopping down from Zippo's shoulders.

She had an exasperated look on her face, but also the ghost of a smile. She shook her head. "Unbelievable. It's okay, Vudi," she said. "They're with me."

Jeremy felt a strange sense of *deja vu*.

* * *

"So how did you get here? You weren't on the flier," Jeremy said. They sat on speaker boxes backstage while Plumpy's Pudding performed. From what Jeremy could hear, they weren't very good. *They must be doing something right, though, gauging by the sound of the audience's approval!* Probably the fact that the band was all dressed in Pigpimples uniforms playing Cobblestone-themed songs made up for their musical shortcomings.

"After your little—incident—at the club, you mean?" she turned to Moe with an arched eyebrow of disapproval. "I'm fine, by the way!"

"Hey, Miss Starruki—" Moe leaned in close, putting an arm around Rhonda's shoulders. "You know I'll always be there to rescue you!"

"Ugh," Rhonda said, shrugging Moe's arm off her shoulders. "I'll be in *serious* trouble if I ever need your dumb butt to rescue me."

Zippo chuffled.

"That's right, baby. Because I know you can take care of

yourself," Moe winked. Rhonda scoffed.

He continued, "So did you ever listen to those future tracks I gave you? I thought some of them were right up your alley, musically—"

Rhonda rolled her eyes and turned away. "You will just never get it, will you?" She looked at Jeremy. "In answer to your question, Pigasus Rising had to drop out at the last minute. Rumor has it their lead singer contracted slug-limb from a cursed Follypop."

Jeremy locked eyes with Zippo. *See?*

"My contact knew the right people, and so here we are. Not a lot of offworlders touring this system, and we worked up a pretty good buzz from our run at Heavy Nova. The festival organizers thought an alien act might help boost Cobblestone brand awareness with the offworlder market." She sipped from a straw placed in a bottle of Nova Pop.

Moe squinted. "I don't get it. Since when do you like Tommy Cobblestone?"

"Oh, I don't. That is," she leaned in close, "I've never actually read it!" She made a cute surprised face. "But if it helps me break into the Terran market, I'll memorize every issue! My drummer, Mase, got me this jacket." She stood, slipping on the blue denim jacket and showing it off. On the back was a big red heart made of rhinestones, with the names *Georgina + Elmer* inside it. [*Translator's Note: a reference to the on-again, off-again relationship between Cobblestone fan-favorites, Georgina Best and Elmer Pineneedle. —ChatterBot 3.6*]

"Waow, det vary sparkle!" Zippo complimented Rhonda, petting her jacket.

"Thank you, Zipponio! But the real question is," Rhonda turned to Moe, "what are *you* doing here? I thought you two had black holes to dip, nightclubs to open."

"We do," Moe said. "But first, we need to save the world real quick."

"Wanna help?" Jeremy asked.

Rhonda laughed. "Oh, you boys! Can we talk later? I have a gig to get ready for!" She picked up her electric kithara by the neck. "We're on as soon as Plumpy finishes up." She pointed at the stage with the instrument.

"All right! Perfect! I just need to go on before you!" Jeremy exclaimed.

"What is this kid talking about?" Rhonda turned to Moe.

"He...uh...does a *funky* magic set! This could be his big break!" Moe said.

She looked to Zippo. He gave a thumbs up. "*Vary* funkee."

"I guess if anyone asks, we could just tell them you're my opening act..." Rhonda sighed. "But if you bomb out there, I'm telling security I don't know you."

"Deal!" Jeremy beamed.

* * *

They searched around backstage until they found a very fancy phonograph player. "Zippo, let me see your backpack," Jeremy asked. Zippo bounded over, handing Jeremy a pink backpack. The front was emblazoned with a flying Pigasus. "This is Sally's!" Jeremy looked up.

The Felinian mewed. "Oh! I liek Sally BECK-peck, so we trade." Jeremy shook his head and unzipped the pink backpack, pulling out a very special album—maybe even his all-time favorite. *Xavier Arnito Presents: Salsa Galactica.*

"All right—this is it," he murmured to the record. "If I don't see you again, just know that I couldn't have made it without you." He gave the cover a smooch. "Put this on when I give the signal, okay?" Zippo agreed, taking the record in his paws. After a brief discussion of their plan, Jeremy took a deep breath. It sounded like Plumpy's Pudding was wrapping up.

"THANK YOU, COBBLE-CON! AND REMEMBER:

REAL MAGIC IS THE POWER OF LOVE IN YOUR HEARTS!" Jeremy cringed at the dreadful catchphrase from the comics. "GOOD NIGHT!" the singer's voice echoed throughout Central Park, met with applause and cheers from the crowd. The band emerged backstage as the golden curtains shut. The stagehands scurried around, quickly dismantling the instruments.

Members of Plumpy's Pudding headed to the craft service table, where they stopped to converse with the Zig-Zags. Nobody seemed to be paying attention to the stage. *It's now or never!* "Here we go," Jeremy said, sweating buckets.

He pointed at Zippo, who dropped the needle onto the spinning record. They'd rigged a microphone up to the record player, and within seconds the air swelled with mystical Latin rhythms. Jeremy pulled out his wand and made his big entrance.

He entangled himself in the curtain almost instantly.

The lighting crew, not realizing the next act was already starting, quickly swiveled a spotlight onto Jeremy as he fumbled with the curtain. He spun around several times, finally falling to the floor with an audible thud. Once free, he hopped up and danced his way to the front of the stage. The darkness of the night and the blinding spotlight in his face made it mercifully difficult to see the thousands upon thousands of fans in the crowd. He tried not to think about them, and just kept dancing.

The audience, puzzled by the new style of music they'd never heard before, were not exactly sure how to react. The fact that there was a strange boy dancing on the stage in a Pigpimples uniform only added to their confusion.

"Who's that kid?"

"Oh, I get it!—he's a Tommy Cobblestone impersonator?"

"Hey wait a minute—"

"He's the kid from the movie preview! It's him!"

"But why is he dancing around like that?"

"And what's wrong with his costume? Why is he so filthy?"

(At this point in his adventure, Jeremy's school uniform was covered in a variety of pink and green slime splatters, plasma scorch marks, and gooey marshmallow stains.)

"This kid!" Moe said, elbowing Zippo in the ribs as they watched from the wings of the stage. "He knows how to work a crowd, I'll give him that!"

As Jeremy did his dancing handkerchief routine, Zippo noticed something else: the scary-looking wizard in the red robe was standing up from his seat in the floating skybox. It looked like he was arguing with Tiny Tim. The first song on the record came to a close, and the crowd applauded. Jeremy adjusted the mic stand, lowering it as he spoke. "Good evening, ladies and gentlemen! My name is Jeremy Fletcher—and I am the Mambo Wizard!"

"WE LOVE YOU, JEREMY!" a voice screamed from the audience. Everyone chuckled.

Jeremy shielded his eyes and looked out into the audience, copying the gag from that M.C. in Heavy Nova. "Oh! Why thanks, grandma!" he joked, hamming it up for laughs. Everyone chuckled. The crowd was warming up to him!

"For my next trick, I'll need a little help from an audience member." He looked up to the skybox. "I know! Why don't we ask Mrs. Craw—"

Just then, a blast of green energy shot right towards him with a terrifying *skeeeyYEW!* Jeremy dove to the floor as the bolt exploded behind him.

The audience *OOOH*-ed.

A scorched hole burned in the curtain, right where his head had just been. Jeremy rolled to his left as another blast of plasma rocked the stage. He scrambled to his feet, grabbing the microphone. "Excuse me, but whoever is doing that—it's extremely distracting—!"

The audience gasped as the scary red-robed wizard floated down from the skybox, hovering in front of the stage. Professor Bibliosnuff's wand was extended and his eyes were glowing green with fury. "YOU! You are zhe one who stole zhat ancient tome from zhe Atheneum!" Another green projectile screeched forth from his wand, bathing the audience in emerald light. Jeremy turned to escape, running directly into the curtains again. He couldn't find where they parted, and so he wrapped himself up and hoped for the best.

From out of nowhere, a fireball intercepted the green bolt, smashing into it and sending splatters of energy across the stage.

"Hey, ya big mook! Leave him alone, why dontcha!" a Bronx accent called out from the audience. Jeremy peeked out from behind the curtains. A kid climbed onto the stage! He was holding his own magic wand, and had created a fire shield to block any incoming blasts.

"Bruno!" Jeremy yelled, running to his friend.

The crowd cheered as the peppy samba played on.

A magic missile pierced Bruno's fire shield, shattering it to embers. Thinking fast, Bruno yanked Jeremy into a headlock and pulled him down—narrowly avoiding a green shaft as it sailed over his friend's dome. The young pyromancer let Jeremy go and returned fire, blasting the night sky with streaks of blue flame. The audience was mesmerized.

"Impi-ardus!" Bibliosnuff cast a spell with a wave of his wand. Jeremy didn't care for the sound of it one bit. Three fat little imps, their eyes also glowing green and their skin as black as coal, materialized on the stage. They had little nubby horns on their heads and hoofs for feet. An intricate marimba solo pounding from the speakers provided the perfect accompaniment as the imps surrounded the two boys.

"Why are they *naked*?!" Jeremy cried out to Bruno. The audience laughed.

The imps produced glowing pitchforks, jabbing them menacingly at the air. The two boys stood back to back as the creatures closed in on them. "Back it up!" Bruno said, holding his wand up. A rope of flame sprouted from the wand's tip, growing like a vine until it brushed the floor.

"Back, ya little freaks!" Bruno lashed out at the monsters, the flame whip cracking back and scorching Jeremy across the left shoulder. He patted his jacket frantically, stopping the fire before it could spread.

They were running out of space. Bruno lashed the whip straight ahead, catching an imp by the neck. The demon screamed as it tried to squirm free, its head bursting into flames. Its companions screeched, rushing the boys with their pitchforks and knocking Jeremy to the floor. Maledict Von Bibliosnuff hovered in the air, his evil laughter booming across the park.

Then there was a muffled sound, followed by a flurry of shots from stage right. Electric blue bolts and hot pink pulses *PEW*-ed across the set as Zippo and Moe ran out, phasers blazing. The Felinian *raowed* with fury as he fired shot after shot, finally knocking a spectral pitchfork from one of the imp's hands. Enraged, the devil bared its sharp teeth and ran at him. Zippo squeezed off a final shot at close range, hitting the pudgy creature square in the chest. The imp disappeared in a puff of magic.

Meanwhile, Moe went after the other imp. He cornered it long enough for Bruno to catch it by the leg with his fire whip. The imp screeched and yowled as it writhed, attempting to break free. Moe raised his phaser up, pointing it at the demon's head. He put on his oversized shades with dramatic flair. "*Arrivederci, baby,*" he said in a husky voice, quoting a favorite phrase from *Vince Thorne: Agent of Fortune.*

With that, the imp decided it'd had enough. "Do NOT call us again, Maledict!" it hollered, then disappeared back to whatever plane of existence it had come from.

"Awwww! What was that?!" Moe complained. He turned to the audience. "That was wack!"

The red wizard landed on the stage, assessing the situation before him. "Wolves!" he thundered. "I require your azzistance, *immediately*!"

Bruno obscured the side of his mouth with his hand as he muttered an incantation. "Phoenix fly!" he exclaimed, completing the spell and whipping his wand. The whip crack summoned a fiery bird that screeched into the sky. The creature flapped its wings, turning and dive-bombing the red-robed wizard, who yelped out in anger as he flew back and away.

"*Aaaaarrgh!*"

The audience was loving the scene, laughing, pointing, and shouting as they danced.

"Hey, Jeremy!" Bruno said, helping his friend up off the floor. "How's it goin' pally? Never thought I'd see you at a Cobblestone convention! Didn't really care to come myself, but the food! Mwah!" he gave a chef's kiss to the air.

"Well, you know me," Jeremy said, dusting himself off and grabbing the microphone by the stand. "I've always been a Tommy Cobblestone superfan *number one*!" he pointed out at the crowd. They exploded in applause.

Superfan number one? he thought to himself. *What is wrong with me?*

A shot rang out from somewhere up above. It hit the mic, which screeched with electric feedback before exploding. The shot couldn't have come from Professor Bibliosnuff, as Jeremy could still see him fighting with the summoned phoenix in the distance. Jeremy looked frantically to the skybox.

A deranged cyborg snarled down at him, a look of murder behind the lanky strands of his blonde hair. He stood with one foot on the handrail, his cybernetic arm-crutch supported on his knee. The young man looked down the sights of his crutch-gun, closing his eye to aim another shot.

"TIMOTHY! Stop this! Stop this at once!" Mrs. Crawford screamed, yanking Tim's crutch away before he could fire again.

The audience murmured in confusion.

Professor Bibliosnuff floated back over to the skybox, his

robes slightly singed and smoking. The phoenix must have dissipated. "Now, then!" he shouted, also taking aim with his wand. "You vill see how seriously the Fascination Wolves treat library policy *violations*!"

Mrs. Crawford stood up and slapped the wand out of his hand. "Stop this, you foolish old coot! Are you both *insane*? Seashell Systems has put too much into this franchise for you to murder a child in front of thousands of fans! Can't you see they love him?! We couldn't make this a bigger party if we tried!" She pointed down at the crowd, who were looking more concerned by the second.

The Professor furrowed his brow at the old woman, opening his mouth to speak. She cut him off. "Not another word!" Mrs. Crawford leaned out of the skybox, shouting to the audience, "It seems we had little scare there with some faulty props!" She glared daggers at Tiny Tim. "We wouldn't want to accidentally KILL the STAR of the new Tommy Cobblestone PICTURE, would we?"

She shouted for a new microphone to be brought out. Stagehands emerged, quickly replacing the exploded mic. "Let's hear it, everyone! He's okay!" She called out, clapping. The audience caught on, and soon the buzz of confusion transformed into cheers of approval.

"I knew it! I knew he was the kid from the preview!"

"What a show!"

"He's not exactly the Tommy I imagined, but he'll do!"

Jeremy sighed with relief, giving a half bow. Bruno patted Jeremy on the back. "You owe me big time after that one!" he said.

"How does breakfast sound? On me," Jeremy replied. Bruno laughed, exiting the stage through the curtains. Moe followed.

"Jrr-mEE?" Zippo asked, reluctant to leave his companion alone on the stage. Jeremy reassured Zippo that he'd be okay, thanking him and reminding him to flip the record to side B.

Zippo padded away, slipping gingerly behind the heavy curtains.

"Ahem!" Mrs. Crawford called out from the skybox. "Now then, why don't we all allow our young STAR to wrap up his little show, shall we?" She gave Jeremy an icy look.

He gulped. The plan hinged on this moment.

"You know everyone..." Jeremy spoke into the mic as he looked at the crowd. "How'd you all like to see Mrs. Crawford help me do a final magic trick?"

The audience whooped and cheered.

"Oh, no. Absolutely not." Mrs. Crawford shook her head in distaste.

Jeremy ignored her. "Come on, everybody! Who wants to see the *real* magic of Seashell Systems?!"

The crowd cheered even more.

Mrs. Crawford folded her arms, staring down at Jeremy. She did not look happy.

Jeremy remained all smiles, putting his hand to his ear and leaning out towards the audience. He laughed as they got louder. The old woman finally grabbed Maledict, muttering something into his ear. He obeyed, lowering the skybox to the ground.

The crowd went wild. Jeremy did an enthusiastic dance as Xavier Arnito's trumpets blasted. On the ground, Mrs. Crawford pushed Tiny Tim out of her way and marched out of the skybox. The cyborg tried following her, but she jabbed him with her sharp elbow. He stayed behind, but pointed his crutch cannon at Jeremy menacingly.

Mrs. Crawford waved at the crowd as she joined Jeremy on the stage. She even managed a good-natured smile as the boy wizard finished up his dance.

She then covered the mic with one hand and leaned down, taking a pinch of Jeremy's cheek in her bony fingers. She smelled of dead flowers, and her breath reeked of cigarettes. "Whatever you have planned," she whispered as she waggled his cheek flesh, "make it quick and get me off this stage, or your friends will never even find your *body*." She let go, giving Jeremy's cheek a little pat and smiling warmly.

"Yes ma'am," Jeremy said back, rubbing his cheek. He faced the audience. "For my final trick, I give you..." Jeremy threw down a flash bomb, enveloping them both in a swirl of yellow smoke. He waved his arms apart, dispersing the smoke and revealing a tall, narrow tent with red and white stripes. "...the Tent of Mystery!"

"It looks like a changing tent," Mrs. Crawford observed.

"Of MYSTERY," Jeremy corrected, giving the audience a wink. He saluted with his wand, before ducking into the tent. That was Zippo's cue. He turned up the music, filling the air with the bouncy chords of "Redshift Rhumba."

* * *

Jeremy popped out through the bottom of the curtains backstage, crawling on his hands and knees. Zippo rushed over, helping him up. Stagehands and other crew members went about their business, working around them. Bruno was nowhere to be seen, although Jeremy assumed he'd found food somewhere. Meanwhile, Moe and Rhonda were back at it.

"We don't need their songs, Moe! The stuff I write is better than anything you can fish out of a black hole!"

"But why let them go to waste?! It's not hurting anyone, is it? Baby, they're *proven* winners!"

Jeremy cleared his throat.

"Oh hey!" Moe spun around. "Did you get it?!" he asked frantically.

Jeremy reached into his jacket pocket, hands still trembling with adrenaline, and pulled out the device. It was Mrs. Crawford's Personal Shell!

"Switched," he said. "Let's just pray she doesn't check her pockets for the next five minutes." He shot an annoyed look at

Moe. "Did you really have to put that *Noise Pickle* sticker on our P-Shell?" Jeremy asked, annoyed.

"What, they're a great band!"

Jeremy handed Crawford's Shell to Zippo. They gathered around as he flicked the device on. The little rectangle glowed to life in his paws. The Felininan's pupils dilated as he went into hyper-focus. He scanned through all the files in the Shell's digital datebook. He started in surprise. "Got et!" he chittered. "Got et! Is hear, is *hear*!" He waved the device in triumph. "Look, is hear!" He held the Shell in Moe's face. Jeremy stooped to read the text.

Reminder: P-Shell Shipment aboard THE PERFECT STRANGER

Captain: MIKE MANIA

First Officer: CHARLES IN CHARGE

Estimated Time of Departure: 46 hrs.

Destination: Terra Firma [Luna Port of Entry]

Personal Access Passcode: "dare_2_dream"

There followed a long string of space coordinates.

"Mike Mania and the Personal Shells all in one shipment! Got 'em!" Moe socked Zippo in the arm, working himself up with excitement.

"Yeh! We blow up slobber-tongue naow!" Zippo bared his pointy fangs in a menacing grin, miming an explosion with claws extended.

"Zip—those coordinates...that's not too far from here, right?" Moe asked.

Zippo thought for a moment, calculating in his head. "Yeh. Prabably orbit near...ehm..." he rolled his paw, trying to remember the name, "*Markary*?"

"Mercury?" Jeremy said.

"That's the one!" Moe said.

"Um, Jeremy?" Rhonda said, peeking at the stage. The music was still going, but the crowd was getting restless. Mrs.

Crawford stood, tapping her foot impatiently. "Are you going back out there to finish your magic trick? That lady looks pretty upset."

"Oh, no way. I never figured out how to finish the Tent of Mystery," Jeremy shrugged. "'Redshift Rhumba' should buy us a couple of minutes. Thanks for letting me go on, by the way."

"Don't mention it," Rhonda said. She looked to Moe, perturbed. "So what, you guys are just taking off now? You came all this way and you're not even going to watch our set?"

"Rhonda, it's not like that; it's just that—if we don't get out of here right now—"

"Oh let me guess, more people who want to kill you because you stole something, is that it? Zig-Zags!" she called out to her band mates, slinging her kithara over her shoulder. "Get ready. We're up."

"Don't worry about it, she just gets like this when she's nervous—" Moe started to say before Zippo batted him with both paws. He'd seen something. Up by the tent's entrance, two red-robed wizards were talking with the Volzoid security guard. The guard spoke into a walkie-talkie before unhooking the velvet rope and letting the Fascination Wolves in.

Zippo looked down at Jeremy and Moe. "We are *trap*," he whispered.

"Ay, yo! Jeremy!" a voice called out. *Bruno!* He was standing at the craft service table. It was laid out with all sorts of tiny sandwiches and other snacks. He loaded up a plate with cold cuts as he regaled a gaggle of young fans. He waved at Jeremy, "Jeremy! Get over here—these guys all wanna meetchya!"

Jeremy rushed over, placing a hand over Bruno's mouth. "Shhh! I'm not here!" He looked around madly, seeing if he'd been spotted.

"Okay, okay," Bruno chuckled. "Pipe down! Look at this guy, one show and he thinks he's mister big-shot celebrity!" The other kids remained silent, sipping their complimentary bottles of Nova Pop. "Jeremy, these are all winners who are gonna get tickets to that big movie premiere. Chadwick here scored the final goal in the 'Tardd match, and I believe Philip won the Karaoke contest."

Jeremy grabbed Philip by the shoulders, sizing him up. They were about the same height. The boy had on a white t-shirt that just said TEAM TOMMY in big black letters. "Ugh," Jeremy grunted, then threw off his Pigpimples jacket. He haphazardly unbuttoned his vest and untucked his dress shirt. Wendy, whose prize bunny had won the lapitolo races, looked away, mortified.

"Uh, buddy?" Bruno asked, "Is there a reason you're stripping?"

"I need you to do one last thing for me," Jeremy said as he loosened his tie frantically. "Kitani and Sally are out there somewhere. You need to help them get in touch with their families back in England. Hey! Are you listening?!"

"Yes, yes. I saved your life, and now you need me to help your girlfriend. No sweat, pally!"

Jeremy froze. Bruno just grinned at him and slapped him on the back. They were out of time. Jeremy pulled his shirt off. "Phil," he said, "how would you like your very own Pigpimples uniform?"

* * *

"All right—enough!" Mrs. Crawford shouted, exasperated. She stomped over to the changing tent and pulled it down in a huff. A boy in an extremely disheveled Pigpimples uniform sat huddled inside. He squinted up, the spotlight in his eyes.

"Well don't just sit there!" Crawford hissed, yanking the boy up by his arm. "Finish the trick!"

The boy held up a plate, offering it to Mrs. Crawford sheepishly. On it was a single breakfast burrito.

"What am I supposed to do with this?!" She nearly

screeched, but controlled herself.

"Breakfast is served..?" the boy said half-heartedly.

Mrs. Crawford walked to the microphone, dragging the boy with her. "Wow! Would you look at that? It's a burrito!" She held the burrito up to a smattering of applause. It did little to allay the audience's confusion.

"What happened to his glasses?"

"WHERE'S JEREMY?!"

"That's not the Tommy Cobblestone kid!"

"He transformed himself into a burrito!"

Mrs. Crawford was quite finished with this nonsense. "All right, let's hear it one more time for our big star!" She gave a few claps, escorting the boy to the back of the stage and shoving him through the curtains. "Now then, on with the show! Next up, we have..." She fumbled in the pocket of her jacket, pulling out her Personal Shell. For some reason, there was a scratch-and-sniff sticker of a pickle on the back of it.

* * *

"Rhonda!" Moe called out. He rushed over to her, Zippo by his side. She was with her band, waiting for the curtains to open. The Fascination Wolves were still making their way through the backstage tent, roughing up stagehands and pushing them aside angrily. Tiny Tim was with them, leading the frantic search.

"What is it, Moe? We're going on any second!"

Pulleys squeaked. Stage hands were lowering a starry backdrop behind Rhonda and the Zig-Zags.

"Baby! I'm sorry for being such a jibroni back there! Of course I wanna watch your set. In fact," Moe picked up a spare set of holosynth sticks, "I'd be honored if you'd let us play with you."

Zippo held a tremolo vibrobass. "Plez, RHAN-da?" his face wrinkled as he smiled pleadingly.

Rhonda turned, looking backstage. In a corner of the tent she could see Tiny Tim. He picked up a roadie and casually threw him through a table. She smirked. "They're looking for you. Aren't they."

The backdrop continued descending, inch by inch, dividing Rhonda from Moe. She leaned down as it sank, peeking underneath it. She just wanted to see Moe's response.

"You know," Moe chuckled, "sometimes the only way out of a jam...is *through the stage*. That's what they say, right?"

"I've never heard anyone say that," Rhonda said with an exasperated smile. She waved them on to join her.

Moe ducked under the backdrop and Zippo tucked and rolled just before it touched the floor. They stood in the darkness behind the curtains, listening to the anticipation of the crowd in the park. "Well, it should be a saying. There's a wisdom to it!" Moe exclaimed.

"Just follow along, studmuffin." Rhonda leaned forward, rubbing noses with the Binosian. "We'll start with one you guys know."

The golden curtains parted.

Mrs. Crawfood stood on the stage, the spotlight outlining her against the night. "Where is he?" she demanded. She stomped about, examining each member of the Zig-Zags furiously. "That does it!" Mrs. Crawford nearly screamed. She returned to the microphone, looking out at the crowd. "All of you, listen to me!"

Moe waved at Rhonda frantically, urging her to begin. "Just go! *Go, go, go!* Start!"

"Whoever finds me that Cobblestone kid will win a fabulous prize—!"

An explosion of synth from the cathodic klaviphone rocked the park, cutting Mrs. Crawford off. Mase the drummer came in with a swirl of percussion, the rest of the Zig-Zags joining with their alien instruments. They were accompanied by Moe's holosynth and undertones from Zippo's vibrobass. The lighting crew, realizing the set had started, swiveled the spotlight off of

Mrs. Crawford and transformed the stage into a sea of neon blue lasers and hot pink lights. Rhonda's electric kithara wailed to life, sending the audience into overdrive.

With a *harumph*, Mrs. Crawford stormed off the stage.

* * *

After opening with "Pineapple Spongecake" and blazing into "Lunar Madness," the band worked through a variety of rockers, pop anthems, and disco synthers. The audience was alternately captivated, entranced, and, about three songs in, deeply moved.

"You know what," Moe shouted to Zippo as they tried their best to play along, "these guys would make a great act at our club!"

It may have been the sparkling lights of the city, or even certain planets lining up in space—perhaps it was just Rhonda's sincerity—but there was *magic* in the air. The congregation of fans couldn't help but bob their heads and tap their feet, some of them even shedding their crippling awkwardness and actually *dancing*.

For a few brief moments, it seemed like CobbleCon in Central Park had shrunk the whole galaxy. They were all enclosed in a beautiful bubble under the summer stars, floating at the center of the universe. Nobody knew the words to the songs, but that didn't stop them from singing along and swaying, arm in arm, to the alien melodies.

Moe's musical bliss was interrupted as he noticed the intruders gathering at stage left. A faction of red-robed wizards waited impatiently. As nonchalantly as he could, he looked to stage right. There were even more of the red weirdos on that side. The front of the stage didn't look any better, as Tiny Tim and Mrs. Crawford stood in the crowd with a group of very surly looking security guards. They were surrounded.

"I hope that kid made it," Moe called out to Zippo as

Rhonda's final song came to a close.

The audience roared their approval, Rhonda Starlite and the Zig-Zags bowing graciously and bidding the audience goodnight and farewell. Moe noticed an evil smirk on Tiny Tim's face as he switched on his crutch cannon. The inner barrel glowed as it warmed up. Moe sidled up next to Rhonda before she could leave the stage. "Another!" he shouted over the din of the crowd. "They want another! An encore!"

"We already did an encore!" Rhonda laughed, patting the sweat from her brow and taking a sip of water. She shrugged happily. "It was a great show, wasn't it? You kept up pretty good!"

Moe persisted. "We can't stop now! Look!" He pointed out the wizards and the security guards gathered around the stage. "As long as we're playing, she won't let her goons get us!"

"I hate to break it to you, hun, but we've played pretty much everything we know! We even did a couple of songs from my *Heaven* days," Rhonda said.

"Hey, I know! Me and Zip can do one from *2 Funky Brothers*! 'Platonic Friend,' or how about 'Danny the Dog'?"

"'Gat Chunkee, Gat Funkee'!" Zippo suggested, nodding vigorously.

Rhonda thought of something, holding back a smile. She glided to the microphone. "You've been an amazing crowd," he voice echoed through the park. "We want to do something a little special here. This is a new one." She looked at Moe, biting her lip. "It's called, 'Follow the Stars.'"

Moe's jaw dropped.

She floated over to him, placing a finger on his lips before he could speak. "Just shut up. You were right, okay? I listened to the disc. It's a really good song." She pecked him on the cheek, then pointed at Mase to start. "Hit it!"

Mrs. Crawford scowled. The crowd went wild.

Zippo had practiced "Follow the Stars" many times, and

could play the vibrobass part backwards and forwards with his eyes closed. He was happy to be playing something he knew, prowling across the stage and soaking in the positive energy. They'd radio dipped this track on their very first black hole run. They didn't know how far into the future it came from, but it had that stadium-filling, barn-burning sound of an absolute *banger*.

Rhonda's singing and the Zig-Zag's playing mesmerized the audience within seconds. Everyone in the crowd sensed that something about this song was different, although nobody could quite say why. It was as if they were witnessing a monumental shift in reality. As the chorus hit, Rhonda's voice rang out, forging entirely new timelines—or perhaps just re-aligning old ones. It may have been echoes of the time flux, or the melody weaving in and out of space. Whatever it was, everyone at the convention was too stunned to dance, or even speak. They simply stood and listened in captivated silence, letting the melody reverberate through them.

Zippo grooved along with his eyes closed, becoming one with the song. Then his ears flickered. His whiskers twitched, and then his tail. Despite the resounding decibels of music, he could hear something in the air. It was the familiar whine of a subetheric drive. He looked to the sky, his pupils expanding as they took in the starlight. There, hovering above the stage, was the *Terrapin*.

"Jrr-mEE!" Zippo meowed out, waving at the ship.

＊ ＊ ＊

"Hi there! I couldn't help but notice that it looks like you're trying to descend dramatically onto a rock concert of some sort! Is this accurate?" Mister Squeakeasy chattered from the navi-control screen.

"Yes!" Jeremy screamed. "Just shut up and help me!" His hands were slippery with sweat and he could barely hold onto the flight wheel.

"All right then! Would you like me to turn on the ship's disco lights for maximum emotional effect?"

"Yes, of course! Now help me pick up my friends without crushing them!"

Mister Squeakeasy made an annoyed chirp. "Excuse me, but I hardly think comments like that are necessary!"

As they completed the first verse, Rhonda returned the mic to its stand. She picked up her spirit theremin, closed her eyes, and raised her arms. Her hands undulated and waved, each movement teasing a synthetic note out of the air. As she danced, a light shot down from the sky. It illuminated Rhonda as she played her extended solo.

Moe looked up to see the spotlight beaming from the undercarriage of the *Terrapin*. Colored lights on the ship blinked on and off as it hovered above them. Zippo bounded to Moe's side, pointing up excitedly.

Rhonda, still lost in her solo, played her instrument obliviously as the starship descended.

The rear cargo door opened with a gasp. "Go, Zip! Get on!" Moe urged his companion. Zippo bid the audience farewell before turning and calculating his trajectory with a waggle of his rump. He leaped to the ship, expertly grasping a rail and pulling himself up into the cargo bay. He reached a paw down to Moe, lifting him up.

Holding the siderail, Moe hung down from the back of the starship. "Rhonda!" he called out. She opened her eyes, surprised to see Moe floating in front of her as she played on. "I'm sorry!" He leaned down, his lips next to Rhonda's.

They kissed, breaking the audience from the song's spell.

The crowd went *insane*.

Rhonda smiled beguilingly as the ship pulled up and away, the cargo bay door hissing itself closed.

"They're getting away! After them! NOW!" Mrs. Crawford

screamed, sending Maledict and the other Fascination Wolves after the ship. The wizards rose, ascending into the air—but it was too late. The ship blasted away through the stratosphere, streaking ionized particles across the sky before disappearing into the stars.

CHAPTER 48

THE PERFECT STRANGER

Their breath came out in little white puffs. It was definitely getting colder.

It was clear the *Terrapin* would never intercept the P-Shell freighter in time—at least, not while flying at such a prudent and reasonable speed. In order to crank the engines to max power, they had to cut the auxiliary systems. This included most of the energy to the ship's heaters.

Jeremy sat in a large overturned crate in the cargo bay, bundled up in his father's robe and several blankets. He still had on the TEAM TOMMY t-shirt, but had resolved to shoot it out an airlock the second they'd had a chance to do some laundry. "You know, this actually isn't half bad," he said, referring to Kitani's gifted copy of *Jeremy Fletcher: Magic Boy.* "The storyline is convoluted, but some of the jokes are kind of funny!"

"Huh?" Moe fumbled with a crate lid. It was hard to get a good grip with the mittens he was wearing. His brightly colored windbreaker crinkled as he rummaged through crate after plasteel crate. There were copies of issue #52 scattered everywhere. He could have sworn they had some spare battery packs buried in one of the crates, but had not found any. His pulse phaser was pretty much spent, and they couldn't risk recharging it by using energy from the ship's power core.

Jeremy put the comic book down. It was no use trying to read anyway; his vision kept fogging over. He removed his spectacles and found frost forming at the edges of the lenses. "We should have brought Bruno," he said. "Could have kept a nice cozy fire going." Moe grunted in frustration as he dug through layer after layer of comics.

"Hay guise," Zippo mewed over the ship's intercom. "We are get cloze. I see *Parfect Strenger*, so I slow down." He gave them an estimated time of arrival and switched off.

"Best news I've heard all day." Jeremy said. "Good thing, too, because my eyeballs are about to freeze."

Moe looked up from the crate. His face darkened. "Yo! How's our magic potion looking? It's not frozen, is it?"

Jeremy reached into another pocket, producing the Philter of Forgetfulness. He swished the purple fluid around, holding the vial by its cork. "Looks keen-o to me."

Moe sighed in relief.

*   *   *

"Uh, Mike?"

Mike Mania looked up from his captain's chair, setting down his clipboard and checklist. He gave his chops a lick, but said nothing. They hadn't even started on their journey to Terra Firma, and already his idiot brother was pestering him.

"Someone's hailing us."

Mike bared his teeth in annoyance. "What in Hades are you talking about?! Nobody even knows we're out here! Don't tell me it's another raider ship!" He flung the clipboard to the floor, then his ears shot up. "Actually, come to think of it...a battle does sound like a pleasant diversion!" He rubbed his paws together eagerly, hopping down from his chair.

"Mike—they say they're from Seashell Systems!"

"What are you talking about?! There's nothing in the itinerary about visitors!"

Charles shrugged, nearly wincing as his litter brother stalked towards him. "They transmitted the passcode! And they knew our exact coordinates! They said they have an important message from Mrs. Crawford, that they can only tell *you*!" Charles made a whiny sound of protest.

"Put them onscreen!" Mike barked, hopping back into his chair and smoothing down his doublet.

The image of the Binosian Class-1 transport tug flickered onto the bridge's immense screen. Mike squinted, then growled. Then, he started to laugh. "It's the mangy little pups who came back for more!" he grinned fiercely at Charles, who panted with concern. "Oh, this is going to be RICH. What do you say, Charles? Up for a disembowling? Actually, a quick evisceration might be more fun. Start thinking about it!"

Charles clearly had no idea what his brother was talking about. "You're useless, and you sicken me. Just let them on!" He bared his incisors as he curled his lip. "They're in for a little surprise."

＊ ＊ ＊

"Thank you, uh...*Terrapin*," Charles' voice came in through the ship's comm. "Please dock in landing bay nine dash four."

Jeremy remembered the *The Perfect Stranger* from their fateful encounter at the Massif Prime archive. The ship was at least ten times bigger than the *Terrapin*. Its hulking frame and dazzling array of weapons gave it an ugly, imposing look. No space pirates would ever mess with such a craft.

Zippo slowed the *Terrapin* down, swinging them around to face the front end of the *Perfect Stranger*. Giant horizontal doors opened on the lower half of the freighter's bow, the lights within glowing menacingly. For a moment, Jeremy imagined that they were flying into the wide open jaws of some horrible demon.

Zippo's ears flattened. He gave Jeremy a sidelong glance. "Dis...a little bit *scary*," he whispered.

Moe remained as cool as a Binosian dewcumber. "Once we make it onto their ship, all we need to do is find a way to get Mike to drink the potion. Pour it into his water bowl, or something."

"He liked Toastee Mums," Jeremy remembered the Cerberon's order from that night at Heavy Nova. "Blueberry, I think."

Moe snapped his fingers. "You're a genius! Whip us up some Toastee Mums and put 'em in here." He unzipped Sally's pink backpack, dumping its contents to the floor.

Zippo glanced down, cocking his head but not saying anything. He was too focused on finding a spot to land, which was proving more difficult than he'd expected. Once he maneuvered the *Terrapin* through the forceshield, he discovered that the inside of the docking bay was filled with hundreds of thousands of cargo crates, many of them stacked nearly to the ceiling. Zippo hovered and rotated the *Terrapin* above the landing pad until he found an opening just large enough to nestle into. He mewled with relief as he shut off the subetheric drive.

"Sorry...uh...about the mess in the docking bay," Charles's voice chimed back onto the comm. "We ran out of room in the cargo hold." Charles instructed them to exit their ship and come up to the bridge, where Mike wanted to have a little chat with them.

"Let's boogie," Moe said, putting on his shades.

* * *

"Waow! Vary big. Vary cool!" Zippo meowed in wonder at the enormous cargo hold.

"Say what you will about GRIS—but they sure know how to

design a starship! Look at this layout!" Moe pointed at a schematic posted on the wall by the elevator. "Subetheric drives, nanoparticle luminators, an etheric glimmer bank as long as our ship! Funky!" Moe insisted they eschew the elevator, remembering their mishap at Bolero Station. "Too easy to get trapped." He opened a narrow closet door nearby. It revealed a vertical maintenance shaft with a ladder in it, leading up through the bowels of the ship.

"Aww yeh!" Zippo meowed happily. He loved stuff like this and led the way, his nimble frame scurrying up the ladder.

"Homie! Slow down!" Moe called out, panting as he climbed.

"Shh!" Zippo hissed. His tail flicked. "I hear sound! Wat is..?"

Jeremy listened. The climbing had made him rather warm, and he wished he had left his wizard robe behind. "I hear it, too," he said. He couldn't tell if the sound qualified as music, or if he was hearing the inside of some horrifying GRIS torture chamber. Zippo climbed the final rungs to the next level, getting off and beckoning them up.

A look of recognition spread across Moe's face. He smiled lopsidedly as he hurried up the ladder. "I know that! That's *Magma Contusion*! Listen to those drums!" Zippo nodded, headbanging gleefully as he traipsed along the corridor. Jeremy was not familiar with *Magma Contusion*, but it sounded like that dreadful "heavy metal" music the offworlders sometimes enjoyed. Jeremy didn't get the appeal at *all*.

"I only know one guy with a *Magma Contusion* recording," Moe said, depressing his thumb on the door portal. He then punched in Mrs. Crawford's master override password. The door slid aside, revealing an inner corridor of empty cells. "This must be the brig. Be careful," Moe warned. Zippo ceased his headbanging. They followed the sound of the music down the corridor until they reached the last cell on the left.

DJ Nebz stood within, his head down as he ironed a shirt on an ironing board. The Amphibion's clammy green body gyrated as he headbanged along to the music, which blared from a portable jam box. He was still nearly naked, clad only in a pair of *tightee whiteys*. He was working on a big stack of laundry that needed ironing.

"Nebz!" Moe shouted, startling the Amphibion.

DJ Nebz looked up, recognition dawning in his bulbous eyes. An enormous smile spread across his massive mouth. "Get da grok outta here! Hey, tadpoles!" He set the iron down, walking up to the front of the cell. "Ya'll came to rescue me!"

"Das rite!" Zippo meowed. "We get out of hear, DJ Nabz go beck to radio!"

"You said it, buddy," Moe reached up to give Nebzs a high-five, but an invisible shock barrier zapped him. He yelped, more in surprise than pain.

"Oh, hey! Sorry about that! I furgot that grokkin' shield was on." DJ Nebz poked around a control panel with his long fingers for a moment, switching the shock barrier off. He stepped out of the cell.

"Wait—why do you need us to rescue you if you can just walk out?" Jeremy asked.

"Hey! Cobblestone boy! Love dat t-shirt, kid! Boggy as *grok*!"

Jeremy looked down at the "TEAM TOMMY" shirt. "Oh right, boggy. Thanks." He closed his wizard robe, tying it shut with its silver sash.

"Anyway...uhhh," Nebz stopped, regaining his train of thought. "So—those GRIS guards, they don't got any more prisoners right at de moment. So they jus' let me use the whole wing. Long as I do their laundry." Nebz walked them to another cell, where a washing and drying machine was set up. "I got a sleepin' cell, an eatin' cell. They even let me listen to muh music. Front door is always locked, though. You guys musta hacked the code, didntja!" DJ Nebz slapped Zippo and Moe on their backs. "You two are a couple of grokkin' space pirates!"

"I'm glad we found you, homie. But you'd better bounce. Take the ladder down to the cargo bay and wait for us in the *Terrapin*. You can hitch a ride with us when we split."

Nebz gave Moe a squishy hug, blorping his appreciation. "Can we stop somewhere to get some grub? These GRIS guys— they're pretty nice, ya know...but they's food is grokkin' *nasty*."

"Yes, but you'll need to hurry up," Jeremy interjected before they could get off on a tangent about junk food. "This whole place is going to get destroyed pretty soon. Just take what you need, and get out of here."

"You guys are da *best*!" Nebz walked over to the dryer, taking some clothes out and folding them into a basket. "Jus' lemme finish up this last batch."

* * *

"*It's time for a refill!*" Moe shouted the catchphrase of Tommy Cobblestone's friend, Nicholas, as he brandished his phaser and burst onto the bridge of *The Perfect Stranger*. Several of the *Stranger*'s crewmen looked at him and his companions, confused by the intrusion. Most went about their business, having not heard a thing.

A GRIS engineer in a slate-colored jumpsuit wandered over. "Hi, can I help you? I couldn't help but hear you come in. Sounded like you were quoting *Tommy Cobblestone*, huh?"

Moe pointed the phaser at the crewmember, who raised his arms in surrender. "Sorry! Just wondering why you chose to quote that catchphrase! It seems to have almost zero application to this situation!" He backed away, hands raised.

Jeremy reached over, forcing Moe to lower his gun. Meanwhile, Zippo aimed his rifle at a female intern who was working quietly at a navicomputer. She gasped in dismay and started to cry. "Oh, oh no. Sarry—sarry!" Zippo put his rifle down, patting the young woman on the head and moving away.

The captain's chair in the center of the room looked out over a giant viewscreen that faced the stars. "So. We meet again." The chair swiveled around. Mike Mania sat there, his furry pantalooned legs crossed casually.

"Okay, now that was pretty cool. See?" Moe pointed with his pistol. "I wanted to do something like *that*."

Mike Mania smiled and bowed in his chair. "Good evening, mongrels. I have no idea what you think you're doing here, but you have about ten seconds to explain yourselves before I blast you and toss your carcasses out the airlock." Mike gestured to Charles in Charge, who stood behind him in the shadows. He held a small neutrino cannon, aimed squarely at them. "On my mark, Charles."

"Mrs. Crawford is about to be arrested!" Moe shouted.

Mike stopped. "I beg your pardon?" He sniffed the air.

"Your boss, Mrs. Crawford! Planetary League authorities are on their way to arrest her right now, and she knows it! Someone in her organization leaked to the Cosmic Beacon that these P-Shells are manufactured with Velitovian tech, and are therefore illegal under the laws of the Planetary League."

Mike grunted. "Terra isn't IN the Planetary League."

"Well...yeah!" A few of the crew members had left their stations and were gathering nearby to witness the exchange. "And they're not ever *going* to be if the League gets wind of this. Seashell Systems - Terra Firma Division will be ruined! So she sent us here to make sure all the Personal Shells get destroyed. Before the authorities or anyone else gets their hands on them."

Mike nodded thoughtfully. "And why didn't she just tell me about this? We could have destroyed the cargo ourselves."

Jeremy and Zippo turned to Moe, awaiting his explanation.

"She said she didn't want to risk any official communications that could get used as evidence against her!"

Moe said, acting exasperated. "So she paid us to get here as fast as we could and take care of it. *Nobody* can find out! They need to be destroyed! All of them!"

Mike mulled the Binosian's words over. "And...I assume she sent you here with some kind of proof that you're working for her, right? Or am I just supposed to take your word for it?"

Zippo unzipped his fanny pack, pulling out Mrs. Crawford's Personal Shell and holding it out for Mike. Mike's muzzle twitched. He hopped down from his chair, scurrying over to the Felinian. "Hmm..." He took the P-Shell in his paws, inspecting it. "Well I'll be the son of *Cerberus*! Looks like the real deal to me." He handed the device back. "All right! You heard them, Charles!" Mike pointed theatrically at the big star on the main viewscreen. "Set the controls for the heart of the sun!"

His brother rushed over to the navicomputer, pushing the crewmember aside as he typed rapid keystrokes. "All right, Mikey! Our flight path has been altered."

Mike picked up the comm receiver by his chair, speaking into it so the entire ship could hear. "Crew and staff of *The Perfect Stranger*, may I have your attention please? This is your captain speaking. It seems I have some bad news for you all— our mission has been compromised. As such, I am putting out the order to abandon ship, effective immediately. Repeat, *abandon ship*. Now. There's no need to panic; we're running with a skeleton crew and there are plenty of lifepods for everyone. Just get in one and set the trajectory to Mercury. Let gravity do the rest." Mike covered the receiver with his paw, speaking to Charles. "Say—do you want to go and see mom this weekend? The Hades portal is fifty percent off for the next ninety days, and we haven't been home in a while."

Charles mumbled something about mom being on vacation with a new boyfriend, to which Mike growled in disgust. "Eh, we can talk about it later." He uncovered the comm receiver. "Of course, GRIS will compensate you standard daily rate for aborted missions. You've been a delightful crew to work with, and I apologize for the inconvenience. In fact, let's make that...TEN minutes to abandon ship. But you'd better all do it now. Captain Mike Mania, over and out." Mike returned the comm and pressed a button that sounded off a periodic alarm.

Jeremy and Zippo exchanged puzzled looks. "What's going on?" Jeremy whispered. "Why was this so easy?"

Moe looked at Jeremy over his shades. "Because you're witnessing a *professional* getting the job done, that's all. Stick with me, baby—you'll learn a lot. All the loose ends tied up nicely." Moe pushed his shades back into place with his phaser.

Crewmen scrambled to get their belongings before abandoning ship. All of them had stopped paying attention to Mike or Charles in the middle of the bridge. Mike pulled Charles down by his ruffled collar. "Before you go, set all the lifepods on the ship to auto-eject in..." he glanced at his wristwatch, "ten minutes. Actually, better make it eight and a half. It'll look more realistic if we lose a few stragglers. Just make sure you get on one yourself, you big lug!" Mike ruffled the fur on his brother's head. "Let's meet down at that little bar in the Lava Gardens...what's it called..."

"The Solar Flare?"

"That's the one! We can get our stories straight from there. Now go! We're going to be set!"

Charles ran off, tugging at his pantaloons as he scampered away.

"Hey! What happened to giving everyone enough time to abandon ship!" Jeremy objected.

Mike turned, fury flashing in his eyes. He whipped out his glazer, pointing it at Jeremy's head and firing a shot. The bolt whizzed by, only missing by a micron.

"I don't need a bunch of witnesses telling the galaxy that a GRIS Blackhull Galleon got raided by a discount TOMMY COBBLESTONE impersonator and his merry band of imbeciles!" Mike ran up to Jeremy, grasping him by the t-shirt and growling in his face. "How STUPID do you think I am? Do you mangy little pups think I don't know what you're doing?! I saw you on the security televid down in the brig, helping that disgusting Amphibion friend of yours! You're here for more P-Shells to sell on the black market!"

"No! That's not true!" Jeremy shouted, shoving Mike off. Mike barked in frustration, but regained his composure. He adjusted his collar in a reflection as he calmed down.

"I don't know how you got that device from Crawford, but if she ever found out you stole it..." he shook his head, tittering. "Let's just say they don't call her *Grandma Gelding* for nothing! Believe me, I'll be doing you a favor by killing you!"

"We don't want to steal your stupid Shells!" Jeremy protested.

Mike bit a claw thoughtfully. He started talking, more to himself than to the others. "I couldn't have planned it better! I'll tell them the boy wizard stormed the bridge and took control of the ship using his dark magic, or something. You fought valiantly to the death, but I was ultimately the victor." He grinned. "They might just buy it!"

"We don't have to fight!" Jeremy said, backing away from the Cerberon's glazer. "Why not just get in that escape pod with your brother?"

"Ha!" Mike barked. "You've obviously never had to share an enclosed space with Charles! He reeks. Ugh, his breath alone—!" Mike sniffed the air in disgust, his tongue lolling out as his nostrils flared. "Besides, I can fit more P-Shells on your ship than I could ever fit on an escape pod!"

Moe nodded in understanding. "I get it. You're gonna use this as an excuse to jack the merchandise yourself."

"Please don't misunderstand me," Mike said, placing a paw on his doublet. "It was a good plan on your part! So good, I decided to take it! Ha!" he barked happily. "Now let's fight! I could use some authentic battle scars to sell the story!" Mike shot at the trio with his glazer, missing on purpose to get them started.

Zippo lashed out like a hairless pink tiger, distracting the Cerberon by slashing at his jerkin and giving him a good kick before scampering away to join his companions. He knew his claws were no match for a fully-charged glazer.

"Dude!" Moe exclaimed from behind a computer console. He continued shouting between glazer shots. "We're not here to steal the cargo! We're here...to...*destroy* it!" He reached over to Zippo's fanny pack, pulling out Crawford's P-Shell and peeking up over the panel. "These things are *wack*! Let's make a deal!" He tossed the Shell out. It clattered across the floor of the bridge.

Mike stopped shooting. "All right, all right!" he shouted. "I'll jump through your little hoop! Why in *Hades* would you want to destroy the hottest new tech on your podunk little planet?"

Moe peered out tentatively. "Just let us explain."

* * *

Moe and Jeremy (with some helpful imagery mindspoken by Zippo) recounted their dealings with the Personal Shells, the use of the professor's magic to mask Velitovian tech, and the disappearance of future Terran radio waves. "This means all that stuff we talked about before, you know—the black hole—radio dipping," Moe started.

"Opening up a nightclub?" Mike grumbled suspiciously.

"Yeah. If you start selling these babies, you might make a little quick cash, but Crawford'll stop you. And you can kiss the nightclub goodbye," Moe said, nudging the Shell on the floor with his foot. "I think we can put aside our differences, don't you? Help us trash the Shells, and we split the profits from the black hole..." Moe gulped, "...fifty-fifty. What do you say?"

Mike panted slightly as he pondered on the new information. "Well then. What are we waiting for?" He picked up Crawford's P-Shell, slamming it onto the floor as hard as he could. It shattered into pieces, startling Zippo. "It's a deal!" Mike barked, extending a paw. Moe shook it. Jeremy sighed in relief. Mike sniffed. "Now how about a snack to celebrate?"

"Wat...snek?" Zippo mewed, worried. "Wat snek are you mean?" Mike was staring right at him, licking his chops and salivating.

"That little backpack of yours! I've been smelling it since you walked onto the bridge! There's *Toastee Mums* in there!" He sniffed the air rapidly. "Blueberry ones!" Mike walked over, wresting the backpack from Zippo's shoulders. He unzipped the front pocket. A toastee mum waited inside. "A-ha!" Mike barked, spying the pastry.

Jeremy's eyes darted to Moe. The pastry in the front pocket was the one he'd sprinkled with the forgetfulness potion! They held their breath, waiting for the Cerberon to eat it.

"Hey now, wait just a moment!" Mike barked. He unzipped the main zipper of the backpack, revealing a whole trove of pastries. "You little mutts have been holding out on me! Ha ha haw!" Mike overturned the backpack, dumping all the pastries, including the enchanted one, onto the floor. "Five minute rule!" he shouted, shaking the remaining crumbs out of the backpack and tossing it aside gleefully. [*Translator's Note: The Five Minute rule is an ancient Cerberon custom, stating that food that touches even the filthiest of floors may still be ingested as long as it is retrieved before the passing of five minutes, after which the blessing of Cerberus is withdrawn. —ChatterBot 3.6*]

Moe, Zippo, and Jeremy stared at the Cerberon as he dug through the Toastee Mums, setting aside the ones that looked the most "Toastee Fresh." Suddenly, he stopped. "Oh my Cerberus, pardon me—where are my manners? Please, take some! All of you."

Jeremy lifted a hand, "That's all right, I'm kind of sick of Toastee Mums..."

Mike lifted his glazer, his eyes widening with rage. "I...INSIST." He smiled insanely. "It's not like they've been POISONED, right?" he gave Jeremy a murderous look.

Jeremy gulped, picking up a pastry. "Cheers," he said, taking a bite of the Toastee Mum. Considering he knew nothing about the black hole or its location, he guessed he would never know whether he was eating the enchanted one or not. Moe and Zippo, on the other hand, looked visibly nervous as Mike urged them on. They each picked up a pastry, taking small bites and chewing as slowly and as thoughtfully as they could.

"Mmmm," Zippo finally mewled out. "Das...pretty gud."

Mike Mania, satisfied that the pastries were not poisoned, got started on his short stack. He tried to eat neatly at first, but his insatiable appetite got the best of him. "Aww!" he spoke through a mouthful of pastry, sprinkling his doublet with crumbs. "Now *that* is simply divine! I gotta hand it to you Terrans!" he swallowed, slapping Jeremy on the back. He picked up another Toastee Mum. "Your little peasant world is pretty disgusting, but you sure do toaster pastries right!" He broke the pastry in two, shoving half into his jaws. "...And the televids! Speaking of which, do you guys have any bootlegs of *Laika: Space Dog*?"

"Oh... no. We don't do pirated televids," Moe looked down at his pastry, forcing himself to take another bite. He and Zippo looked like they were going to be sick.

"That's a shame! *Laika* is truly a masterpiece. Every episode I've seen is a work of Terran art!" Mike went on to recount the plot of the televid series, which featured a border collie who gets inadvertently shot into space as its protagonist.

They sat on the floor of the bridge for a while, Mike recalling the details of seemingly every episode of *Laika* he could remember. "And THAT'S how Laika saves the

International Space Station! Anyway, you get the idea—it's a great program!" Mike stood. "Anyone want the last one?" he said, pointing at the final toaster pastry on the floor. "Good! I was going to take it anyway! Ha haw!" Mike scooped up the pastry, attacking it as he walked over to the navicomputer console. "All right, I think most everyone has gone. Time to send this thing into the sun, how's that sound?" He pushed up his slightly puffy sleeves and typed in his captain's authorization code. He then increased the ship's engines to maximum subetheric speed.

The Perfect Stranger groaned as its heavy inertial dampeners kicked on. Its engines were incomprehensibly more powerful than anything on the *Terrapin*, which resulted in Jeremy feeling a bit spacesick.

"That should do it," Mike Mania called out. "At this speed, you and those stupid little Shells will be roasting in the core of the sun in...let's see..." Mike glanced at the time, "A few hours."

"Pardon me?" Jeremy said. He wasn't sure that he'd heard that right.

"What are you talking about, homie?" Moe said, standing up.

"What I'm saying, *homie*, is that I'd better get going before I end up toasted myself!" Mike brushed the final crumbs out of his fur, then pulled out his glazer. He pointed the gun at the navicomputer console, blasting it to pieces as he snarled. It exploded in a burst of plasma and vapor. Zippo yawled in surprise, jumping to his feet.

"Hey now! Wait a minute, wait just a minute!" Moe shouted. "Why'd you go and do a kruddy thing like that?! What about our deal?"

Mike snorted. "As if I would *ever* make a deal with filthy infringers! This is payback for your actions at Heavy Nova." Mike strode across the bridge towards the elevator.

"Hold up!" Moe looked to Zippo, who seemed to be

mindspeaking something to the Binosian. Moe shrugged, hustling over to talk to Mike. "How are you going to even use the black hole?! You don't know anything about radio dipping! You don't know how to decrypt magtapes!"

Mike pressed a button with his gun, summoning the elevator. "Why do you think I kept your little froggy friend alive?" He scratched the inside of his ear with the front end of the pistol as he spoke. "Because I enjoy watching slimy green weirdos walking around in their underwear? Heh." Mike pointed the gun at Moe. "As they say back home: *see you in Hades*." Mike fired three quick shots in succession, scattering the trio.

"Okay, okay!" Moe called out from behind a set of databanks. "We do it your way! What was it you said that night? Seventy-five percent of profits, right? You got it!" Mike made no response. Moe peeked out tentatively, then ducked back down. Jeremy, crouching a little ways away, pointed his thumb at the ceiling as if to say "higher."

"All right, fine—eighty percent! We'll do the legwork!" Moe shouted.

Mike still made no response. Zippo peeked out from under a desk. The three moved stealthily towards the Cerberon, who remained standing stock still, as if awaiting a better offer.

"Okay!" Moe pleaded. "You can keep *all* the money, dude! It's yours! Just let us three run the club! All we really need is a place to crash at night. That's fair, right guys?" Zippo and Jeremy nodded vigorously.

The elevator arrived with a chime, its doors opening. Mike remained unmoved. Jeremy wondered whether it was some kind of trap. Growing impatient, Zippo stepped up. He walked over to Mike, claws extended and ready. He placed a paw on the Cerberon's shoulder. Mike turned around, as if noticing Zippo for the first time. He smiled wide.

"Hi!" he said, his tail waggling. "You sure do have an interesting smell! Who are you?"

CHAPTER 49

BREAKFAST IS SERVED

Moe and Zippo wasted no time disarming Mike, who handed over his glazer gladly. Then, using some leftover speaker wire from Zippo's fanny pack, they tied Mike's paws behind his back. The Cerberon continued smiling amiably. "Guys! That tickles!" he chuckled. They shuffled onto the elevator, ordering it to take them to the cargo bay.

"Zip—memory check," Moe said as he secured the knot around Mike's wrists. "Do you remember the black hole?"

Zippo clenched his eyes shut, then reopened them happily. "Yeh! All der," he tapped a claw at the side of his head.

"Right. I remember it, too. How about you, chief?"

"I remember us talking about it, although to be fair I never knew where it was to begin with. That is..." Jeremy tilted his head, "I don't *think* I did. Did I?"

Moe leaned over. "Say, Mike, do you know about the black hole?"

Mike grinned and panted excitedly, assuming Moe was talking to him. "Are we going for a walk now?" Despite being bound, he still appeared quite cheerful.

"Well, Sally," Jeremy removed his spectacles and polished them with his robe. He looked through them to see if they were clean, which they were not. "You make one heck of a potion." It only took a few seconds of talking with Mike for Jeremy to realize that the Cerberon had most definitely forgotten the location of the black hole. Other things he had forgotten included: where he came from, why he was on a starship, and who he was. There was one thing, however, that he seemed to remember quite well.

"I remember you!" Mike said to Jeremy, his eyes wide and shining with love. The elevator arrived, its doors opening onto the cargo bay.

"Yeah? You remember me?" Jeremy said.

"Of course I do!" Mike leaned in close. "You're Tommy Cobblestone!"

* * *

DJ Nebz made himself at home in the cockpit of the *Terrapin*, his feet up on the dashboard as he played *Jessica Gelato*. He called out to Zippo and Jeremy as they entered the ship through the cargo hatch. "Heyyy! How y'all doin'? Took ya's long enough!" As they ushered Mike on board, Nebz nearly fell out of his chair. "Why da grok did you bring *him*?! I don't like dat guy!" Nebz scooted back nervously.

"Relax, Nebz," Moe said. "Mike is...well, he won't hurt you."

"Hi!" Mike barked. "I'd shake hands but I'm a little tied up at the moment!" he waggled a paw behind his back.

Nebz croaked with laughter as Moe climbed into his captain's chair. "All right, homies and gentlefrogs. Let's boogie on out of here before we all get turned into crispy critters, shall we? Squeaks—" Mister Squeakeasy appeared on the navi-control screen. "Tell *The Perfect Stranger* to open her hangar bay door."

"Aye aye, cap'n!"

Within seconds, the enormous door slid aside. The yellow orb of the sun blazed at the dead center of their starfield. For a moment, its brightness nearly blinded everyone in the cockpit. Thankfully the windows adjusted, automatically dimming the view. Jeremy squinted at the gigantic star. The sun had never looked so big.

"Dang, homeboy, you weren't kidding!" Moe said to Mike. "Your ship is haulin'!"

Mike smiled and nodded, unsure of who Moe was talking to.

"Zipponio: take us outta here," Moe saluted with two fingers to his brow.

Zippo switched on the navigational controls, lifting the lever to spin up the hoverthrusters. But as he pulled the flightwheel back, nothing happened. He depressed a button, flicked a few more switches, but the ship remained unresponsive.

"What in da blorpin' heck are you waitin' for?!" Nebz croaked.

"Zip, what's going on?" Moe asked.

"We are...*stack*!" Zippo let go of the flightwheel, flabbergasted.

The A.I. mouse reappeared on the screen. "Sorry about that, fellas! Looks like the *Terrapin* still has a safety tether strapped to the bottom of her hull! As long as that tether is attached, all flight controls will remain disabled. Might wanna remove it before trying to take off!"

"Then remove it!" Moe shouted. "Tell *The Perfect Stranger* to de-tether us! Now!"

"Right away, sir!"

Moe shook his head and sighed. He cracked his knuckles. It's been a long day, eh chief? Can't wait to hit the starways and switch to autopilot. I feel like I haven't showered in days."

"You haven't," Jeremy said. "None of us have. Except Zippo, I guess. If licking yourself counts."

The mouse returned to the screen. "All set, captain! Since

the tether was specially ordered by Captain Mike Mania of *The Perfect Stranger*, I'll just need his authorization code to proceed!"

They all looked at Mike. "Who's Mike Mania?" he said, smiling.

Moe let out another, bigger sigh. He then removed his shades and massaged his temples, keeping his eyes shut.

"You..." Jeremy started, putting a hand on Mike's shoulder. "You don't know the code, do you," he said flatly.

"What code? Tommy, what's going on?" Mike whimpered.

Outside, the incomprehensibly humongous fireball that was the sun, grew larger.

"Why don't we just go back to the bridge and steer *The Perfect Stranger* outta da blorpin' way?" Nebz asked.

"Because," Jeremy answered, "I believe Mike here shot up the navigational controls."

"Mike again? Where is this guy?" Mike asked, looking around.

"Then let's turn on an emergency broadcast!" the Amphibion croaked. "This thing's gotta have an etheric glimmer signal, or somethin'! There might be ships out there that could hear us! Pirates! Anyone!"

Zippo shook his head, looking up. "No, Nabz. We are too cloze to star."

"He's right," Moe muttered. "Our signal would never get through the noise. The sun's blasting out too much interference." He drummed his fingers along a control panel. "You know what, we'll be so rich we can buy a new ship!" He patted the Terrapin's dashboard. "We'll just have to squeeze into one of *Stranger*'s escape pods and drop to Mercury, assuming the sun doesn't pull us in. We can hitch a ride from there. Computer, how many pods are left on *The Perfect Stranger*?"

Zippo looked at the number flashing on the monitor. "Ehm... Zee-RO."

Moe slammed a fist down on the navi-control console. A startled Mike grabbed Jeremy's arm for comfort. "Fine. Forget it!" Moe snapped. "Who needs an escape pod? We'll de-tether manually. I'll get out and unhook the stupid thing!" the Binosian flailed, exasperated. He jumped out of his seat, rushing to the cockpit's top hatch.

"Moe, *stahp!*" Zippo cried.

Zippo and Nebz tackled Moe to the floor before he could open the hatch.

"Get a hold of yerself!" Nebz ribbited. "Where da blorp do ya think yer goin'?! You can't go out there without a vac-suit!"

Moe rubbed his elbow, which he'd landed on. He looked annoyed. "I'll be fine! The forceshield is still up!"

"Computer mousey guy!" DJ Nebz called out. Mister Squeakeasy appeared. "Tell the *Stranger* to shut that big ol' door!"

"Captains?" the mouse awaited confirmation from either Moe or Zippo.

"Yeh, yeh. Jus do et *naow!*"

As the hangar bay's door slid closed, DJ Nebz croaked. "The forceshield only seals off the vacuum; it won't do nothin' against radiation from a star this close! You'd get mutated, or somethin'! The grokkin' microwaves alone would cook you in a nanosecond!"

Jeremy looked up.

"Oh. Right," Moe muttered. He got up, grabbing a mechanizer wrench. "Zippo, come with me."

"What are you going to do?" Jeremy asked.

"There's gotta be some way to pry that tether off manually. We'll check it out. Jeremy, you have the helm."

* * *

Mike Mania lay sprawled out on the bench, tongue lolling

out the side of his mouth. He was panting heavily, most of his fancy clothes strewn about the cockpit. DJ Nebz's clammy green body sat splayed out in the captain's chair, one webbed foot on the dashboard, the other on the headrest of the second chair. He made little sickly croaking sounds, trying his best to not move. Jeremy had shed his robe, and was down to just his TEAM TOMMY shirt and a pair of undershorts.

Every room in the ship was suffocating. Jeremy didn't know how much longer they had until they flew into the sun, but if this brutal heat was any indication, it was probably soon. He sat on the floor, as the metallic walls felt slightly cooler on his skin. He was determined to think of a solution, but the sweltering temperature made rational thought difficult.

The rear cargo hatch hissed open. Jeremy rushed to the back to meet Moe and Zippo. "Any luck?" he asked. His throat felt dry and he wiped his brow with the back of his arm. The co-captains trudged back to the cockpit, grim looks on their faces. Zippo flopped down onto the floor, defeated. Moe shook his head, running his fingers through his sweat-soaked hair.

"Nope. It's impossible," he gulped. "There's no way to reach that *stupid* tether. It's attached to our undercarriage somewhere, blocked off by component housing. I tried crawling under the ship but it's too tight a fit, even for me."

"Moe es too *fat*," Zippo mewled unhappily from the floor.

Moe dabbed himself with a towel. "Short of getting out and pushing," he smiled weakly, "I am out of ideas. We're stuck, dude."

Nebz blubbered to life. "So that's it! It's over! We're all jus' gonna burn up inside the sun! We're gonna *die*!"

"Homie, chill!" Moe said, pushing Nebz's foot off of the captain's chair. "That's not true. Not even a GRIS ship is built to withstand that kind of heat. We'll most likely burn up *millions* of miles before we make contact with the sun."

Nebz croakled a sob. He sniffled for a while, peeled himself out of his chair and plopping down on the floor next to Jeremy. "Hey, magic kid," he blorpled, "how about a last meal, eh? A little Sir Donk's for old times' sake?" He held up one of the many empty cereal bowls that littered the cockpit. "Heck, I'll even take Branno-Bix!"

Something clicked in Jeremy's fevered brain. He looked up, amazement in his eyes. "That's it, frogman!" he shouted, hopping to his feet. "Get up, all of you! Come with me!" Magic wand firmly in hand, he led the way.

* * *

Jeremy flipped open the lid of one of *The Perfect Stranger*'s plasteel crates. The box was filled with hundreds of Personal Shells in shiny new boxes, all stacked in neat rows. Jeremy pulled a box out. Words were printed on it in a sleek, futuristic font.

The Personal Shell
by Seashell Systems
Dare to Dream!™

Jeremy kicked the crate over. Shiny white boxes tumbled out of it and onto the floor. He opened another crate and knocked it over, and then another.

"Uh...why are you doing that?" Moe asked.

"Come on, what are you guys waiting for? Just help me!" Jeremy called out as he overturned another crate. "We need to make a big pile of boxes back here, right behind the *Terrapin*."

"Big pile of baxes?" Zippo asked, puzzled.

"Yes! Just do it!"

Jeremy continued knocking over crate after crate, as Mike and Moe pushed, kicked, and herded hundreds of the white boxes into a large pile. Zippo and Nebz took turns climbing up stacks of crates, gleefully knocking the top ones to the floor, sending their contents scattering. Working together, the gang was able to overturn many of the crates in the hangar. The large pile of P-Shell boxes grew into a hill, then a sort of blocky plateau, and finally an all-out butte. In fact, the pile of boxes was so high that Moe could no longer see over the top of it. He clambered to the top of the box pile, looking out over the hangar. "There's still a few more crates over there!" he pointed, sending Zippo and Nebz to fetch some that they'd missed.

Whether it was the intense heat having an effect on Jeremy's brain, he did not know, but he kept envisioning himself and his companions as crazed elves working in Santa's workshop, chucking packages to and fro into the biggest pile of presents he'd ever seen. When the pile was so high that not even Zippo could see over it, Jeremy called out. "Okay! I'm going to try it now!"

"Try what?" Moe called back, jumping down from the top of the pile.

"Novo collazio!" Jeremy shouted, dabbing and tapping his wand at the boxy mountain.

With a flash of magical energy, several of the boxes in the pile transformed into mounds of colorful pebbles and flakes.

"Breakfast cereal?" Mike Mania sniffed the air excitedly as he stood beside Jeremy.

"Novo collazio! *Novo collazio*!" Jeremy shouted again and again, transforming more and more boxes.

"Hey! I know dat! Sir Donk's Cave Crunchers, now with more Martian Mallows! Nice!" DJ Nebz reached out and scooped up a handful of multi-colored cereal.

Jeremy slapped the Amphibion's hand with his wand. "Quit it! We're going to need all of it if we want to make it out of here alive!"

Nebz opened his hand and dropped the cereal back into the pile, a sad look in his eyes.

"You can have the oat bits, but leave the Martian Mallows! Novo collazio!" Jeremy continued enchanting the boxes as Nebz gathered up some of the non-marshmallow pieces. He passed some to Zippo and Moe, who all stood munching oat bits as they watched the boy wizard.

"Hey! Can you do toaster pastries, too?" Mike called out, his tail wagging.

Jeremy was sweating profusely. It felt like the hangar was getting even hotter. Also, all this spellcasting was wearing him out. He'd never attempted to create so much breakfast in one go. "Novo collazio! Novo collazio! *NOVO COLLAZIO!*" he cried out, sweat trickling down the back of his neck. He used the front of his t-shirt to dab his forehead, scoffing in disgust when he realized it still said "TEAM TOMMY." His brows furrowed in concentration as he danced around the pile, attacking it with all the mystical stamina he could muster. At one point he stopped, his outstretched hand dropping his wand to the metal floor.

"Jrr-mEE! You are okay?" Zippo called out, rushing to his side and catching him as he staggered backwards.

"Yeah...just..." Jeremy panted, "all this cereal...it's...it's too much..."

"Dude—take a little break!" Moe pleaded.

"NO!" Jeremy pushed himself back up. "I cannot stop now! MUST...CONTINUE!" He grabbed his wand from the floor, climbing up a stack of empty crates to get a better view. The boxy mountain was now mostly cereal, with only the occasional P-Shell box poking out here and there. Every untransformed box he could spot, he attacked with ever-weakening blasts of magic. Again and again he did this, until, at last, the cereal mountain was complete. It rose far above the rear of the *Terrapin*, looming like a candy-colored volcano.

"Out of the WAY! Give him some space! The kid just made like four tons of Martian Mallows!" Moe pushed Nebz and Mike Mania aside. Jeremy stumbled up the cargo hatch's ramp, one arm around Zippo's shoulders for support. He was nearly delirious.

"Nebz!" Moe shouted, "Go get him something to drink! I think there's some cold water in Zippo's fridge!"

Jeremy slumped down on the jumpseat bench, panting and trembling slightly. Nebz handed him a plaztek bottle of cold water. Jeremy took it gratefully. After a few sweaty gulps, he tossed the bottle aside. He pointed out the cockpit windows with his wand. "Open the hangar bay doors...now!"

"Com-PEW-ter! Open hangar door, *naow*!" Zippo mewoed.

The hangar bay door slid aside. The sun's titanic, all-encompassing sphere had nearly doubled in size. It filled the interior space of the hangar with its terrifying white hot light. Everyone in the cockpit of the *Terrapin* shielded their eyes as the windows adjusted. Just as Nebz and Zippo had predicted, the *Perfect Stranger*'s forceshield did little to stop the sun's nuclear blast of particles.

The cereal behind the *Terrapin* reacted instantly. The hundreds of millions of marshmallows expanded in all directions as they soaked up the tsunami of radioactive microwaves.

Within seconds, an all-consuming ball of rainbow fluff enveloped the entire stern of the *Terrapin*. And the mallow sphere grew. It lifted and pushed all the crates in its path, like so many empty cereal boxes carried on a tidal wave of high fructose corn syrup.

In the cockpit, Zippo flinched. "Wat det?" he meowed.

Then they all heard it. There was a high-pitched scraping sound coming from the rear of the ship, followed by a wobbly sensation.

"Did we activate grav-thrusters?!" Moe called out, confused. The controls were still unresponsive.

"I think..." Jeremy placed a hand on Zippo's shoulder, stumbling as the ship lurched upwards and forward. "It's *working*! It's the marshmallows! They're pushing us out of the hangar!"

Zippo wasted no time, grabbing the flight controls. The *Terrapin* was moving fast, a force more powerful than subetheric drives carrying it towards the hangar bay door. Moe shouted at Zippo as he buckled himself into his seat. "That's it! You got it, homie! Just ride the mallow wave! *Ride the mallow wave on outta here!*"

Zippo concentrated, paws gripping the flightwheel as he waited to regain control of his ship.

Jeremy glanced out the cockpit's side windows. The mallow blob had expanded so quickly that the hangar was already completely filled. If they didn't get pushed out fast enough the blob would engulf the *Terrapin* itself, trapping them forever. "*I knew I shouldn't have gone with two times the Martian Mallows!*" he shouted.

For a split second he had a vision of himself roasting marshmallows with Dad on one of their camping trips.

He remembered the way he used to put his mallows close to the embers, seeing how hot he could get them before they inevitably burst into flames. The scene shrank away as he rose into the atmosphere. His spirit flew past innumerable stars, all of which began to inflate and fuse together until they became one giant marshmallow. And then, there he was—entombed in the eternal mallow cube, as he and his companions fell helplessly into the sun.

The shriek of a ripping cord jolted Jeremy back to reality.

"I think the tether just snapped!" Moe shouted.

"Naow!" Zippo yowled as he punched the accelerator forward. The sub-etheric engines exploded to life, blasting the ship free from the encroaching wall of mallow. They propelled out the hangar and into open space.

A colossal bubble of marshmallow erupted forth from the

docking port, the colorful goop alternately boiling and freezing as it hit the cold vacuum of space. The *Terrapin* zipped away amidst the eruption, barrel-rolling out of *The Perfect Stranger*'s trajectory.

"Yeeeah! We maed it!" Zippo mewled with joy, looping the *Terrapin* in an about-face that put the sun and the black-hull galleon behind them.

"BREAKFAST... IS... SERVED!" Moe screamed triumphantly. He pointed at Jeremy. "What do you think of my new catchphrase?"

"I love it!" Jeremy shouted as he hugged Zippo from the side. "Hey, guys!" he yelled at Nebz and Mike, who were still huddled together and sobbing hysterically. "We're alive!"

Moe got focused. "Zip: drop everything we've got into subetheric and move us away from that star!" He typed a few keys on the navi-controls. "I'll get us onto a trajectory with Mercury, if this thing even works." Moe swiveled back to the main console and flicked a few switches furiously. "I have no idea how long our little baby is gonna hold out—luminal burners appear to be plugged up with mallow slime, and can't tell if our pulsator is offline or just fried." He swiveled back around. "Mike: are there any self-service ship washes on Mercury? All that goop on our back-end is really wrecking our sensors."

"Are you talking to me?" Mike sniffled.

Moe ignored him and moved on. "Nebz: please get up, and get some pants on! Shorts, anything!" Nebz croaked in the affirmative, leaving the cockpit in search of clothing. "Jeremy— how we doing on hotcakes? You know they help me navigate."

The escape had given Jeremy a second wind. "Coming right up, captain," he saluted with his wand. "Zippo, do you want anything?"

"Hotkeck good, yeh," he gave a thumbs up without looking away. "SY-rup. Liek, LOTS SY-rup." Zippo then used an extended claw to press the play button on the ship's stereo. The sound of Xavier Arnito's *Salsa Galactica* blared through the *Terrapin*'s comm system.

"What the—where did you get this?! I thought I left it at CobbleCon!"

"I made ya'll a copy when you guys were visitin' last time!" Nebz blorped happily as he walked into the cockpit. He was wearing Jeremy's towel wrapped under his pot belly. "What a boggy jam!"

The cockpit was soon transformed into a breakfast buffet, the whole gang enjoying syrupy hotcakes and jamming along to "Redshift Rhumba" as the *Terrapin* sailed into the night.

CHAPTER 50

THE LAVA GARDENS ALL-YOU-CAN-EAT
INTERPLANETARY SYNTHETIC OCEAN BUFFET

September 7th, 1919

Dear Jeremy,

I'm so happy that you're alive and working on Mercury!
The Lava Gardens All-You-Can-Eat Interplanetary Synthetic
Ocean Buffet sounds SMASHING! When are you going to take
me and Sally? (HA-HA!!!)

When you left on that spaceship in the middle of the
concert, I thought maybe that would be the last we ever saw
of you! EVERYONE was talking about your big stunt for
weeks! It was in all the papers! Lots of kids at school said
that they were at the show (LIARS!!!) and I tried to explain
that it was really you! Nobody believes me, though.
Christopher Lionspark and Janine Wintershade told everyone
that it was just Denny Diamond, the boy actor who plays
Tommy Cobblestone in that STUPID movie that's coming out.
They claimed that they know him personally because they all
worked together over the summer. (YUCK!!!)

Sally and I both made it back to PigPimples, thanks to

Bruno and his parents. Professor Chamberpot held a tribunal about whether or not to expel me and Sally for all the trouble we caused, but we got out of it by telling him that you actually kidnapped us and forced us to break into the Atheneum, and that you and the offworlders threatened to blow up the school if we didn't cooperate (I hope that this is OK!).

When are you coming home? I can't wait to see you again! Sally and I have been working on a new story cycle about our adventures together! I can't wait to show you!

Well, I'd better run along! All the new eighter-tots from House Fluffernut are meeting in the Trough for dinner (and to show off the dances we came up with over the summer)!

Be safe out there!

Your closest friend,
Kitani "Kit" Kawaii

P.S.
I've enclosed a photo of me and Sally! We got to see Rhonda Starlite perform in London!

P.P.S.
Sophie says hello!

Jeremy looked at the black and white photograph. In it, Kitani, Sally, and Bruno were standing in front of an amused Rhonda Starlite. A surprised Madi Nabo was tucked under Sally's arm. Kitani and Sally were doing the bunny ears hand signal of House Fluffernut, while Bruno held a record album. It appeared to be a copy of *Heaven*'s self-titled debut, autographed by Rhonda Starlite herself.

"Yo, Mambo," Moe peeked into Jeremy's quarters, drying his hands on a towel. He untied the back of his apron as he spoke. "Do you know if Nebz is working tonight?"

"I think he's DJ-ing a wedding party down at the Solar Flare."

"Another one?"

"They say it's the season for it."

"How about you? You doing a show?"

"Nah," Jeremy said. "I gave the slot to Frriekzhi. He's that stand-up comic from Qhoz'eik."

"Oh yeah! Have you checked out his set?"

"Nah. Is he any good?"

"Absolutely wack. Hey! Is that the letter from your chica?"

Jeremy reddened. "If you mean from Kitani, then yes."

"Hold up—is that Rhonda?" Moe snatched the picture from Jeremy's hands, staring at it lovingly.

"We're just friends!" Jeremy protested. "Friends can write letters to each other, you know." Jeremy wondered why he always took Moe's bait.

"I guess since you're just friends, this doesn't bother you," Moe scrutinized the photo.

"What doesn't bother me?"

"Looks like Bruno is mackin' on your cutie, dude."

"What?!" Jeremy grabbed the photograph back. Upon closer inspection, Bruno did indeed have his arm around Kitani's shoulders. Jeremy looked up, started to say something, then looked back at the photo. "Well that's..." he attempted a scoff. "They were obviously..." he stared at Moe, who looked like he was holding back gales of laughter. "They were just posing for the photo!"

"If you say so, chief!"

Zippo walked in, swinging a bucket of leftover coconut shrimp as he purred happily. He still had on his hairnet and apron from his shift at the Synthetic Ocean Buffet.

"NiiiRRiyaEew, " he called out to Donut, who was asleep in her cage. He dropped in a few leaves of Snorrian spinach from the Buffet's salad bar. "Derr you go, NiiiRRi." Tucked under his arm were some rolled up blueprints and a newspaper.

"There you are!" Moe said. "Show him the thing!"

"Wat, dis?" Zippo tossed the newspaper onto Jeremy's bed. It was a copy of the Cosmic Beacon. Jeremy picked up the paper, reading the headline aloud:

"*Anita Cosgrove Announces Official Title for TC Motion Picture—TOMMY COBBLESTONE: JUSTICE IS SERVED!*" Jeremy folded the paper shut, falling back on his bed in disgust. "Could they NOT have thought of *anything* else?" he sat up. "Do either of you have matches? I need to burn this real quick."

"Zippo, you jibroni! I told you not to show him that! I meant the *other* thing! The thing we were working on last night!"

"Oh yeh!" Zippo pulled out one of the tubes from under his arm. "Look at dis ting!" He unrolled the blueprints onto Jeremy's desk, pulling Jeremy over. Spread out before them were the complete plans for the night club.

"See, we'll put the bubble room here, and the fizzy strobes can be over here, by the sanis. And then I think we can even fit a laserdance aquarium along the back, just like we talked about! And here's where the stage will be..."

"Guys, what's all this?"

"It's the building plans, dude!"

"We are *approve*!" Zippo smiled.

Something about the sketch looked different to Jeremy. Then he realized the wording above the entrance looked off. "Future... *Magic*?"

Zippo covered his smirk with both paws.

"I thought we were calling it Future Pop?"

Zippo chuffled his weird Felinian laughter, patting Jeremy on the head.

"Zip suggested we change it, and I agreed," Moe said.

"Is for Jrr-mEE Faltcher, *MAGIC boi*!" Zippo yelled excitedly, throwing his arms around Jeremy and squeezing him tightly.

"You guys changed the name...for me?"

"Of course! You saved our butts, multiple times! *Future Magic*! Has kind of a funky fresh sound to it, don't you think? We're gonna build it right on that spot that we showed you, back on Callisto!"

"But what about money? We've barely saved up enough credits to buy new clothes," Jeremy said, examining his worn out "TEAM TOMMY" shirt.

"We're done washing dishes! We'll have fat stacks the second we get radio dipping!" Moe declared happily.

"Does this mean..." Jeremy whispered. "Is the future music *safe*? Did we do it?"

"Only one way to find out! How's the marshmallow situation, Zip?"

"Marsh-MELLON all kleen, all sensor are *vary* nice. Vary smooth. *Terrapin* is reddy to go."

"The black hole awaits!" Moe exclaimed.

Jeremy jumped to his feet. "Then what are we waiting for?" With their starship repaired and the marshmallow cleaned out of the sensors, there was nothing to stop them from leaving.

The boy wizard pointed to the sky. "Let's get starside!"

THE_END.TXT

FINAL NOTE FROM TRANSLATOR

Wow! What a ride! Didn't I tell you it was a great story? I personally enjoyed the part about the time-traveling caveman!

However, if you're like me, you were probably left scratching your virtual head with a few questions, such as:

Will Mrs. Crawford get her revenge? What about the Fascination Wolves and the Velitovian threat?

How will these guys ever run a nightclub?

Why didn't DJ Nebz have any pants?

Not to worry! The next volume of this historic saga is on its way. Our team is compiling historical memoirs, interviews, blog posts and chat logs as fast as our processors can compute 'em! All these queries and more will be answered when Jeremy Fletcher, Zipponio, and Moe return in *THE MAMBO WIZARD: HOT SALSA!*

See you then! And stay keen-o!

ChatterBot 2000 (ver. 3.6)

ABOUT THE AUTHOR

Giordano J. Lahaderne was born to an Italian mother and an American father. A graduate of BYU-Idaho, he originally came up with the story of Jeremy Fletcher in Miss Bollinger's creative writing class in the seventh grade. He lives in Montana with his attractive wife, Rachel.

He has never read Harry Potter.